FALL

FALL RIVER

Meredith Miller

HONNO MODERN FICTION

First published in Great Britain in 2024 by Honno Press
D41, Hugh Owen Building, Aberystwyth University, Ceredigion, SY23 3DY

1 2 3 4 5 6 7 8 9 10

A catalogue record for this book is available from the British Library.

Published with the financial support of the Books Council of Wales.

ISBN 978-1-912905-98-0 (paperback)
ISBN 978-1-916821-00-2 (ebook)

Cover design: Mad Apple Design
Text design: Elaine Sharples
Printed by 4edge Limited

This is a work of fiction and no resemblance to persons living or dead is
intended or implied.

For my daughter, Maia

h is the muscle of anger
p is the muscle of sorrow
g is the muscle for biting
g n m is the same muscle
o t is the muscle of anger
                    Leonardo

2016

Chapter 1

You might not have noticed her. You'd be distracted, maybe, by the spectacular curve of river and steel resolving out of the dark, the black hills hulking against the sky either side. The bridges, old and new, thrust into the rock of the banks. From, say, high up and god-like on the bridge tower observing the whole grand sweep of it all, one hunched-over girl with her hair tucked into her hoodie slouching her way down from South Pill to the landing stage wouldn't necessarily catch your eye. Less important than a sparrow, really.

She has tucked in the hair on purpose, because no one ever misses that. Even in security footage it looks ginger. Her trainers blur a glow into the air, but that blends into all the visual noise of the streetlights, traffic lights, bridge lights, the red and green sparks on the channel buoys, the porch lights, the strings of bulbs on the floating docks. Saltash doesn't get dark. The surrounding hills disappear after sunset and the rest of the Hamoaze looks like fallen sky. Even the bees get night and day confused here.

Alice throws her upper body back and lets her feet fall down the hill the way people do, having grown up on these tall banks best friends with gravity. The river is flat below her. *Like glass*, they say, *like a mill pond*. But the river Alice knows is full of screams and sharp edges, oil fires and boilers exploding and the whistle of bodies falling at gathering speed, the hard slap of the surface.

History silts up below the bridges. Alice can hear it.

She steps onto the mud without taking her trainers off. The river is cold, but it doesn't shock her. Her body forgot how to shiver weeks ago. Muddy water seeps in, gritty between her toes, and Alice remembers three sets of painted toenails resting on the open window of her bedroom. Three colours of cousin hair hanging off the bed: hers, Jo's and Khadija's. They are laughing

3

and the sun is warm on the bottoms of their feet, blinding into the blue behind them.

Her memories are so full of heat and light they force her pupils into pinpricks even in the dark. They burn up out of her skin in red blotches. Pictures of her life, flashing past. So that turns out to be true.

The sky is lightening behind Normandy Hill but the river is still thick with dark. Ernesettle is a starless place across the water. In the world outside of Alice, nothing appears or disappears below the lights at Royal Navy Air Defence.

The riverbed is soft under the shallows. She moves across it quickly, in up to her thighs and the pulse beats through her skin into the freezing current.

It rises cold over her belt, like Charlie's cold hand on the small of her back. Charlie with his tongue in her mouth. The heat then, coming up through her stomach and into her breath, the gasping and the letting go. She can remember it, but she wouldn't be able to get there again. Her skin still sends her messages, but Alice isn't listening anymore.

She is used to the way her body lies, wishing to be touched, to be warm and fed and clean and anything other than what it is – crying for quiet all the time. All you need to shut it up is trust. Trust in the nothing, in the invisible inevitable, in whatever airless, waterless, dark hereafter is there, after.

She rests her chin on the river so that its surface fills up most of the world, then the hills and one slice of lightening sky.

Jo buried Alice up to her chin on the beach once. Alice was six years old, so Jo was maybe nine or ten, Aunt Jan's sunglasses falling down the sunken little-girl bridge of her nose. Through those glasses Jo saw another world for them, full of cocktails and liposuction and paparazzi shots of the three of them climbing out of a hire car laughing and flashing their pants. Then she took the glasses off and they were in Cornwall again, temporary summer toffs sneering down at them in the sudden painful light. The burn on the skin of Alice's nose, the sun bleaching the fire out of her hair.

The river will put her out like a candle.

She will tumble into the current and one cold rush will wash away everything that flashes and sparks behind her eyes.

She dips her mouth below the surface and sees a cold girl on a metal table. A crime drama girl, covered in cuts with bruises on her neck. Her skin is the colour of the television dead, the colour Alice's skin has always been. There is a picture like that every night on every channel. Someone with private troubles and a crumpled coat will break the rules to find out why the girl is on the table.

But nothing happens unless she dies first. There is no story until the girl dies.

Bye, bird. Bye. Then the empty river against the sky.

Some gulls have found a bin bag somewhere up Fore Street. Their screeching rides high up over the river, above the sleeper train clacking through the cutting from St Budeaux and out onto Brunel's bridge.

Below the A38 extension, Alice's body sends the water up and out in circles from the point at which the last of her has disappeared. Then the surface lies flat while the muffled sun rises and the traffic begins to move. No one thinks to look for Alice until noon.

Inside the train, a woman sleeps sitting up, head resting on her balled-up mac. Leaves, torn by the open window from railway sidings somewhere in Somerset, are sprinkled over the table and snagged in her hair. She looks old enough to buy vodka without answering questions and young enough to be able to sleep soundly sitting up on a train. This is Khadija Sleep, coming home.

Her eyelids are still; maybe she isn't sleeping at all? When a voice from the tannoy in North Yard drifts in through the train window, the muscles tighten at one side of her mouth. She turns her body away, lifts an arm to cover her ear. Of course it's no use. Khadija takes a breath and turns her head to look.

At 6:30 on leap year morning, the Navy yard is the brightest thing on the river. It's lit up like Hollywood or heaven, like no one ever dies there. There is a personnel carrier in Weston Mill Lake, sitting so high it rises in front of the council flats at Barne Barton. From a distance the layers flatten out, as if you could jump from one of the balconies and fall through the cancerous air right onto the top deck.

Apart from the new smokestack pouring a darker shadow out against the sky over the estate, six years have made no difference at all. Khadija stands up and shakes out her coat. She twists her hair into a knot that won't stay and moves between the carriages to stare down at the Union Pub, one hand out to steady her suitcase while the train clatters over Brunel's bridge.

It curves round toward the Cornwall bank, aiming now at Wearde Quay and the big house on the hill. Khadija puts a hand up to her neck and digs her fingers into the ache there. You'd think she was older just then, watching her shrink in the face of that view.

At first glance, the water is blank below her, covering the riverbed and pretending it would float you. Khadija knows the muddy bottom underneath, waiting to hold your ankles so the river can choke you. Mud two metres deep, made of rotting grass from up the valley, pesticides carried downstream, animal guts and blood hardened into the iron on the bridges. The rows of pleasure boats strung along the moorings are bobbing on top of all the bones and plastic trash and piss and nonsense that make up every river on this island, twisting down to open their mouths and sick into the sea.

A rippling circle on the surface of the river catches the light under the road bridge. A cormorant diving maybe, or something heavy tossed from a car. Or maybe it's the Tamar swallowing one more stranger's sadness, turning another person into a body, putting somebody else to sleep.

Khadija feels for the receipt crumpled in the pocket of her coat, signed by the server in a Russian restaurant in Primrose Hill. Farah might once have wanted it, to put with all the other till receipts she used to keep stuffed in a boot box at the bottom of her closet. She used to say she'd be able to reconstruct, years from now, where she'd been and what she'd done on any given day, from the receipts. When they first met at uni, she'd get the guards to let her through train station turnstiles so her tickets wouldn't get swallowed, ask for a paper receipt every time she bought a bottle of water or a KitKat. In addition to the boot box, there were several plastic grocery bags full of older receipts tied up under Farah's bed in halls.

The other night, Khadija paid for the whole dinner just to be sure she'd be the one to keep the record of it: £43 at 21:52 on a particular Wednesday. What was eaten, how much was drunk, at the last supper.

The carriage lurches over the points and Khadija's suitcase rolls away. When she ducks to catch it the automatic door stutters and disturbs the weekenders, trying to sleep until Penzance. No one on holiday needs to wake up before Bodmin. The stations in east Cornwall release a different sort of people, people pushed inland, people who reached up the line and got pulled back again, riding standard class. All over the country, train lines are ending stories just like this one.

She almost misses the sight of her mother's window, half-covered in street light, Aunt Tammy's in the shadow of the bridge. Apart from one, every person Khadija loves is on that hillside, breathing into their pillows in the dark. Jo and Alice and Beth Kennedy, all connected by their parents and their past. Her mother and Aunt Jan, Dylan and Aunt Debbie and Tammy, all strung together with dead relatives and bridge cables. None of that is important enough to stop the *Night-time Riviera*; the sleeper flies right through Saltash station.

She'll get off at Liskeard and wait for the up train, drinking crap tea and looking at sheep. Looking at others like her, who have moved to London and back again, failed and fallen in on themselves. All the pathetic backdrops are still waiting at all the stations, ready to swallow everyone who comes home for Christmas or Eid, for funerals or birthdays or babies. For good. Back out to the edges, back down under the rain, where all the trains are above ground and all the money washes away up the line.

In Liskeard station, she will enjoy her last few minutes of invisibility, the last time she'll be far enough from home to disappear into her surroundings. No one is expecting her; even her mother doesn't know she's on the sleeper. The talk will start soon enough, why ring ahead? Somebody will spot her on Fore Street and get straight on the phone.

Guess what, me lover? I just seen Khadi Sleep outside the chippy. Yes, I'm sure! She's back.

Wonder who'll die this time?

Here she is, cutting into the middle of things once again, like a misplaced full stop. Ending shit. She passed the eleven plus, broke the surface of the river and leapt like a fish up into the London air. This is her, falling back down again.

Nothing to see here. Just gravity. Splash.

It in't daylight yet, but that don't make any difference round Saltash. Tammy Williams comes out the back of her house and looks up at the bridge. In around the sound of traffic overhead there's some other rumbling, and a feeling, too. Like it's almost ready to storm, or it's 1941 and a doodlebug just finished whistling and went silent. Like the wind is sucking into itself, getting ready to blow them all over.

Tamara Williams is little and wiry, with hair the colour of the river. Lines like estuary mud all down her cheeks and her arms. Sixty is older in Saltash than it is in Mannamead, but livelier too. The women don't drawl here; they shout and cackle and some of them whine. Not Tammy, of course.

She looks down at her namesake, meaning the river not Tammy Wynette. It's smooth as sheet metal and acting like it has nothing to tell. Tammy isn't fooled. Fooling Tamara Williams isn't easy.

"Course, Tammy doesn't remember 1941, just the grown-ups talking about it, back when the cottages were still standing against

Brunel's pylons and the A38 bridge was brand new. The way people go on, you'd think everyone remembers. You'd think it was last year.

The rumbling from up the hill gets louder now. Someone is dragging a case over the cobbles in the mews.

Lots of people living round here have seen blitzes, of course. They've seen houses implode into rubble with families underneath, roads full of craters, people running with their bloody screaming children in their arms. But none of that is in England and people don't talk about it at all. The kids go off from here into a blank silence and come back again missing limbs, but it stays in their dreams. Meaning Tammy is the one who has to deal with it. Sometimes she wakes up screaming too, with all they things in her head.

Or they come back like Craig Kennedy, broken mostly on the inside and in love with some drug or somebody they think will make it fade. Craig's drug was Khadija Sleep.

Whatever is rumbling through the mews comes out into the road now, louder than the helicopters from HMS Drake and the early traffic on the bridge above Tammy's roof.

She turns to look and there is the girl herself, Khadija, rolling a case heavier than she is down toward their terrace. She's taller than last time she came home, but it wouldn't be Khadi's height or her eyes or the shape of her face that Tammy would recognise in the half light. It's the way she holds her shoulders up and her chin sideways, like there's just been a loud bang, or she can't quite stand to look you in the eyes. Been away all that time and she's still holding herself that way. Distance done her no good at all.

Maybe it was the sleeper train coming past that woke Tammy. Usually, she don't even notice it. She's been hearing it every day but Sunday for most of her life, so it tends to fold right into her dreams.

'Khadi,' she smiles and holds her arms out. 'Hug, right now.'

'Hey, Aunt Tammy.' Khadija takes a bit of a look at her own house, like maybe she'll get used to it one glimpse at a time. 'How you been keeping?'

9

'You come on the sleeper? Where's your taxi?'

'I waited at Liskeard for the up train.'

'Your mother know you're here?'

'I didn't tell her the train. She'd've been up all night.'

But Carol hears, of course. Between their terrace and the bridge towers, sounds bounce around the road and back against themselves like gunshots in a western film. No such thing as a private conversation in their road. Carol Sleep opens her front door in a football shirt and pants, showing the world her teenager's legs. Her face, though. Carol has a smoker's face. Right now, it looks like she's about to cry.

'Hiya, Mum.' Khadija gives a small, sarcastic smile and waves.

'Well, I got to go up to Mrs Osborne,' Tammy says. 'Come over for a cuppa later and tell me everything, Khadi. I'll do your cards.' Tammy turns away. God knows those two need some time.

If Khadija hadn't turned up, Tammy would have said something. Knocked Carol up and told her something was wrong. Or, if it had been anyone else coming down the hill, she'd have stopped them and tried to raise an alarm. Because something is wrong, isn't it? It wasn't Khadija dragging that suitcase that woke her up, and be honest, it wasn't the sound of the sleeper. What woke Tammy up was the river. A wave of something cold and hollow come up off the water and blew right into her. Someone told her to get up. Shouted, even. She was gasping into the dark before her eyes were all the way open, sat up knowing something had happened down there. You could call it a bad dream if you like it better that way.

It wasn't till later that day it would occur to her. The coincidence wasn't half unsettling, Khadija Sleep coming home after so long right at that particular moment. Just when Tammy had thought her name, and Craig Kennedy's. And, as it turned out, later, just when Khadija's cousin Alice disappeared.

Chapter 2

Tammy uses her key to open Mrs Osborne's door at a quarter till eight, then takes an extra minute to herself on the doorstep. If you don't remember to gather in all your breath before you face Nora Osborne, she'll take it away and leave you gasping.

The fridge hums far away in the kitchen and the case clock just next to her ticks against the foyer tiles. Tammy turns to look down the front lawn and over the roofs above the boatyard. The river stares up at her from between rows of moored boats without blinking or rippling. She gives it back her best poker face, not letting on about the falling men and drowning girls and the poison leaking into the water behind her eyes. She's been pretending like that all her life. The trick to living with a soul like Tamara Williams' is learning to fake it early and never forgetting how. If you can't, the world moves back and forth through your skin until you don't know where the end of you is. Until you fall apart like wet tissue in the rain.

'Close the door, Tamara. You'll let the mizzle in.'

'Sorry I'm late.'

'The only one who minds about that is you. Why don't you make some tea? My son left those revolting doughnuts.'

Nora is in the wingback chair facing the closed curtains, barefoot in her nightgown. There is no point giving her a blanket or asking where her slippers are, so Tammy lays out the tea things and starts on the kitchen while the kettle boils. You have to use a whistler, and a bunch of unrelated crockery from around in the cupboards. Nora hates for things to match. Tammy wipes the wooden tray with linseed oil before she piles everything on. You can't smell the tea through the chemical stink.

When she puts the tray on the coffee table and starts moving things

11

from the rest of the surfaces, Nora barks at her to sit down. Tammy takes the sofa, looking at Nora's profile and her thick yellow toenails.

'How you keeping, Mrs Osborne?'

'Exactly as I was last week. It's very relaxing, this stagnation. One day you'll see.'

Not likely. Tammy'll die first, but she doesn't say it. 'I'm going to open these curtains. The light is good for you.'

'You are not a nurse, Tamara. What's good for me is none of your business.'

'Well, I'm doing it. Get up and fight me if you like.'

'Don't be vulgar.' She doesn't mean that. She likes it when Tammy talks back to her.

'Guess who came home today?' It slips out as soon as Tammy lets the sight of the river in through the window. She wishes she'd left the curtains and her mouth closed.

'I have no way of knowing. Will I care?'

'Khadija Sleep. Carol's daughter. She came on the sleeper without telling anybody first.'

'Well, that fits, doesn't it? Thoughtless girl.'

'You've not met her, have you?'

'I know *about* her, don't I? We all do,' Nora sniffs. 'And the mother, as well. Not much of a chance for the girl, raised by that one.'

'Go on and take the blanket. You're making me cold.'

Tammy holds out a crocheted thing that clashes with the chair and the sofa, wondering who made it. Certainly not Nora.

'Carol Sleep is the sort of woman who doesn't mind what she ruins.' Nora ignores the blanket. 'Probably doesn't even notice everything crashing down around her. The kind that never looks around or behind.'

'Carol's had a tough time. She can't let herself be loved.'

'Ha! You must be the only person in town who believes that.'

'*That* isn't love, and you know it. She's all right.'

'Tell that to any woman around here with sons.'

'We've all got old, Mrs Osborne. None of that matters now.'

12

'I'm going back to bed.' Nora puts a hand on the arm of the chair to push herself up, then stands for a minute steadying herself before she turns and shuffles away.

She won't be sleeping, just reading a Georgette Heyer in the bedroom with the curtains drawn. She hates the light. She's like a rat or a cockroach, but slower. Well, the hoovering is easier without her in the way.

Tammy does the front room and the dining room, careful to leave some dust bunnies behind the radiators. The smell of burning dust will comfort Nora when the radiators kick on. It's not something she ever said, but she don't hide much. Not from Tammy, anyway.

The siren goes at North Yard while Tammy is running some laundry and doing the kitchen floor. The washing machine drowns out the sound of that awful hallway clock, but not the siren. That's how Tammy knows it's 11:30 when the spin cycle shakes the dishes on the draining board and makes the light shimmer on the wet floor. No one needs a clock on the Hamoaze, even if a clock could tell you how time works here.

Tammy takes a deck of playing cards from a drawer and brings it to the table, shuffling it while she waits for the washing. Three of spades is the card she pulls first.

Cards and kitchen tables are what Tammy knows best. Wheelback chairs and rush seats, particle board from IKEA, old farmhouse salvage and new-money upholstered dining sets. And the women, women, women, sitting at them with all their questions written right on their faces, lipstick leaking into the cracks around their mouths, the streaks in their hair that tell Tammy everything she needs to know about the state of their marriage and the callousness of their selfish children. They gasp and nod at each other when she repeats back at them the things they've only just told her with their wringing hands and the shape of their mouths.

Three of spades. A conflict. Something tipped off balance. Heartbreak. She leans the card up against the bag of doughnuts Nora's son Anthony has left on the table. Nasty piece of work,

Anthony Osborne. The kind of man Tammy's father called a crafty idiot. Whatever Nora may be, she doesn't deserve that man for her only child. The washing machine whines, then shifts the sheets back and forth one time before it goes still and the light blinks off.

An hour later, Tammy comes into the master bedroom with the washing basket. Nora is dressed and peeking through a crack in the curtains.

'Leave that, Tamara. I'll put the sheets away,' she says to the sky over Torpoint.

She's upset; something's unsettled her. 'Go on. Tell me.'

'I don't like that Sleep girl,' Nora says.

'Well, she didn't come back to bother *you*. Don't worry about her.'

'I've never believed her story about Craig Kennedy.'

There's such a knot of denial and resentment in those words, Tammy wouldn't know where to begin to talk back to it.

'I put fresh curtains up in the front room. I'll drop the others at Johnson's this afternoon.'

'Thank you, Tamara. Anthony will collect them.'

There is an envelope on the hall table with Tammy's full name on it, written in a palsied hand. The paper smells of Yves St Laurent, even though Nora Osborne only ever smells of musty skin under Pear's Soap. The three of spades is still on the kitchen table and the clean curtains are open. By afternoon everything will be gone and closed.

Drops of moisture sit still in the air in Nora's front yard, not quite heavy enough to fall. There is a flash of copper on the river, but when Tammy turns her head it's gone. She closes her eyes and sees long hair streaming in the current like bloody watergrass, takes three steps in the dark before she looks again. There is the water lying like slate, lying like a politician at the door.

You have to watch that river. You have to watch it all the time, or it plays tricks and tells you things you don't want or need to know.

When Tammy pushes the light switch in her own hallway, nothing happens.

'Breaker's off, Aunt Tammy.' It's her nephew, Ben, up a ladder in the sitting room.

'Look at you, mister.' Tammy tilts her head back to see him, bent below the ceiling. 'I remember when your dad fit between the sofa cushions.'

'You squished Dad in the cushions? That's mean, Aunt Tammy.' Ben lowers his drill and laughs.

'I lay him in the crook so he wouldn't roll off. It was my job to look after him while Mum cooked tea. He had a pushed-in nose and skin like a pillow all over.'

Now little Harry has Ben and two others, a wife and a car full of plaster dust, big steel-toed boots and scratch cards on the passenger seat. Tammy remembers when he widened his eyes and opened his mouth in shock if you only hid a ball of wool and brought it back again. When he smelled of Calpol and snot. When the rest of them were still here in the house, in the body.

'Come down off the ladder, Ben. It's nearly dark; you can do that tomorrow.'

He's putting a brace to the old light fixture so he can earth it properly.

'Nearly done, old bird.'

She can see him falling, been seeing it for years. Ever since he was little, she could never stand to see him on top of things. But Ben was always a climber. He used to shimmy up the street light and come in through her upstairs window when he was nine.

'I want you to sit down and tell me about yourself. Ain't seen you in ages.'

'Seen you last week.' Voice like his mother's, not Harry's. No matter how close he is it sounds far away. 'Listen, Aunt Tammy, you should hoover up and wipe down everything in here with a damp rag, in case Uncle Micky used asbestos.'

'In here?'

'He might've. Lads bring all sorts home from the dockyard. Asbestos brown board all over in these houses round here.'

It was the white stuff, not the brown, that killed Tammy's husband Micky. They put that in the paperwork like it mattered. There's kinds of asbestos, apparently. The white stuff takes years to suffocate you, but it does the job in the end.

Nothing about Micky broke up or broke off, just stiffened and got heavier until he couldn't move his ribs, until he gasped every word and lived flat on his back next to a little explosive tank of oxygen. At the end, they let him stay right in his own room, his heart pounding through the covers, trying to make up for what his lungs weren't doing anymore. Tammy put her cards away for months and made Victoria sponge for the home care nurse. Most people came once and quickly, and then didn't come again.

Well, even Micky's been gone more than fifteen years, and anyway, when he was here in the body he took up a lot of space with everything but his brain. Back when he was upright and walking, he used to turn sideways to get through doors. It was a pain in the neck to clean around him. He voted for Thatcher and shook his head at everyone under thirty like it was all their fault. All what? Well, he wasn't specific. Tammy don't vote at all. It's hard to convince yourself voting matters when you can hear the future coming.

Micky wasn't the only one to die like that, with his own body making rocks in his lungs. Craig Kennedy's father, too, half of the fitters and most all the laggers who worked down the dockyard in the seventies.

Tammy screws up her eyes and rubs them with a thumb and forefinger. 'It feels like ages since I seen you, Ben. How's Jo, anyhow?'

'She's fine, glowing. You going to congratulate me? I'm having a baby.'

'Jo's baby. Girl, that one.' Jo with the little jewel inside her belly, sparkling. Emerald? She'll be named for something shining anyhow. Green eyes. 'How far along is she?'

'Thirty-eight weeks. Coming any day now.'

'She'll be a good little mother, just like mine. Smiling and doing her hair and skipping up and down the stairs with her little baby girl.'

'My baby, too. Whatever is Jo's is mine. You told me that years ago and I didn't listen to ya.'

He holds the fixture up against the ceiling and the battery-powered drill screeches into the wood, so loud she can't hear her own reply.

'Well, people find their own way. It's when they don't I have to hear about it.' The drill stops and the rest of the room gets louder. 'Please get down, Ben. You're spooking me.'

'I stand on ladders all day, Aunt Tammy. It's my job.'

He used to climb the pylons under the railroad bridge at high tide, jump off into the river and swim round to Town Quay, go up Kingsmill Lake to zip back and forth on water skis. Like frogs, the boys round Saltash, grown up around so much mud with so much in it. So many half-water girls like Alice Tregidga. Like Tammy.

'Ben, something's wrong. Something went wrong this morning, in the river.'

'You worry too much. Sometimes it turns out to be nothing, in't it?'

'They won't find her. They won't be able to see.'

'Won't find who?'

'Alice. She'll be wearing a boy's hoodie. Wearing bright shoes.'

'Alice Tregidga gone walkabout again, has she? She upsets Jo, I'll—'

'No one knows yet. Her hair come out of that hood, all loose. It turned around her neck and picked up all the thickness in the water.'

'Don't think about it, lovely. You know what Alice is like, just likes to wind people up. Been driving Jo nuts ever since the other cousin left.'

'Well, Khadi's back now and all.'

'Khadija Sleep? What's she doing back just when everyone's got over her?'

'She's all right. Try and understand her. She's your family, now.'

17

'I know if you love someone you gotta love their family and all, but bloody hell, Aunt Tammy, that lot are intense.'

'Them girls crossed over each other like wires this morning, coming and going. Tangling up, under and over. I'm worried, Ben. It was me should've helped that maid.'

'Who, Khadi Sleep? She helps herself, don't she?'

'No. Alice. She's like me, Ben. I should've helped her.'

'You do nothing *but* help people. Stop worrying just for a minute. Tell me about something else instead. How's that old bag up the hill keeping?'

'Mrs Osborne? She's fine.'

Ben carries on talking, but the rest of them are speaking, too. The spirits are all talking at once this morning. They're agitated, excited even. It's like this when the river swallows someone; they rise up, chattering. 'Tar and tangled, it's on her skin like blood, red veins on top of the blue. She's out of the blue.'

Did she say that out loud?

Ben comes down off the ladder and it goes quiet for a minute. Tammy's lungs open up. He's come down on his feet, step by step. He's fine.

'Sit down.' Ben puts a hand on her, acting just like his father now. Looking straight in her eyes, fixing her back to the floor.

'Now I'm done, how about a cuppa?' he says.

A while later, he's in front of her holding a cup. He puts his hand on her shoulder again, acting like she's ill.

'You don't know, Ben.' She can't see his face in the shadow of the sky and the water behind him. 'You can't go in the river. Not if you're like us, me and Alice.'

'We don't know where she went, Aunt Tammy. She'll probably be home by now. Drink that. It's OK.'

'The river is loud; you can't imagine the noise. She can't hear us. She's nowhere here, nowhere near us.'

'You're upset, Aunt Tammy. I get it. But you can't do nothing till you're asked, so relax for a bit.'

He sits down beside her and puts an arm around her shoulders, stretching out his boots. When did he get to be another one with long legs, stretching his dusty boots along her carpet? Another one who tells her it isn't real? She leans her head on him and looks at the hills turning the colour of old pennies in the falling sun, the river shrinking up toward Calstock, and past that where it gets too small to swallow anybody's children at all. Up there, sad girls can wade in up to their ankles, shiver and tiptoe until the cold pulls all the poison out through the souls of their feet. But Alice grew up down here, where the water is full of mud and roped-up spirits, where it's a full-time job to resist the sucking force of the channel, pulling the rest of the world in and out, in and out.

Chapter 3

There is rain collected in all the depressions on Upper Fore Street, the seventies mosaics and the cracks in the pavement and the benches left over from when benches were benches and not strips of aluminium designed to tip rough sleepers off onto the ground. The wet air smells of grease from the chippy, sweat and laundry soap from the Air Ambulance Charity Shop.

You'd notice Khadija in the Saturday morning crowd by the bus stop even without anyone pointing her out. She looks like a summer person, out of place in March. Her clothes are from London and she holds herself as though she's trying to shrink away from her own bones, staring at the fogged windows of the Kitchen Café.

She is trying to see how many people are in there and whether one of them is her cousin Jo. She can't see through the windows, and the only way to clear them is to open the door.

The plastic tablecloths have changed, but not the brown sauce dispensers or the all-weather carpet. Jo is there, sitting right next to the window with her phone in front of her face, filming the event of Khadija coming through the door. Jo lives with that camera between her and the world. Now she's got that pregnant belly for a buffer as well.

Khadija knocks some chairs aside coming through. She doesn't fit the furniture here anymore, as if she's blind and they've moved it. Everything is closer together than it should be. She opens her arms and makes Jo stand up to hug her.

'Fuckin' hell, you look amazing,' Jo says. They squeeze together with Jo's belly between them, then pull back for second looks.

'You too. The bump suits you. Like, really suits you.'

'Tammy Williams says I'm gonna be prettier as a mum, whatever that means. But you, bird, looking all indie and London and shit.'

'Shut up. In London I felt Cornish as fuck. The whole first year up there, I felt like I was wearing a sign that said: "Ask and I'll show you my six toes." Then I realised it was all about my face and my name. Everyone just assumed I was from Chigwell or somewhere, long as I kept my mouth shut.'

'The don't-give-a-shit look is fit, though. You're like one of those actresses that looks even better when they get caught without straighteners or make-up. Like you didn't bother to put anything together, but you don't even need to.'

Because Jo remains Jo. She says whatever occurs and it all just bounces off and floats away. No one minds.

Everyone in the café is still looking at them. They're all saying to themselves, *them Sleep women are trouble. Spooky, the lot of 'em.* Then there's Jo's baby that Ben didn't give her and everyone in town knows that, too. But it doesn't matter now.

'I forgot how much better everything feels with you around.' Khadija pulls out a chair and throws her coat onto the wide windowsill. 'How is that not Ben's baby? What the hell?'

'We broke up for a while. I explained this already.'

'Slag,' Khadija laughs. 'You're supposed to be little. I'm supposed to say something all wise and helpful right now. This is too weird.'

'You look different,' Jo says, 'the same but different. People would say a bit middle-class, but that in't it. Just, you've been somewhere else and it shows. Your accent keeps going in and out.'

'I'm from here, Jo. I'm so absurdly from here it's not even funny.'

'That's depressing. Listen, bird, Alice didn't come home last night. She never turned up at school yesterday but nobody noticed till lunchtime.'

'I heard. You know she'll be at a friend's. Aunt Debbie'll be losing it until she comes home. Little shit.'

'I don't know, Khadi. She's got worse lately.'

'How's your mum?'

'She's fine. The same. Tell me about London. It looked awesome in your posts.'

They look out over Fore Street at all the people who never cross the bridge and never bother with umbrellas because the rain is sideways and nothing will ever dry out.

'It wasn't awesome, Jo. I know you think everywhere else is better, but it isn't. In London, you spend half your life on the tube and the buses. There's loads of cool stuff to do, but you can't do it because once you pay the rent you're utterly skint and it takes an hour to get anywhere from your flat. All you can do is stay home, make toast and use someone else's Netflix password. Literally the only nice thing about London was that nothing happened to me there. It was dead restful, but then it got … I don't know, kind of suffocating.'

'Yeah, but things were happening right near you. Things that matter. No one makes films in Saltash, Khadi. No one writes songs about it.'

'What difference does it make being right next to something if you can't reach it anyway?'

'Deep. Where the hell am I supposed to stay if I get an internship now?' Jo smiles, but only to take the sting out. She sounds annoyed, like it was Khadija's job to give her a line to somewhere else. Somewhere Alice and Ben and the babydaddy weren't happening.

'I have a few mates. So tell me what the hell's been up with Alice.'

'Oh, you know. On one level it's the same as always, except now she's older and she's gone all emo and is probably shagging Charlie Osborne.'

'Jesus. That's just weird.'

'It's just Alice. She grew up exactly how you'd have thought she would.'

'I didn't think. Don't hate me; I sort of imagined you two would always be little.'

'Remember the thing with the hamster?'

''Course I do. I'm the one had to explain it to that lot. I hate that you remember it, though.'

'Well, that was just the beginning, mate.'

'At the time I thought you were young enough to forget.'

'I still have pictures of the hamster blood running down the wall.'

'I notice you're *still* filming everything. Maybe you should try the world in real time.'

'Yeah, I guess. Anyway, there was so much more while you were away. You missed a whole lot of Alice.'

'I should have told someone about that night so they could talk to you. And Alice. I just kind of panicked and thought they'd send her away or something. And it wasn't as if she tortured animals for a hobby. Alice isn't mean.'

When Khadija goes for more teas, the woman behind the counter says, 'You back for a visit with your mum, me lover?' Khadija has no idea who the lady is, but she knows Khadija. Everyone seems to.

'We missed you at the memorial service.' The woman doesn't even try to hide the accusation in her voice. 'For Craig Kennedy.'

'Yes,' is all Khadija says. What else is there? She winds back between the tables more carefully this time, trying to make herself small enough.

'You got a notification.'

Khadija looks down and lights up her phone. 'Weird. Mohammed Magdy just followed me on Insta.'

'Who's that? Is he famous?'

'Nah, it's just I hardly know him. I mean, I only met him a couple times. If he looked at my account, he must have seen I've left London.'

'Seriously though, Khadi, weren't you afraid to come back here?'

'Meaning, *what kind of tragedy will you cause this time, you psycho?*'

'No. Meaning, aren't you worried you'll get stuck?'

'Never mind. I can see everybody's thinking it. They're all staring at me like people might start falling off the bridge just because I'm here. I might push somebody off, maybe.'

'Well, you're back after a commercial break, bird. 'Course everybody thinks about what happened when you left. They'll get over it. Nobody reckons it was your fault, Khadi.'

'But they do. You know they do.'

'It was a weird coincidence, him lying there on the mud and when they looked up from that, you'd left the same night. Everyone knew he was into you. It just sorta goes together in people's minds.'

Two blokes in yellow jackets push their plates aside and stand up. Khadija scoots her chair in to let them pass.

'London cops came to question me, did you know that? First week of classes, I had cops knocking at my room in halls. After that, Farah was the only one who'd speak to me. She thought it made me cool or something. Everyone else thought I was a terrorist.'

Khadija had disappeared from the wrong place at the wrong time, and near as anyone can figure out, she was the last person who saw Craig Kennedy breathing. But that isn't why people in Saltash blame her.

'He was obsessed with you, wasn't he?' Jo says. 'Looking back it must have been intense, but I didn't really get it at the time.'

'Well, apparently, if some older boy starts clinging onto you like he's drowning and you try to shrug him off so you can fucking have room to breathe, it's your fault and not his. Go figure.'

'Is that why you left?'

'I left because it's what you do after A-levels. Craig was all right. He was pathetic, not creepy. But he was all up in my head before I turned seventeen.'

'You seemed practically grown-up to me.' Jo laughs.

'Well, it messed with me and then it ended horribly and now it's been done ages. The memorial service was six years ago and people are still blaming me for not coming.'

'What do you think happened?'

'I don't know, Jo. They concluded accidental death.'

'Yeah, but—'

'He was still himself when I saw him. He wasn't more depressed than usual, if that's what you're not saying.'

She looks inside herself to see a picture of Craig Kennedy on her doorstep, holding his jacket out to her. Of herself visibly shaking him off so she can turn away. Herself sparkling in a new dress while he fades into the dark of the hillside.

'So, you staying, or what?' Jo asks.

'What? Oh, I don't know. What difference does it make? I'm gonna get stuck somewhere. Might as well do it here with you lot.'

The windows have steamed up again and cut them off from the rest of the world. The air inside the café is warm and greasy and safe. Any minute now Khadija will choke on it.

'You say that now,' Jo speaks the thought for her. 'Wait a few months.'

'I got a job,' Khadija says.

'What, as a solicitor? I guess you *are* a bit middle-class.'

'I'm not qualified yet. Working admin at Bright and Tunstall till I pass the exams.'

'Then you're going back?'

'No! Whatever. You and Ben are OK, though?'

'Yeah, it's all good. He'll look after the baby. You know Ben, you can't fault him. That's what's so boring.'

'Tell me about this Max guy, the dad? Never saw a single picture of him. I find that a little suspicious, you being you.'

'Just a random. Posh totty. It was fun, but.'

Jo wipes a hole in the steam on the window so she can take a picture of the bus shelter. A pair of OAPs are sitting on the thin little seat smiling at each other. Some lady on an electric scooter is parked across the pavement, sitting inside a plastic tent covered with raindrops.

'Everyone grew up while you were away, Khadi. Ben spends all day doing building work with his dad and Jarek. We only go out Saturdays and bank holidays, like we're fifty.'

'Count your blessings. At least he's got work.'

'Yeah, when he can, but they lost their biggest job. At the school. Now it's part of the academy trust, Mr Osborne says they can't hire just whoever they want. They take bids and get contractors from up the line. They pay 'em ten times as much. Go figure.'

'You mean Mr Osborne in my road? Charlie's dad?'

'Yeah, but he's headmaster now.'

'I know. He's mum's boss, remember?'

'More to the point, babe, he's Alice's headteacher. He's the one rang Aunt Debbie saying she didn't turn up Friday. He has to ring every time because Alice is "at risk". Or possibly "a risk". Can't remember.'

Khadija sits up a little straighter. 'What's it called?'

'What's what called?'

'The academy. What's the name of it?'

'@Saltash, with the 'at' symbol. So lame.'

'I mean the company, the trust. Is that the same name?'

'Oh. Resolve Logistics. That's what it said on the final payslip. Why?'

'Because when the Osbornes are part of something, it's usually dodgy. Surely people know that?'

'Charlie's all right, though. He proper loves Alice.'

'They're fifteen, Jo.'

'I was fourteen when me and Ben hooked up.'

'Yeah, that went real smooth.' Khadija looks at Jo's belly with dramatically raised eyebrows until Jo puts two fingers up at her. 'Charlie's mum rung Aunt Tammy trying to get *information*; she's that worried about him. He's all curled up in his room apparently, feeling abandoned.'

'Poor Charlie. He's a sweetie. Nothing like his dad.'

'Tammy's coming apart and all,' Khadija says. 'You know what she's like.'

'She might help. You know her. Just when you think it's all bollocks, she comes through.'

'Little cow, Alice, winding everybody up. Wait till I see her.'

Chapter 4

Lower Fore Street is empty when Khadija gets home. The smell of fags and vinegar hangs around the doorway. She stops by the door to take off her shoes and drape her coat on the radiator. The walls are a new colour and so is Carol's hair. It's all too much to think about.

'Crap, I'm freezing! Have you got the windows open?'

Silence.

'Mum!'

'Hiya, babe. I'm in the kitchen.'

Carol is kneeling on a tea towel cleaning inside the cooker. That's why the vinegar.

'The house smells like fags, Mum.'

'I went out the back, I swear.'

'Well, if you stand half out the door it just blows into the house.'

Carol puts the kettle on and stands.

'Vinegar and bicarb,' she says. 'It's brilliant; you could use it to strip paint. Seen it on Instagram.' She stands up and pulls off her rubber gloves finger by finger. Her nails are a mess.

'I've seen Jo,' Khadija says. 'Is Aunt Debbie OK?'

'Give us a hug, lovely.' She comes around and leans her weight onto Khadija. 'Thank God you're my daughter. I'm so lucky I got the level-headed one.'

'Yeah, that's me. The level-headed one. Fun. Have they heard from Alice yet?'

'No, love. Just got off the phone with your aunt. I think you've come back with a broken heart. It was a boy, wasn't it?'

'It was not a boy, you know that. And we're not going to talk about it. What the hell happened to Alice lately? And why haven't you been telling me?'

27

'She's in some trouble. Well, I mean, she isn't always well.'

'Mum, say what you mean.'

'She's got mental problems. Emotional problems, I guess.'

'I know that.'

'She tried to – you know. Once before.'

'Christ.'

'Tamara came to my door jibbering at one in the morning. Time I got to Debbie's house the ambulance was driving away with her.'

'Where would she go, do you think?'

'I don't know. Debbie has to wait twenty-four hours before the police'd do anything, now there'll be a mountain of bloody paperwork. Tammy says she knew yesterday morning. She says that now, of course. Didn't say a word earlier.'

Khadija pulls out a chair and sits at the immaculate table. Everything in her mother's house reflects empty light. She'd forgotten how exposed she feels here.

'Drink this.' Carol holds out a mug with the 'Saltash for Success' academy logo on it.

'What is it? It smells of vinegar.'

'Vinegar and honey. You need it, after you've gone running about in the freezing rain.'

'I do not need it. I promised Aunt Tammy I'd go over for a cuppa. Want to come?' But Khadija doesn't move to stand up. She carries on staring at the empty light caught in the kitchen table.

'You gonna stop here for five minutes at some point?'

'Yes, Mum. In fact, I'm stopping indefinitely. You'll get sick of me, don't worry.'

'We're all being TUPE'd at the school.'

Khadija looks up. 'What the hell is too-peed?'

'It's a job review thing. There's gonna be redundancies. They want to get rid of all the support staff.'

'Crap, Mum. That sucks. They sacked Ben and Mr Jinks and all. Jo told me.'

'Signing on is a nightmare these days. I might have to move out and rent the house or something. I don't know what I'm gonna do, Khadi.'

'Mum, you're not listening. I'm here. I told you, I start at Bright and Tunstall on Monday.'

'I'm worried you're throwing away your degree, maid. You worked so hard to get there.'

'Well, I couldn't have got this job without it. It's crap money until I pass my CILEX exams, but it'll buy us groceries and pay the council tax. Stop worrying.'

Khadija lifts her arms up over her head to hug Carol behind her.

'Jesus, girl, your hands are freezing!'

'You smell like the cooker.'

'Drink that before you go to Tammy's or I'll lock you out the house.'

'Fine, you hippie witch.'

'You ask me, Alice does all this just to frighten her mum. She's controlling.'

'This is disgusting!' Khadija puts down her cup and pushes it away. 'Alice hasn't posted anything since the day before yesterday, but that's not so odd. Sometimes she goes quiet for a few days.'

'You have no idea what that girl's put Debbie through.'

'Right, I don't, because you didn't tell me.'

'I was trying not to weigh you down. Sue me.'

She means it. Every time her mother lies to her, she thinks she's doing a kindness. It all comes anyway, just Khadija doesn't see it coming till it falls on top of her because her mother's curled up in a corner having a breakdown.

'I changed Alice's nappies, Mum. She's my family. It's not weighing me down.'

It is weighing her down, of course. It's stones in her pockets and chains around her neck.

'Khadija, I need to give you something.'

'Oh, here we go. What?'

'Finish that and I'll show you.'

'I'm not gonna finish it. Tell me.'

Khadija looks at herself in the shiny perfect window, smiling like anyone normal until Carol comes back with a big square Cadbury's tin. She's cradling it against her chest, with a pack of cigarettes balanced on the top edge.

'Beth Kennedy left it. Craig's sister.'

'I know who Beth is, Mum. I had a degree course, not amnesia.

'She said it was for you.'

Carol puts the tin down on the table and lays her fag pack on the worktop next to the kettle. A train blows a warning on the Devon side of the bridge, about to follow the green signal over.

'How is Beth, anyway?'

'She's working over at Millbay. They got her on drugs. She never got over her brother dying. First she was so angry, and then she just turned it all inside herself.'

'If people know she's working over there, why isn't anyone trying to help her?'

'You're right judgemental for someone who hasn't bothered to visit no one in ages. Of course, people tried. Last time she came round here, she pawned her mother's flat screen.'

'God, why did I come back?'

Khadija has to hug the tin to her body in order to get her nails under the lid and lift it. When it pops off she nearly drops the whole thing. She can feel the heaviness and lightness of the things inside, crushing each other.

'Khadija? Milk or not?'

'Milk, Mum. Since when do I take tea black?'

'You used to. Said you felt sorry for the cows, because they fed them hormones and took their babies away to get to the milk.'

'You're making that up.'

There are coins sliding on the bottom of the tin. Lifting the lid, Khadija sees a little bird's nest, some papers and printed photos tucked along the side. Something made of cloth, folded.

No, not now. She puts the lid back and leans her arms on it.

'I am not making it up,' Carol says. 'You refused to drink milk for two whole years. My mum told me this would happen. You'd grow up and we'd remember everything in two different ways. I didn't listen to her.'

'What's Aunt Tammy saying? About Alice, I mean.'

'I don't know, Khadi. The last thing we need to do right now is listen to Tamara Williams. You going to open that?'

'I will, but not now.' Khadija puts the tin on a spare chair and stands up to push it under the table.

There is not enough gravity on earth to account for the way everything inside it pulls on her. It feels like Craig is in the room, making sad eyes in the corner. *Please Khadi, lift me up. Make me less dead.*

Fuck off.

'Poor Craig,' Carol says. 'I liked him.'

'Hello? I'm your daughter. Can you maybe be the one person whose first thought when they look at me isn't, *poor Craig*.'

But Khadija smiles, a real smile this time. Carol is sweet, underneath it all. She means well.

Khadija will have to sort through Craig's things eventually. There might be something in there, something about Mr Kennedy's pay-out, the class action suit maybe. Some link in the chain of things that led to Craig lying lifeless in the mud. Something that isn't in the Lexis files or Hansard. Could be that tin is the reason she came back.

'Khadi?' Carol has a hand on her shoulder. 'I put milk.'

'I'm glad to see you, Mum. I am.' Khadija takes the teacup in both hands and leans sideways into Carol.

'Right, I need to ring Jan.'

'Tell her I'll go round first thing tomorrow. Tell her I love her.' She picks up the tin and heads for the stairs. 'I wish somebody had filled me in. This is a lot, even by Saltash standards.'

'Nothing around here has changed, maid. You know it all already anyway.'

Chapter 5

The one long breath of day begins to rise off the river while most everyone in Saltash is still sleeping. Charlie Osborne lies curled on the sofa next to his mother's empty wine glass, waiting even in his dreams. Dreaming of Alice ringing, returning. His father's exasperated sigh drifts past without disturbing him.

Anthony Osborne shakes his head at the sight of his son nestled under a fleece blanket and pulls the door to. He can picture his wife, Tina, unsteady on her feet after two Chardonnays, sliding gently out from under the boy and tucking her perfectly coordinated throw up under his chin. Always wrapping you up, that woman. Anthony reties his robe and steps through into the kitchen. The sky is only just lightening; the house will stay quiet for an hour at least.

Maybe that ridiculous girl has gone home in the night. Maybe when the rest of the world wakes up it will all be over and he can have his Sunday. Somehow the media hadn't got wind of anything yesterday, thank God. No 'Headmaster Claims School Took Appropriate Safeguarding Measures' headlines. Not yet.

A slice of river appears in the growing light beyond the Union Pub, a dinghy slipping out toward Mount Edgecumbe. He fills a cafetiere and leans over it to inhale the smell that rises up.

His father should be there. He was never frightened by the press or the unions or the parliamentary committees. Barristers didn't faze him. The only thing that ever unsettled Anthony's father was Anthony's mother, and she unsettles everyone.

She'll want him up at the house today, his mother. He promised to cut back the Virginia creeper and trim the box hedge. She'll watch through the window, looking pathetic from behind the glass like a ghost or an abused child, pulling out of him some sympathy he didn't know he had. His authority will leak out into the early

March mizzle and fall sodden on the grass. By the time Anthony heads home he'll feel heavy and dirty as the mud along the walkway.

When the landline rings he's at the breakfast table, looking out at the campanula between the paving stones in the patio. The second ring of the telephone cuts through the kitchen, but the yard on the other side of the glass remains quiet and still. On the third ring Charlie runs in through the kitchen door.

'Don't, Son.'

'It might be Alice,' Charlie says.

'And it might be the papers, or BBC Southwest, or some community support idiot. Leave it.'

'Good morning to you too, Dad. Thanks for your concern; I'm fine.'

'I know you're taken with that girl, Charlie. I sympathise. This town is full of women like her. Don't think I don't understand.'

'But?'

The phone rings a fourth time and Anthony gets up to refill the kettle.

'But we need to be careful who we speak to. This is my job on the line here.'

'This is a girl's life on the line! Jesus. Anyway, she wouldn't ring the landline. I need to charge my phone.'

'Listen to me, Charlie. This is very important. If you fall for their melodrama, they'll control you. You'll never be rid of it.'

'I get what you're not saying, you know. I'm not stupid.' Charlie sits bent over the glow of his phone so that Anthony can't make out what's in his eyes.

'No one thinks you're stupid. I just want to give you the benefit of my experience. I want you to start one step ahead. Tell me, how that is wrong?'

'Ahead of what?'

'See? The ringing's stopped.'

But the front door bangs at the same time. Not the smallest interval of peace between. Anthony's hour of civilised quiet evaporates into the light outside.

'Morning, me lovelies.' Tina is dressed and has lipstick on. Lipstick at eight in the morning, that is Tina in a nutshell. 'Who was that on the phone?'

'We don't know because Dad wouldn't let me answer it.'

Tina picks up the handset and dials 1471.

'Withheld number. Muffin, babe? Porridge?' She leans over and kisses Anthony from behind Charlie's chair, all the time with a loving hand on Charlie's head, owning him.

'There, you see, Charlie?' Anthony says. 'Withheld number. Journalist.'

'What's going on?' She turns on the tap and reaches for a sponge to wipe the worktop that's already clean.

'Bloody Alice Tregidga still hasn't turned up. It's been 48 hours.'

'Oh, poor Alice. Charlie, you all right?'

Anthony blows out a breath and counts to three. 'Poor Alice! Who do you think is going to catch hell if she's done something to herself? Who do you think will have to talk to the bloody *West Briton*? They'll be on about how academy comprehensives aren't succeeding, no support services. They'll quote my salary on line three, no doubt. As though making a living and balancing the budget is some sort of crime.'

'Anthony! Alice is Charlie's friend. He's worried.'

'It's a control tactic, Tina, as you know perfectly well. How many hours have you spent at the Samaritans listening to people claiming they're going to do themselves in?'

'Give up, Mum. He has no feelings. He was just born that way.'

Charlie heads for the door, hating him again. The women in Anthony's life exist to make him look bad. It doesn't matter that he's done nothing at all.

'He doesn't mean it, sweetie. Everyone's tense.'

And there she is, posing as the reasonable one. Tina slips into every available crack, turns any colour. Everybody falls for it, even Charlie. She's in the house five minutes and he's on her side. He'll be in his room with the door shut for hours now, swiping through Snapchat and posting about his soulless father.

'Well, if I'm going to spend Sunday morning being insulted, I might as well go to my mother's.' Now he is the one who sounds like a petulant child. How do they do it?

'No one's insulting you, love.'

'If the news ring, don't tell them where I've gone.'

'You need a shave, handsome.' She rubs her cheek against Anthony's.

If you didn't know any better, you'd think she meant it. She hands him an old jumper from the front closet before he can think to ask for it, then stands behind the kitchen island looking as though she's in a washing powder advert. She likely stands like that the whole time he's away, waiting for the curtain to go up again so she can say her lines.

'Alice is troubled, Anthony. Whether it has anything to do with your salary or not. What will they do?'

'No idea. Depends how far the stupid girl's gone and when she decides to turn up.'

'Poor Alice,' she says again.

Anthony opens the front door and looks back at her still posing with her hands on the work surface. She has exactly the right look on her face. Her hips are perfect and her breasts are ageless.

Witch, he thinks. *Siren*.

He turns round to see Carol Sleep standing in her front doorway and thinks the same thing again. *Witch*. *Siren*.

Good God, the daughter's back as well. There she is, saying goodbye to the mother, and Carol Sleep right on the front step in nothing but a T-shirt and pants in broad daylight. In front of her boss. She's wearing what looks like some man's football shirt. Lord knows whose, could be anybody she picked up in the Brunel. Whoever he is, he won't stay long. Probably a pupil's father; it's happened before. She's been with at least one of the staff as well. Now Tina has crept up behind him, pressed into his back with her chin on his shoulder.

'You forgot your work gloves.'

'Morning, Anthony,' Carol says. 'Tina.' An afterthought. Carol doesn't speak to women if she can avoid it.

'Morning, Carol.' Tina, on the other hand, talks to anyone. Little old ladies, homeless men, pathetic strangers on the phone at three in the morning.

'And Khadija!' she says. 'Lovely to see you back. How you keeping, sweetie?'

'Hi Mrs Osborne. How are you?' Khadija says.

Khadija is far enough away right now so Anthony doesn't have to see into her eyes, but if he could he knows what would be there. A picture of himself as some kind of creep, a letch. Blame everything on men, those two. And sometimes other men believe them, fall into their trap and go charging around like knights in armour. Look where that got Craig Kennedy.

If it weren't for women like the Sleeps every town in England would run more smoothly. There'd be less violence and probably fewer drugs, too.

Whose idea was it to let Carol Sleep work in a school? If Anthony had been headmaster then, he'd never have hired her. Everything that's wrong with education, right there. Schools have become workhouses for fallen women, all sitting in the staff room talking about *Celebrity Blind Date* and making angels out of toilet tissue rolls. Thank God the academy trust is planning to get rid of the TAs. Sound strategy. Waste of money, paying someone to do what the teachers ought to be doing already.

'Well, I'll leave you to it.' Anthony gives a general wave. Let them all stand there, looking their meaningful looks at each other. It nearly makes him glad to be going to his mother's house.

When he turns to look back from the top of the hill, Carol Sleep's front porch is empty. The row of cottage windows reflects back jumbled pieces of the bridge. Relic of the nineteenth century, that row, had outdoor toilets not so long ago. Shabby, and sitting between Anthony's house and the view upriver.

What is Khadija Sleep doing back, anyway? The whole family is full of unhinged women and their spooky daughters, walking around town like ghosts, making men feel haunted. As soon as one disappears another one pops up out of nowhere.

The sun is thin on the hill. Down in the hollow at Wearde there's still a frost in the shadows, rime on the dark side of the council house roofs. Anthony walks up through the trees to his mother's house, remembering when it was all open space, when his father owned everything right down to the river. Before their family shrunk up into the side of the hill, before his father died and his mother fell into that wingback chair, so glad to be left alone that she couldn't hide her relief. She'll be perched up there now, like a crow, drinking in the shadows and watching everything, squawking out at Anthony whenever he comes close.

'Morning, Mother,' he calls out before he puts a foot over the doorstep.

'Son.' Her voice is so close it makes him jump. She's in the kitchen passage, wearing a Windsmoor skirt and a T-shirt that looks as if it could be Charlie's.

'Good Lord! What are you doing, Mother?'

'I was in the pantry, sorting things. Found your father's Henderson's Relish behind some tins.'

'Where did you get that T-shirt?' There is a wrecked ship lying on the hem and a diver floating near a line at the top that is the surface of the water. 'Scapa Flow' it says beside the wreck.

'I don't know; it just appeared. Nothing but sugar, this.' She waves the Henderson's at him.

'Pieces of clothing do not just appear, Mother. Have you been to the charity shops?'

'Possibly. I don't recall. Why are you interrogating me? Haven't you come to do the gardening?'

'Yes. As it happens, I'm your son as well as your gardener. Would you like to know how I'm doing?'

He can see it pass across her face, *not really*. But her voice says, 'Of course I would. Stop being hostile and come through.'

They stare at each other across the kitchen table while the kettle roars into the air. The look between them is frank and open, also blank. Anthony thinks of Tina and Charlie around the table at home, sharing confidences and sympathy, drawn into that circle of theirs that can be felt even from the next room. He looks away before his mother does, then gets up to make the tea.

'So,' she says, 'Charles' little girlfriend is missing again.'

'She'll turn up, though I'm sure she'll do her best to ruin my chances at promotion first.'

'What is promotion for a headmaster?'

'The trust owns half the schools in England, Mother. There's plenty of room for me to move up.'

'Tamara doesn't think she will turn up.'

'The T-shirt is one thing, Mother. If you start listening to Tamara Williams' nonsense, I'll have you evaluated.'

'This isn't 1953, Anthony. You can't put every woman who rubs you the wrong way into an institution.'

'Don't I know it.' Anthony lifts his eyes to the ceiling.

'Not dead either, Alice. According to the *voices from beyond*.'

'Imagine if the voices from beyond could say something useful? A grid reference would be nice.'

'Charles will feel it,' his mother says. 'He's obsessed with that spooky girl. You should talk to him. Try to sympathise.'

'Yes, I've already had my own lack of feeling explained to me once this morning, thank you. He'll feel it again when I lose my job and he can't have the new iPhone.'

'Don't be ridiculous. He'll always have the new iPhone. Even I know that.'

'The TAs are bloody unionising.'

'What?'

'I need to cut the staff budget. Every kid with nightmares or toilet issues gets a one-to-one these days. Bunch of ignorant women who sit in the staff room all day talking about *Celebrity Desert Island*.'

'Talking about what?'

'Please stop saying "what". I don't know what it's called. They trap a bunch of page three girls and footballers with permanent injuries somewhere with palm trees so women like Carol Sleep can watch them talk about sex and behave horribly to each other. I hear about it all day long while kids with heroin addicts for parents are pulling the blinds apart and throwing the desks through the windows.'

'I believe those are the children who bring the most money. Isn't that what you told me when you took up the post?'

'Bloody pupil premium. Absurd waste of public money.'

'Not public anymore, is it? It's in your wallet. The other Sleep girl is back too, you know.'

Is she trying to make him uncomfortable?

'Yes, I saw her just now. You never leave this house; how on earth do you know everything that happens down the hill?'

'Will she cause you trouble, do you think?'

'Who? Khadija Sleep? Why would she cause me trouble?'

'Don't you find it odd, her leaving the day Craig Kennedy died and then coming back just now?'

'No, it isn't odd. Her mother lives here. London is expensive. What kind of skills can that girl have? She'll be in a flat in Saint Stephen's with three children before you know it.'

'The one appearing and the other disappearing feels like providence, a god in the machine.'

'Mother, you sound mad. But I do grant you the world would be far less disturbing without all the girls in it. No offence.'

'None taken. I gave up being a girl years ago. It didn't suit me at all.'

She stands at the window while he does the gardening, watching like a waif from Dickens. So much smaller than she used to be. From far away, she almost looks vulnerable. Anthony doesn't remember the gardening gloves until he scratches himself and starts to bleed. When he does put them on, he can feel the dirt inside them rubbing into the scratches and poisoning him, making mud out of his blood.

He cuts the vines from the side of the house and piles them on what's left of the slope of the front lawn. When he was a child he could run and slide all the way to Wearde Quay. Now there are grey roofs and rows of garages in the way; he can't unimagine them. The world has been steadily shrinking since he was fourteen.

Doing the box hedge is soothing. He loses himself making perfect planes with the clippers, tightening the green horizon in front of him. When he looks up, Nora is gone from the window. The sun is round behind Trematon and it's time to burn the vines. He hasn't stopped for lunch and feels shaky, unanchored. Tina will be cooking and fielding the phone calls. Charlie will have been online all day, passing panic around among his friends. You can't stop them.

It takes four long matches and two advertisers to get the branches alight, even though he begins with dry things he cut months before. The new green at the top of the pile smokes and stinks. Anthony looks through the haze at St Budeaux Wharf smudging into the river.

Just along there they found him, wedged half under a two-masted boat. That wasn't where he'd gone in; the tide had carried him down and left him. Currents in the Tamar are fickle; they pull people under and then either throw them back up into the light or they don't. No telling where or when. Craig Kennedy happened to wash up close to home and barely rotten.

Anthony's eyes fill with water and the world before him tips ... Devon rising and himself falling back toward the Lynher. What is the matter with him? The women have got under his skin today. He coughs the smoke out of his lungs and shakes his head to wash the wet memory away.

He needs food, and then a strong drink.

It's the Sleep girl, landing like a loud accusation, making him feel pulled and pushed at the same time without her having to say anything at all. *Don't you find it odd*, his mother said, *her coming back just now*? But it isn't odd at all; the parts fit perfectly. He can just about hear them, clicking into place.

Chapter 6

Nora Osborne's house is squat and sprawling. She likes to think of it as a bungalow with pretensions. It sits alone among the usual shrubs up on the hill above Wearde, wrapped round the slope making room for windows with views. Nora enjoys the views but not the sunlight. She waits until Anthony is long gone and it's full dark to turn out the lamp and open the drapes on the big picture window.

The first thing she sees is Khadija Sleep, crossing the bridge walkway. She shines into the road lights with bits of her hair and her clothing tossing about in the wind blowing off Rame. Anthony is not wrong about the Sleep girls; they're loose and unsettling. They don't tie anything up, don't seem to have edges.

The river has disappeared, leaving only the shining streets and the square windows, the corner of her son Anthony's roof showing between the other roofs below. Nora spoons in the last of her pea soup and sits back with her cognac, keeping her back straight and feet on the floor, because even when there's no one watching you imagine a watcher. That is how it's done. Was done. The way Nora does it still.

If her husband Jon were here, they would have the overhead light on and the bridge would be invisible. There would be more than soup, and she would wait until the sitting room for her cognac. If Jon were here, there would be an acid jangle running up and down her spine like strychnine, and she'd be wearing shoes.

When Nora met Jonathan Osborne, she'd counted on him not being trained in the private cruelties of her mother's family, and was partly correct. He certainly did not understand the lounging and the drawling, having gone to Malvern. Nora thought she could live in the breeze created by his rapid movement. She thought she was

41

shaking up the world, but gently so that it would all flutter down around her like the silver dust in a snow globe.

Jonathan's cruelties turned out to be public and impersonal, and she managed to ignore them for years.

Every night of their marriage he came home, opened himself and let the world out. It settled down on her like coal smoke, leaving a gritty residue. Nora was not intended for that kind of thing. Ideally, the world and her marriage would have been safely isolated, but her grandfather had invested in the green revolution. Hundreds of thousands of people starved in places that were still just about colonies. Executive jobs were lost and he didn't move his money out quickly enough. Nora, with some of those accounts attached to her, married a man with a position. A career, even. She saved her family and then they spent the rest of their lives looking down on her.

This is the house where those tides left her. Here is what remains of her marriage and of the time before. A few pieces of Chinese porcelain and a set of drawers someone once suspected of being made by Hepplewhite; what the law calls her paraphernalia.

Nora wiggles her bare toes and turns back toward the window. Across the blank darkness below Khadija and the bridges, she can see Saltash Passage curving around into the trees. She can see Craig Kennedy falling. He tumbles into the light with one arm out of his jacket, sheepskin lining flapping behind him. The invisible water is high; it takes only a moment to embrace him and erase him. The stretch of his skin, the organs inside, the sacs of his lungs like bunches on a vine, working so perfectly they open to the river water without complaint.

It happened in that hour no one seems to remember. Ask anyone else, they'll tell you they woke up suddenly at one in the morning. They drank too much, took a hot bath, had a long day, fell asleep on the sofa in front of a film, woke an hour later not knowing how they'd gotten where they were. Ask Nora and she'll tell you nothing, of course. In fact, she had found herself with her head in her arms at the dining table, curtains still drawn.

No one saw Craig Kennedy that night, apart from Khadija Sleep, but Nora sees him often now.

There he is again, sliding down the bank this time, with his feet flexed, heels digging channels into the mud. Going in feet first and slowly, unconscious. He takes five full minutes to fail to save himself.

Behind Craig are other, older men. Men who might take longer to drown because they are already suffocating. Craig's own father, lying at Derriford for two months. If Nora ever met him, she doesn't remember it. Why would she? She went to the funeral, of course.

She does remember every day he was in hospital, because it was during that time that she first understood what Jon and the others had done.

She remembers Tamara's husband, Micky, at home with his oxygen tank. On the sofa in the front room smiling at everyone else's children because he and Tamara had none of their own. He even smiled at Anthony, fourteen years old when they went in to visit. Nora couldn't bear to bring grapes, which reminded her of lungs even before all that. She brought clementines and Anthony sat sullen on the edge of a chair. On the way back up the hill, he'd made a nasty joke about their kind of people and been very pleased with himself. It wasn't the first time Nora hated her own son, but perhaps there was reason not to hate him just then. A teaching moment, the books call that. She might have said something; he was hers to teach after all.

Fruitfulness is very much overrated.

She looks out and Craig Kennedy is rolling sideways this time, still unconscious. He must have been unconscious. It isn't easy to fall into that river sober, and Craig hadn't drunk much, they said. Now she can't see a jacket at all, or shoes. Was he planning to swim? At the end of September? Was he going after something in the trees?

There is Khadija Sleep on the bridge walkway, and Nora cannot tell what time she's in. Is she the Khadija from before or the one who has returned? Is she walking above Craig's falling body, or walking home from the Ferry Inn right now? Tonight, or that night? The floodlights from the bridge are shining down the right side of her, and her shadow falls away through the wire grid of the walkway cage.

Whenever she is, it is certainly her. Nora can tell by the hair and the way she holds her body up, with her shoulders climbing to her ears and her eyes turned away, pretending to be afraid of her own power, her own pull. She is thoroughly her mother's daughter, the grammar school and the pre-Raphaelite hair don't alter that.

Nora keeps quiet about these things. Bragging about them turns a woman mad and obvious like Tamara Jinks, who has been Tamara Williams for decades now.

Yes, it could be Khadija who left Craig Kennedy to fall. He would have followed her to the edge, or anywhere, and that would be easier to believe than other things. Everyone knew Khadija might have saved him from his odd loneliness and his river wandering. He was begging her to. But she walked away above the river and left him falling, didn't she?

Nora will let herself believe it. She will.

Once Nora has gone to bed, the moon swings up over the house. Cooling air makes its way round the corners and forms in drops on the glass behind the drawn curtains, river clinging to the walls. The big clock ticks against the hallway tiles and something settles in behind the airing cupboard. Nora has no dreams, black hours like blankets layer up.

Her grandson, Charles, comes in the morning while she is looking through the kitchen window, out across the Lynher. He is standing on the porch with his hand on the electric bell, about to ring a second time, when she opens the door.

'I'm about to hug you, Grand. Get ready.'

'I'll endure. There. Now come in and sit stiffly on the sofa like a good middle-class boy.'

'No, you sit stiffly. I'll make the tea.'

'How old are you now? When can we graduate to cognac?'

'It's ten in the morning, Grand. We're having tea forever if it's before noon.'

'Forever before noon. How lovely. It sounds like a lost novel by Rebecca West.'

'OK. Sit.'

'I do not respond to dog commands, young man. You clearly need a retriever. I have told your father this.'

The sound of him moving about the kitchen disturbs Nora. No, it comforts her. That is what is disturbing. He is so determined, so loud and direct. You'd know he wasn't Anthony or Tamara even if you hadn't looked. Underneath, he's only just holding it together, dying inside over the Tregidga girl, but he doesn't want Nora to see. He comes back with two cups, a packet of Garibaldis and her brother's boarding school chess set.

'Go back and get a plate, please.'

'The plate is pointless, Grand. The biscuits will be gone in two minutes and then someone will have to wash it.'

'The same can be said of everything we do. Humour me, Charles.'

And he does. She can hear him pushing a kitchen chair over to the cabinet. He comes back with a Sheffield cake plate that belonged to her parents.

'So, if I get a retriever, will you walk it with me up to the castle?'

'That walk would take me hours. I'd fall ill with sunstroke long before we got there.'

'Dad could drop us off part way. You need some sun on you, Grand. There's a rumour going around that you're a vampire.'

'Well, you obviously like vampires, judging from your girlfriend.'

'Don't, Grand.'

'Right. I'm sorry. I am actually sorry. But do please rethink her.'

'Rethink her? You can't rethink a person. People just are and you don't get to control it.' He holds out two fists and she picks the black queen. 'I'm gonna play the way you do. Mad chess.'

'I do not play mad chess.'

'You never have a plan, but you always win.'

'There's a lesson in there, young man. Anyway, why are you not in school?'

'Mum didn't make me go. I just can't today. Everyone will expect me to know something. About Alice, I mean.'

He leads with bishop's pawn and they are quiet for some time, going through a set of opening moves they both memorised when Charles was five. The thing in the air between them is love. Nora loves Charles and neither of them has to say so. He is the one mistake she didn't make. Imagine a whole life in which everything one had done were as right as Charles.

'Grand, do you like Dad?' As though he'd heard her thought.

'He's my son, Charles. Liking doesn't come into it. I like *you* very much, which is more relevant with grandchildren.'

'I like you, too. You don't like Dad, do you?'

'Has no one told you we don't discuss those things?'

'Didn't you ever think that's what's wrong with us?'

'No. There is so much more wrong with us than that. Since everyone pretends this is America these days, I'm going to "plead the fifth" with regard to your father.'

Nora is not keeping silent out of a sense of maternal duty or general decorum. There are things about Anthony that Charles is better not knowing, that he will never know from her.

'Wow. I almost feel sorry for him. Everyone blames him. What about Mum? She sits there all day pretending things are normal, bleaching everything and lighting scented candles from Waitrose, as if that's gonna make things more real.'

'Charles, you are exhibiting teenage angst. You've no doubt caught it off the vampire.'

'Grand!'

'I'm sorry again. Or possibly still sorry.'

'She never turned up at school on Friday. She didn't come home over the weekend either. I can't stay at our house waiting for her to text me. I can't take it.'

That is why he has come. For comfort. Nora is his comfort.

Something twists inside her. Her heart, her womb, some organ related to progeny and triggered by a vestige of procreative hormones. It is painful to see the look on his face. Physically painful.

'Why not look for her?' she asks. 'You know her best.'

'I've been all round Saltash this morning. I've thought of every possible thing that could be found already. Trust me.'

'Do you want to tell me? You could, you know. I won't be flip, I promise.'

'She didn't even message me, Grand. Why didn't she message me?'

'People don't, in most cases. I mean— No, forget I said that.'

'Which is going to be worse? Finding nothing or finding something?' Charles looks into her eyes. 'Why do so many people disappear here? It's like we live next to a hole in the bottom of the world.'

'A boy went missing once, when I was very young. They found him, eventually.'

'Dead?'

'No, he was fine. His mother never seemed to get over it, though. And they both died soon after.'

'I didn't think you lived here when you were small?'

'I didn't. I was visiting over at Antony House. It's one of my earliest memories, the day little Thomas Bone went missing.'

'Antony? In Torpoint? I knew you were posh, but I didn't think you were *that* posh.'

'Very funny. We weren't. Well, I don't know. Perhaps we were, but the money had gone, and my mother hadn't married any more of it. We used to get invited, I suppose out of pity. I don't know.'

'So,' Charlie says, 'your life was like some kind of period drama, basically.'

'Ha! In no way whatsoever.'

'What happened? With the boy?'

'I was at the back of the lawn that day, lying near the adults. One of the Antony people had a wiry little terrier called Rodney, who kept putting his wet nose on the backs of my legs. I could hear all the adults talking, but it was just garbled nonsense, the way it is when you're a child. It wasn't the words that caught my attention, it was the panic. Most of the time, those people lounged in the garden as though it were a vocation; they drawled like they owed it to the national effort.'

Charles settles back. He likes for her to tell stories, has a listening stillness Anthony never had.

'Some of the grown-ups got up and started to pace about. The women, I think. It felt as if a blanket had been torn off the afternoon. Then someone lifted me up and carried me up to the nursery, shut me in with the other children. The grown-ups were acting as if a hole that swallowed children had opened in the world and Thomas had dropped through it. As if they needed to be careful the rest of us didn't fall through it, too.'

'I think Mum is like that right now. She keeps putting her hands on me like I might rise out of my chair and slip away.'

'Funny you used those words. *Hole in the bottom of the world.* That was just what I thought at the time. Check.'

'Crap! Sorry, Grand. It was Alice who said that to me first, about the hole in the world. Was Thomas Bone your friend?'

'Oh, no. I had no idea of Thomas Bone before that day, what he looked like or which things he could and couldn't do.'

'What was wrong with him?'

'Nothing at all. I think Thomas Bone was a new category of people for me. He belonged out of doors. It was another year at least before I realised people like the Bones had houses of their own into which they could go.'

'Jesus, Grand!'

'What shall I do, pretend it wasn't that way? I went to the Bones' house later, with my mother. The place was little and very clean, with wear at the edges of everything.

'The afternoon he went missing, we could see the grown-ups from the nursery windows, fanned out all over the grass and the water. Someone brought us a cold supper much too late. I was still watching through the dark when they brought Thomas up Tomboy Hill, wrapped in a blanket.'

'Your move, Grand.'

'There was a cluster of lanterns around him when he came over the top. All I could see of the man carrying him was arms, the rest of him faded into the shadow. The whole group of them disappeared toward Butland and then the big people stayed downstairs murmuring for hours.'

'So the kid was OK? Where'd he been?'

'Curled up under Wearde Quay. Lost. He was fine, yes, but not for long. A few years later, he and his mother went shopping in Plymouth and then into the bomb shelter at Portman Square. Tamara Jinks says everyone in the shelter that day died with their clothes on fire. She says it smelled of burning sugar. Tamara thinks she knows these things.'

'I had no idea you ever stayed at Antony. Is that why you named Dad that?'

'Your grandfather named him. I wasn't consulted so I've no idea why. If it was for the house, it's spelled incorrectly.'

'I can't believe Dad never told me you hung out with baronets. Seems like the kind of thing he'd brag about constantly.'

'It was all long before he was born. I'm sure he'd blame me for not keeping up the connection. Your father would no doubt sacrifice a limb to be invited there, though of course he's exactly the sort of person they'd never notice.'

'You *don't* like him.'

'Well, I believe my grandmother would say that the family have "sadly declined", but I'd say your father is just the sort of thing that happens when we're left to our own devices.'

Chapter 7

Khadija stops to look at Debbie and Pete's house. It's Monday evening and all the cars are lined up obediently in all the driveways. The little cul-de-sac full of Barratt Homes that look like a set from *Harry Potter* – like the people who hate magic live there. The last thing it looks like is a box that would hold Alice. How the hell did they *not* think she would run away?

Khadija will go indoors and comfort everyone, make tea so it can go cold, untouched while she tells them Alice will be fine. Because Alice isn't with Charlie Osborne and she still isn't home. Khadija can't panic with everyone else because she is the one who doesn't.

She stands in the middle and turns in a circle, looking past the houses and down the road. Could that be the shadow of Alice, fading through the passages between shrubs, taking her pigeon-toed high-tops down the middle of the road at sunrise, lying right here on the asphalt, looking like Micky Williams, like Mr Kennedy, like a person without a person inside? Like Craig? This is home, shadows of the dead layering up on top of each other until sometimes you don't know which is which. Who's still here and who isn't. She never tried to explain it to anyone in London, because how would you? But she spent the whole time there trying to find out why. Why us? How did they do it? To Tammy's Micky, to Mr Kennedy. To Craig.

Debbie and Pete's front door stands open but there are no lights on downstairs. The patio doors are open too. Maybe they think Alice will wander back in like a missing cat. Wet air blows through over the carpeting.

The loft stairs are new. They made the conversion for Alice when she was thirteen, put her up there where she'd have to sneak past them before she could disappear. Where it's farther to fall. Khadija closes the front door and heads up the winding stairs.

They've got the Velux window open, too. Someone has tidied Alice's room, which they probably shouldn't have.

'It's getting dark.' Aunt Debbie hugs herself and looks out the window at the yellow light on the pavement.

Khadija puts a hand on Debbie's back and thinks of a wing sprouting there, for some reason. 'Listen, Aunt Debbie, she'll be fine. She's always fine, in't she?'

She's not going to be fucking fine because Khadija is going to strangle her, but no need to say that now. Also, she's never been fine. They've all known that since back when Alice still lived in her little girl room on the first floor. Khadija did as much as anyone to help sweep it under the carpet, but Alice was always the same. Now she's turned into a creepy little emo, listening to Marilyn Manson while she posts photos of her trauma on Instagram. No surprise really, but you can't say that to her mum.

'I'll make tea.'

She heads back down, then stops on the stairs to listen. Nothing but silence coming from Debbie and Pete. A very large silence. It feels different this time, but Khadija isn't going to admit that. Not yet.

Down in the kitchen the air is lighter, free from that anxious invisible fluid that breathes from the skin of mothers. It hangs around Jo already too, a cloud of something about to rot. Like the baby inside her is a fruit gone off. One day it will be Jo standing there like Aunt Debbie, helpless in front of some terrible absence. Why is Jo having a child when there are perfectly good pills for that?

There are forms pinned to the corkboard, a registration for doing the Ten Tors with the school next to Alice's therapy appointment card. Aunt Debbie said it took eight months to get Alice into counselling after the last time she disappeared. According to the card, she's supposed to be at an office in Liskeard in two days' time.

The police knock before the kettle boils, and the sight of Khadija in the hallway throws them. For a minute, they look confused, wondering whether they've knocked on the wrong door. Khadija laughs and then apologises, trying to look grave. They are some kind of special assessment officers, come out after hours because Alice is considered high risk.

'They're up in the loft, in Alice's room. Follow the stairs all the way up.'

'Are you a friend?'

'Cousin. I'm making tea?'

They shake their heads and say no thanks, then take their equipment belts up to the loft.

She makes the teas for Debbie and Pete with two sugars, even though Aunt Debbie normally doesn't take any. Sugar for shock, in't it?

The cops leave with Alice's laptop, her mobile number on a post-it stuck to it. Then it's time to stand by while Debbie really falls apart.

Once they've got her in bed, Khadija heads home down Fore Street. She winds through the people carrying bottles of wine out of the Co-op and under the blue light from inside the number five bus, pulled up outside the chippy. Opposite the Guildhall she stands looking into Lower Fore Street.

The daphne bushes are blooming their old lady perfume next to the turnstile from the bridge walkway. Khadija remembers coming through there with Beth Kennedy the night before she went to uni, but she can't remember anything for at least an hour before that.

She was legless, everyone was. It was the Friday before Freshers' Week and everyone was out – girls from Plymouth High together with people from the comps and people who hadn't done A-levels at all. Everyone's life was about to change, so of course the thing to do was get as pissed as possible and go ride the Torpoint Ferry. Khadija remembers the ferry toilet and then stumbling off the bridge walkway right here, with Beth Kennedy of all people. Everything in between is a blank.

Along their terrace the front windows are lit and the cars are perched on the slope, everyone back from work and turning on the telly. There will be no way to avoid her mother's hippie tea, unless she goes next door for Tammy's dramatic portents. No, and no. She turns her back on the bridge and the space below it, heads downhill toward the green.

The wind blows south from Bere Ferrers, full of sideways rain that runs into her collar and down her face. It feels cold and clean. Her trainers sink an inch into the squelching grass.

She bends over with her hands on her knees, feeling dizzy from the sudden change of pressure. Farah and London and wanting to be anything else rise up off her shoulders and release her. No one here is going to surprise or enchant her. There is nothing here to want, and no one left that she needs to refuse. A space opens inside her, a little something comes out with her breath. She leans into the sparkling night and lets herself go.

'Khadi Sleep.' A voice drawls her name in the darkness.

She says nothing, tightens her shoulders without noticing.

'I heard you were back.' It's a bloke her age in skinny jeans and a jacket. His head is uncovered, the drops of water in his hair shining red in the bridge lights.

She should probably know his name. She doesn't, which is why he'll think she's a snob.

'Hey,' she says.

'Nah.' He spits. 'Not hey. Whyn't you go back where you come from?'

'Uh, I come from here.'

'I don't mean that and you know it. Nothing good happens when you're about, Khadija Sleep.'

He does mean that, of course. That and all the rest of it. She carries on walking, shaking a little now. He doesn't follow.

And no, he isn't why she wants answers. She's spent six years telling herself it isn't her fault. She pretty much believes it. She wants the answers for herself.

She'll keep looking, keep tugging until she finds the end of the thread – of the boards behind companies and the companies on the boards, the liabilities and the bankruptcies and the drowning and suffocating. The asbestos mines in South Africa and the asbestos factories in Yorkshire, the procurement contracts and the shell companies.

Four hundred and twenty-three men on the Hamoaze had died when Khadija last counted. One of them was someone she loved, with a gravelly voice and watery eyes, who lay in bed for two years listening to Khadija read books about magic owls and pretending to be interested while he was slowly crushed to death by an invisible weight.

People have paid token liabilities, but not enough to weigh the scale against Micky Williams. Or Craig's dad, let alone four hundred and twenty-one other people. Mostly they hid the money and leaned on their mates in the higher courts.

Bright and Tunstall were thrilled when she applied; high street firms love a CILEX candidate. Cheap, at least until she qualifies. She'll work on conveyances and do probate, and nothing will ever happen to her again. The people there are nice enough. The office is full of dusty silence and, as far as Khadija can tell, no one called either Bright or Tunstall. They even let her interview by phone. It will be a lot of filing, a bit of research and full access to LEXIS.

Khadija stretches out her arms and lets the cold air in between them, opens her hand with the dinner receipt from her pocket crumpled in it, breathing deep until the ink runs onto her fingers and the paper melts. Her body softens into the wet dark. Some of the rain is tears, water she has carried inside her all the way down the line, running off her face and soaking into the green.

She makes sense here, whatever kind of sense it is. There is an empty space in the shape of her and its edges take some of her weight. She spins on the wet grass with her arms out and her feet squelching. Lighter and cleaner, hiding herself inside the person they all think she is.

Alice will turn up somewhere, spend a week or so looking thin in a hospital gown. All eyes on her while Khadija makes the tea, then everyone else will go quietly to sleep. Khadija will shut the door to her room and search until she finds answers. Beyond that, her life stretches on as blank as the water. Loveless and comforting.

She might have her own torts practice. Do union work, file some cases for the wives and the mums. There is far too much law in London and not nearly enough anywhere else. She could help change that.

She wipes tears and raindrops from her face and lets her shoulders down.

And then Craig falls out of the sky.

Nothing good happens when you're about, Khadija Sleep.

Craig splinters through the raindrops and slides through the sheets of darkness over the Ernesettle rails. His ghost voice whispers her name out of the electric light and cold metal around her. She turns toward Saltash Passage as though she might see him, still lying there with the river in his lungs. But it isn't that simple. Of course not.

That feeling of lightness fades into the rain. It was only a shadow on the river, a trick.

That last night, she let go for maybe two hours. Got pissed like normal people, got off with someone maybe, had a laugh. Forgot to remember. Wound up stumbling home with Beth Kennedy. And Craig picked that moment to fall. Six years later and people still blame her. He'd found a way in the end, to mark her forever and make himself her job.

Khadija turns her back on the river and starts climbing home through the laden air. It's as if Craig never hit the surface at all, just vaporised into the steam from the heating systems at North Yard and the clouds lying on the water. He is in front and behind her and falling all around.

At the top of the hill Tina Osborne is pulling out of her driveway. Khadija stops so they can both stand waiting for the window to slide down. Then they can say awkward hellos, and goodbye, take cares. See you soons.

'I'll come down for a cuppa with you lot,' Tina says, turning the car with the window still down. Odd because as far as Khadija can tell, Tina and her mum haven't spoken in years.

She doesn't ask what Khadija is doing home, doesn't look suspicious or judgemental. She is the first person in Saltash who doesn't seem to want anything from her, or want to lay anything down on her.

'Go hug your mum, bird.' Tina smiles and holds a hand out into the rain before she pulls away.

She is off to the Samaritans, where she'll spend all night talking to desperate strangers. Because who wouldn't choose that over sleeping in a house with Anthony Osborne?

Chapter 8

Tuesday morning, Tina drives back across the Tamar with the sun in her rear-view mirror and the wind banging into the side of the car in gusts. Wind like that, it's lucky they haven't closed the bridge. Anthony'd blame that on her, some way. She'd drive around to the ferry and be late home. Anthony would worry but he wouldn't say that. He'd say he couldn't find his washing or Charlie needed something he didn't have time to give. Anthony was raised to view a wife as somewhere to put your blame and your illegal bank accounts.

In the wind and the sunshine falling across from Devon she can see other days on the bridge walkway, other kinds of light, times when she was younger and less tired. Laughing or crying, or in a bunch of girls with cold legs, drunk-singing all the way home from the R.A.B.I. One of the girls would always be a Sleep. Carol or Debbie usually, because Jan would be somewhere else, glued to some useless bloke.

The first time Tina found out she was pregnant she stood right there on the walkway, looking through the railroad bridge at Wilcove, wondering what to do. She had the sort of parents who would have shouted about ruined opportunities and what the neighbours would think of her, pretend she'd got pregnant all by herself on purpose. No one has that sort of parents anymore. Well, maybe Charlie has one. If he got Alice pregnant, Anthony would call him trapped, a fool. Blame is the river they swim in. The river that drowned that little baby inside her, then drained away leaving her washed up in a new build with Anthony Osborne.

Turned out that while Tina stood there on the bridge walkway, dreaming she could still travel and maybe move to London with a lovely milk-smelling baby in a basket, Tammy Williams was up at the big house, talking to Nora Osborne about her and Anthony.

57

Those two cooking up the rest of Tina's life between them without even asking her.

Well, if Nora Osborne made her son marry Tina, it was Tina who said yes. Tina turned her back on the river, the Channel, the continent, the chance to wrap her baby in a rainbow-striped blanket and take her to the south of France, to Slovenia and Turkey. That isn't how you do in Saltash. You mend your seams and iron your jeans and bleach the worktop. The blankets are white or pink or blue, made by the knitting circle at St Nicholas. Tina does all that, and then for a holiday she spends all night over the bridge talking to urgent, fading people. A bit like Tammy really, if the other end of the phone was the spirit world. Down the phone line, needy people feel blurry and thin. It's a relief from the smell of bleach, and the rest of the sharpness in the house.

All she had last night at the Samaritans was a breather and the man who hates himself because he wants to have sex with his dog. He calls most nights, the breathers, too. You're supposed to hang up without saying anything, to protect yourself and not encourage them. Sometimes Tina just rests the phone gently down and goes for a tea. They're just as sad as anyone, having to wank down the phone at strangers.

Being at the Samaritans all night turns her personal clock upside down, but she's used to it. Mornings look different to her than they do to everyone else.

From the bridge, she can see the dirty little two-carriage train chugging over to Mill Pond. There is a girl on the walkway, heading through behind the betting shop onto Fore Street. The sun breaks out onto her hair and Tina sees that the girl is Alice, wearing Charlie's jacket. Her dark ginger waves light up like a dying fire and the girl straightens her shoulders into the warm sun falling on her back. She's been gone almost three days, but she doesn't look hurt or bothered at all.

Tina swerves left and lets down the passenger window. 'Alice!' A big pillow of wind pushes the name back into her throat. 'Alice!'

58

Alice ignores her, moving behind the fence and through the stile. The traffic light at the end of the bridge goes red.

'Shit!'

When the light changes again, Tina swings round onto Lower Fore Street and waits for Alice to come through the little square in front of Bet Fred's. There is a man with one metal crutch there, and Owen Moss with his bacon sandwich from the Kitchen Café. Tina waits a minute, two, three, but the pathway is still empty.

Alice would have to come through the gate at the end of the walkway, unless she's stopped on the bridge. Tina gets out of the car, leaves the door hanging open, and runs across the road. The daphne bushes by the stile are sending their dishonest perfume out into the cold. Over the rise onto the bridge, and the wind slaps Tina like the back of a hand. The view is clear all the way down to the bridge office. Two joggers heading for St Budeaux and someone dawdling, looking at the view with a freezing spaniel beside them. That's all. There is nowhere Alice could have gone without Tina seeing her.

She shakes her head while the rest of the morning disappears, the morning in which she would come into the kitchen with Alice, toast muffins and wake Charlie up, the two of them bringing happiness and safety and the light from the bridge with them indoors. The morning in which the men would change places; Anthony would fade back and Charlie would take up his space but all careful and soft, the way he is. For a minute that other morning was clear in front of her, just the way the life of her first child was, that other day on the bridge. Now all of it drops down past Tina's feet, splashes into the water and tumbles away.

The only things she's bringing home are the name the river has pushed back inside her, a bottle of bleach, a bottle of wine and a candle that smells like those daphne bushes, a lie told in the wrong season.

Alice has melted into the gold air over the river, with her skinny arms in Charlie's jacket and her promise of actual love.

'Charlie!' Tina shouts up the stairs with one hand on the newel post.

Silence. He's up there and he's awake, resting against the wall behind the bed with his head on his knees. Tina can see him without looking. She leaves him there and starts on the house.

When she does lean through his bedroom door, the smell nearly knocks her out.

'I'm opening this window. And I need you to help me shift the sofa.'

'You hoovered under the sofas yesterday, Mum. You have OCD.'

Charlie's window faces up the hill. The master bedroom has the view, past the bridges toward Tamerton and the morning sun.

'I do not have OCD. I like a tidy house. I'm a housewife; it's my job.'

'That is so 1950s. Don't you ever want to do anything else?'

'Not really. Come on. I need ya.'

Charlie bumps into the glass coffee table sitting in the hallway with the side tables piled on top of it. He's so tired, walking like someone's filled his arms and legs with sand.

'You're going to have to go to school tomorrow, lovely.' She says it while they're lifting the sofa, so he doesn't have to look her in the eye. 'You know your dad'll kick off if you take another day.' They rest the sofa down and she turns on the Hoover so he won't have to answer.

By the time she turns it off again, he's disappeared. She pulls the cushions off and attaches the upholstery nozzle. She can call him when it's time to put things back.

At the Samaritans, Tina deals with people's pain for eight hours at a time. Here it is now, in her own house, the kind of pain that beats out into the silence in waves you can feel from the next room. You push them out and give them your milk and build them up for years and then there's this. They're taller than you and they smell of some unfamiliar hormone, and they're dying inside but you can't help them at all.

She hears a little gasp from behind the sofa. Charlie hasn't gone upstairs. He's sitting behind there just like he sits all night in his bed, trying to sob without making any noise.

'Oh, sweetheart!' He tries to shrug her off and the springs are digging into her knees but she hangs on, stretched awkwardly over the back of the sofa to put her arms around him and rest her cheek on his hair.

Fucking little tart. Does she not care what she's done at all?

'She's dead, Mum. Everyone knows but no one will say it.'

'No babe, everyone doesn't know it. But we might need to start thinking what if.'

'Don't laugh at me?'

'I couldn't laugh right now, Charlie. Not when you feel like this.'

'She said she loved me. She lied.'

'I'm sure she meant it.'

'If she meant it, she wouldn't have left, would she? Dad says it's attention seeking. She's doing it to control people.'

'Get up here.' She throws the cushions back on and sits down. 'Come on, I need to explain you something.'

When he pulls his feet up on the sofa, Tina pushes them down before she can think about it. He flinches like having his stomach exposed to the air is painful. The dog next door starts barking hysterically and the post comes through the letter box.

'I'm so stupid,' he says. 'I can't believe I fell for it.'

'When people are depressed, they lose perspective. It's hard to tell what's right or what anybody else feels. Someone on the phone said to me once that it's as if you fall into a big hole in your own head and then you can't see out of it. You don't even remember there's a world out there. It isn't that Alice doesn't love you. She's probably convinced herself you're better off without her. Have you thought of that?'

'Dad said if I give in to it, women will always control me.'

'Your father thinks everyone is out to get him personally.' She shouldn't have said that, but it's sort of an emergency.

'Why did you marry him? He doesn't even like you.'

'That's not very nice. Not true, either.' But it is, half the time. 'I'll tell you what, you take a shower, put on some clean clothes and eat something. If you do that, I'll go up to see Tammy Williams and Carol Sleep. They might have some news.' He pulls his knees up again. 'Deal?'

He doesn't answer, but he does go up and turn the shower on. She heaves the sofa back by herself, one side at a time. It's nearly one o'clock; hopefully Anthony will have lunch at work. She's only just managed to get everything sorted and moving. If he blunders in now, it'll all grind to a standstill again and Charlie will curl back up in a ball on his bed.

Yes, she'll talk to Tammy, and Carol too. They've all lived with death together before now. They've all looked for the missing before. Tammy lost Micky and Carol lives like a widow too, because she banished the only man who was ever good to her.

From behind the kitchen worktop, Tina can see across to the houses along the top of Normandy Hill. The sky above them is the colour of wet river mud, the colour of Micky Williams' eyes, wide and lost over the oxygen mask. That brings the memory of the shape of Micky's hands, lying on top of the duvet, caressing each other. The sight of Tammy, wiry and efficient, making everything all right.

This is what they do, the women in Saltash. Sift through the trouble and make the houses quiet for people to die in. Move the furniture and wash away the poison dust.

Carol Sleep never comes to the door the first time you knock. She hears you all right, the house is tiny. She just never answers the first time. Even when they were kids, you had to ask her every question twice. Today it takes three rings on the bell, then Carol leans in the door frame and doesn't invite Tina in. She's wearing jeans and a T-shirt that looks like she borrowed it from a teenager. She has an unlit cigarette in her hand.

'Tina.' She looks guilty and accusing at the same time, flinching overdramatically like there's a hand about to come down on her from above.

'For fuck's sake, Carol. I know you slept with Anthony and I don't care. It was nearly ten years ago anyhow. Get over it.'

Carol looks as if Tina just dropped a brick on her toe but she's trying not to scream at the pain.

'You gonna bloody let me in?'

'Why? What do you want, Tina?'

'I want you to come round Tammy's with me. Charlie's in bits. I need to bring him back something.'

'And you think you'll get it from Tammy Williams?' She's whispering now, so Tammy won't hear from next door. 'Charlie don't need that. He needs the truth.'

'Let's just assume I'm the one who knows what Charlie needs, yeah?'

'What do you want me for?'

'Carol, I've known you my whole life and your niece is missing. I made a mistake and married Anthony Osborne. You gonna keep blaming me for it until we die or what?'

'Bloody hell.' Carol steps back and crushes herself up against the wall in the hall. 'Come in while I have a shower.'

'You have work later?'

'Not today. Monday, Wednesday and Thursday afternoons. Until your husband sacks the lot of us, that is.'

'He says you've got the union in. Good luck to ya.' She puts on a supportive face so Carol won't think she's being sarcastic.

The house smells old, but not bad. Like old wood and vinegar and hippie incense. The view from the sitting room is amazing; Tina had forgot that. The great big girders on the A38 bridge slice the landscape in half, but through them you can see all the way out past Kingsmill Lake. Across the river, the train comes out of Warleigh Wood and crosses the Tavy Bridge, carrying people up to Calstock. It'll be full of cider drunks and OAP ramblers, young mums on their phones having drama. Everyone wrapped in their different pleasures while the hills slide by the windows.

The shower stops and Carol moves around above her. It's only then Tina remembers seeing Khadija in the road the night before.

Carol's daughter, who got on the up train, rode away from the sudden absence of Craig Kennedy and didn't come back for years.

Carol comes down the stairs and stands by the back window towelling her hair.

'Is it nice having your maid back?' Tina says.

'Well, yeah, but then she won't tell me nothing.'

'She OK?'

'I guess, but what's she doing here, really? Who'd live here when they've got a perfectly good job in London? I don't even know if she ever had a bloke up there. I think I maybe put her off the whole idea of love.'

'Or Craig did that. Don't you think that's more likely?'

Carol picks up the same unlit fag from before. 'Let's go through the back and I can smoke this on the way.'

And then they're at the back wall wreathed in smoke, like Tina is seventeen and Carol is just that glamorous couple years older, like nothing ever broke them up or weighed their bodies down.

The hill slopes gradually enough you could walk it if you had proper shoes on, but leaning your arms on the wall you can't see that. All you can see is a sheer drop right down to the landing stage on the other side of the bridge, the bridge itself thrust into the side of the hill like a sharp blow to the heart.

'She'd have been nearly as old as Khadi is now.'

'Sorry?'

'My girl. The one I lost.'

'I'm so sorry, Tina. I wasn't thinking.' Carol holds the fag out, and Tina shakes her head. 'I guess she'd be in her twenties, eh?'

'It was Tammy; did you know that?'

'Tammy what?'

'Tammy went and told Nora Osborne and she made Anthony marry me.'

'Then you lost her. God, Tina. Life, eh?'

'Another eight years until Charlie. That was the longest eight years of my life.'

'You never talk about it,' Carol says.

'How would you know what I talk about? We don't speak.'

'I didn't think you'd want to. You went to a different world. And then, you know.'

'I told you, I don't care about that. No offence, bird, but Anthony would shag anything. Just doesn't get many chances. But you're right. I never talk about it to anyone. Charlie stirred it all up somehow, seeing him break this morning. Or maybe this thing with Alice made me think about having a daughter.'

Which is what Tina's really doing, isn't it? Looking for herself. The girl who cried in Carol's bedroom and then let Tammy save her. The girl who wanted to leave her treacherous body behind, drop herself from the bridge walkway and spend two and half seconds pretending she could fly before the water hit like concrete. The girl who talks like them.

'Two little birds on my doorstep!' Tammy looks delighted, but not surprised. 'What you two doing here?' She's wearing pedal pushers and a green sweater that makes her look dead.

'Hello, Tammy. Ya'right?'

She could use a little powder at least. Tammy isn't so old. Or maybe she is, and they all are and it's time for Tina to give up and stop putting on lipstick like Louise in *Thelma and Louise*.

'Just come for a chat,' Tina says. 'You gonna make us a brew?'

'Just a chat, eh?' She smirks at them. 'Good to see you two together. It's like we're all twenty years younger again.'

'I was just thinking the exact opposite. How you keeping, lovely?'

'Same as yesterday. Tickin' over. Come in and sit.'

Tina walks through, then turns to see Carol, still standing on the back step like a girl outside the headmaster's office. A forty-five-year-old girl.

Sometimes you just want to shake her and say, *fuckin' stand up straight and live your life, you stupid bird*. But if you did that, she'd just tell you how she can't and she's broken and it isn't her fault that it's all her fault, she just can't help being a screw-up. She tries. Then

65

she'd lie down and let you walk right over her if you wanted to. So then you don't want to shake her because some way that would mean she'd won. You'd be the one that's a cow.

Tina keeps telling herself she isn't angry with Carol, but all of a sudden she is. Not because of Anthony, because of Mo. Because Carol is the one of them who could have had the beautiful thing. She just tossed it away, like an arrogant bastard burning hundred-pound notes in front of homeless people.

'Your hair looks nice, Tina.' Tammy is standing in the kitchen doorway with the kettle going behind her.

'Ta. Got it over the river at Whispy Tyler. Mad place. They got parrots, and a fountain indoors.'

They all sit round the table in the kitchen. The shape of the house is the mirror of Carol's, but it feels newer somehow. The view through the back is shifted just a bit so you're looking at RNAD instead of the Tavy Bridge.

'It's good to see you two being there for each other.'

'You said that,' Carol says. 'Tina wants help. Charlie and Alice were together.'

'*Are* together,' Tammy says. 'Alice ain't gone.'

'Yeah, well, that's nice for you, Tammy, but she won't do Charlie no good without she's got a body, will she? 'Course you'll be chatting to her all day long, so that's OK, in't it?'

Tammy doesn't even look insulted by the way Carol's talking to her.

'I done some peanut butter cookies for your maid, Carol. She always loves 'em.'

'All right, then.'

Jesus, Carol sounds like she's fifteen. Stroppy. Tina looks at the lamp that's tucked under the cupboards in the corner of the worktop. The shade has the shadows of seashells painted on it. When you turn on the bulb the shade circles round and the pictures move.

When Tammy touches Tina's hands it makes her jump.

'You keep chasing them away, lovely. You keep telling them they're not welcome. The spirits don't like all that bleach.'

'Never mind me. What do I tell Charlie?'

'You tell him to hold on. Tell him to wait. The river is real loud. It frightened Alice.'

'Christ!' Carol breathes out the word and shakes her head. For some reason Tammy smiles at her.

'Hold my hands, bird.'

'No.' Carol actually sits on her hands.

'Just for a minute. Humour me?'

Carol wiggles her butt and pulls out her hands. She puts just the tips of her fingers on Tammy's palms. Her nails are painted but short; Khadija must have done them. That's Carol. Making herself look neglected when no one's there to baby her. Her whole body is whinging all the time. *Poor me*, until someone says, *let me do your nails, let me fix your hair, let me buy you a drink, let me kiss you and make you forget how you feel.*

Tammy takes the tips of Carol's fingers like they're made of spun sugar, if you hold them too tight they might snap. If you love them, they'll crumble.

'Feel that on your shoulders, Carol? That isn't yours. Shrug it off. Let your bones down, let them loose. Look up. It's time to look up.'

Tammy buys the whole poor Carol thing, just like everyone else. Even the spirits of the dead are buying it, apparently. She looks back and forth between Carol and Tina.

'There's still a hole between you two. A river running, a whole river. There's the current sweeping you both apart. There's the bridge flung out between you, *like a blow to the heart*. In't that it, Tina?' Tammy repeats those exact words Tina said to herself in the garden, as if there's an echo in the air between the houses.

That's the thing about Tamara Williams. Just when you've put her safely in a box she knocks you sideways, says something you can't explain away.

'I can't help it,' Carol says. 'I swear, Tina. I know you're angry, even though you're pretending not. I just break things. Always have.'

'You had a lovely man, bird.' Tammy lets go of one hand and

67

smooths Carol's hair. 'And he gave you a lovely girl. Nothing's broken. You're just looking in a broken glass. Remember when they used to say a mirror was foxed? Foxed. Spots in it like rot. Foxed, fooled, seeing a thing the way it isn't. Something between you and yourself, something green and rusty in front of your reflection. Spreading.'

'Okay, lovely.' Tina lifts Carol's other hand out of Tammy's. 'Let me do the tea. You sit, Tamara.'

When Micky was alive, he used to calm Tammy down. He'd talk to her as if she was ill or a child, all she needed was looking after. He'd open something in himself and quiet would wash out into the room. Tammy would settle then. Tina tries to hit that Micky note.

'You want builder's tea, ladies?'

'Lemon and ginger if she's got it,' Carol says, as though nothing Tammy's doing for them counts or even is real.

'Tell him, in the shower,' Tammy says.

'OK, lovely. I will.' Tina lays two hands on Tammy's shoulders. 'I'll put half a sugar in yours. You could use it eh, you skinny old bird?'

'Tell Charlie, talk to her when he's in the shower. She's far away, not gone. She'll hear him best through the water.'

Chapter 9

The house is empty when Khadija comes in from her second day at Bright and Tunstall. She can feel it before she calls out. There's no air moving around. No fag smoke blown in from the back and sitting in the corners. She lifts one foot to take her wet shoe off and falls sideways into the wall. The washing up is half done and the gloves are crumpled over the side of the sink. Her mother never does that. Christ, what's happened now?

The back door is unlocked. Khadija has to put her shoes on again to go out and see. She takes a breath and sits down on the back step to tie them, feeling like she's five years old.

'Aunt Tammy!' she calls over the wall.

Tammy is with someone in the kitchen. No one answers, but Khadija can hear voices through the side window, so she goes round back.

It's 5:30, the sun has already thrown itself down on the river like it's tired and can't be bothered with the sky anymore. The gate in the common wall is rotting, but someone has replaced Tammy's crumbling back doorstep with new wood. It'll be Jo's Ben who does those things for Tammy now. All grown up and proud of looking after his women, like.

'Aunt Tammy?'

'Come through, maid. Your mum's in here.' She says it like, *can you believe your mum's in here?* But it isn't just Carol; it's Tina Osborne, too. Double weird.

In the kitchen, all three of them are wearing the same look, as if they agree on the situation for the first time ever.

'You lot ate my peanut butter cookies, din't ya?'

They look embarrassed, like she's caught them smoking a spliff or looking at porn.

'You don't think I put any by?' Tammy gives Khadija a little shove. 'Get on, you. You been away so long you don't even know me anymore.' Tammy stands on a chair and takes a tupperware from the top of the fridge.

Khadija peels off the lid and stands against the worktop with one arm around the container. Three cookies in it, laid out flat. 'These are all mine, people.'

It almost feels like she's still the golden girl, the shooting star. Like no one ever died and she never went away and found out that nothing sparkles anywhere, no matter how far you go.

'What you all doing?' she says. 'Why is everyone sitting around like it's a funeral?'

'Khadi!'

'Shit, so sorry. I didn't mean it like that.'

'We're just having a natter. Charlie's upset.' Tina has on brand new jeans that look like she irons them, possibly while they're on her legs. She never has roots or a chipped nail. She smells of Dettol instead of perfume, just like always.

'Jo told me Charlie and Alice are a thing,' Khadija says around the cookie in her mouth.

'Well, yeah. He reckons he loves her. He's heartbroken she would disappear without telling him.'

Tina looks as though she has little sharp objects stuck into her all over, but she's trying to ignore it. Whatever goes on with the rest of her, Tina's face is always real. She may be house proud, but she's ten times more honest than Khadija's mum.

'She might not have done it on purpose,' Carol says.

'She would've though, wouldn't she? I'm sorry but we all know Alice isn't always a nice person.'

'Khadija! What is the matter with you?'

'Well, we're not going to find out what happened to her by pretending she's an angel. I love her, but she's selfish. You lot know that.'

'She does have funny turns,' Tina says. 'Anthony calls her mad. He's got Charlie half convinced she's some kind of *femme fatale.*'

'Anthony would say that, wouldn't he?' Carol looks at the floor while she says it, pushes her chair back and stretches her legs.

A long silence then. Just long enough for Khadija to curse herself for coming home at all. The whole place is perpetually suspended at some kind of horror film climax. Fucking everybody is about to die or go mad, all the time.

'You gonna gobble those cookies without any tea even, you little glutton?' Tammy sounds like the most normal woman out of the three of them, which in itself is nuts.

'I better go,' Tina says. 'I promised Charlie I'd bring him news if there is any.'

'Tell him what I said.'

'What did you say, Aunt Tammy?'

'Never mind, you. Eat your cookies before I take 'em back off ya.'

Carol still won't meet Tina's eyes, even when they say goodbye. She stands there looking scruffy beside Tina's molecularly smooth jeans and her expanse of uninterrupted blondness. That is when Khadija realises what it is, what her mother did to Tina. Because *of course*. Why is she even surprised?

Tina goes out the front door and up the hill. She moves along the road in perfectly even steps with her hands swinging in time against her legs and the whiteness of her trainers shining in the shadows. The trainers look like they don't belong on her feet. Maybe she borrowed them from Charlie.

'Stop twitching my curtain, Khadija. It's only Tina Osborne. You seen plenty of her in your life.'

'Mind if I stay for a minute, Aunt Tammy? Mum, I'll come over soon and help with tea.'

'Am I being dismissed, then?'

'Yes. You left the washing up half done and I need to ask Aunt Tammy some stuff.'

'What stuff?'

'It's only questions to help with my exams, like. Please?'

'Right, I'm making Bolognese. See you later, Tammy.' Carol pulls a bent fag out of her pocket and stands up. 'Khadi, try not to upset people, eh?'

'I'm glad we chatted, bird.' Tammy lays a comforting hand on Carol.

'Yeah,' Carol says. 'Ta.'

Khadija takes her mother's chair. 'You're happy to see me, Aunt Tammy, in't ya? I can tell by the cookies.'

"Course I am. What a silly question. I made those this morning.'

'No one else is happy to see me. They still think it's my fault. About Craig.'

'Maid, the only one who ever thought it was your fault is you. Good Lord, you were seventeen.'

'Did Micky get the IIDB payment when he got sick, Aunt Tammy?'

'*Those questions*, you're talking about. Yeah, I still get the IIDB. It helps a bit.'

'So then he got the government compensation, too? Through the Asbestos Victim Scheme?'

'Yes. Why are you asking me about this, Khadi?'

'You know if they decide you get the payment it helps you in a lawsuit?'

'First off, the company offered to pay me. Second, I got no interest in a lawsuit.'

'They made you an offer? Did you sign something? Can I see it?'

'Yes, yes, and no. I didn't keep the paper.'

'Aunt Tammy! Are you serious? You threw the papers out?'

'Yes. Which I had a right to, missus. I'm not your textbook case.'

'People have been compensated. Craig's mum got into a class action.'

'I got the state money, and some private company come round with the offer. I told that girl in her New Look suit to piss off.'

'No offence, Aunt Tammy, but it's that attitude that let's them get away with it. Hundreds of men died. They're gonna keep dying, too. Lots of people who knew it would happen got clean away with it, or a slap on the wrist fine. They should be made responsible.'

'You spend all your energy trying to make somebody pay, you find out in the end they just took more years of your life. You have to let go of things, Khadi. That's how you win.'

'No, that's how *they* win! They killed people we love. They knew they were doing it. You reckon I should just let go of that?'

'So that's what this solicitor thing is about, eh?'

'Solicitor is a good job, Aunt Tammy. I need to take care of Mum. She might lose her job, did she tell ya?'

'You need to take care of a man and a couple babies, is what you need. Carol's still young. She don't want you giving up your life.'

'Jeez, Aunt Tammy, listen to yourself. It's 2016. Anyway, I'm not like that. I don't want a man and babies to take care of.'

'Well, how about you let somebody take care of you for a change?'

'Can I ask you the name of the company? The one that wanted to pay you?'

'Rock Group? Stone? Something. Service contractors.'

'Slate Group?'

'That's the one.'

'Yes! Oh, sorry,' Khadija says.

'Some of the women died and all, you know. From doing the washing with the dust on it every week.'

'Yeah, I read about that.'

'GP checks my breathing twice a year.'

'Jesus, I never thought. Is it OK?'

'It's fine. Now that you *are* thinking, maybe think what it feels like you bringing all this up to me?'

'Crap. I'm really sorry. I just care, lovely. When I went away to uni, I didn't even mind if I passed the course. I just wanted to learn enough to know whose fault it was, who was supposed to pay for what they did to Uncle Micky. And Craig's dad. Never occurred to me solicitors and the unions been trying to do just that for a century already.'

'Bless you, lover. It's always somebody's fault. That don't make no difference.'

'Know what my lecturer told us in first year? That we needed to understand, it isn't justice. It's law. What the hell!'

'I could've told you that, without charging you tuition fees neither.'

'Ha, ha. But they owe you, Aunt Tammy.'

'They owe me something they can't never pay, maid. Anyway, I'm happy. Look at me. Micky was a right obstacle in this tiny little house.' She cackles like a witch in a cartoon.

'It's only 'cause I love you, you mad old bird.'

'I love you, too. Even when you pester me. Give me your hand.'

'You know I don't like that.' Khadija puts her hands out and hunches her shoulders up.

'Don't be cross with me, but you're just like your mum. Trying to close yourself up. As if that'll keep anything out. OK, do me this. Big breath in.'

Khadija takes in a breath and looks away past Tammy's shoulder. It's evening now. The kettle has steamed half the kitchen window into a perfect curve of mist over the dark outside.

'Come on now, me lovely. A real big breath.'

'Fine.' Khadija fills her lungs and her shoulders rise even higher.

'Now out. Slow as you like.'

It's easier to do it than to argue.

'Make me happy, maid. Just let go.'

'I'm all grown up, Aunt Tammy. Not a maid no more.' But she lets herself relax while she says it.

'I remember you from an infant. All curled up on Carol's chest like a little kidney bean. I'll call you what I like.' Tammy's hands are softer than they look.

'Did I sick up on her lots? Hope so.'

'Oh yeah, you're hilarious. You're afraid, bird. You don't like people up close to you.'

'That's not true, Aunt Tammy. I just don't like people trying to suck the life out of me. I don't like needy.'

'Like Craig, you mean? Boy loved you like an addict.'

74

'I was seventeen! It wasn't fair.'

'You're one of those that makes people want to be close to you. Your dad too, you know. He misses you. He wants to know you.'

'No, Tammy.' Khadija pulls her hands away. 'You're out of order.'

'I'm sorry. I just wish you'd let it in. You have relatives that have passed, you know. They don't speak English, but I can feel them all the same.'

'You're making this up now. You saying spirits speak in English and Arabic? Seriously? Cornish too, I suppose? Piskies, maybe?'

'Say what you feel, sweetie. We'll all still be here.'

'Shit. I'm sorry.' Khadija leans back in her chair. 'I don't mean it. It's just a lot, being here.'

'It's love, Khadija. It's just love.'

'Love is creepy. Even when *I* feel it, I feel like I'm being creepy.'

'And spirits do speak Cornish. Or Welsh or something. Sometimes, if you're asking. I dunno what it is, 'cause I don't bloody understand it.'

'OK, all right. I said sorry. Can I have another cookie?'

'That was the last one, greedy.'

'Mum says you knew about Alice.'

'Well, I knew something. The river woke me up, but no one's said nothing since. I'm waiting.'

'Not dead useful, them spirits, are they?'

'They're not useful or un-useful. They just are.'

'I got to go back. Mum's guilt-tripping already and I only got here four days ago.'

Khadija walks through the gate to find Carol standing at the back wall holding a burning fag.

'You fucking slept with him, din't ya?'

'Slept with who? And hang on, why are you speaking to me like that? You don't get to ask me who I slept with.'

'You slept with Mr Osborne and Tina isn't speaking to you. That's utterly disgusting. I really don't need that information in my head.'

Carol doesn't turn to look at her, just keeps staring upriver with the smoke curling up from her hand into the twilight.

'You just seen Tina speaking to me,' she says to the bridge.

'Oh, yeah. It didn't seem awkward at all, neither. Here's a thing to ask yourself. How come I could tell why right away? Why's that the first place my brain went?'

'What do you want me to say? I'm a person. I get that you hate me for it, but it's not like I can help it.'

'You can help it! You can. You just put the fag out and don't light another one. You just keep your bloody legs closed. And you could cover 'em up when you're standing out in the street and all.'

'I can wear whatever I want in my own front garden.'

'OK, Mum. Classy.'

'You wish I looked like Tina? Like they moulded me out of plastic and I can't use my own face muscles anymore?'

'You slept with Mr Osborne, Mum. You don't get to push that back onto me or Tina. That's on you.'

Maybe she was shagging Tina's husband downstairs on the sofa while Khadija was revising upstairs. Maybe she went to his house when Tina was at the Samaritans, or just had him up against the wall behind the Brunel. Fucking hell.

'When was it?'

'When was what?'

'You know what.' They are both facing over the wall, talking to Devon. The pillboxes over at RNAD are standing out yellow in their little pools of light. 'Or are you still doing it?'

'Enough, Khadija. You're twenty-five years old. You telling me you never shagged a bloke just because you couldn't figure out how not to?'

'Uh, yes I am. I tend to look for basic respect before I sleep with someone. You know, makes a change in our family. When somebody's good to me, I don't push them away and head to the pub looking for the nearest creep.'

But she does. Push.

'Give it time, lovely.'

'Ok, nice parenting. Well done. Who pays you?'

'What? What did you just ask me?'

'At the school. Who is it on your payslips?'

'The academy trust. They took over a couple years ago because the school was failing.'

'You got that backwards. They fail the school *so* the academy can take over. I'm asking, what's the company name on the payslips?'

'The trust is called Aspire Academy Trust. They have schools right up the line to Somerset.'

'Different name.'

'Eh?'

'Ben and his dad get paid by Resolve Logistics.'

'So?'

'Never mind. I'm going for a walk. Try to keep it in your pants till I get back, yeah?'

She should feel bad saying those things, like she's being nasty and the other person is just lonely. Just alone. Khadija is trying to feel that. She really is.

'I was hoping we were gonna be able to be mates,' her mother says, 'now you're grown up.'

'Mates tell each other when they're acting like tarts. Love you, though. I'll be back.'

You can't really storm out the back gate. It's hanging from the hinges and sticks on all the wet leaves and mulch piled up by the wall. You can disappear down the hill, though. Take ten steps and no one in the gardens can see you until you're halfway to the green. The world around Saltash is built for disappearing into.

Next morning, Khadija's alarm rings an hour later than it would have in London, but it still feels too early. She isn't out of her dreams and tied back to her body yet. She pulls her bedroom curtain over the goldcrest nest sitting on the sill.

Will the sun damage it? She moves it to the chest of drawers, where it trembles every time she opens a drawer. When she cleans out her brush and throws the hair away it falls into the same twisted shape at the bottom of the bin. Everything discarded in the world takes the same twisted form, all the threads and hairs and fibres. All the blood in their veins and the water at the river mouths.

She takes the hair back and puts it on the outside windowsill where a bird can find it and use it to line a nest. Craig would like that. It's probably something he said once, about her hair. Maybe about her being like a bird, or a home for birds. Whatever it was repeats itself in the air, half heard.

Showered and dressed and still she doesn't feel clean. Her limbs aren't doing what she tells them. Her tights get twisted and she spills tea on the carpet.

Packing things back in Craig's tin to put under the bed, she notices a print-out from the *Herald*. Double-sided, with a photo story about Saltash Regatta on one side, and something about businesses moving into Royal William Yard on the other. Must be a few years old then, from back when the Royal William development was big news.

Which side of the paper is it? Which of those articles has Craig saved, and why did he think it mattered? Everything else in there is either about his dad, or some secret signal for her. He imposed all his signs and symbols onto her life like they should mean things to her as well. Birds' nests and the names of boats and old pitch pennies they'd used, like it was all the beginning of some beautiful story they'd cherish together in fifty years' time. Maybe some seventeen-year-old girls want that.

Anyway, the papers are mostly to do with Craig's dad, so the article must be about him. Pictures of posh people with their boats on the Tamar? Green development companies buying repurposed warehouse space? Who knows where he fit those things in? She puts the print-out in the tin with everything else. She'll want to look over Mr Kennedy's compensation papers soon. The rest of it will keep.

From the front door, she can see old Mrs Osborne's house on the hill, across a lake of milky light. Here they all are in the clouds. Maybe this is heaven, but heaven turns out to be really boring, all made of up little pockets of asphalt and metal and fearful ignorance.

Chapter 10

Tuesday at 2:15, Tammy has an appointment in Bodmin; it's a train and then a bus. A Cornish bus. She waits forty minutes in the little station café that sits above the platform at Bodmin Parkway. If she'd told Ben or Harry they'd have drove her, but she hasn't told anyone. Not about the appointment, nor the support group neither.

'Funny being in a hospital for myself,' she says to the doctor. Mrs Brady, she's called.

It isn't really for herself; she's here for Alice as well. Because the world is different these days, and Alice is not the girl Tammy was. Being half in the spirit was always difficult, but it's tougher now than it used to be. Alice's parents are no help to her, bless them.

'Well, technically, this isn't a hospital. This is a clinic.' The doctor has designer specs that make her look pretty and smart at the same time.

'I know. It said "outpatient" on the letter. I seen enough clinics with Micky to know all the terms.'

'Micky was your husband? You've said you're widowed.'

The office window looks out on a car park and some roofs, the part of Cornwall no one would pay to see. The Londoners skip right over Bodmin, even the train they come down on is out on the A38. The buildings across the way were built in the sixties, when everything was trying to be ugly on purpose. The big tourist attraction in Bodmin is a gaol.

'Asbestosis,' Tammy says. 'Eventually he died from the pleural thickening, but it took a good long while.'

'I'm sorry. That must have been very difficult.'

'We managed. He died at home, months in bed with the oxygen and the nurse visiting. That was years ago now.'

'Let's talk about you. You say you're here because you hear voices. You've always heard them, you've said. So why now?'

79

'Well, I'm on my own and I'm getting older. What if it gets worse? What if I start to not know people in the body from the people in the spirit?'

This is a lie, but only a little one. She's mostly come because everything she ever tried to say to Alice slid right off, and now Alice is in big trouble again. So what do the doctors say to people like them? How do they get them to understand? She's after something she can use to help the maid, words or pills or anything they've got that'll slow her down long enough to listen. To breathe out.

'So, the voices are the spirits of people who have passed away?'

'Died, yes. Hate that phrase, passed away.' She laughs. 'Sorry.'

'That's OK, Mrs Williams. Can I call you Tamara?'

'Everyone calls me Tammy. Ever since 1968, anyway.'

'1968?' Mrs Brady smiles and it isn't fake. Tammy decides to like her; decides all by herself because the rest of them are quiet as the actual grave today.

'"Stand by Your Man",' she says. 'Tammy Wynette. You probably weren't born yet. I was only twelve.'

'Ah. I thought it sounded American. Tamara is like the river, isn't it?'

'Yep. They always told me it was an old goddess. Mrs Osborne says that in't true. She says Tamar just means dark and winding.'

There's an addict out in the car park, looking skinny and lost.

'The same as the Thames. That's interesting; I hadn't heard that. I'm looking at your questionnaire. You say you have no trouble sleeping?'

'Not more'n other women my age. Sometimes I wake up before it's light and can't go back.'

'Is it the voices that wake you?'

'Sometimes. They woke me up when Khadija came home and Alice went in the river.'

'Was that recently? Tell me about that.'

'Khadija is my neighbour's girl, but a bit like my own, too.'

'You don't have any children?'

80

'We couldn't, which is just as well I guess.' Half a lie again. They might have tried harder, but what if they came out like Tammy? They both thought it, but Micky never said. Give him that.

'And Alice?'

'Khadija's cousin. She's disappeared and everyone thinks she's dead. She isn't. This is probably where you start to think I'm mad. I am a bit, but she isn't dead. You'll see.'

'And the morning she went missing the voices woke you up?'

'Yep. And then I heard Khadija coming down the hill. It wasn't an accident, that. I mean, I guess I do believe in coincidence, sometimes. Like if you bump into someone all the way down Plymouth, or you play your mum's birthday and win the Lotto. But that? No. Khadija appearing and Alice disappearing right at the same moment? That was something else.'

'You seem upset by it.'

'I just can't figure it out. Sometimes I'm supposed to do something, and I don't know what it is this time.'

'That is a common feeling among people who hear voices. Has anyone talked to you about that?'

'Yes, a few times. Whatever you call it don't mean I can just sit back.'

'Why you?'

'Well, that's the million pound question, in't it? I don't know, Doctor; it's just always been that way.'

She's scribbling, probably something like *grandiose delusions*. They wrote that once when she was still at school.

'Maybe it isn't your responsibility?'

'Wouldn't that be lovely?'

'You've said that you were on medication previously. For the voices.'

'Oh, yeah. Years ago. Sulpiride.'

'And how did you get on with it?'

'It din't make the voices go away, but it made me not care about them. It also made me sleep all day and my left arm went funny.'

'Those are fairly common side effects with the first-generation therapies. There are better medications now.'

'Could you tell me about them? I think Alice could use it.'

'I can give you some literature, but you'd have to go back to the psychiatrist to talk about that. I can't give prescriptions. You can see us both, for CBT and medication. Many patients do. Let's fill in your background first. What was it that made you try the medications before?'

'I didn't try them. My parents did. The school made them.'

'Tell me about that.'

'A man went off the bridge. They told me he was up there and I tried to wake everybody up. My mum called the police, but they didn't get there in time.'

'That must have been distressing.'

'I was fourteen by that time. I was used to it.'

'But your parents thought it would help if you saw a doctor?'

'No. They knew how it was. I'm not the first woman in my family to hear the spirits. What I did wrong was tell some girls at school.'

'You talked about it with your friends? That must have been tough. People didn't understand as well back then.'

'They understood better than they do now. My family never called me mad.'

'But they knew you had this ... they knew you heard the voices.'

''Course they did. I was seven the time they called me down Wearde Quay. It was nearly dark by the time they found me.'

'They *called* you?'

'There was a boy lost, but it wasn't that day. The spirits don't see time like we do.'

Tamara's mother had burned some milk on the stove. She was making cheese sauce and Harry started crying upstairs. Her mum ran up to sort him out and left Tamara kneeling on the sofa, looking out the window up the river. When they started calling from behind her, she leaned her chin on her arms and pretended not to hear. Sometimes they said her name but mostly they said names she'd never heard before. They tried to say nice things, 'Pretty little maid!' 'Look after the baby.' 'Isn't it lovely to feel the sun on ya?' Sometimes they couldn't help it, though. Sometimes somebody moaned and said, 'I can't get out!' Or begged, 'Please, tell them to stop.'

Upstairs, Harry was wailing and her mother was singing, stepping back and forth, back and forth on the floorboards above Tamara's head. Tamara breathed the cinder smell of the burning milk and smiled. She turned her head and laid her cheek down on her forearm, closed her eyes and opened them again. Sleepy. Tamara was always sleepy in the day; night-time wore her out.

Soon the burnt air made it up the stairs. She watched her beautiful little mother come hopping down with one hand sliding along the wall. She was wearing pedal pushers and a big jumper that belonged to Tamara's dad. It made her look like she might be her own child. Maybe Tammy would look like that, one day. She hoped so; she couldn't picture nothing better than looking like her mum. Having those hands. Having that necklace she wore at Easter.

Irene grabbed the saucepan and ran it out the back door. She put it down on the brick path at the back of the house, where it sat smoking into the daylight.

'Din't ya smell that, maid?'

'Yes, Mum. I smelled it.' She was proud of herself and her mother laughed.

'Next time call me, eh? I got to start over now. If I bring Harry down, will you sit with him and dangle a toy while I do the sauce?'

Tammy only nodded, turned her back to the river and slid down with her legs out in front of her.

Harry was nestled in the crack between the sofa cushions so he couldn't wriggle out. 'Sweet little man,' someone said. 'You look after him lovely.' He went all peaceful and she got up and went outside. Just for a minute. There was a burnt skin on the pan of milk with rainbows shining in it, flies landing and circling. You can't boil milk; it burns and then you get flies and dirty brown rainbows. She stored that picture away and believed it for years, thought milk would burn like that every time you boiled it. Facts tangle up when you're little and odd things stick, even if the only memories you have are your own. Which Tamara's never was.

She was crouched over the saucepan looking close up at a fly when they began to insist. The fly had two great round eyes on its head, shining with rainbows like the burn on the milk. 'Got to show you, Tamara,' they said. 'Sorry little bird, you're the only one.'

'No. Because my brother.' She said it quietly to the ground because it didn't matter where she said it to. Inside the house, her mother was singing again. Tamara went to the back door and put her head in. Everything was fine. 'I don't want to,' she said to her sleeping baby brother.

'Got to show you, Tamara. There's time. They can't find him, but if you show them, there's time. He's someone's little brother and all.'

'My little brother,' somebody said.

They didn't stop talking until she got to Wearde Quay.

'Tide's coming up,' they said. 'He's trapped underneath.'

'Show them, Tamara. Show them before he's drowned.'

Tamara looked at the mud under the quay, and the little channels of water cut into it. At the green sludge that lay shining in the rock pool, smelling like cabbage and dead cats. The tide was not coming in. You wouldn't be able to drown so much as a kitten there for another four hours at best.

'They don't see time the way we do,' she says to Mrs Brady again.

That day when she was seven, there were so many of them, wringing their hands and whinging, grabbing at each other and wailing, all insisting at once. The only thing to do was curl up quiet, hide her head and wait.

Tamara was cold through by the time they found her, hunched into the side of the boathouse with her hands covering her ears. As if that would help. People must have been stood right there calling her name for ages before she realised one of them was her mother.

Her mother in the body, all the way real. Her dad, too. He said her name, then lifted her up higher than he needed to. The world

84

tilted and shimmered before he brung her back down against his jacket. It was going dark and the water was up to the edge of the quay. Irene smelled like the burned milk still.

Later that same night, a boat came into North Yard with the tide, carrying men back from North Africa, hanging their heads and sorry to see their own mothers.

'My parents never gave a name to what happened,' Tammy says to Mrs Brady. 'They never asked anyone else to neither. You didn't back then.'

There was already a name and a shape for things, made out of the river and the mud and the grass. There'd always been girls like Tamara. People made them half into saints and half into village idiots. They fit.

'Turned out the lost boy was Thomas Bone. He'd gone missing more than twenty years before they called me to come save him. It's like that sometimes.'

'You say this made it hard with friends at school?'

'Dead people talked to me and my family name was Jinks. I guess you can imagine how it went for me at school. It was them called the Social and told my parents if they didn't get me some help I might get took away. Help. That's what they called it.'

Mrs Brady holds up the information form. 'You say here you've never wanted to hurt yourself or anyone else.'

'I'm not like that, never have been.'

'The reason we ask is because for some people the voices are very distressing. It's OK to feel like that. Sometimes the things they say aren't good.'

'It's like that for Alice, the one who's gone away. Me, I find people in the body more upsetting. In the spirit, they tell me what's wrong and I try to help. If they wanted me to do something bad, I wouldn't listen.'

'That sounds sensible.'

'That sounds patronising.'

'I'm sorry. I didn't mean it to.'

85

That is the first time in her life Tammy ever heard a doctor say sorry. She points past Mrs Brady's shoulder to the bloke outside the window.

'Is that your patient? He looks a bit lost.'

'Don't worry. There are people downstairs at reception.'

'What they say isn't always pleasant. The spirits. It's about upset, getting hurt, dying, sadness. The kind of things that leave an impression. Sometimes happiness, too. Love and contentment and babies coming, all they things.'

'Well, so why have you decided to try CBT? How do think I can help?'

'At my group someone told me about it. They said go to my GP and insist on it. Don't take no for an answer. It took nearly a year. Here I am.'

True. It did take a year and someone did tell Tammy to insist, but not for herself exactly. Tammy went into support group one day crumpled up and shaking all over. It took her half an hour and three cups of stewed tea before she could say anything at all.

That was the day after the spirits woke her up to show her Alice. One of those things she saw instead of hearing it, cutting into the back of her eyes like a migraine. Alice in bed with her blood soaking into the sheets, with her eyes rolled up in her head. Debbie Tregidga shouting down the phone like it was Tammy's fault, because Tammy had called the ambulance. Without that ambulance Alice would be as dead right now as everyone thinks she is.

Alice has never been the same since Craig Kennedy died. Everyone else in Saltash lost a piece of that night, even the people who aren't normally sensitive. Even Tammy. One of the hours around midnight just got skipped over, a bit of time slipped down into the river and away. Ask anyone; none of them seem to remember it. Except Alice. She was nearly as young as Tammy had been, that day at Wearde Quay. But it was worse than that. What Alice hears is bloodier, somehow. It all goes right in through her skin.

And yes, it's true what Khadija says. Alice can be cold as stone when she wants. Sneaky, too. But the river gets loud when someone goes into it. The poor girl was awake through everything that night, everyone on the other side shouting in her head at once. Pulling her under and squeezing the air from her lungs, crying for help. She was nine years old.

Chapter 11

Khadija has two windows open on her work desktop, one for Land Registry, which is what she's supposed to be doing, and one for LinkedIn, where she's chasing the names of board members registered at Companies House. When you look into companies, you have to grab a thread and hang on to it, follow it back. They aren't exactly hiding things. They just tangle them up, because every knot is an hour's billing and who's got the money to pay a solicitor to trace it all? Nobody who needs it, anyway.

And you find things like this: two directors on the board of Aspire Academy Trust are former board employees of Slate Group. This is how they do it. Perfectly legitimate robbery. It isn't justice; it's law. It would take hundreds of legal hours just to find the cause of a single, unimportant death. The reason more people don't make them pay is they've made it too much of a faff. Simple, but very effective.

Weak sun comes through the plate glass into Bright and Tunstall, but it will never reach Khadi's desk. From Fore Street, you wouldn't be able to make her out, sitting in the gloom behind the glare. There is a faded blue velvet sofa and a load of dark wood bookshelves, all calculated to make them seem venerable and trustworthy.

How many years will Khadija spend here, looking at Saltash through the glass, searching for leans and registering covenants? Forever would be fine.

But it won't be quiet or soothing, of course not. There are already three messages from Jo on Khadi's phone.

There's CCTV of Alice. You should go to Aunt Debbie's.

I'm working, Jo. It's only my third day.

Go straight after. I'll meet you there.

And the rest of the day is pictures of Alice running through

Khadija's head – Alice hanging, drowning, mangled on the sidings, smirking at them all because she's everywhere now; she's filled up all the negative space.

In the police station, Khadija finds Aunt Debbie and Uncle Pete at the window of the front desk. She takes Debbie's hand and murmurs some nonsense that won't help. Once Jo arrives, they all crowd into a family room. There's stewed tea and some kind of support lady and an actual telly on a rolling stand like they used to have in school when they still showed films on VHS.

A lady cop holds up a DVD and tries a joke to lift the tension. 'When was the last time you saw one of these?'

Aunt Debbie visibly winces. Khadija's mum comes in then, breathless from rushing up the hill without a jacket. She makes a small noisy fuss getting herself settled.

'What this will help us do,' the officer says, 'is establish a timeline. We can't read anything into it until we have more information, but it will help us build a picture of Friday morning. Does that make sense?'

She's talking to Aunt Debbie because Debbie is the one she thinks is most unhinged. Can't she see Uncle Pete's lips? The way he's holding his spine? He's obviously the one about to crack. Mothers and mad girls are a standard type of agony, at least round here they are. Fathers can't handle that type of thing at all. They haven't got the words to tell themselves about it. They don't hang out with Tammy Williams.

When the video starts, everyone looks but Aunt Debbie. She digs her nails into Uncle Pete's thigh and closes her eyes, then whimpers like she can see it on the back of her lids anyway.

First there is a blank stillness for twenty seconds, a dark empty street with cars parked along the fence and lights shining on the fronts of the houses. Then she looms in from the left and starts to get smaller, moving down into the frame. It's odd how you can tell someone from the shape of their body, from the way their legs move.

Alice has her hair tucked into a hoodie, everything else on the film is a kind of greenish-grey. Something shines on one of her shoes. She isn't hurrying; she doesn't turn her head to look about. Eventually, the last piece of her disappears behind a house on Glebe Avenue.

'It's her,' Khadija says to the support lady, because it seems like no one else is going to.

Eventually, the WPC comes back to explain that there are no cameras further down the hill.

'She isn't...' Aunt Debbie can't finish the sentence, but she doesn't have to.

She isn't heading for the bridge. Debbie doesn't break down crying like she would on telly. She looks like she's holding her breath, because Alice is still neither alive nor dead. Her mother is still stretched on the rack, wondering. Uncle Pete is still doing his best to behave like the architecture Debbie lives in.

Jo follows Khadija to the police station toilets. They're lit with blue anti-junkie light like the loos on the ferry, as if someone would actually try to shoot up right there in the cop shop. Which they probably would. It's Saltash, remember.

'Let's walk back, yeah?' Jo says it like they're at a party full of strangers in someone's parents' house and she wants to leave before things get out of hand.

Their voices echo back over the toilet stall, bouncing around off the stainless steel in the creepy blue air.

'Jo, they need us right now.'

'Yeah, I know,' Jo says. 'We can follow them lot. I just want a breather.'

'You? That lot call me all day.'

'Yeah, bird. I know how it feels, trust me. The whole time you were in London, it was me.'

Outside, the world is another sort of blue, the kind that comes just before black. The wind cuts through their clothes.

'Do you think Alice is somewhere warm?'

'She wouldn't head for the bridge, Jo.' Khadija stops in the road and turns, standing with her feet apart.

'What?'

'The bridge is covered in cameras.'

'Oh.'

'If she went in, she went in off the green or over to Wearde Quay.'

'She wasn't headed toward Wearde.'

'The green, then.'

'Cheerful, Khadija. Good to have you back, you and your positive attitude.'

'Tammy keeps saying she's alive, but that doesn't mean she is, Jo.'

'OK, OK, I hear you. How does that help?'

'Well, if she's dead it'll be us holding the world up while that lot fall apart, as per usual. You know that, right? What the hell will Aunt Debbie do?'

'Yes, Khadi. Like I said, I been here the whole time. Again, how does that help right now?'

Khadija laughs then; she can't help it. 'Fuckin' hell, you are so grown-up it's spooky.'

'Speaking of which, the council called today. We're getting our flat soon.'

'You and Ben? Did you tell them he's the dad?'

'Nah, I gave the CSA Max's name. Fuck 'im. His mum came to take me out for posh coffee and demand a paternity test. I said, "Yeah all right, send me the appointment. Also, maybe buy your kid some condoms instead of hassling me."'

'Swear to Christ, Jo, when does it stop? Posh boys trying to use us for wank towels and their mums blame us for it.'

'Who we talking about now?'

'Not me!' Khadija puts both hands up. 'I'm just saying.'

'What the hell happened in London and why are you back, Khadi?'

'Never mind that right now.'

'You'll tell me eventually. You know you will.'

'I'm only saying, it's the story of my mum's life and all. And Tina Osborne, and people I knew in London.'

'Mr Osborne's mum don't blame Tina. They're thick as thieves, them two. Anyway, Max is all right. He's a sweetie, actually. He's just from Mannamead. Never had to try for anything in his life.'

'You didn't love him or what?'

'Ben is the other piece of me, Khadi. You know that. It sounds naff but he just is. Max was a blip. Fucking awesome shag mind, but that's probably why and all.'

'You saying Ben is boring in bed? Wouldn't have pegged that.'

'I'm saying everyone's boring after a while. It's about other things, long-term.'

'Oh my God, you *are* like a fifty-year-old. That bump is affecting your brain; it's so sad.'

They stop at Lower Fore Street and look down the slope. Jo slips her arm through Khadija's and lays her head against her shoulder. 'I'm glad, you know. Really glad you're back, babe.'

'Me too, bird. Now get off me.' Khadija shakes her arm free.

'You don't seem glad to be back. Tell me what's the matter?'

'Seriously? Everything. Nothing.'

'Bollocks. I mean, what's the matter with you.'

'I don't know, Jo. I keep feeling like a sticky video, like something's moving me back and forth and I can't step out of it. London wasn't right, but I don't know if this is either.'

'You have to be somewhere. That's what I tell myself every morning before I get out of bed, anyway.'

A gull comes screaming out from under the bridge and the bell at St Nicholas rings just once. Or maybe Khadija imagined that. Maybe it's just the echo of the bird bouncing off the water. When she looks over, Jo has her phone out, taking a video of the darkness below the road and the orange light on the wall of Khadija's house. The front door is open, her mum standing there already, waiting.

'You know,' Jo says, 'every time I pass by, I imagine you in your

92

room sitting with the light off, looking out at everything from the dark like you used to.'

'I didn't. Anyway, if I did how would you know? You wouldn't see me.'

'You did. You were so much older than me then.'

'Uh, I'm still the exact same number of years older than you, genius.'

'You know what I mean. You were all soulful and seemed like you had the answer to everything. Proper uncanny, like you knew it all from a baby. Like Buddha or something.'

'That's weird and untrue. Also, low-key racist.'

'Shut up. You hundred percent seemed like you knew all kinds of stuff other people didn't. That's why they let you in the grammar and all.'

'Well, I might actually have a few answers, soon. But they won't be comforting.'

'Think you know where she went?'

'What? Oh, Alice? No idea, but whatever she's done it'll be to cause the maximum of drama. She's the one should have belonged to my mum. Peas in pod, them two. I meant about Craig and his dad. And Tammy's Micky.'

'Is that what you're doing back?'

'Well, it's what I was doing in London, anyway.'

'Let that shit go, Khadi. It in't your fault and it never was.'

'You don't know, Jo. Not all the details.'

'All right, keep it close to your chest then.' Jo squeezes her arm. 'Khadi, I'm gonna tell you something I never told no one.'

'Please don't.'

'It's important. I mean it might make a difference, about Alice.'

'Don't tell me you know where she went. I'll bloody strangle you.'

'If I did, I'd have her by the scruff of the neck already. I have another name.'

'What?'

'Another identity, I mean.'

93

'Stop tripping, Jo. There's enough going on here, don't you think?'

'Listen, will you? My videos. I post them under another name. I have almost ten thousand followers.'

'OK ... That's weirdly predictable, but is it relevant?'

'Look, you dozy bird. What if Alice does, too?'

'I get where you're going, but the cops will have been through her laptop and her phone records. They'll look for that kind of thing. They're cops, but they're not completely stupid.'

'Yeah, but they don't get Alice, do they? Debbie and Pete don't get her neither. We're the only ones who do. She'll have done it all on some other computer.'

'At school?'

'Or a friend? Charlie? Somebody who'll get in trouble instead of her if she posts some messed-up crap under another name. That would be so Alice, right?'

'Can I see your account? What's your ID?'

'Don't laugh, right? It's RubyMae. I'm gonna name the baby that but no one knows. I decided years ago. Nobody else even knows it's a girl.'

'Tammy said it was a little jewel you were carrying. Jesus, I hate this place.'

Khadija stops at her open front door to hate it some more. She scowls at the purple light on the water by Saltash Passage. She has always imagined it staying purple even inside Craig's lungs. The rust on the railroad bridge that seems to get all over everything, invisible and gritty. The six bloody pubs you can see from the doorstep without even craning your neck, because it takes that much alcohol to keep the Hamoaze from breaking apart and blowing sky high.

Jo's Vimeo account is strangely fascinating. It goes all the way back, seven years at least. At three in the morning, Khadija is still sitting up in bed scrolling through it. She's forgotten to close the bedroom curtain or get undressed.

It makes sense Jo has 10,000 followers, but it would be hard to explain why. Mostly there are videos of random strangers. Jo follows them around, making up stories about what they're doing. But she has also filmed Saltash and everyone in it, people through their windows, even. Surely someone should have reported the account? There's one of Khadija's mum, smoking at the back wall in the bridge light. She closes that one and clicks past, feeling like a creep even seven years later.

What would Jo's voiceover sound like if you were some stranger in Preston who'd never heard her talk before? The whole country thinks everyone with their accent has learning difficulties. But when you heard this, you'd think, *this girl is so clever, why isn't she writing for television?* Because actually, she is really funny. And she sounds grown-up in a way she never will when Khadija is in a room with her. A stranger would think, *Wow, wish I could meet her.*

For Khadija it's like hearing an echo, an uncanny repeat that makes her scrunch up her shoulders and pull the headphones out from her ears.

The Vimeo doesn't start until halfway through 2010. First, she was on Deviant Art, posting still photos with all the emos. Those go right back through 2009 and carry on for a while after the Vimeo starts. There are pictures of Beth Kennedy, of the bridge walkway and of kids in the bus shelter at Carkeel, popping NO_2 canisters in the cold halogen light. There are pictures of Khadija, coming out of the R.A.B.I. at dusk, sitting on the bench under the bridge thinking no one was watching. Her interrupting the sun on Lower Fore Street, a long shadow falling into the river in front of her. In the spring of 2010, there is a series of Anthony Osborne and his mother, framed through the kitchen doorway at the big house, a silhouette of the back of her and him with blurred hands and open mouth, waving his arms. In 2011, the page is filled with pictures of all the empty spaces in Saltash where Craig would be if he hadn't died the year before.

She opens her phone and types, 'You're a creepy stalker' into WhatsApp, then keeps scrolling back. There is a close-up of Craig's sister Beth before her hair was black, when she wore a studded belt and ripped jeans and cobalt blue eyeliner. Looking at it, people would say it was obvious where Beth Kennedy would end up. People always do say that, after it's already happened.

Was Beth just trying to wind Khadija up, leaving that Cadbury's tin? Trying to hurt her? Tell her something? No doubt she had a tenner off Carol while she was round dropping it. Useless, Khadija's mum. Cruel by omission, but a pushover when someone comes begging.

Khadija looks away from Beth's face, out to the bridge. Nothing on it now but light. No traffic, no dog walkers, no jumpers waiting for their moment. No girl with over-extravagant hair walking along the line, no limping soldiers.

But no, there they are, she and Craig looking out from the bridge walkway as if the thought brought them, as if one of Jo's photos has bled through dimensions, ghost-like. She can see herself, with the long cloud of hair blowing around her, looking a bit younger, a little rounder, so full of fresh blood that men like Mr Osborne could smell it. There is Craig half hidden behind her, with the helpless anger coming off him like steam in the cold. The sheepskin collar on his jacket is turned up around his neck.

Craig lifts a hand and holds it above her shoulder, then turns his face away and lowers it again without touching her.

Khadija shakes the vision out of her eyes and looks at her phone. 3.57, the minute the river gave her that gift, showed her the thing that happened behind her, the resurrected hand of a dead man, rising. She remembers that moment now, remembers herself looking out from it, blind to what was happening behind her. It hasn't frightened or surprised her. She is home now. This is how home is.

She should never have told Craig about Mr Osborne. It wasn't any big deal or trauma. She was too young to understand how angry and full of crushed desire Craig was, how much better and also how exactly like everyone else. She didn't want him then and she wouldn't want him now, but she pulled him anyway. Like a trigger.

2014

Chapter 12

Khadija felt like their flat in Chiswick was home, until the day Farah invited Will's parents into it. Two bedrooms, a shared bathroom, a car park with a fox living in the shrubs behind it, and a kitchen. Sort of. She and Farah slept in beds that previous tenants had already slept in. Other people had sat on their sofa and spilled things on their IKEA table. They ate takeaways and went out less than they had in halls. The energy it took to study and pay the rent started to weigh on them. Home most nights, they started to weigh on each other.

Khadija's bedroom window faced the car park and the backs of the houses on Dolman Road. Nights she stayed up late reading case law, she'd see the fox slink by at three in the morning. She'd never seen a fox before moving to London. It looked skinny and maybe ill. Will, the boyfriend, said that was because Khadija expected it to be shaped like a dog. That it was fine and urban foxes were perfectly good at living behind car parks. He said people who wanted to rescue animals usually didn't understand them, which was a response to something Khadija hadn't said. Didn't want.

That fox was the one thing Khadija did understand. It crouched there on the edge of something, avoiding the light and looking hungry, surrounded by bright windows framing people who seemed to know what they were doing with their lives. Mr and Mrs Brotherstone came to the flat just the once, to spend five minutes walking through the rooms while Farah put on her boots and found a scarf, before the four of them headed out to Gaucho to eat some misunderstood animals.

'So sorry; I'll only be a minute!' Farah called from her room.

To be fair, Farah hadn't quite invited them in, but apparently that wasn't necessary. Will stood aside and the two of them circled the sitting room before turning and heading right down the bedroom hallway. Mrs Brotherstone stopped at Farah's bedroom door while her husband kept on walking with his shoulders hunched like there wasn't enough space for him to swing his arms properly.

He stopped at the door of Khadija's room to look in at the desk and the diagram on the wall.

'Farah says you're studying law?'

'For my sins, yeah.' Khadija was trying. She smiled even.

'What's all this about, then?' He waved a hand at the wall.

'Oh, it's just a couple of torts cases that might be connected. A lot of company boards, employment histories, financial filings. It's hard to keep all of it in my head at once.'

'Interesting approach to coursework. All about "learning styles" these days, eh?' Mr Brotherstone did air quotes.

'It isn't coursework. Not exactly.'

He raised an eyebrow.

'Just some stuff I want to get right.'

'Law won't be easy for a girl like you. Tough game, the pupillage.'

Khadija said, 'Oh no, I'm going to be a solicitor,' instead of everything else she could have said to that. She *was* trying, mostly because she knew Farah would accuse her of not trying later, and she wanted her to be wrong.

Mr Brotherstone turned from the wall then, and looked Khadija up and down, glanced away when his wife's voice came down the hallway.

'You look really lovely, Farah.'

Farah came out of her room in some Fenn Wright Manson something she'd got at Designer Warehouse Sale. The instant you stopped looking at her it was impossible to recall. Spies should wear Fenn Wright Manson. They probably do, which is why you don't know it.

Before they'd been in Chiswick a month, Will had moved in through Farah's skin like a ghost or a virus. The two of them watched films in Farah's room with the door closed. He'd usually leave before Khadija got back from work the next day, then Farah would come and get under Khadija's duvet, watching her at the desk and dozing, exhausted.

'Well?'

It was nearly April and it had snowed. You couldn't see it from the window, but there were beautiful pictures of the parks all over social media.

'Well, what?' Farah opened her eyes and pulled the duvet up to her neck.

'You never go to his flat.'

'He has a housemate.'

Khadija opened her mouth and let the silence out. On the other side of the car park there were two people moving across a kitchen window. Someone turned off a tap and tilted their head, listening. Their splashback was made of red tiles with knives hanging in row.

'You know what I mean! You're you. His housemate is just a housemate.'

'I'm me. Are you sure? Have you checked lately?'

'Khadi, don't get weird.'

'I'm just saying, an alien virus could hijack your friend's body and make them do mad shit. It's been known to happen.'

'Subtle. And piss off.'

'What happened to your hat?'

'It got manky. I gave it to the British Heart Foundation.'

'You brought them a manky hat?'

'I brought them a bunch of stuff. I was feeling charitable. You don't like Will.'

'Bollocks.'

That night Khadija dreamed they were all in the sitting room with a takeaway and the giant Jenga from the pub. She reached out a hand and looked through a space between the blocks, calculating, and then gravity turned upside down. She was on the bridge walkway in Saltash, looking at herself through somebody else's eyes. Things tilted and slid around her. She woke up thinking she'd fallen off the bed. She went and threw up in the bathroom then walked to work with her coat open, hoping the cold would shrink her.

A few days later Will and Farah had their first row, outside the pub. Then they had another one in Farah's room in the middle of the night. Khadija lay awake in bed like a child with alcoholic parents.

Chapter 13

Jo was on her way to college the morning she saw the knitting lady at St Budeaux Square, on the bus that would get her to the nine o'clock lecture with fifteen minutes to spare. She had her webpage project on a USB and a fiver for chips and hot chocolate at Caffeine Club after. The government had seen her coming and scrapped the EMA, so she usually got the fiver from her mum, or Ben if her mum was skint. Best of Britain, Jo, pulling herself up by her New Look bootstraps, dreaming of buying a Next suit and getting a job at a public relations start-up.

Not.

The knitting lady was too good to pass up, with her bag on wheels and her cloud of hair the colour of the lighting on the on trains and in dodgy toilets. By the time they got to North Cross, Jo had decided to skip the lecture, which was pointless anyway. She could get notes. She got off behind the wheelie bag lady at the stop above the market, followed her down Mayflower Street, through the Tesco subway and past the uni. The wheelie bag lady headed into the museum. Jo waited five minutes before she went in and walked across to the toilet, checked her make-up and went out on the street again, talking into her phone.

'Here we are at the museum,' she said to the camera. 'Today's topic is a blue-haired lady with a wheelie bag. What's with those wheelie bags, eh? Like you get to a certain age and you suddenly have to carry around two square metres of crap that's too heavy to even lift or what? She's gone in here.' Jo points a thumb at the granite arch behind her. 'The museum. So, why? What is she doing in there? What's in the wheelie bag, a bunch of artefacts from her South Pacific expedition? Some fossils from Siberia? Unexploded ordnance from underneath her allotment? Let's find out.'

She pushed the door with her back and held the camera up as she slid through.

In the foyer was a little machine, a glass box with a mechanical posh lady in a jungle inside, wearing old-time clothes and carrying an umbrella. When you put tuppence in, a tiger came out of the grass and the lady beat it back with the umbrella.

'Hiya,' Jo said to the bloke at the desk. 'My nan's in here somewhere. Did you see a lady with a wheelie bag come by just now?'

He smiled and spoke to her tits. 'Knitting circle's through the natural history room. Just there.' He pointed past the umbrella-lady machine.

The natural history room had a stuffed raven and a bunch of fish skeletons, some smaller birds with shining glass eyes and a table full of corals and fossils you could touch. Across the corridor at the back were double doors with two little windows in them. One of the doors said, 'Community Room'.

Jo turned her camera back on. 'Knitting circle, they say. Likely excuse, in't it? I'm suspicious.'

She panned her phone from a stuffed frog and a puffer fish around to the community room doors, then held it down so she could show how she stood on her toes to peak in.

'They appear to be knitting, but what are they talking about, eh? It's the perfect cover. Knitting circle, my arse. You don't need a bag that big for a ball of wool and two plastic needles, do ya?'

She went back to the museum hall and sat on a bench behind a display case full of old crockery.

'I say we pursue this lead, Gov'nor,' she said into the camera. Then she closed it and waited in front of a map of the air strikes that had hit Plymouth in April 1941.

Eventually the ladies started dribbling out in twos and threes, then a whole gaggle at once, including the wheelie bag lady from St Budeaux. Once they were out on North Hill, Jo pushed through the first set of double doors and turned on her camera.

'Next week, I'm going all the way in,' she said. 'I'll bring some decoy knitting. Young girl interested in the traditional craft thing. They'll eat that right up. Just call me Double-O-Genius.'

The ladies had almost disappeared around the corner of Exeter Street, heading round past the old post office onto Royal Parade. They were going to the Cavern, of course. Old people loved sitting under that weird plaster cave eating greasy custard pies. At the traffic light by Debenhams, Jo was close enough to hear them.

'I don't know,' said a lady with an actual basket over her arm, 'I think there's plenty of good that happens, too. People are basically good.'

Hippie.

'You'd never know it, watching the news.'

'Well, they don't want you to know it, do they? They want you to be worried all the time. They want us all to distrust each other and vote for them.'

Deep.

'Hey, Jo Sleep.' So quiet Jo almost missed it.

She spun around with her camera still on.

'How you keepin'?' Beth Kennedy's voice didn't match her eyes, brittle and glittering.

'A'right. College and whatnot. You?'

'Working at the Devonport Social. *Behind* the bar, if that's what you're thinking.'

'I was thinking exactly nothing, bird. Not a big thinker, me.' Jo raised her palms and shrugged. 'How's your mum?'

'Lost, basically.' Beth patted herself here and there, looking for a fag.

'Beth, I keep thinking how I need to say I'm sorry.'

'Bloody hell, Jo. It's been four years. Leave it.'

'Not about Craig, about the other thing. With John Killian.'

Did everyone have things they'd done that they couldn't think about without cringing? Jo did. So did Beth, surely?

'Seriously, Jo? The hell you bringin' that up for?'

'Because I actually am. Sorry for what I did. And about Craig and all. 'Course.'

'It wasn't you. It was me. I attract that sort of shit. One thing I'm not doing is helping you convince yourself you're a good person after that. Save it, lover.'

'Nah. I'm leaving it here. An apology. You might want it later.'

Ben rang while Jo was out on Royal Parade, looking through the Cavern window. She ignored him. He'd call again. He called every day. She should never have shagged him; he'd gone full lost puppy and stayed that way ever since. In the Cavern, the knitting ladies got two booths and a lot of custard pies, sitting with the greasy stalactites poking down at them. Everything was painted orange and covered with sticky dust.

'Stalactites are the down ones,' Jo said to the camera. '"Tite" because they hang on tight to the ceiling. Stalagmites are the up ones, "mite" because they're mighty. I learned that at Cheddar Gorge in year six. The stalactites in there,' she points over her shoulder, 'were made out of *papier maché* in around 1973 and haven't been cleaned since. *Why*, you ask? Who knows? It's Plymouth, mates.'

It took the old ladies ages to drink their coffees. Jo was cold, but you had to follow the story till the end. Other people watched TV, Jo watched the world. By filming it. Once the knitting ladies paid their bill and emerged onto the pavement, she held her camera high to show them all walking away behind her.

'That was it, the big excursion to the "knitting circle".' She used one hand to make scare quotes in front of the camera. 'We are no closer to the vital information. What is in the wheelie bags? What are they really doing in the museum? And that concludes Chapter One of *Knitting or Not*. Next week, I bring some wool and go undercover.'

Everyone from the lecture was in the Caffeine Club. Ben rang again while she was eating her chips but she was busy showing the new video to two guys from BA Film.

When she didn't answer, Ben texted to say he loved her. Massive turn-off.

'It's weirdly compelling, but I don't know why,' one of the film guys said. Nathan. He had a beanie hat and ironic seventies trousers. Tartan.

'Because this is life right here. It's full of mad weird shit and everyone ignores it. There is literally no need for screenwriters. No offence, *bhey*.'

Nathan's nameless friend just shrugged.

'Yeah,' Nathan said, 'but what do you do with it? How do you get it out there?'

'People love it on Vimeo.'

'That only gets you so far, though. Once you have a big following, you need something to produce. Something people with money will get. Money people are thick as pig shit.'

'Yeah, but. If you're already famous, people give you stuff.'

'There's famous, and famous enough people give you money,' Nathan said. 'Two different things.'

'Two ways a bird who's not from London can get proper famous. Do a sex tape with someone who already is or post the craziest shit she can think of on social. I don't even have to do the thinking bit, though. Look.'

Then the nameless guy spoke up. 'It isn't the knitting ladies. It's you. It wouldn't be interesting if it weren't for you.'

She called Ben from the toilet, before it got awkward.

He was lovely, but he was like the wallpaper. After a while it just started to bother you, and you'd think, *an accent wall with big metallic flowers, that's what I need*. Probably you'd regret it, but after you have that thought one time it comes back every time you look at the wall.

She went to the computer suite with everyone to edit the knitting ladies, feeling well professional lining up a Rudimental track with the titles while Drake Circus hulked outside the window in the rain.

In her room that night Jo posted two videos, *Knitting or Not?* and a second one titled *Glimmer/Sorry*, two seconds long. The camera spinning round, a flash of seagulls and the blur of Beth Kennedy with concrete facades turning behind her.

Chapter 14

Khadija began to find herself walking nowhere. Evenings after work she'd turn for home then turn away again, swipe her card without thinking, step onto a bus or an overground, get out again after an unspecified while. In Greenwich or Finsbury Park, she'd carry on walking, eating a roti or some chips from her hands. Wind up in King's Cross maybe, when the commuter people had gone and the late-night people hadn't arrived yet.

The big dirty pub and the Ethiopian restaurant on City Road were empty. The only people around were waiting for buses that would take them to other parts of London, with houses and parks in them. Tower blocks. Also of course, there were the permanent people in the plaza in front of the station, selling God.

Not what Khadija was looking for, but what was? Could you look for nothing? Maybe that feeling of being in halls that she hadn't stopped to appreciate at the time. Monday of Freshers' Week when everyone else was still shiny and new, Khadija was already old. Bereaved. Guilty. *Out out, damn spot.* Once crowds of drunk people started pushing doors open, she followed them through without looking first.

It turned out there was another London, where you passed in and out of doorways without ever seeing the spaces in between. Everyone rode in private hire cars and you bought dresses from the Topshop on Oxford Street, wore them with the tickets tucked in and returned them the day after so you'd able to stand next to girls who didn't have to. Between the doorways and the hire cars, the cold touched you but it didn't hurt. Everyone's eyes were half-covered with a layer of water and chemical shine. Twenty-year-old men wore £10,000 watches and university students had maids.

Khadija made friends with Nikhil at the Student Union Bar

because he was sweet instead of flash. His job was to invite her to club nights where she dressed up and let men buy her £100 bottles of champagne. In between dragging Farah away from her books to go out for food and walks by the canal, she read torts and corporate liability and rode around the West End with Nik and a bunch of forgettable girls. Everyone back home saw the pictures and thought she had the perfect life. Now Khadija seemed to believe her own social media history. She was wandering around looking for sparkly London, missing something that had never happened.

Or maybe she was looking for the foxes, looking to hide behind car parks, come out only at night and forget human language, so she wouldn't understand what was happening on the other side of her bedroom wall.

Apart from all that, she was looking for an address. In behind the Euston Road at 8pm on a Tuesday, Marylebone was full of empty light, a daytime place abandoned now. She found the building, glass and chrome vestibule that might have been made in the 1980s, though the transom above the door was Art Nouveau. Khadija saw herself in the doors, layered in the reflection of the dark windows of the lunch place over the road, the lines on the asphalt, the light that never went out in the hair salon. Hackney cabs and ambulances driving through her body.

The building was thin and stretched, sandwiched between a bank and designer start-up. It had three floors and forty-seven letter boxes. This was the address listed at Companies House for Slate Group, who had filed for bankruptcy and ceased trading in 2004.

And? Slate were found liable for loss of bodily integrity at the dockyard. They shared three directors with companies where one of the Osbornes, son or long-dead father, had held directorships, one where the mother had been a secretary. But of course their letter box was long gone. There was everything from Alta Holdings through CN Incorporations to Resolve Logistics, but no Slate Group. It had been broken up and reconstituted like some sort of chemical salt. Somewhere in those forty-seven boxes was a letter addressed to someone who was once a director of Slate Group and who now officially lived on the Isle of Man, no doubt.

And? That was what companies did. You could start literally anywhere on the Companies House site and find a web of connections just like that one. They didn't kill people with their actual hands and they didn't break any laws. They made those, so they didn't have to.

What was she looking for?

'How do you see yourself in that thing?' Farah said, pointing at Khadija's mirror, scattered with post-it notes.

'It's good practice, seeing through the confusion.'

'Deep. Or maybe, you're just making it more difficult for yourself than it needs to be?'

'Can I borrow that Rees dress?'

'What, you're going to Royal Festival Hall or something?' Which was meant as a joke because only Farah would go somewhere like that. Only then. Only with Will and his parents. 'On a random Wednesday night?'

'I'm going out. I'm twenty-three years old, for fuck's sake.'

'Where? With who?'

'Whom.'

'Where are you going, Khadi? *Friends look after friends*, innit?'

'Nik is doing a couple of weeknights in a club off Brick Lane.'

Being alone was better in the club, or any place that was not her bedroom, anywhere you couldn't hear what was on the other side of the wall because the bass was far too loud. If she didn't want to be alone, if anyone bothered her, she could walk over and slide into Nik's table.

So then she was looking at another crowded mirror, behind a bar, rows of bottles full of coloured water on glass shelves in front of it. There were two barmaids who'd taken hours to dress like they didn't give a shit how they were dressed. Nik was aiming at the indie crowd, the baby *Guardian* readers.

'I like that you don't use straighteners.' He spoke from behind her and it was only then that Khadija realised there was a stranger behind her in the mirror.

'No point.' She looked away at the DJ booth.

'You'd be beautiful with no hair at all.'

Seriously? That was a line? There was nothing desperate behind it, though. Lack of effort, maybe. Craig used to make her more uncomfortable when he asked if she wanted a cup of tea.

'You don't want to eat my soul, do you?'

'What, like a vampire?' He laughed.

She waved a hand at the mirror and raised an eyebrow. He looked nonplussed. She was drunk and he wasn't dead clever. She kept talking into the mirror, where everything was clean and lit from below. No fingerprints and no shadows. He asked her name and she answered.

'Never seen you here before.'

'You probably have. Nik's a mate.'

'Trust me, I'd remember.'

'You live in London?' Not that she cares, but it's getting awkward.

'Sometimes. What can I get you?'

'Something green. Bright green. Something that looks like it's glowing.'

'Is that how you decide what to drink? By colour?'

'I'm feeling toxic.'

'Sorry, didn't hear you, darling.'

Because the Shy FX remix of London Grammar is unnecessarily loud. Well done, Nik. Bang on the target market.

'Well, it has to happen sometime,' Khadija says to the mirror.

'Sorry?'

'You said that. Never mind.'

Later they went through the cold and into an Uber that took them to a house in St John's Wood. There was a magnolia shining in the dark on the lawn and a driveway that crunched underneath the car. They went in a side entrance, so it was only after they were indoors that Khadija realised it was all one house.

'Your parents live here?'

'Yeah, but nobody's home. Well, maybe my sister and my cousin.'

Khadija took her heels off; there was carpet everywhere so thick it would tip you over. He disappeared for some kind of time and she lay down and dug her fingers into the pile. On the wall beside her was a painting made of two humming squares of colour, blurred at the edges and ringing against the background like two notes that were almost but not quite the same.

Then he was next to her, and all over her skin. He said her name and turned her over. For a while she looked from his face to the painting and back again, trying to sort out her breathing. Then she realised she wasn't supposed to and shouted instead. He made her a coffee while she waited for the car.

'Not that I'm complaining, but you should be a little more careful in clubs, lovely. Something bad could happen.'

'Well, it didn't,' Khadija said. 'Mohammed Magdy, eh? Mohammed is my father's name.'

'That's creepy, woman.'

'No, I've never met him or anything. I just know his name.'

'Creepier. We could be related.' He laughed.

She lay back against the sofa like a person with no bones and that seemed to make him happy. They chatted while she waited for the hire car. She'd been unfair; he was quite clever. He hugged her at the door and told her to look after herself, that she was beautiful and probably special. Nobody offered their number; it was too weird by that point. She'd bled a little on the carpet but he hadn't noticed.

Farah was sleeping when she got back to Chiswick. The house was quiet and the fox was gone.

Nik messaged at eleven the following morning.

OK?

He was just waking up. She'd been at work for three hours already.

Fine.

...

Go back to sleep, you lost-it.
Nothing bad happened, right?
Nothing bad, Nikhil. Apart from that Fleetwood Mac remix.
It was ironic.
Nah. It was like being home with my mum.

...

But thanks for checking, hon. Proper paladin, you.
Something good happen, then?
Straight-up neutral.
Mo Magdy's dad owns a fucking airline.

...

a small one like, but still.

Nik had grown up in Tooting and had been trying to make that eight-mile journey to the centre of things since he was fifteen.

We didn't take numbers. Slow your heart rate and go back to sleep.
Things happen to you when you're pretty.
Really? Things like what?

Chapter 15

Around midnight one Saturday, Jo took her shoes off to stand on the rim of a toilet in Revolution. She turned on the video and held her phone above the cubicle wall.

'Seriously though, does it gag ya?' said one of the girls in the next stall.

There were two of them in there, which is why Jo had turned on the video. Women's toilets on Union Street were pure gold, and these two were far too pissed to notice the camera.

'Yeah, but I'm not a lesbian,' the second girl said. 'Fannies always gag me.'

Jo put a hand over her mouth to keep from laughing out loud, then fell sideways into the wall. The two girls in the next stall didn't even pause. They were practically shouting. You could hear everything they were saying, even over the sound of 'Fancy' banging on the sound system.

'Even your own? I like my fanny. When it's bald.'

'Perve.'

'But look, though. I can't go home with no one. Not with all this bush. It's minging.'

'Why didn't you think of that earlier? You took about five hours getting ready.'

'Yeah, but I was pissed already. Not a good time to be near my business with a razor blade.'

'Anyway, it's not a bush. It's stubble.'

'It's scratchy.'

'The state of you! Honestly. Chlamydia would be a blessing. At least it'd keep your legs together for two seconds.'

'You *say* that.' And they both fell over laughing.

Jo sat down on the toilet to put her shoes back on, then rested a hand on the shiny brown door and stood up. The mirror over the sink showed a row of cold red legs behind her while she tried to fix an eyelash, a repeating image of straps and sequins and cascade chains. Someone had left their hair extensions by the sink.

At the bar, a floppy-haired posh boy was trying to make his nerves look like superiority. He was afraid somebody was gonna pull him outside and break his face any second, you could tell.

'I think you took a wrong turn at the Gin Factory, mate.'

'Hi.'

'Smooth. Witty.' She spat out the 't' sound.

'I'm Max. And I came in here by choice. With my friends.' He put his hand out.

'Then they fucked off and now you're stuck?' She looked at his hand like it was in the wrong place. 'Buy me a drink and I'll show you something hilarious.'

'Are you with someone?'

'No. I had a boyfriend until about an hour ago.' She put her purse down on the bar and laid her phone on it.

'Why am I looking at the ladies' toilets? That's a bit creepy.'

'You have to hear it. Come out to the smoking area.' She necked her vodka and grabbed his arm.

Outside it was January. Everyone in Plymouth was skint and zingy, with extra Christmas weight on and chapped skin. Everyone but Max, who looked like he moisturised. They pushed up against each other's shoulders and leaned over the phone.

'Anyway, it's not a bush; it's stubble,' said the girl on the phone.

'Christ,' Max said. 'Who are you?'

'It's my final project for Film Studies. It's about spying and about Plymouth.'

'That's blatantly illegal. Trust me, I'm a law student.'

'My cousin's a law student. And they'd have to see it and prove it was them before they could sue me. It's like, can anyone prove anything is really them anymore, you know?'

'Profound.' Max does sarcasm in that way that means you're never quite sure it is sarcasm.

'My project's about how you can make all the stories in history out of random people in the street. Like they're all different, but there's only so many stories and they're interchangeable.'

'What happened with your boyfriend?'

'He got boring. It took me a while to notice, because on one level he's a nutter. We both like excitement, that used to be how we bonded.'

'Then what?'

'Nothing, really. It's just, when you repeat something a hundred times it's not exciting anymore. I've known him since I was eight.'

'Not to be funny or anything, but you're gorgeous. I wouldn't have left you here.'

'Save it, lovely. I don't do posh tottie.'

They'd made up by Monday, of course. Ben apologised, so Jo had to as well. Those were the rules; one thing triggered the next, like pinball. He wrapped his arms around her from behind and everything fit inside everything else. She nestled back into Ben and Saltash and Vimeo, carried on making a video life inside her life, and didn't talk about it.

Chapter 16

On a warm night in October, Khadija rode back from Alu Nak with Farah and Will. Graduation was weeks past. Khadija was supposed to be a grown-up now. Farah was on a four-year course. The three of them looked out three different windows of the Uber, as though if any two lines of sight met inside the cab it would blow up.

Will was cross. Another row, one of those teeth-clenched, calm little rows where people grind their emotions out of thin lips. Where there is urgent murmuring in restaurants and eye-rolling in the car, but you'd only notice if you were watching very closely. Which every housewife in Alu Nak was, because Will was white and Khadija and Farah were obviously not Iranian (Persian) and what were the three of them doing there? Food tourism does not go down well with the clientele in Alu Nak. Farah said, 'screw them,' the dressing on the Shirazi salad was what protected her from winter colds.

Khadija chatted to the Uber driver, trying to escape the situation in the back seat. He thought she was Afghani at first and opened right up even after he found out she wasn't. He told her about meeting his wife in London and their daughters who spoke Polish and Farsi and English. She told him her dad was Moroccan, but not that she'd never met him.

When he pulled over on Chiswick High Street, Khadija handed Farah a fiver for her account and climbed out. There was someone living in the doorway next to theirs; he'd been there for a week on and off. Community cops moved him on once a day. She had no cash left and didn't know his name. If she'd asked him, Farah and Will would have thought it was because she was ignorant and didn't know how to live in London. As if Armada Way at home wasn't full of rough sleepers, kipping in the doorways of boarded up shops.

Khadija looked back at the car. No one was moving inside it. Asadullah the Uber driver was acting like nothing was weird and he was just taking a little break, he and Will and Farah looking out three different windows. Khadija was the only one looking at Farah. Farah disintegrating, Farah silently burning up.

Khadija unlocked the door, went through and left it open.

She was shut in her room by the time she heard them come in. Even through her headphones she could hear every word they said, which was partly the shitty walls in their flat and partly that her body was listening, whether she wanted it to or not.

'I'm just saying you have to try with them.'

He meant his parents. Will and Farah had three rows and this was one of them.

'Why? They don't want to know, Will.'

'They do. They've just never known anyone like you before.'

'That's not my problem.'

'It is though, isn't it? You're blaming us but you're the one who's got an attitude.'

You certainly couldn't accuse Will's parents of having any kind of attitude. You had to dig through several layers of polish just to uncover their disdain.

She waited in her room for Will to leave. He didn't slam the door. He liked to walk away like Farah wasn't worth raising his blood for. In rows he'd go very calm and reasonable, waiting for Farah to make herself look hysterical.

Khadija knocked on the door as softly as she knew how. 'You OK?'

'I'm fine, Khadi. Find something else to fix.'

'I just want someone to have a cuppa with.'

'Bloody hell. Come in.'

'What were you rowing about?'

'Nothing. I'm just adjusting to the whole thing. My family is different. People shout and hug each other.'

'They're normal, you mean?'

'It's just different, Khadi. It's not wrong.'

She wanted to say, *it's wrong for you and you know it*, but instead she made tea. They sat up and acted like nothing was weird or difficult and no one ever hurt each other quietly.

'I don't know what I'm doing, Farah.'

'You're doing what you always do. Working and swotting and being an excellent housemate.' Farah waved her half-empty mug.

'Not being melodramatic, but I feel like I'm fading or something. I have days when nothing is clear. I can't remember the reason for anything I'm doing.'

'It's two in the morning, Khadi. I need sleep. Can we talk about this tomorrow?'

'We don't need to. It's no big; I'm just having a shit night.'

'I want to know, Khadi. I do. It's only, this is a bad time.'

Back in her room, Khadija sat on her bed with her back in the corner of the wall and opened Fairchild v. Glenhaven. Out the window, half of the view was quilted with another set of windows, yellow and red and the bricks between.

It wasn't true that the city never got quiet. It did, around 3:30 in the morning. The silence bounced off the asphalt into Khadija's open window and the traffic sighed like the sickly ghost of the bridge traffic at home. She had the Companies House website open on her phone then, following a string of corporate boards from Slate Group, PLC, who were listed as directors on the board of the holding company that owned part of the logistics firm that contracted the pipe fitters at the dockyard between 1963 and 1980. A guy called Orcutt sat on the board of Slate and two other companies described as 'marine logistics'. Maybe it didn't matter anymore. Everyone was already dead, but she needed to know how they moved the law like that. Exactly how, all the details.

Khadija went home for the holidays, on a train crowded with uni students and the dirty washing they were taking home to Mum. On Christmas day, Farah messaged a picture of the trash outside Angel tube. *Angel We Have Heard on High*, it said. That was when she knew Farah hadn't gone home, and also that she was still in there somewhere underneath the Marks & Spencer jumpers and the pastel make-up. Still herself. Farah sent two more messages, saying *when are you back from Cornwall*? Khadija answered the first one, but Farah asked again two days later.

When Khadija got back to Chiswick, it was the 28th of December and the flat was quiet. She put a tin of Aunt Tammy's cookies on the worktop and knocked at Farah's room. No answer and no music playing. She wrote on her train ticket and slipped it under the door.

I'm back. Obvs. Wake me up when you get in.

Sometime after midnight, Khadija fell asleep on top of her duvet with LinkedIn still scrolling behind her eyes.

The next afternoon at one o'clock, time came scratching at the walls and Khadija rolled over. Farah hadn't woken her coming home because she'd been home all the time. Khadija stumbled into the hallway and tried the handle, then leaned in to put her mouth against the crack of Farah's door.

'If you don't let me in, I'm calling people.'

When was the last time someone checked on her? Where the fuck was Will?

'I'll call lots of people. Parents and shit.'

By the time the door swung all the way open, Farah was already back on the bed with a book in her lap. She was wearing a long T-shirt and manky slippers. The heat in the room was baking and she looked sweaty.

'Farah, what—?'

'Revising.'

'Where's Will?'

'Greece. With the parents. They invited me, but in a *please don't say yes* way.'

'Why are you in bed at one in the afternoon? And why the hell didn't you answer last night? I thought you were out. Scared the crap out of me just now.'

121

'I'm focussed, Khadi. I have exams in February. Scary ones.'

'Thanks for the Christmas card.'

'We're Muslims, Khadi.'

'You're a Muslim. I'm out on a limb with all that what happens after death, how big is the universe stuff.'

'Not now, Khadi. Please?'

'Will was in Greece? What did you do all day?'

'Walked around a lot. There was no one on the roads but people who have to be, nothing open. When the leaves are off, the trees are the same colour as the buildings and the sky. You ever notice that? I hardly ate for two days because there was nothing but takeaway.'

'So when was the last time you ate?'

'Calm down, Khadi. I was exaggerating. I ate.'

'I'm staying here until you take a shower and come outdoors with me.'

You couldn't see anything outside Farah's window because she'd covered it with new drapes.

'Okay, stand up.'

'Seriously? Go back to your combine harvester.'

'You're losing your shit, Farah. Stand up or I'm gonna call Living Support and tell them you're a danger to yourself.'

'You wouldn't do that. Anyway, we live in private accommodation now. I'm not their problem.'

'One time I phoned the police on my own cousin. Don't push me. I'm putting that T-shirt in the washing.'

Khadija pulled the duvet off the bed, sending Farah sideways into the wall.

'Leave it! Shit, I can't believe you just did that.'

'Arms up.'

'Oh my God, just have a baby already. You're creeping me out.'

'Arms up, you pathetic bird.'

'Bird?' Under her socks, Farah's toenails were painted the colour of someone else's flesh. Her wrists were bare.

'Don't move.'

122

Khadija had to take three pairs of tights out of the shower before she could turn it on. She combed out Farah's hair until steam came through the bathroom doorway. Just like Alice. Like Jo. Like her mother. The people who needed Khadija turned her inside out until she became the person who combed their hair and put them in showers and made them tea. Even Craig thought she'd fix him. Be his fix.

Farah wasn't asking for Khadija to care, though. She was asking for nothing at all, at least not right out.

She shoved Farah under the running water and shut the door, then she went back to her own bed and let all the air out of her lungs, wrapped her arms around herself and felt like running away outdoors.

'Hey. I actually do feel better.' Farah stood over her with her hat and coat on. A new hat. 'All day breakfast, right?'

'Crap, I must have fallen asleep. The water reset you, didn't it? It makes you new.'

'Yes actually, West Country witch. I want greasy mushrooms.'

'Yeah, witch. That's what I am. I got it from my mum.'

'Also fried bread. Maybe just mainline some grease right into my arm.'

'We live on the edge of town and when anything goes wrong, they all think it was us who did something. Isn't that how it worked with witches?'

'What? Get in this conversation, Sleep. We need grease, not gluten free vegan bollocks. Where we gonna get that shit in Chiswick?'

It sounded like her, but she was dressed like some other Farah. All of the clothes that made her real had gone to the British Heart Foundation, apparently.

Will came back from Greece looking more like himself than when he left. Full of colour and puffed up with salt water and fried octopus, healthier than anyone on this island had a right to look. Khadija went back to wandering, hanging out with uni people. She started spending the weekends in the London Library instead of reading in her room.

One night she found herself in a hire car at three in the morning with Nik and someone called Rhian who was never going to pass for a Londoner.

She didn't seem to care though, Rhian. She went on in her own accent, talking too loud and sparkling like mad. That was the other way to do it, the way Jo would do it if she had half a chance. Act all the time, like you were in a play starring your hilariously regional self. It was exhausting just to watch.

Khadija looked out the window at Tottenham Court Road, trying to think of something she could do besides go home. That was when she realised it wasn't home.

Chapter 17

'Thought you might need a lawyer.'

The bloke looked around Jo's little gallery cubicle and then threw himself down in Tammy Williams' comfy chair. It was Max Randall, the guy from Revolution. Jo hadn't seen him in months.

'Cool, a stalker. I can tick that off my getting famous list.'

Jo had separated off her own space in the gallery for her final show, set up two screens and a camera opposite the chair, like the Diary Room on *Big Brother*. Ben had brought the chair from his Aunt Tammy's sitting room in his dad's van.

'Because like I said, this is blatantly illegal,' Max said. 'How do the college let you get away with this?'

'I faked a bunch of consent forms. They could probably tell, but they're covered because they required them.'

'Jesus!' It wasn't the consent forms. Max had just noticed the video of himself running on the bigger screen.

'Check that guy out, right?' She pointed at his image. 'He's well judgemental. Totally up himself; let's vote him off.'

'How does one random girl turn out to be as strange as you?'

'When I was small it was easier to turn everything into a film, trust me. B Horror, mostly.'

Max Randall was not a person who had any idea what to say to that.

'Anyway, I'm not strange. I'm a flippin' creative genius. Ask Nathan.'

'Who's Nathan?'

'Mr *Hoxton* over there.' Jo pointed across the gallery at Nathan, wearing skinny jeans and a T-shirt with a picture of a blank screen on it. 'He came to see my stuff, so get out of the chair, stalker.'

'Your stuff is going to be him, looking at your stuff? Deep.'

'My videos are here, too. They'll be on the little screen below. It's just, the audience is the spectacle. Because the internet, get it?'

'Amazing how you can be shallow and meaningful at the same time.'

'Hang around and watch me do it. Just don't piss off my boyfriend.'

'The boring one?'

'He's not boring; I just got a little bored. Anyway, none of yours, *Mark Lewis*.'

'Right over my head.' He made the motion with one hand above his floppy hair. 'Who's Mark Lewis?'

'He's the psycho stalker in this brilliant film I watched with Nathan. He follows women around with a camera then murders them.'

'So, a bit more like you than me, actually.'

'Burn. Cameras, though. They do shit to people's minds, right? You're uncomfortable right now, aren't you?'

'But is it you or the camera?'

'You're not the first person to ask that. Now piss off.'

'Good luck. I hope you get a distinction.' He stopped to type his number into her phone.

The next person to sit in the chair wasn't Nathan, it was Vicky Harvey, the Film Studies lecturer.

'Oh, this is quite nice. Clever as well, but I really needed a sit down!'

'Happy to help.' You were supposed to call her Vicky, not Miss Harvey, but that still felt odd, so Jo left the name out.

'This is great work, you know.'

'Thanks. It was a laugh, really. I mean I worked hard, but it didn't feel like it.'

'You'll get better at the production side. And the artist's statement. You have to learn to go slow sometimes, go over all the small details. That takes a lot of quiet time, without anyone bothering you.'

'Yeah well, I have a little brother, so that in't really on the cards.'

'Kids, yes. I know you're not supposed to say it anymore, but they do make it harder to do your own work.'

'You have kids, then?'

'Yes, but I waited until I had some work experience and a bit of savings.'

'Is this a talk or a *talk*, Ms Harvey? Vicky.'

'I was only thinking out loud.'

'That's bollocks. You think because I drop a letter here and there I'll be pregnant in a Mount Wise tower block any minute. What a waste of a person, you're thinking.'

'Well, I'm certainly going to miss you either way. In the past two years, I've never heard you say a single thing that doesn't need to be said.'

'What a terrible loss it would be if I wound up like my mum, eh? Beyond saving.'

'You need to be heard, Jo Sleep. I'm not going to apologise for saying it.'

'I'm supposed to say thanks now, I guess.'

She meant well, but in that way where it was all mixed in with feeling better about herself. It was a wind-up.

'You have to be selfish to do work like this,' Vicky said. 'You know?'

'Newsflash. Some of us don't consider selfish a virtue. If people like us win the lottery, we're poor again three years later, did you know that? Know why?'

'No, and I'm not sure I believe you.'

'We read about it in GCSE Sociology. It's because we divide it all up with the family and people we love. The article didn't say love.'

'Generalisations don't have to define you, Jo.'

'You're not getting me. I'm saying we don't keep it all to ourselves because we don't want to. I'm saying there's people got my back. No matter what.'

'I meant selfish in a good way. You have to look after yourself. Be jealous of your time and your space.'

'OK, get out of my chair.'

The look on Vicky Harvey's face was reproduced on the screen across from her. She saw her own shock and closed it right down.

'Not being rude,' Jo said, 'but Nathan from BA Film wants to see my work. He thinks we could make something people would pay for.'

'Oh! Well, I guess I'm late to the party. I'm really glad you've got a project in the works. Well done, Jo.'

'Not like, regular people. Like the Arts Council or something.'

By 8:30 the gallery was emptying out, but Jo's space was packed. Tammy Williams sat in her own chair, Jo's mum perched on one arm and Ben on the other. Aunt Debbie stood awkwardly in the entrance with a plastic cup of wine, looking at Alice and Dylan sitting on the floor.

Alice was moving her hands and watching them on the screen. Dylan shoved her and she shifted over, leaving a smudge of brown rust on the lino floor. Uh-oh.

'You guys hang out here and get pissed. I'm gonna show Alice the editing suite.' Alice didn't hear Jo, or pretended not to anyway.

Jo had to pull her up by the scruff. She took her down a half-lit, echoey corridor before she said, 'you need to sort yourself out, maid. Wait, I guess you're not a maid no more. When did this happen?'

Alice slumped against the wall and looked at Jo with unfocused eyes.

'My insides are peeling off,' she said. 'It hurts. Don't tell my mum.'

'Oh, this is the first time?'

Alice slid down against the wall and laid her hands on her little womb.

'Get up, you ridiculous bird. This is gonna happen to you every four weeks until you're as old as Tammy Williams. This level of drama is not appropriate.'

'It feels like this?'

'Yep. Nice, in't it? Now get over it and let's go sort you out.'

She took Alice to the all-gender toilet on the other side of the

Media suite, shoved her in there and ran back to the gallery for her purse. The only people left were her family, a couple of tech support guys and Vicky Harvey in the doorway arguing with Aunt Carol's boss, Mr Osborne. What was he doing here?

'Where's Alice?' Aunt Debbie looked like maybe Jo had lost her or helped her jump off the roof because she'd taken her eyes off her for five seconds. No wonder Alice had issues.

'I left her in the editing suite. She's well into it.'

'Someone should be with her.'

'She's thirteen, Aunt Debbie. Anyway, I'm going back now.'

She had to push past Vicky Harvey and Mr Osborne to get out of the gallery.

'Now this girl,' Vicky Harvey grabbed Jo like she was a life raft that could carry her out of the conversation, 'is one of your home-grown Saltash talents. Talk to Jo Sleep if you want to know why Arts education matters. Jo, say hello to Anthony Osborne, one of our governors.'

'Sorry, Ms Harvey, no time. I need to go explain to my baby cousin exactly where her vagina is and how to put things in it.'

Alice had left the toilet door cracked open. She'd pulled her jeans down but not her pants, which were soaked. Her left hand was covered in dark blood, and her fingerprints were smeared across the wall. She was rubbing her bloody fingers together and crying.

'Fuckin' hell, bird. Wake up.'

'This isn't my period, Jo. I'm coming apart. I can feel things coming loose inside.'

'It *is* your period. That's how it feels. Now let's deal with it, before someone comes looking for us.'

'How do you make it stop?'

'You don't.'

'They're not allowed. They can't do this to me. It's supposed to be my body. It's never mine, Jo.'

'It is yours and this is the package. Christ, Alice, didn't they show you the film in school?'

'I don't remember. It doesn't matter. This isn't my body. I don't need instructions for it.'

Khadi should have bloody been there. What would she do?

Focus on the practical. Get those pants off and put them in the bin. Forget cleaning the wall. Get the jeans back on her and wrap her hoodie around her waist. Shit, *and* get a tampon in her.

Alice was rubbing the blood into her thigh now. 'Outside. Inside,' she said.

This.

This was the thing Jo would trade her twenty-million-pound lottery jackpot for. This was what she had in place of riches.

Jo's mum looked up at her when they got back to the gallery, 'Give it to us one more time, babe?'

She sat Alice down and patted her shoulder, then realised she was treating her like a puppy. Like Aunt Debbie did.

'I'm saying we have it all round here, Mum. We're dramatic, tragic, struggling, daring. Definitely hilarious.' Like Alice, hiding her blood in the corner from her mother who thought she wanted to die. 'There's a story wherever you point the camera. It's just that no one ever points one at us.'

'Is it meant to be funny or sad?'

'It's meant to be whatever. That's why the screen that shows you watching. You're making the story while you watch, and you're part of it too. We read a bunch of crap about that in Film Studies AS.'

'People would laugh though, wouldn't they?' Debbie said. 'If you put this on telly, they'd laugh as soon as one of us spoke. Can only be comedy when we're speaking.'

'Telly is over,' Jo said.

Chapter 18

One late spring morning, Farah went with Khadija to the bus stop. She had been following Khadi around lately, like there was a string between them and if she let go she'd float away. The rain was warm and you could smell the winter cold breathing itself out of the stones. They stopped in Café Nero and threw their coats onto the leather chairs by the front window.

'I'm getting it,' Farah took out her wallet. 'My access grant came through. You are loanless now.'

'I have a job, though. An actual job.'

'Internship.'

'Job. My internship ended last week. They're keeping me.'

The man in front of them was wearing All Saints jeans and a Pete Doherty hat. Khadija nearly shouted out 'double espresso!' before he had a chance to say it himself.

'Nice suit,' she said to Farah instead.

'Thanks. It was on sale at Next.'

'Is it you, though?'

'Yes Khadi, this is me. Sorry I don't live up to your indie standards. Incidentally, you don't live up to them either.'

'Do you need a receipt?' the barista asked.

'No, ta.' Farah picked up her cup and turned her back.

There were drops running down the inside of the window and someone else's half-empty cups on the table. The two of them stared out at the High Road with a feeling like waves between them. Like soaking ground and sinking rivers.

'No receipt?' Khadija asked. 'Who are you and what have you done with my friend?'

Farah rolled her eyes and sat down. 'I can't save you, babe.'

'I don't want saving. I'm trying to save you, you silly cow.'

'That isn't true, Khadi. You screwed up a load of things at home. You've been haunted since you got here, and you won't even talk about it.'

'If you don't need saving, why did you follow me to Café Nero?'

'I thought we'd hang out for a minute, have a coffee. Don't make me regret it.'

'I just give a shit, Farah. You're letting yourself drift away. It sucks and I'm the one who knows who you could be.'

'No, hon, I'm the one who knows who I could be. Can't you even hear yourself? What is happening on your bedroom wall?'

'Subtle change of subject. Well done.'

'It isn't a change of subject, Khadi. The reason we're always talking about me is because I'm your crap telly. I'm your celebrity mag, the thing that helps you avoid thinking about your own shit.'

'Since you have all this figured out, why didn't you tell me sooner?'

'Because I love you and I've been trying to hang on. I'd like to have a life now if it's okay with you.'

'I'm not trying to stop you having a life, Farah. I'm trying to stop you not having one.'

'Not your call, babe. Answer my question. What the hell is that on your wall. Will's dad thinks you're a nutter.'

'It's just some liability stuff. It's well complicated. I needed a map.'

'Do you have to do it serial killer stylie? Couldn't you just use a notebook?'

'It helps me think. I'm a visual thinker. There are so many connections, a web diagram is easier. I do have a question you might know the answer to, actually.'

'Go.'

'I need to know the rules on financial filings. Like how often and how much detail. How do they hide stuff?'

'Dude, are you gonna do some Erin Brockovich shit?'

'Unlikely. It's all over. There was a class action suit. Negligence, personal injury, corporate liability. A bunch of people died and a couple companies paid out some crap little amount and that's it.'

'So, why the map?'

'I want to understand it.'

'You're staying up every night till all hours making a map of something that's over, something you can't do anything about, and you think *I'm* not living *my* life?'

'It's part of me, Farah. It happened to people I love and the people they love. I need to put it to rest, like. I just do.'

'What happened? Talk about it for once.'

'Asbestos. A bunch of men where I live spent years breathing in asbestos. Hundreds of them died and they knew. The management at the dockyard knew, the supply companies knew, the government knew, and nobody did anything because you don't die from asbestos until years later. They thought they'd get away with it.'

'Wow.'

'And it isn't over, actually. People are still dying. Maybe not just from the asbestos.'

'I'm so sorry, Khadi.'

'Yeah? Well, you're in training to be the person that gets those sort of bastards off paying out. Congrats.'

'That's a bit of a stretch, Khadi. You know I wouldn't do something like that.'

'That is literally the point of what you do.'

'Sorry I'm such a disappointment. I have to go; I have a revision session at ten.'

'It's horrible.'

'Well, it's what I'm doing. Take it or leave it.'

'The way they die. It's horrible. They suffocate, but it takes years. It happened to my next-door neighbour. I really loved him.'

Khadija waited for Farah's bus to leave before heading for the tube. She wasn't wandering this time.

The Islamic Centre had probably been in a nice spot, before they built Westway on top of it. To get there Khadija walked from

Ladbroke Grove tube under the roadway, blanketed in a sound as loud as military airplanes.

The mosque was like a school. Well, it actually was a school; they taught all sorts of classes there. The prayer room had shelves for your shoes and wall to wall carpet. People sat around on it like they were in their own living rooms, but someone had taken away the furniture. In one corner, a girl with a long skirt pulled over her jeans had her face buried in her phone. The imam was called Mehdi and he didn't look much older than Craig.

'Thank you for talking to me.' Khadija looked at him and he looked away.

'I'm happy to, sister. It's what I do. Have you been in a mosque before?'

'No. It seems lovely. So relaxed.'

'Not like on telly, eh? So if you think the mosque is lovely, what's worrying you?'

'This is going to sound rude, but I don't mean it to be. Are you from here?'

'Was I born here? No. I was born in Sheffield.'

'My dad was from Morocco. I never met him. I want to, but I don't know what to do.'

'Ah.'

'I know. I literally googled "where do Moroccans go to mosque". It's lame, but I thought you might know how I can search for someone there? Or how I write to a mosque there or something? He was religious, my dad. Is religious, I guess.'

'How about you? Do you believe in God, sister?'

'I don't know. Not being disrespectful, but it seems a little childish to me, expecting someone else to tell you what's right and wrong.'

He smiled. 'I'd go with humbling, but OK.'

'Have you? Always?'

'Well, I chose to a long time ago. Do you know how I know I was right?'

'How?'

'Because you came here when you didn't know what else to do. That's why we're here. If I can help, I will.'

'You sound just like a priest.'

'Some of my best friends are priests.' They both laughed, and the laughter sank into the rug. The girl on the phone didn't even look up.

'Anyway, it's the part where I'm supposed to accept all the terrible unfair things that happen. That's what gets me. I just think if there was some loving parent in the sky they'd take better care of us, you know?'

'Well, tell me what you know about your dad. I can try writing a few letters for you.'

'That would be amazing. Thank you so much.'

'Here you are, needing help. Allah tells me to help. Also, I want to know what you're doing about your education. That's the price of my service.'

'My uni exams are finished. I'm doing my training now, to be a solicitor.'

'Ah, maybe one day you can help someone here. See how that works? I like to think it's a plan.'

Later, Khadija put her shoes back on and walked all the way to Westbourne Grove station in the falling dark beneath Westway. Late delivery traffic rumbled between her and the brown sites and the construction along the roadway.

'Go home!' She jumped and the sound of laughter from a car window telescoped in and out of the rushing wind. They were gone before it faded. She'd forgotten to take the scarf off her hair.

Warm lighting fell in long rectangles out of the few shops that had survived under the motorway, stretching onto the long empty pavement. This was a world too hostile even for pigeons or graffiti artists. Surely in a universe with a god, there would be less concrete.

After that day, the Jenga dream ended on the railing along Westway. It hadn't even occurred to her, walking under it, how much it felt

135

and sounded like the bridge walkway at home. In her dream, shadows of people came rushing through the sound of the traffic.

One night, Farah announced she was making stuffed grape leaves. She made Khadija promise to stay in for them, got lost in the middle and had to call her dad for help while they steamed in a covered pot. There was wine from Marks & Spencer and Will was somewhere else. Khadija could feel an announcement in the air, silence with substance like a pillow pressing in around her. She spoke just to push it away.

'I was thinking it might be time for me to have a dad.'

'I thought you didn't know where he was?'

'I don't, but I could look.'

Farah pulled a chair out and sat down. She looked at the pot on the hob and then at the phone. She looked at the floor for a while and then back at the cooker.

'What?' Khadija said.

'I— I wasn't expecting that.'

'Me either. It's what you said, though. It's my life that's messed up. If yours is too, it's none of my business.'

'Of course it's your fucking business!'

'Ok, now I'm lost, Farah.'

'Will wants me to move in with him.'

'Yeah, I kind of got that from the Marks & Sparks wine.'

'Should I do it, Khadi?'

'Why not? You do everything else he wants you to do.'

'Please stop being cross with me. I really don't know what to do.'

Khadija leaned back against the kitchen wall and looked at the red splashback across the way. The light was on but there was no one in the kitchen, no one cooking any Nigel Slater bollocks and smelling each other's necks. They were probably in the bedroom shagging before dinner because they were so into each other they just couldn't wait any longer. Life was like that on the other side of windows.

'What do you want to do?' Khadija said at last.

'If I knew that I'd do it, wouldn't I?'

136

'Farah, I get the point you were making the other day, but I still don't think you're this person. London eats people. I'm thinking I should leave, before it eats me.'

'I feel like I can't see anything properly anymore, Khadi.'

'I feel like you can't, too. I've seen a lot of women be right where you are, though. Dunno about you, but where I'm from women are in this situation all the time. They don't try to deny it. You'll move in with him.'

'Why?'

'Because you're not done until you're done.'

'How will I know, though?'

'You'll know.'

Farah was right, of course. About the inside of Khadija's head. It wasn't Farah's shadow falling from Westway in her dream. It wasn't the smell of her, blowing over the millennium bridge. Khadija hadn't even known you could dream a smell, before her first week at uni.

She was wrong about why she cared about what happened, but she was right that it was Khadija's life that was the problem. It wasn't the ghost of Farah's jacket she saw from the corner of her eye, lying on the mud along the river at Richmond.

It was the same for everyone Khadija knew in London. Each of them had run away from somewhere, even if it was only another part of the city. The thing was, everything had followed them. Of course. In all its random corners, London was piled high with cast-off shadows and angry ghosts.

2016

Chapter 19

On Thursday morning Fore Street closes up and everyone joins the search. Mrs Halden at Bright and Tunstall lets Khadija leave after barely an hour, even though it's only her fourth day on the job.

Aunt Jan, Jo's mum, lives at the back of Wearde, just by the footpath that leads up past the Osborne's house and over to St Stephen's churchyard. The whole little estate lies in dip in the hill, a bowl of shadow full of grey houses with white council signs by the doorways.

'Morning, sweetie,' Jan says at the door. 'Thought you said you were bringing your Aunt Debbie?'

'They're dropping her off in a bit. Uncle Pete wants her out the way while the police go through Alice's room. Again.'

'All right. Get in here, you.' Aunt Jan leans down from the doorstep and kisses her.

'How are you, *Grandma*?'

'Not a grandma yet, cheeky. Brew?'

The television is turned down low. Khadija can barely hear the women in bodycon dresses talking about last night's *Britain's Got Talent* with the Thames stretched out behind them.

'Dylan in school?'

'Nah, the school has let people out to help with the search, so I kept him home. Don't worry, you can shout loud as you like. It won't wake him.'

'Does he smell yet? Teenage boys usually smell disgusting.'

'The room smells even worse than he does. Have a teacake. There's still some jam left I made in the summer.'

'Thanks, I ate breakfast. Don't have much appetite, anyhow. I'm getting too worried to eat and all.'

'Well, imagine how Debbie feels. Sit down and tell me all about London, maid. I haven't had a chance to ask you anything yet.'

Aunt Jan turns to the kettle and the cups on the worktop. She has on jeans and a bedazzled hoodie. From behind, she could be nineteen. Looking at the back of that jacket, it could be 1996. She's done her make-up and has the Hoover out. On the kitchen table, there's a basket with some crochet in it.

'London doesn't seem important right now, Aunt Jan.'

'You never think you're important, Khadija Sleep. I want to know what the bloody hell you're doing back here.'

'I don't know. London was just done. You know sometimes you just know something's over? Anyhow, Mum needs me.'

'Or maybe you need her, eh?'

Khadija laughs out loud. 'Sorry.' But she can't manage to look sorry. 'You know in one way I made sense there, my name and the way I look and all, but you lot are my belonging. We may not be as inbred as everyone thinks, but we're right tangled up, in't it?'

'All families are, Khadi.'

'We're not like all families, though.'

They're saved by the sound of the car door. Pete walks Debbie in and sits her down on the sofa. She's high as a kite, trying to smoke a fag but she keeps forgetting to pay attention to it. Jan takes it away.

'You can't have that in here no more, lovely. Jo's pregnant, yeah?'

'Yeah. Tell her not to keep it. Tell her not, Jan.'

'Stop it, Debbie. You don't get to say that, not even now.'

'All your kids are perfect, yours and Carol's. You two have no bloody idea.'

Khadija wants to say that Alice is perfect, too. That she's beautiful and nothing's wrong with her, but she can't. Ever since she was small, Alice could drain the comfort right out of a room. She always made you feel like there was one more person there you couldn't see, and whoever they were they didn't mean well.

Khadija walks Jan and Pete to the door.

'The doctor gave her something, Uncle Pete?'

'You noticed that, eh? She can't take more until this afternoon, but they are helping. She slept a bit last night.'

'What about you?'

'I'm fine, Khadi.'

'Don't worry, I'll look after her.'

'Get something down her,' Aunt Jan says. 'Start with water, then see if you can get her to drink something sweet.'

'All right. Leave us to it.'

'Tell Dylan I'll be back to do tea.'

In the sitting room the ladies in fitted dresses are gone. Caroline Quentin is wearing wellies, walking through a derelict house with a lady who owns a riding school. They're talking about oak beams and lime plaster.

Aunt Debbie looks like someone's stripped the surface off her. Whatever she's covered herself with since she married Uncle Pete and moved into that Barrett Home, it's gone now. Been pulled off like a blanket and left her swearing and dropping fag ash on people's carpet.

Khadija turns away to the kitchen so she doesn't have to see her looking like Craig's mother looked at the funeral. She clicks on the kettle and puts Jan's jam with some teacakes on a tray. From the kitchen window, all she can see is a slope of grass falling towards her and a row of garages, one thin piece of white sky behind the roof of old Mrs. Osborne's house. Aunt Debbie has wandered in behind her, searching for something in the basket of wool on the table while the kettle roars like an aeroplane.

'What ya looking for, Aunt Debbie?'

'Pink.'

'The blanket's gonna be green. Aunt Jan thinks the baby's a boy, but she's playing it a bit safe.'

A little current of normal passes over, or maybe just the shadow of a bird from the bridge. Khadija tries to pass her smile across the room, but it falls onto the lino between them.

'Couldn't put pink on Alice. Not with that hair. We made her blankets white.'

'Did you guess she'd be ginger?'

'Tammy told us.' Debbie laughs one breath of a laugh.

'You reckon Aunt Tammy knew Alice was ginger before she was born? Jesus, my whole family lives in the Middle Ages.'

'She didn't say ginger.' Debbie winds a ball of wool and puts it back in the basket. 'She just told us to make the blankets white.'

Khadija remembers the white blankets, of course. She remembers the ginger fuzz on Alice's soft head and the way her feet turned blue if you held her the wrong way. She remembers them all crowded into Tammy's sitting room, Alice sleeping in the corner while Micky Williams breathed into a plastic mask upstairs.

'Charlie ever talk to you about the old lady?' Khadija points up at the Osborne house.

'He loves his nan. Talks about her all the time. I'm sure she's better than either of those parents he's got.'

'Did the husband leave the house to her, or the son?'

'I don't know. Not the sort of thing you'd talk about, is it? Charlie wishes he could live at our house, anyway.'

'How long have he and Alice been a thing?'

'Not sure. Cagey at that age, in't they? He loves her, though. You can just smell it on him.'

So now Charlie is the boy clinging onto Alice, breathing in the soul that comes off her skin, drinking everything out of her eyes. No wonder she's disappeared. Gone into the water just to get away from the air that's full of him, maybe. Sometimes the river lies there asking to surround you, pretending it will protect you. Khadi's heard it herself, but she always knew not to listen. Or tell anyone.

Aunt Debbie roots around in the basket, looking for a thread that isn't there.

So is Khadi. Nora Osborne's name turns up on at least three company boards, always at one remove from the husband and the son. On the papers it says Eleanora, but it's her. She's on one board with a guy called Orcutt. The name jumped out because she's seen it somewhere. Whatever that lot were up to, the old lady knew about it. Planned all of it, maybe. Who knows?

144

'Sometimes I don't love her, Khadi.'

'Sorry? Oh, Aunt Debbie, that's not true. You're just upset and confused.'

Why do the Sleep sisters say this shit to their children? If they hate their own kids, why can't they tell each other about it? Get a therapist, for fuck's sake?

'You don't know, Khadi. Daughters try so hard to make you stop loving them.'

Sudden sounds of shooting come out of Dylan's room, making them startle and look away from each other. Khadija smiles and shrugs, but Debbie looks like someone's actually been shot.

'What about sons, then?' Khadija says.

'Who can say? They don't talk to you at all, do they?'

Out of Aunt Jan's kitchen window Khadija can see something dark with wings, lifting off the roof of Nora Osborne's house.

Chapter 20

Below the surface Alice hears the scream of metal against metal, the chewing of two-man saws, the hissing of water into steam.

Her head breaks through again, into the quiet dark. She will have to swim. She'd thought the current would pull her away into the cold, that everything inside her would stop. But the river refuses to help her. She needs to get to the channel, where the water compresses into swallowing force.

One arm over, one ear in the water and the sound of someone's child cries up from the mud. Alice dips her head and dives into the roaring. A storm and seven Cornish boys chained below the decking, one sobbing, one cursing and one just moving his lips. Not a prayer, a nursery rhyme. The other boys are silent, pissing into the dark.

There is oil in Alice's mouth, grains of metal and a sick green bloom on her lips.

When she reaches the channel, it takes her feet first and tumbles her under. Five bullets and a splinter of bone slice through the water. Someone falls in, blood leaking from the lips of a knife wound. There are a dozen girls with baskets, carrying bottled gooseberries and linen and vials of lovage cordial, carrying the mouths of foreign generations between their legs.

She draws the backs of her hands together above her head and then sweeps them out to part the water, pulling herself down through the noise. Still hoping to make the river make it stop.

More water in Alice's nose and her mouth, and with it the taste of pitch and burning coal. A sound like thunder or January waves, like a star bursting next to her ear, and the body of a stoker rains down on her in four hundred pieces. Chunks of hot metal hiss through the water and she dives after them.

Pictures too, of three hundred Americans rolling out toward France, of two stolen West African children riding upriver dressed like dandies, already too numb to cry for their mothers. The strong arm of a shipwrecked Spanish blacksmith who'd made a bad choice.

The current turns Alice slowly and her hair coils around her neck. She feels the tightness and the pounding on her eardrums, then the cold seam of nothing below.

Chapter 21

Friday morning at Bright and Tunstall it's all title searches. Khadija reads through a covenant a page and a half long, without a single comma. 'Premises will not be used as a hotel beerhouse tavern nor will goods be advertised for sale in any place on the property.' It goes on like that. Mrs Halden says you know from the missing commas that it was written around 1900. Someone lost a lawsuit over the placement of a comma in 1895 and no solicitor in Britain used a single one for the next ten years.

Solicitors have been making words for centuries, piling them up line by line and stacking the pages on top of each other. Studying law is like drowning in an ocean of language, without commas to let you breathe, even.

'So,' Mrs Halden says, 'They found nothing yesterday? That's good in a way, isn't it?'

She's trying to be kind, so Khadija doesn't say that of course they didn't find anything because the bodies round here go in the river, whether they walk in, jump or get pushed.

'Yeah, I hope so. It's like she walked out of that video into thin air,' is what she says instead.

Mrs Halden makes a caring, mourning face.

Khadija responds to three requisitions from Land Registry before lunch. By that time it's raining. Outside the window, people are walking on Fore Street like they don't even notice the water running down into their ears and washing up through the stitching on their shoes. She stays at her desk revising on the duty of care and unbroken chains of causation, waiting for the sky to stop and take a breath.

Around 4:30 she begins to feel like nothing can breathe, not even her. She picks up the phone and dials Jo.

'Where you to? Meet me after work.'

'Aunt Debbie's. It's pissing it; I'm not going nowhere. Sorry.'

'How are they?'

'Hang on... OK, I'm in the toilet now. Pete's *being the man* and Debbie's kind of dead behind the eyes, you know. I guess how would we be in their situation? It's been a week now, Khadi. The search turned up nothing. We're gonna have to stop pretending it's all going to be fine, in't we?'

'Well, for what it's worth, Tammy says she isn't dead.'

'Oh OK,' Jo says, 'should we tell the cops spirits told Aunt Tammy everything's fine?'

'She didn't say everything's fine. She said Alice isn't dead.'

'What will the cops do next?'

Khadija sighs. 'It just drags on, I guess. On telly they always say the first twenty-four hours is the crucial bit, don't they? After that the odds go right downhill.'

'Jesus, Khadi. There has to be something. What did Charlie Osborne say?'

'Dunno. He talked to the police, but I guess he didn't say anything useful. Jo, how long has Charlie's dad been at the school?'

'What, Mr Osborne? Couple years, I think. It was after I went to college and they turned it into an academy.'

'How'd he get the job? Is he on the academy board?'

'I don't know, Khadi. As soon as they academised he was the head. It came out in the same announcement. Why?'

'Does Ben know who else is on the governors?'

'Doubt it. Why would he? Bunch of people Mr Osborne has dinner with at China Fleet, no doubt.'

'Standard. He's creepy though, Jo. I wouldn't want him in charge of my daughter.'

'Well, he's a dick,' Jo says, 'but I don't reckon he keeps kidnapped girls in his basement or anything.'

'That's not even funny, Jo. Meet me after work, please? My mum's driving me nuts. I need an excuse to be out.'

'Come by here. We can tidy and things for Aunt Debbie. Make them eat. I'm pretty sure she's eaten nothing but Temazepam all day.'

'Right, I'll stop at the Co-op.'

'No need. My mum's filled up the slow cooker. Actually, get me a Viennetta.'

'Jesus. OK.'

Out the window the water still runs down Fore Street, carrying anything light enough to be washed away. Alice certainly didn't vanish into thin air. There is no thin air around Saltash. The wind outside is overloaded with moisture and grit and the dirty past. One way or another, every pair of human lungs on that hill is heaving, trying to pull it in and push it out. Even without the asbestos.

The front hall at Debbie and Pete's is full of post, stacked up on the floor by the wall. Aunt Debbie is on the sofa with the patio door wide open. She's watching the 1950s in colour on ITV. Or rather, she isn't watching, she's looking out at the back garden.

'No Viennetta, sorry, bird.' Khadija half whispers it.

'You got something else, right?'

'Sorry, I didn't know what you wanted.'

'I'm pregnant, Khadi. I want fat and sugar. It in't rocket science.'

'Calm down.'

She moves into the room at the front of the house, beckoning Jo to follow.

'Now, you grumpy cow,' Khadija says, 'fill me in. Anything?'

'Nothing here. Exactly what did Aunt Tammy say about Alice?'

'Oh, you know. Weird shit about water and how Alice can hear Charlie through the shower.'

'My mum's the only one of them lot that ever believes her. Sorry I snapped at you. Can I blame the hormones?'

'You get one pass. Look, if Alice is alive, that means she went somewhere. We just need to find her.'

'What, now you want to track her down?'

'It's worth trying at least.'

'How the hell are we supposed to find her, Khadi? She stopped posting on all her accounts the same day she disappeared.'

'You were right, she probably hangs out somewhere under a different name. Believe she's on some secret chat with a bunch of kids from Bridgend or somewhere.'

'Thank you,' Jo says. 'I did say that three days ago. You told me I was a creepy stalker.'

'You so are. But also, you have a point. So, let's find the silly cow and get her to come home.'

'Maybe you should've been a private detective instead of a solicitor.'

In the sitting room Aunt Debbie is still in the same position. Not even her eyes have moved. On the screen she isn't looking at, a girl in a pencil skirt is crossing the green of some Oxbridge college. A skinny posh boy in a gown stares down at her from a Gothic window. It won't be him, then. Too obvious. Fade out, and then back in, to a riverbank in the morning. The same girl has turned a sickly cold white, lying with no shoes and a bloody bruise all down one leg.

'Did you have your tea, Aunt Debbie?' Khadija turns the television off and Jo slides the patio door across.

'Leave it,' Debbie says. 'It gets stuffy in here.'

'I'm pregnant; you can't freeze my bump.' Jo smiles, but Debbie isn't looking at her. 'Khadi said, did you eat?'

'Your mum put beef stew in the slow cooker earlier. It should be done.'

Jo sits on the sofa and puts a hand on Debbie's arm. 'Tell us what happened today?'

'All the days are the same. I call them at eight in the morning, then again around teatime. They tell me, try to be patient. Even they know it's a ridiculous thing to say, but it's probably in the *How to Deal with Hysterical Parents* manual.'

'She's OK, Aunt Debbie.'

'You don't know that, maid. Don't insult me.'

'I'm not insulting you,' Jo says. 'Have you ever known Aunt Tammy to be wrong about anything?'

'No, because I've never heard her say anything definite. That's how them people operate.'

Khadija looks over at the two of them, sitting in front of Aunt Debbie's bowl of decorative balls like tragic figures from a Grayson Perry tapestry. Sideways rain is pounding on the patio doors. Something out back triggers the security light and everything beyond it disappears into the sudden glare.

'The stew's lovely,' Khadija says. 'I'll go get Uncle Pete.'

While Debbie and Pete are pretending to eat, she pulls Jo over to the sofa and turns the television back on. The detectives are standing over another girl now, this one in pedal pushers with ugly bruises on her neck. Her shoes are gone, too. That'll be the key, but it'll be another twenty-three minutes before someone figures it out. The posh detective looks at the rough and ready detective with unfathomable sadness in his eyes, a guilty sense of responsibility because they're missing the vital clue. There will be a complicated past that made the posh one take the job in the first place. No doubt all the mums could explain it, but Khadija never watches ITV.

'OK look, he sort of tried to touch me up once,' Khadija says to the television.

'What? Who?'

'Anthony Osborne.'

'Christ, are you fuckin' serious? When you said creepy, I didn't think that.'

'Seriously? Have you met him? I was seventeen so it wasn't technically illegal, but it was still vile, for a bunch of reasons. And that's all I'm saying about it, so don't ask me.'

Chapter 22

After the nothing there is a sky so white it half-blinds Alice, even through the layer of muddy river that lies like a cat's extra eyelid between her and the world. She sees two faces in front of the heavenly emptiness. Three hands reach toward her through the water; the fourth is busy covering someone's mouth.

A small wave of current takes Alice on its tongue and spits her through the surface.

And the river has refused her twice.

Chapter 23

There are announcements about the girl on the radio now. 'Parents plead for information regarding the whereabouts of Alice Tregidga, fifteen, of Saltash', etc. Nora switches off the set, grateful there is no picture. She sits down in the wingback facing the closed drapes, so much more soothing than the river and the open sky, or the roof of her son's house.

Charles brought the girl to meet Nora, just a few weeks ago. She understood that this was very sweet of him and did honestly try to give the sweetness back. That girl though, sugar would burn if it touched her. Brimstone and treacle. Nora gives a dry laugh to the curtains.

Alice. If you twist it a certain way it sounds like acid, which is apt. Charles rang the bell and the girl stood on the step with the river behind her, refusing to meet Nora's eyes.

'Nice to meet you, Mrs Osborne.' She looked past Nora at the light leaking from the front room into the hallway.

'Well, you'd better come in and sit down before you get washed away out there.'

'I'll make tea, Grand.' Charles went directly to the kitchen, the little traitor.

The girl slumped into an armchair and gave Nora a smile like watered-down oil. You could see right through her skin. She was ginger, for heaven's sake.

'I like your house.'

'What a ridiculous thing to say. You've barely seen it and it smells like burning dust.'

'I like the smell.' She meant that. It probably smelled like that whenever she touched things. The girl was corrosive; Nora could see that right away. If she sat there long enough, she'd probably eat through the chair.

154

Charles came back with a tray. He is a good person, which must have something to do with Tina Simpkin. Tina Osborne. Charles' mother has raised a far better boy than Nora has.

'There are biscuits in the tin, Charles.' He went back for those, and brought them on a plate.

'Grand only likes Garibaldis,' he said.

'Why are you called Grand?'

'Because I am.' Nora gestured magnificently at herself, the way she would if only Charles were there. She was trying. 'Also, grandmother is ridiculous and I'd never pass for anyone's nan, would I? Charles won't eat the Garibaldis. He says they're full of crushed flies.'

The girl relished them like that was true.

'She gets to be Grand but I'm not allowed to be Charlie.'

'I knew a horrid girl named Charlie. She became a horrid woman named Charlotte. What if that were to happen to you? I'd be devastated.'

'You never told me that.'

'I've never told you many things. You are all unknowing, little boy.'

'Tell us about your friend Charlie?'

'No, sir. It's a woman's story.'

The worst day with Charlotte was the day little Thomas Bone went missing. They were shut in the nursery together for a whole afternoon.

As soon as Charlie knew the adults were occupied, it began.

'How fast can you move, then?'

'You can move faster than I can, Charlie.'

'Let's give you some practice.'

She made Nora lay her hands on the table so she could bring the ruler down on them. Nora could move away if she were quick enough. She wouldn't get hurt if she weren't so slow.

The big people had fanned out all over the grass and the water; Nora could see them from the nursery windows, but they were too far away to hear her voice. Anyway, what would she say? They'd laugh and shake their heads and tell them to 'make it up'.

'I'm learning to box, you know. I'm a pugilist,' Charlie said.

And she backed Nora into a corner with flying fists. One stopped an inch from Nora's face and pulled back while the other came crashing in, over and over. Nora's eyelids blinked and twitched and Charlie called her a spastic. It took her the whole afternoon to get bored.

When they were older she became Charlotte, and her cruelty grew decorous.

'How about Grandma?' the girl said then, in 2016, sitting in Nora's armchair.

'I'm sorry? Oh. You'll have to meet me at least twice before you're allowed to change my name. Didn't your mother tell you that?'

She and Charles both looked embarrassed, or perhaps frightened. Then he said, 'She's winding you up, Alice.'

'I do not wind people, Charles. It's a vulgar habit.'

They had all laughed at themselves then, playing their roles together. The girl had come in like the weather; there was no point fighting her. Charles looked at her all the time like she was on a high wire and he was the spotter.

Now Alice Tregidga is gone. Perhaps part of Nora was hoping she'd stay and marry Charles. Simply because it infuriated Jonathan so much when Anthony had 'married down'. He'd always accused her of arranging it. Which she had.

'Mother!'

Good God, it's noon already. Alice Tregidga has been gone for a week and she hasn't seen Charlotte in decades. Anthony will see her daydreaming in her robe and imagine he's one step closer to putting her in care.

'I rang the bell, didn't you hear it?'

'I was thinking,' Nora says, sleepily.

'Would you like to explain this?' He is waving a letter.

Anthony has inherited his father's smallness, his love of leather sofas and yacht club food, the vulgar creases ironed into his sleeves. He has a Jaguar and a motorboat, and a wife named Tina. Less vocabulary and more money than he ought. He lives in a sea of people just like him that seemed to flood the country some time in the late 1990s and has not yet receded.

In the late 1990s Nora still had a few brown hairs, a waist and a book group. They read the Booker shortlist and drank Merlot once a month, until one day Nora realised she didn't have to go. She didn't ever have to ring any of them again.

'Mother?' He tosses the letter in her lap. 'You resigned from the board of CNI without asking me about it?'

'I don't have to ask you about it, you know. Do sit down.'

'I'm your son! These are the family interests.'

'I'm sorry, I can't understand you. You're shouting.'

He marches away into the kitchen then, and turns on the tap. It runs for ages, but of course he doesn't put the kettle on or ask if she wants anything. He is not Charles.

'Why do you hate me?' He's back, holding a tea towel for some reason.

'I do not hate you, Anthony. If your wife said what you're saying now, you'd call her hysterical.'

The wife named Tina is in fact the best thing about Anthony. Nora had known she would be.

'My *wife* doesn't say anything to me, though God knows what she says to you. You two seem to be best friends. Does she know about this?'

'Why are you interrogating me? I want nothing more to do with company boards. Really, it's fairly simple.'

'What did you do with the shares?'

'I donated them.'

'Christ! You do hate me. And you hated him, too.' His father, he means. 'What did we ever do to you?'

'Nothing much at all. You've done rather a lot to other people though, haven't you?'

'We've kept this house, and the fat pension you're living on. Don't you like our money anymore?'

'My money, I think you mean. I like it just fine, thank you.'

'What about Charlie? I know you care what happens to him.'

'Charles will be fine.'

'His name is Charlie, Mother. And what is it about him that's so much better than me?'

'Really, Anthony. Perhaps you should try yoga? We all waited a long time for Charles, and Tina has done a wonderful job with him.'

Because in spite of Nora trying to intervene, the world took that first baby away without any of them asking it to. Anthony has hated Nora ever since, for tying him to Tina Simpkin's empty womb. By the time Charles came, eight years later, the hate was a habit.

The boy's name had come to Nora like a blow. As if it were deliberate, as if somehow Anthony knew about the other Charlie.

Chapter 24

Alice comes to with three hands reaching down to pull her head above the water. She is angry and relieved at the same time. Angry she isn't dead, but glad to be saved from all that noise. They grab onto the shoulders of her hoodie and haul her high enough to spit and puke. Her body does that without asking her, emptying her lungs and crushing the muscles into her guts. After that, she can't see anything at all. Nothing but brightness in her eyes, no shape or colour.

'Just get it out. You'll be weak, but we'll have you up and dry in a minute,' someone says. A woman with a scratchy throat.

Alice's vision begins to sharpen, but then her bones dissolve. She goes soft and starts to sink again.

'No, no, no,' another voice says, and the hands pull harder. Two brown ones and two pink ones now, belonging to two women, all four hands covered in sailors' calluses pull her over onto the deck.

'Laura, where's the phone?'

'I dropped it.'

'Fuck. I'll get the other one.'

'Wait!' Alice spits and coughs some more of the river. 'Please don't call anyone.'

'You need the hospital, love. Your lungs could be damaged, and you'll definitely need antibiotics.'

'Did you fall, sweetie?'

'No. I walked in. Listen...'

But she retches again and can't finish.

'I'll make tea.' That's Laura. The one without a name pulls her up against the boom. It is furled but uncovered. The engine is off board. They're going somewhere.

'What's your name, hon?'

'Alice.' She should have lied but her head is muddled. 'What's yours?'

'I'm Sue and that's Laura. We're getting ready for a trip, but we need to be sure you're OK first. You came back up for a reason, Alice. You know that, right?'

'I went in for a reason.'

Alice shakes the light out of her eyes and takes her chance. What's the worst that can happen? They can ring the cops and send her home, maybe find out she lied. So what?

'There's someone at home,' she says. 'My stepdad. If I go back, he'll hurt me.'

'Jesus. OK, listen. We can stay with you while you talk to the police.'

'You think I didn't tell the police already? I've been telling people since I was eight. I'm seventeen now. No one can make me go back.'

Alice is not seventeen.

'Sue?' The lady with dreadlocks is halfway out of the hatch with a cup of tea in an enamel mug. 'Can I talk to you?' She climbs up and hands Alice a wool blanket. 'Get under this and take your wet clothes off.'

They move forward, but there's no privacy on a twenty-one foot boat.

'You heard that, didn't you?' Sue says.

'Yes. Just let her recover for a bit. She's alive and breathing,' Laura whispers. 'We don't need to do anything right away.'

The bones in Alice's wrists feel soft. Her fingers aren't working and she has to grab at the blanket with her fists like a baby. A milky sun sits behind the cloud cover above Pottery Quay. They must be at Cove Head. She's come a mile down the channel and still fucking lived. Well OK, she's in a boat on the water with women who can sail her out of the river's mouth, at least. A day from now, she could be anywhere. Anyone.

'We are not taking her with us, Laura. Absolutely not.'

'Did I suggest that?'

'You're thinking it. Don't lose perspective.'

'So, what are you thinking? Let's give her back to the abusive stepfather because it's easier? That's perspective?'

There's a key in there. The world was made for liars and Alice is a good one. If you tell the one that sounds like whatever the person is missing, they never suspect.

She lies in a berth all day while they tack along the Devon and Dorset coasts in weak sunshine and a stiff wind from the south. At one point, they'd make her sit up and swallow antibiotics from the first aid kit. She sits with her back against the side for a bit, trying not to sick them back up. Trying to think of a better story, something to add. She falls back to sleep listening to their hushed conversation and searching for weak spots.

It's dark when she wakes again.

'I can't think straight until we're in.' That is Sue. 'This is a complicated pilot plan, you know that.'

They're heading out of the coastal current and in toward Poole.

'But we have to help her, Sue. What if she were ours?'

'She isn't ours, is the point. If she were, I'm going to hope she wouldn't be throwing herself in rivers without us even noticing.'

'Well, we fished her out. We can't throw her back now.'

'She isn't a mermaid, Laura; she's somebody's daughter. We're going to get bloody arrested. Can you picture the red tops? *Lesbian Sailors Abduct Vulnerable Teenager, Head for France.*'

'That's far too many words for the *Sun*. Also "abduct" and "vulnerable" are pretty advanced vocabulary. Just go with "kidnap" and "tragic".'

'Yes, very amusing. We need to call the police before they find us on their own.'

'I'll say it again. Taking her with us and calling the police are not our only two choices. We could call someone at Social unofficially. Janice, maybe? Get some advice at least. Just give her time to recover first. Then we're sort of covered and she stays safe for a while.'

'Sort of covered? Seriously?'

Alice puts her head through the bulkhead and sees Laura winding a sail while they argue. She can already tell that the end of the argument won't suit her. Time to go, but nearly dark and they're moving between a bunch of empty little islands. She slides herself into the prow, in front of the bulkhead with the spare life jackets. Twenty minutes later, she knows more about Laura's life than she wanted to. No wonder the woman is obsessed with rescuing random girls. She'll probably be reliving her own childhood till she dies.

There are boats ahead and to starboard, strung along moorings. They're coming into sheltered water and soon they'll be furling the rest of the sails. Sue will be on the radio any minute. She turns out to be the business in the relationship, adding up possibilities like a futures trader. Getting around her would take more time than Alice has.

The rest of the boats should be empty at the beginning of March, or full of men. So much easier.

They pass a trawler so close she can hear them on the deck shouting in English and something else. Polish, maybe? Russian? Meanwhile Sue and Laura's boat bumps along, square to the wind. Alice times herself with a swell to disguise her movement, then slips over and in.

She doesn't notice the cold because someone is screaming. Moaning. She hears the murmuring sound of a crowd of people milling around.

Lovely little maid, someone says.

He died peaceful, sitting in that chair. Someone else.

The water covers her and her body wants to breathe it in, to gasp brine and burn its own throat. She goes under and her arms and legs jerk without her permission, sending her back up. All the language around her loses its edges and its meaning. Something unseen pushes from below until her head pops through the surface and she coughs everything up. She has an urge to cry, to heave her lungs in and out. Her skin is cold now, and it makes her angry.

You look helpless, someone says. *I like that.*

She's buried in the back. The family have all passed over and no one remembers.

They hid her. The little mother went back to school.

And then her own name. *Alice?* He sounds shy and desperate. *Alice? I'm so bloody angry with you.*

There are tears on Alice's face, but not from inside her. Every drop ever shed from the earth and all its eyes is holding her up. She is cradled in salt, and someone else's gravity.

Let go, maid. Water won't never drown you, no matter how many times you beg it to.

She can still hear them talking on the trawler. A boat full of men in their own bodies, talking meaningless, comforting shite.

Just let go.

She could shout and wave, think of a story to tell them.

But instead she listens to the others. *Not you.* For once she listens, and then she lets go. *You don't get to go home early.*

Alice opens her mouth and the harbour fills it. She bumps against a rope. There is a little windmill above her, and the words *My Kathleen*. A stern line clipped to a buoy.

She tells her arm to lift and it does. The air blows over her skin and turns it into glass. It looks like china clay in the distant halogen light, shivering out of focus when something coats her eyes.

Drink it all. Drink everything until it disappears, Alice.

No, not Alice. Your name's not Alice.

It is.

Alice Malice. Alice Hopeless. Ginger Alice Jealous.

The rope is slick and prickly. It is real.

'Someone will do what I want,' she says to the water. 'I'm good with people.'

But there are no people. All the boats are empty, put back in at the weekend and left until Easter. She unsnaps a corner of the canvas cover on the *Kathleen* and rolls her body inside.

By noon the next day, the inside of the boat is heating up and it smells. It's been sealed up all winter and not cleaned properly first. Alice drinks their bottled water and eats their stale energy bars, with a centimetre or two of plexiglass between herself and everything in the water.

Finally, thirst drives her out. Her clothes are dry, but soon they'll be soaked again. It is at least thirty metres to the nearest floating dock. She piles her hair up and ties it with a piece of rope. There is a pair of plimsolls, but they're a size too small. She slides her hands inside them and ties an old jumper from the boat around her shoulders. Rolls into the water again.

Imagine, Alice. Imagine you get caught in that engine.

The swim takes at least ten minutes, sideways to a current instead of into it, hoping, this time, it will not erase her. The nights are still cold. She'll have to get dry quick.

Imagine your blood churning into the water. Imagine the pieces of you.

There will be someone. There is always someone.

Crabs will eat the pieces and no one will know. There'll be nothing big enough left to recognise.

Alice shouts with her chin above the water. 'Shut up!'

Kick. Kick. Be sick.

Don't kick. Calm down. Nice deep breath.

You're not really here. You're home in bed. You're not really you.

'Don't fucking care.' Alice falls hard onto the edge of the dock and feels blood vessels break inside the layers of her skin. She spits up bile and salt water while the air peels everything off her bones.

She turns her head back over her shoulder and says to the water, 'I don't have to be Alice anymore.'

Chapter 25

Khadija tilts her office chair back, eyeing a letter from the Cadbury's tin. Her method has been to take out one object a day and try to deal with it. That mostly involves deciding whether to save, burn or chuck off the bridge. Save the bird's nest, burn the photos of herself, throw the pitch penny in the river. One decision per day, act on it and done. The papers are a tangle, though. How many of them actually mean something, lead somewhere, and how many are just wishful thinking, fodder for conspiracy theory YouTube videos?

This letter is a cease and desist, addressed to Craig by the management of a holding company. She spent her lunch break searching the board member profiles on LinkedIn. Now what to do with it?

Why has she come to Saltash at all? Everything she needs is online. What kind of idiot thinks, in 2016, that she has to be in a place to find out about it?

But it's worse than that, isn't it? She thought they'd need her. She was so tired of being surplus to requirements that she'd rather come back here and be the local bad luck. She told herself she had unfinished business, things to face up to. That her mother needed her. That she didn't want to be the London kind of solicitor; it was crushing her soul.

Which it was, but so is this. She looks at the letter in her hand, then picks up the phone and dials Jo.

'Where you to?'

'Town,' Jo says. 'Why?'

'Awesome. Meet me in the plaza. I'll be there in half an hour.'

'I'm sorry. Was there a question in there?'

'Sorry. Please meet me in the plaza?'

'If you're going out, I can't drink. I'm pregnant, remember?'

'I don't want to drink. I'm going to see Beth.'

'Beth Kennedy? You can't do that, Khadi. How are you even planning to find her?'

'Just meet me, OK?'

'I need to sit down. I'll be in the Café Nero in Dingles.'

'There's a Café Nero in Dingles? The fuck happened to this place while I was away?'

'Very funny. I want about five banana muffins. You want me to order you a coffee or something?'

There's figure skating on the big screen in the plaza. No one's watching it. Across Royal Parade, kids are skateboarding along the edge of the reflecting pool and the coffee kiosk is closing up. The set of Goths by the fountain are emos now, or maybe something else. They look pretty much like always. It isn't the clothes or the make-up, it's the body language, that weird combination of tension and lethargy, the way the boys lean in and the girls slouch.

Khadija can see Jo through the window with her phone out and one hand on her belly. She only has one muffin, and a coffee getting cold on the table across from where she sits.

'I said don't bother.'

'I heard you. I had points. And I don't have to listen to you anymore. I got you a double soy latte because you're all London and shit.'

'That's disgusting. Why would I drink soy milk?'

'You didn't used to drink milk.'

'Everyone keeps saying that.'

'Because you spent years preaching at us about it. Drink it anyway. I spent my points.'

'You know, the pregnancy thing is weird, but it's kind of useful, you being all grown up now.'

'My pregnancy is not weird. Don't be so middle class.'

'I'm not judging. I meant it's strange on you because you used to be my little cousin. You used to wear your mum's sunglasses when they fell down your face because you didn't have a nose to hold them up. Now you're preggers. It's cool, but also strange. Sue me.'

166

'I'm glad you're entertained. I have to piss every five minutes and little old ladies will not fucking leave me alone on the bus.'

'We can be friends now. Come with me to see Beth.'

'I don't even know where to start with that, Khadi. How about, why? Why do you want to see Beth? What do you have to say to her?'

'She left some stuff for me at my mum's. And she's in trouble, Jo. I get that no one cares. My mum filled me in.'

'Now you're being judgemental. People care. Sometimes you can't help a druggie. You just have to let them go through it and hope they don't die.'

'What if everyone said that about each other? We have to at least try.'

'All right, Mother Teresa. Where are you planning to find her?'

'Millbay, duh. The stuff she left, it was all things from Craig's room. I have questions. She didn't have to save it for me. Since she did, I'm guessing she'll talk to me about it.'

'You think every working girl in Plymouth sits on the corner of Durnford Street waiting to be interviewed? What if she's somewhere else?'

'Give me some credit, bird. My mum keeps in touch with her.'

'If some drug dealer stabs my unborn baby, you're explaining it to Ben.'

'Don't be so middle class.'

They laugh and Khadija can see the glamour still shining out of Jo, bump notwithstanding. The flash and spotless world she keeps alive behind her eyes. It's her antidote for all the postwar cement, the piles of last night's sick on the pavement and the seagulls tearing open the trash bags that are only being picked up twice a month now.

'Where were you to when I rung you?'

'Down here. I told ya.' Jo casts her eyes down and to the left. She's lying, or leaving something out.

'Doing what?'

'Just stuff. I got claustrophobic.'

'I hear that.'

There's an onshore wind blowing up Armada Way and a couple

of guys making their beds in the doorway of Sports Direct. Jo points her bump west down Royal Parade, her jacket flapping in the wind. She looks like a ship in full sail.

They've repackaged Millbay for yuppies, converted some warehouses and put up chrome and glass blocks of flats with balconies. From the balconies you can probably see Cornwall. From where Khadija and Jo are standing, you can see the Millbay bridge, an odd little park in the middle of a turning and the old pickle factory, sitting on its tide-marked wall behind Princess Yachts.

The working girls are standing in a loose group, kicking the curb below a stack of balconies, waiting for early business. Six girls and one coat between them. The girl with the coat has thigh-high boots to make up for it. That girl is not Beth.

It takes Khadija a minute to realise which one *is* Beth because her hair is black as crow feathers. Then she waves the back of one hand through the air in front of her face and shakes her head, breaking the invisible wire between her eyes and the world. That is Beth's gesture, her way of dismissing whatever it is you're saying that she doesn't want to hear. It is her, standing in front of the line of seaweed crusted onto the seawall with the pickle factory behind her, and a crescent moon behind that. Beth and a bunch of skinny women with their heads down, talking to the sidewalk. The chrome balconies stacked above them are full of orange light.

'See, told you she'd be here,' Khadija says. 'Let's go.'

'Nah, lovely. I'll wait right here.'

'Jo, she's your neighbour. You've known her your whole life. Say hello at least.'

'Get a grip, Khadija. This in't London, where people's parents pay for their drugs and everyone gets abortions. Somebody's running her or she wouldn't be standing there. She don't have time to hang about with me and you talking about the good old days.'

'Yeah, you're so hard. Nothing means anything, right? Plenty of people exactly like you in London, trust me. Wait for me, at least?'

'I said I'd wait.' Jo takes out her phone and turns her back.

Somewhere between the Chinese grocery and the little park is an invisible line. It's made of street light, or the shadows from the balconies or just the breeze that curves around the marine barracks. You don't cross it unless you're working or a punter. Khadija knows when she's stepped over it because all the girls go still.

'Hiya, Beth. Ya'right?'

'No, Khadija. Absolutely not.'

'I just wanted to say thank you. For the box.'

'You're welcome. Now fuck off.'

She doesn't look starved. She doesn't look blank-eyed or full of needle holes. Mostly she looks like she's graduated to a different world, seceded from Saltash and set up her own country with a different language. For a minute, Khadija wants to be there, and then that's another reason she can hate herself.

'My mum only just gave it me. She never told me when you dropped it off.'

'Why are you here? You're supposed to be in London.'

'It didn't work. Or, I don't know, it worked for a while. I'm done with it.'

'Well, no one wants to see you here. Whose life are you gonna ruin this time?'

This is where the other person says, *how many lives are* you *ruining*? But Khadija can't make herself say it.

'I didn't do anything on purpose. You know that, Beth.'

'I didn't leave you the stuff so you'd thank me. It was yours.'

'It was Craig's. It makes me sad but I'm glad you left it.'

'Sad? Are you kidding? It's yours because that's what's left. We didn't get a note, no letter, nothing off the police, even. There was just a box full of crap under the bed that was supposed to add up to you. Why should we have to look at it?'

A line of Audi sports are driving past on their way to Royal William Yard. Media content storytellers with asymmetrical haircuts are staring at them out of the car windows. It's like London shook its oily hands and the drops fell on Millbay.

'There's a cease and desist, in the box.'

'What?'

'There's a cease and desist letter from a company called Rame Holdings. Did he say anything to you about it?'

'Are you seriously pumping me for information right now? Wow, that is rich.'

'It matters, Beth. I'm trying to find out what happened.'

'You fucking happened, babe. That's what.'

'I didn't ask for it, Beth. I was seventeen.'

'Aw, diddums. Delicate wee thing. I was seventeen too.'

'I didn't go after him.'

'Girls like you don't though, do you? You just sit there looking mysterious and the whole world ties itself in knots trying to get you to look over and smile. I'm sure it's rough.'

'That is such bullshit! Have you met my mother? Have you met my father? Because I haven't.'

'You said something to him, Khadija. The night before. He came home all red in the face and breathing fast, thinking he was gonna be your hero.'

'I di—'

But she had, hadn't she?

'Yeah. Remember now? So just drop it and piss off again. Climb right over us to wherever you're climbing to, but don't ask us to feel sorry for you while you're doing it.'

'You don't have the faintest idea what it was like for me when I was away. Everybody seems to think they do.'

'Yeah, it looked like a nightmare on Instagram.'

'We all have stuff to deal with, Beth. You're just too lazy to deal with yours.'

'OK, thanks for stopping by, babe. I would offer you a cuppa but the kettle's broke.'

'I didn't mean to have a row, Beth. I only wanted to say I'm back and if you need anything, you could message me.'

'Don't need anything, ta.'

The sky has gone dark and all the girls are drifting off into the back streets. When Khadija turns to walk back across Durnford Street, Jo is pointing her phone at her.

'Are you videoing? Seriously?'

'No. Well, yeah.'

'That's twisted.'

'It was twisted, but not because I filmed it, bird.'

It's two buses home but they both have day riders. By HMS Drake the bus stops for a lady in uniform and a junkie with tobacco teeth, then waits five minutes for the timetable to catch up. The neon in the chip shop window bathes a gaggle of school kids in red and blue light. Khadija is suddenly tired.

They get out at the bottom of Admiralty Street and walk around the corner to Camel's Head for the Saltash bus. Behind the fence is a bunch of desolate allotments that smell of the Southwest Water treatment plant. People are growing vegetables to eat like that smell isn't happening.

'What did I come back here for, Jo?'

'I already asked you that. Don't look at me.'

'You said we're both adults now and all. You said don't treat you like a kid, so I'm not. What am I doing here?'

'Maybe the fresh air?' Jo waves a hand at the sewerage tanks. 'The *Coast Magazine* lifestyle?'

'I'm serious. It made sense when I was still in London and now it's like that dream logic that falls apart when you wake up.'

'Going out on a limb here, but maybe everything that happens to people round here isn't about you?'

'You think I'm selfish and all.'

'Little bit?'

'I'm trying to find out what happened to Craig. You think that's about me?'

'Um, yeah? It was six years ago. Fuck knows why you feel guilty about it, but you don't want to feel that way anymore so you're stirring it all up.'

'It matters, Jo. People made other people die.'

'OK, but why are you raking it all up with Beth Kennedy? You don't think she has enough to worry about? Also, there is a little something else going on right now.'

'Don't even. I'm worried about Alice, too. And I'm trying to help. Holding everybody's hand and making the tea, as per usual.'

'OK, you want to know what I think? You're not finished, bird.'

'I really am, promise ya.'

'No, I mean you're not finished with it. You haven't done whatever or stopped feeling whatever. Blaming yourself is my guess, if you're asking.'

'I am finished, though. I thought I'd be a solicitor so I could help people like Micky Williams and Craig's dad, but I don't even think that anymore.'

'If you're so finished with everything, what the hell was that all about back there?'

'Farah would call it closure. I need to know what happened. I guess that's what you're saying?'

'Farah's the accountant, right? Your housemate?'

'Actuary. She has therapy speak. It does her precisely zero good at all.'

'I don't even know what an actuary is. No, don't tell me. I don't care. How many lawsuits would you have to win to make you feel better about Micky Williams dying? It don't make sense, Khadi. Let it go.'

The number five bus pulls up and the doors hiss open. This bus waits too, above the tracks at St Budeaux station, where trains never stop. There's an apple tree getting ready to blossom where someone once threw a core onto the siding. Jo holds her phone up and focuses on the queue spilling out of the fried chicken place onto the pavement.

'It was horrible, seeing Beth,' she says without taking her eyes off the screen. She pans her camera over to the slave gang at the car wash, nearly ready to close up for the night.

'You didn't see her, Jo. You turned your back.'

'You're judging?'

'You've known her your whole life. You could at least have said hello.'

'Really? Have you thought about what it means, us going down there to *say hello*?'

'Uh, it means we think she's a person?'

'Jesus, who even are you now, Khadi? Did you not see those other girls back away, looking at Beth like she was none of them anymore? She could scream her head off louder than the siren at Babcock in some back alley tonight. None of them girls will even stop to listen now. Well done.'

'You're making that up, Jo. This isn't some gritty Channel Four drama.'

'It in't the *Guardian* "Opinion" section either. It's real life and Beth's a real person. I'm not the one ignoring that.'

Jo moves to the back seat so she can keep her phone on St Budeaux Square as the bus pulls away.

Chapter 26

First, Alice begs twenty pence so she can get into a public toilet, one of those stand-alone ones with every piece made of shining steel. She drinks for a full minute from the tap, throws up in the bowl and then fills herself with water again. The tap keeps stopping, so that she has to wave a hand under it to make it go again.

She follows the signs toward the town centre and finds a bloke with a guitar in a subway. He isn't playing. He isn't exactly awake even; his dog is doing his begging. He has on a Fat Face sweatshirt and rain gear over his jeans, something ground into the fabric that she doesn't want to know about. Alice strokes the dog and sits down without asking.

'You ever been to Plymouth?'

'Got any change, love?'

'Do I look like I have any change?' Alice points to her bare feet. 'I feel like I know you. You been to Cornwall, maybe?'

You have to get people talking, so you can find out how they work.

'Yeah, we went there when I was a kid. Lovely there. Cold, though, but the beach was dead nice.'

'Can you play that?'

He looks around, trying to figure out what she's talking about, like he forgot he was sitting next to a guitar. Druggie.

'That.' She points. 'My boyfriend plays.' She almost laughs out loud, picturing Charlie with a guitar. 'Give us a tune then?'

He grabs the guitar by the neck and the strap, swings it above the dog and into her lap. 'You go on, love.'

'I can't play.' She rests it against the wall between them. 'Where you staying?'

He wakes up a bit then, looks at Alice sideways. 'Around.'

'I'm not being funny. It's only I'm stuck here for a few days. I just wondered.'

'You can get a shelter referral. They do food down St John's at night, ask somebody there. You can stay at the Sally Army, long as you're not gay.'

'Lend me a quid? I've had nothing to eat yet today.'

And he does. She says she'll bring it back and walks away.

For the rest of the day, no one bothers her. She eats a bread roll and goes into the library. If you're not from Poole it costs two quid to go on the computers for an hour. It takes her until tea-time to get that much and by then the library is closed and won't be open again for two days.

She is still in the library doorway the following afternoon, thinking about what she can eat for two quid when the dog from earlier twists around her legs and looks up at her with liquid eyes that make her forget where she is.

'Come on, then,' the guitar man says from behind her.

'Thanks, mate. I don't mean anything, I swear.'

'Yeah, I got it.'

'I really appreciate it. I didn't know who to ask.' She knows that's a mistake as soon as she says it. This bloke doesn't go for helpless.

'You need to keep your shit dry and you need a backpack. Ask at St John's. They might give you a sleeping bag and all. And I'll have my pound back, thanks.'

He walks out of the town centre through the back of an estate. The dog runs ahead, sure of where they're going. Behind the estate is a square with a playground in the middle. One side is full of dirty takeaways and the other is a multi-storey car park, empty. There are a couple of mattresses leaning over the edge of the third level.

'What's your name?'

He holds up a hand without turning round. 'Nope, don't want to know yours either. And don't worry. People here are cool.'

It might be the first time in Alice's life that anyone assumes she can do what she needs to, treats her like she isn't hopelessly broken. How do you get around people who think you can cope?

Mr Osborne, Charlie's dad, he goes for helpless. Alice saw it the first time she hesitated in front of him. The first time she saw him in person at all. She was twelve years old the day he came and stood in Aunt Carol's doorway with everything showing in his face.

They were in the kitchen with Tammy Williams. Tammy chopping onions with a piece on her head to stop her from crying and Alice doing the broccoli. The two of them were teaching her to make pasta bake. Because Alice was still being babysat, right up to last year in fact. The reason was obvious, but no one ever said. It was Carol and Jan who looked after her mostly, but Tammy always seemed to be around.

'Will Khadi come home for the holidays, Aunt Carol? She hasn't been in ages.'

'Don't ask me, maid. She tells me nothing these days.'

'Khadi's all right,' Tammy said. 'She's watched over. She has a journey to finish, then she'll be home.'

'None of that, Tamara.' Carol gave Tammy a look Alice wasn't supposed to understand. 'The tricky bit is the sauce. Don't know about you, Tammy, but I always seem to start with too much milk, then it takes ages.'

'Oh, I don't pay attention much. I find cooking works better if I just sort of let it happen. You gotta feel your way into it. You'll see, Alice. When you're a little older you'll settle into everything and it won't seem so noisy. So confusing.'

'Tamara.'

The knock at the door saved them from a row. Carol went to answer it, left Alice in the kitchen with Tammy.

'Hello, Carol.' Mr Osborne's voice came through from the front door. 'Home on your own?'

Alice knew the voice, though she'd never heard it in person before. The sound of it tipped one world into the other, made Alice feel like a carp frozen into the ice. She went cold and sick and very still. Tammy put a hand on her arm.

'It's all right, maid. You can relax. Let go. I got ya.'

'I'm just making tea with the girls,' Carol said in the hallway. 'How can I help, Mr Osborne?'

Playing it over, Alice can hear the false note. Carol is a terrible actor. At the time though, Alice was distracted, trying to get herself moving. Trying to keep from being frozen inside the sound of that voice. She shook off Tammy's hand, stood up and went to the front hallway, needing to see the face that went with it.

'Congratulations on the new job,' Carol said. 'Is that why you've come, about work?'

But then Mr Osborne was looking past Carol, into Alice's eyes. The hallway was gloomy, but the two of them saw all the way into each other right from the first.

'I'm going to be your new headmaster,' Anthony Osborne said, cheerful and fake like she was five years old. He was saying it for Carol and whoever else was listening, not for Alice.

'I'm going to take your son away,' said Alice.

Now Alice wonders whether she did say that. Out loud. Which part of it was real, how much she imagined, is imagining now. The stories stay the same; she tells them in her head over and over. The thing is, sometimes she doesn't believe herself.

Chapter 27

Three minutes till four. It in't dark in Tammy's bedroom; never dark in Saltash. She fell asleep to the whispering of the bridge traffic, nothing to trouble her and a batch of cookies for Khadija cooling on the worktop. It was one of they evenings when all your little routines fit together like clockwork, not a thing in the quiet but air, nothing waiting to drop.

Until three minutes till four.

Tammy throws the duvet off and goes downstairs to the back window, breathes deep and waits with her eyes full of sky. That's what Alice can't seem to do. If you go still and empty yourself, they tell you whatever it is then go. Mostly.

The sky is black behind the bridge lights, and the water is nothing but the sparkle on its surface. She's looking down at the tugboat dock when the scream comes again. The swearing, the long moan and the puffing breath. *Little diamond girl*, someone says. *Emerald*, another. *Malachite. Moss agate. Tin, copper, china clay. Arsenic, uranium, tungsten*. What even is tungsten? It used to be in light bulbs, but it isn't anymore, like lead in pencils.

Micky would have explained. He did that thing men do with facts, did it all the time and it calmed her. Nights like these. She knew he would calm her, soon as she saw him. Also, his name was Williams. Nice Cornish name to wash away her Jinks.

He was fine, really. He just didn't want any bother, which made Tamara an odd choice. He dismissed all of it like it was an embarrassing tick. Like how you just accepted people who were simple or had faces that didn't work right. Until he got ill it made things uneven between them. Then it was her turn.

For a long while, he walked every day down to the edge of the river and back, sat in the Union Pub just to prove he still could. That

178

last time it took him an hour to come the hundred yards back uphill. He left the house like usual, and Tammy watched from the front window until his round shoulders disappeared beneath the tarmac horizon. He needed to do it alone so he'd still feel he was a man, a dockyard man.

That day, Tina Osborne knocked half a minute after Micky left, like she'd been waiting for him to disappear first.

'Brought you a tuna bake. Thought it'd be nice not to have to cook.'

Tammy put it on the side and came back to look down the empty street. *He'll be a'right*, someone said inside her. *He's happy.* They was always telling her how happy everybody was, in spite of the evidence all round the place.

'Where's Micky to?' Tina looked nervous and sparkly, but that was her way.

'Down the Union. One time soon he'll have to admit he can't make it no more.'

They went quiet while ribbons of wind pushed in around the cracks in the back windows. The traffic on the bridge was light. People'd rather go by Torpoint when the wind was high. Tina had all kind of worry breathing in and out of the air around her, but it was better not to rush people.

Finally, Tammy couldn't take it no more. 'It's a boy this time, lovely.'

The water started to spill from Tina's eyes straight away. Tammy handed her a tissue; there was three boxes right in the living room. She'd known since she was fifteen that allowing folks to cry out loud was the point of her. It was her job, and it wasn't so bad.

'Can you tell me anything, Tamara?'

'Go on.' Tammy reached out both hands and Tina took them. Her palms were dry and her varnished nails pricked into Tammy's skin.

'Who is that with the net curtain? Somebody in the chair. A lady. She likes to play that game of patience that goes in a circle.'

'My nan,' Tina said.

'Sorry love, I don't think she's happy.'

Tina tried to pull away, but Tammy held tighter. 'She loves you, bird. Don't worry. Y. They're giving me a Y. Maybe it's a question: why? Maybe a fork in the road? There's two ways to go here. Two ways. Do you know an Enzo? No? Dapper sort of chap, he's wearing a long coat? No? Keep ahold of him, love. Ask your mum because he's here. Enzo. He's Italian maybe? Spanish? He don't seem like a sailor.'

Tina shakes her head back and forth until it doesn't mean 'no' anymore. She's just doing it.

'This Enzo says there's two ways to go and they're both uphill. You're in a hollow, you can't see very far. Is that how it feels? That's okay. They're with ya. You've got to stop worrying; you've got a little 'un there. Just think on that and keep breathing.'

'I'm scared, Tammy. I can't live through losing another.'

'You'll do what you need to, and it'll be the right thing. You'll hold him. You'll be old with him. Don't worry so much.'

'There's nothing between us anymore, Tammy.' She means the husband.

'Have you told him?'

'Not yet.' Tina took one hand away to wipe her nose. 'If it goes wrong, I'd rather he didn't know at all.'

'You feeling sick? The lady playing patience says ginger and milk. She wants you to drink ginger and milk. She wants you to boil the milk. Oh, that's funny.'

'What?'

'Never mind. She says boil the milk and put ginger in it. No sugar, ginger and black treacle, she says.' Tammy paused and bent her head.

Tina Simpkin, Osborne now, with her hair out of place and snot under her nose. Tammy is the only person allowed to see her like that. It's a kind of privilege.

She went through and made tea while Tina finished up crying. Over the wall, little Khadija was standing at the back of her garden with her arms stretched out to the sides, hugging the wind. She'd be round later, wanting to read her books to Micky. Thinking it was a help. Maybe it was.

He listened anyway, bless him, like the dad Khadi didn't have. Carol had moved with the girl over from the estate as soon as her mother died, leaving her the house. Hiding from that foreign dad, Carol was. Lovely bloke Mo, once you got to know him. But Carol'd tear a lovely bloke to shreds, just how she was made.

Khadija's hair blew up around her wool cap and drops of rain was all on her jacket. The telephone rang, Carl from the pub.

'Your trouble's heading home, Tamara.' But he was laughing; he didn't mean nothing.

'Thanks.' They hung up without goodbyes. It was very near an hour before Micky's head came up over the tarmac. She fed him a bit of Tina's casserole and settled him in, then let Khadija take over while she went to drop some dry cleaning for the other Mrs Osborne, Anthony's mum. She'd been doing bits for the old lady since Micky stopped work.

It was eight years before that, the first time Tammy had gone up to the big house. Someone needed to sort it, and Tina's own mother was gone. Anyway, they all kept telling her Tina Simpkin's son belonged in the big house. Which was why she thought that first one was a boy, and why Nora Osborne never believed anything she said after Tina lost the baby girl.

From the Osbornes' front step you could see past Lowhill to Antony. Was that why they called the boy that? You could see the flat river all around, and right then a boat towering up next to Barne Barton. Standing on that step for the first time, Tammy heard nothing inside herself, no whisper and no comfort. The air was still and the river was fading into the air. She pushed on the bell and it rang a whole tune. One note wasn't enough for the Osbornes.

'Mrs Williams, isn't it?' Eleanora Osborne said. 'How can I help?'

'I'm here about your son.'

Mrs Osborne's eyes got sharper, but she wasn't cross. You could have called that look respectful, even.

'You'd better come in and sit down, then. I'll put a kettle on.'

They went through into the kitchen. The floor was flagged and freezing and the worktops were made of real marble. That kitchen was kitted out like a morgue. The sink was steel with a big curving mixer tap. Still no whispers. Tamara'd never felt alone as she done that first five minutes in Nora Osborne's house.

'Milk and sugar?'

'The Cornish don't take sugar in their tea,' Tamara sang, 'because of slavery.'

Mrs Osborne didn't blink. 'Milk, then?'

'Yes, please. Not being funny, Mrs Osborne, but I'd rather not twist around what I got to say.'

'I appreciate that. And my name is Nora.'

'Not Eleanora?'

'Absolutely not. I come from people who enjoy stretching words, which is why I appreciate your directness.' That was a hint. 'Mind you, I had an aunt called Araminta, so I consider myself to have gotten off lightly.' Which was a joke. Well, she wasn't what Tammy'd expected at all.

'Tina Simpkin is gonna have your boy's baby.'

'Ah.'

'She don't want to tell him, and if you'll forgive me saying it, I don't reckon he'll want to tell you.'

'I'll forgive you. I'll even thank you.'

Nora didn't like her own son. Tammy could tell right away. You sort of couldn't blame her. Tammy blew on her tea and sipped it while she looked around. There was a tea towel folded on the stove handle, but other than that there wasn't a single piece of paper or cloth in the whole room. The tea tasted odd and weak.

'This is the quietest house I've ever been in.'

'Quiet is one of the things we purchase at great expense.' She didn't like the husband either. Nora Osborne had only two people in her family and didn't like neither one. What Tammy meant about the quiet, though, was there was no spirit people. She couldn't hear a thing. It was something about Nora.

'Tamara?'

'If I'm to call you Nora, you should call me Tammy. Everybody else has, since about 1968.'

'Tammy makes you sound like an American.' Nora made that pinched face people like her make when they say the word American.

And then they sorted it all out between them.

As soon as the front door of the Osbornes' house shut behind Tammy, the noise was deafening. The wind had kicked up and the dark was full of shouting. Wet souls from underneath the ships, dry souls with just a trickle of blood seeping out against the dockyard wall, babies whinging and coughing, people showing her their footsteps in the mud, their imprints in the summer grass, their clothes bursting into fire on their bodies, their bones crushed under the rubble. She slid down against the house, looking at Wearde Quay but not seeing it.

'Are you all right?'

Tammy hadn't heard the door open behind her.

'I will be in a minute.'

'A boy nearly drowned down there once,' Nora said.

'*Nearly* drowned?'

'It was long before this place was built. The boy's father worked on one of the farms attached to Antony. His mother worked in the house.'

'He didn't drown, though?'

'No, but he was missing for hours. I was a girl then, visiting over the way.'

'They found him trapped under the quay, didn't they?'

'They did.'

'You're telling me he never died?'

'We all die, Tamara.' But she knew that wasn't what Tammy'd meant. 'He died later, in the disaster at Portman Square.'

'His clothes. His clothes was on fire.'

'I don't know. Will you come back into the house?'

'No, thank you. I have to see to Micky.'

As soon as Nora closed the front door the second time, it started again. They stayed with her all down the hill, a whole bunch of them talking at once. When she opened her own front door, she could hear Micky coughing. That was the first time they went to the doctor for tests.

After Micky couldn't walk up from the pub anymore the nurse came to them once a week, brought the stethoscope and listened to the crinkling and scratching in Micky's chest, the rock building up in between his lung sacks like render between stones.

At the end his lips turned grey and he said he was glad they never had no children. The doctor's surgery had Tammy in and listened to her chest, too. Because she done Micky's washing and breathed in his dust. The last few months, the nurse came twice a day. She ended up crying out her private troubles in Tammy's kitchen and all.

Micky never comes back. He wasn't one with a lot to say, even when he was in the body. Didn't like fuss. The ones that do speak are always agitated somehow, with worry or happiness, something they can't stop doing or saying. They just repeat whatever it is over and over until you want to tear your hair out. Mostly it's ones who've passed, but Tammy hears all sorts about the living, too. When it's really loud, it feels like she knows everything a second before it happens. She can see time before it unfolds.

It in't so bad tonight, here alone in 2016. The river has no one to swallow, nothing stuck in its muddy throat. Inside her they're mostly happy, mostly excited. Someone is falling, but no one minds.

It in't Alice falling. She's still out there somewhere, bobbing in a black tide and trying to use the ocean to stop her ears. The girl don't listen, won't. She slipped the noose and rode the tide away. She gave her copper hair to other waters and left that poor boy pining. She left a hole she was supposed to close. With words. With what she heard.

Another scream and Tammy knows the voice. Of course.

It's Jo Sleep. A shout and a long string of swear words. And then, *why's there so much blood? Is all that mine?*

The eyes are always blue at first.

'Well, you lot are full of fresh information tonight,' Tammy says to the window. 'Anyways, I saw an Italian baby once and the eyes were so dark you'd think they was black.'

They aren't listening. They don't so much listen as dump everything into her head without asking. It isn't unkind, though. Mrs Brady, the therapist, seemed to think it would distress Tammy like it does Alice. It never has, though it sometimes wears her out. She's pretty often tired and forgets about her limbs, forgets about gravity and liquids and keeping warm. But there's family for that.

I can't breathe. It's like a mine shaft. Somebody open a lamp.

Should she ring Ben? What have they woke her for? There tends to be a reason, but not always so it makes sense to people in the body. A spirit reason, and those are usually upside down and sideways.

It's a lovely little maid, Tamara. Don't distress.

She told the therapist about the time they woke her up to bury and unbury a box of baby teeth, but Mrs Brady didn't quite get the point. What was the point? The teeth were in a tin of Anstie's Flake. She took them out and buried them on Beggar's Island, as instructed. Just to quiet everyone down in her head. Still has that tin, somewhere.

One last scream brings her back to the house and the reason she's awake now, tonight. There's a final gush of blood and the sound of flesh tearing.

Ruby. Jo's voice. *Hello, little Ruby Mae.*

Well, it's like Paddington Station around here these days. So many coming and going through the mizzly air she can barely keep track. Maybe they don't want anything. Sometimes she's just a beacon at the edge.

Tammy feels her way upstairs without a light. Runs her hand along that same wall her mother used to lean on, skipping down with Harry in her arms.

She has a good kind of cry and curls back into bed, smiling.

185

Chapter 28

Khadija is home from the hospital an hour before work, time to shower and have toast. There are men working on the railroad bridge, standing out orange against the smoke from Barne Barton. Her mother has gone to breakfast with Debbie and Jan. To celebrate or commiserate? Khadija has already had enough of whatever kind of tears they'll be. Enough of skin, of blood and sea-smelling water from out of her own cousin to last her for a day or two, thanks.

The river has slipped away and won't be back again until lunchtime. She looks from her window out onto the mud. Away over the bridge Jo and her baby are in a ward bed, crying for different reasons, smelling like hospital, staring into each other's eyes. Khadija had no idea how naked it would make her feel, just watching a baby pushed out. How wide open and undefended.

After a night full of pain and rapture and coming and going, the rest of the world seems bloodless, comfortably sucked dry. She opens her bedroom window and shouts Farah's name, just to hear it die on the heavy air.

By eleven in the morning Khadija is starving and grumpy, wired on PG Tips. Out the window, Saltash almost looks like a proper Cornish town. The Tintagel kind, not the Padstow kind, of course. She sits invisible in the gloom inside Bright and Tunstall, watching the stripe of sun fade the blue sofa.

Tina Osborne comes out of Marilyn's Café and takes her sunglasses off the top of her head. Before she puts them over her eyes, she squints down Fore Street into the sun, the better to blind herself maybe. By the time she gets into the shadow of Bright and Tunstall's doorway she has to grope for the handle and feel her way over the doorstep with one foot. Tina doesn't like to see too much, which to be fair is probably a good plan if you're married to Anthony Osborne.

'Ya'right, Khadi?'

'Hi, Mrs Osborne.'

'It was lovely to see you the other day.' She stands with the light leaking around the edges of her. Even Tina Osborne has a few hairs out of place, when she's lit like that.

'Really?' It comes out before Khadija can stop it.

'Yes, really. Let me tell you something, maid, the women you grow up with don't never leave your head. Even when they aren't there, they're there. I love your mother almost as much as Charlie.'

'Hard work though, in't it?'

'She's all right. She just don't know it herself. You should be sweet to her.'

She is saying that about the woman who shagged her husband. One of the women, anyway. If you saw Tina Osborne on the street, you'd peg her as shallow. Nothing is the way it looks, literally nothing in the world.

'Jo had her baby. Girl,' Khadija says, because babies are a definite subject changer.

'Oh! How are they? It's Ben Jinks' baby, yeah?'

'Kind of. They let me in the room during it; Jo asked for me. She seems fine. Tired and a bit goofy. Full of gas and air.' Then they both get to laugh some tension out of themselves. 'So, how can I help?'

'I have an appointment with Mrs Halden, lovely.'

'She's in with someone. Sit down, I'll make you a brew. They won't be long.'

Tina looks down at the streak of sun and sits just next to it, so close to the edge of the sofa she has to use one hand to balance herself.

'I'm not saying what it's about, babe.'

'I'm not asking, so that works. Milk and none?'

'You grew up while you were away, din't ya?'

'Sort of. Wondering why I'm back here if I'm honest. I feel like I might shrink back into a kid. It's keeping me up at night.'

187

'Well, I guess you remember what it's like here. Plenty to keep you awake all night. I don't suppose there's anything new, about Alice?'

'No. If she is alive, I'm going to kill her.'

'Not being funny, but you should trust your Aunt Tammy no matter what anybody else says.'

'I know, I know.'

The little kitchen at the back of Bright and Tunstall has a cracked window that looks out onto Saltash's one arcade. Mews, the sign calls it. Khadija stares at it while the kettle boils, then brings two cups back into the front office.

'Mrs Osborne, can I ask you about something?'

'Of course, bird. We're family.'

'We're not, though.'

She doesn't look hurt. Things don't hurt Tina Osborne; they just bounce off.

'We are, but you can deny it if you like. I'm used to that from your mum. I remember things about you that you don't even remember yourself. If you're not careful I'll tell 'em to ya.' She smiles, but she isn't funning.

'Sorry, I just meant not everyone Cornish is related. We all tangle ourselves up together even when there's no blood between us, and the rest of the country laughs and makes jokes about us.'

'Don't know if you noticed but no one here gives a shit what the rest of the country thinks.'

Has she ever heard Tina Osborne swear before?

'Do you remember, Mrs Osborne? The night—'

'Yes lovely, I remember.'

'Will you tell me? I had a few drinks and the next thing I knew it was two hours later. I didn't hear what happened till I was in halls, in London. No one seems to remember that night properly.'

'I've got a reason to remember it. I woke up after midnight, all of a sudden like. I was alone and I looked out the window.'

'You saw something?'

'No, lovely.'

188

They are quiet together for a minute, remembering the half moon sinking and the late September air.

'Charlie was in his room. He was little then, went to bed at 7:30.'

'It's weird Charlie's a teenager now. He's sweet though, eh?'

'Yes, he's sweet. He was sweet then, too. He still curled up into me in the evenings, but he was getting big. I had to wake him up and make him walk up the stairs himself. He made a sound like a whistling kettle, one long whinge all the way up to his bed.'

'So, you woke up and looked out...?'

'I'd been doing a face mask and my nails and things. My husband was over the river having a drink. I fell asleep and ruined my polish. I'd drunk a glass of wine, but only one, so it was odd. I woke up when I rolled over and realised Anthony wasn't back. It was late.'

Jesus. He was probably with her mum. Or someone else. No doubt Tina was used to it by then. But Khadi doesn't say any of that.

Instead, she says, 'How do remember that was the same night?'

'Everyone remembers, bird. They found Craig across at the Passage next morning. You think back, when something like that happens. For the next six months everyone tells each other where they were at the time.'

'Everybody remembers, but no one remembers. Nobody's got details. Can I ask you something else?'

''Course.'

'Was he a problem? I mean he was a little obsessed, wan't he? Was he bothering you a lot?'

'Well, he wasn't bothering me.' There's more, but Tina doesn't say it.

The door to the back office opens and they look up into each other's eyes, trying to keep the air between them from breaking up. Mrs Halden says goodbye to her clients, an adoption.

'All right, Tina?' she says. 'How's your boy?'

'He's lovely.' Tina keeps her eyes on Khadija while she smiles.

'Shall we go through then?' Mrs Halden holds the office door and stands back.

Tina puts one hand on the desk as she passes. Five perfect fingernails fat with silicon, the colour of the sky over Craig's death.

'Next time, *your* story,' she says to Khadi. 'Come see me soon, bird.

Once Tina's finished her appointment and gone, Mrs Halden asks Khadija to call the other Mrs Osborne.

'Tell her, the documents are ready for her.'

Whatever that means, Khadi isn't allowed to wonder. There was an entire module about why not in the second year at uni. But she spends the whole afternoon thinking about it anyway. What are the two of them signing together? Maybe she's tired, or maybe Ruby Mae knocked down all Khadija's 'ethical walls', tearing her way into the world.

At home the air smells like cinnamon and oranges, and not at all like fags.

'Mum!' Khadija shouts from the hallway. 'I'm home! Slay the fatted calf. Oh, wait. I am the fatted calf, in't it?'

Her mother pulls herself around the kitchen door frame with one hand. She has her hair pulled up, messy. She looks pretty. 'What are you talking about, maid?'

'It doesn't smell like fags in here.'

'I only had two today. I went out back. See? I listen to you.'

'Great. You get that isn't how it's supposed to work, right? You're supposed to sort your own life out, then I have to listen to you.'

'Less of that, thank you. You doing anything tonight? Let's make tea.'

'You're cheerful?'

'I am, yeah. A new baby makes everything better, don't you think? It even made me forget, for a little while. About Alice.'

'I saw Tina just now.' See? She shouldn't have told anyone that. 'What we making for tea, then?'

'I had some fish from Kevin. I thought we'd make fish pie. Did you stop by Debbie and Pete's?'

'No. I rang before I left work. They were going to some kind of meeting. Support group.'

'You're good, for going over there and things. You're a good kid.'

'It's what I do. I even did it in London.'

'I thought you went up there to get away from us and look after yourself?'

Khadi laughs a sharp little laugh. 'Yeah, I thought that and all. But it was like I just didn't know who else to be. If I love someone I pretend they're broken so I can pick up their pieces. It was the only thing I knew how to do.'

'Listen, this is gonna sound pathetic, but you're young. Push back. Just refuse. Be a bit more like Jo. She don't settle for nothing.'

'Some posh knobhead knocked her up and dumped her, in case you didn't notice.'

'Did he, though? Dump her, I mean?'

'When Farah got overstressed about exams and things, I used to feed her and put her in the shower.'

Carol gives Khadija a Tammy kind of look that goes right through her.

She could try to explain to her. That's what daughters do, right? She could try to tell about how soft she felt, all the time up there. All broken and bruised by whatever distance was between her and Farah, even if it was only an inch. But her breath goes out of her throat and she doesn't say any of it. To make words you need air, and there doesn't seem to be any.

'Hey. You.'

'Sorry, Mum. What?'

'Do them carrots. You have to peel 'em good, because there's some chemical that causes breast cancer.'

'What are you talking about?'

'I read it online. We're the only place in Europe where they're allowed to spray that crap on carrots.'

'OK, then.'

'Where were you just now? Talk to me like I'm your mum for once.'

191

'I was thinking about uni. I went away and found out I was still the same person. It wasn't you lot; it was me.'

'Well, but. We made you, didn't we, lovely?'

Out the windows the bridges press down from the sky, dwarfing the two of them and their house and all their pains and desires.

Farah's message comes while the fish pie is in the oven and Khadija is in the shower, watching the water run clear down the drain because it can't get to whatever is inside her. It slides over her and carries absolutely nothing away.

The message doesn't say Farah is done, or that she needs help, or please or thank you. It doesn't say anything except that she is due into Saltash the next day at 16:50. Not even hello, how are you? I'm thinking of coming down, is that OK?

Well, there is one other thing: It says, *What kind of name is Saltash, anyway?*

It's accurate, Khadi types back. *This is a bad time, Farah.*

Then Farah tells a piece of the truth. Just a piece.

I sort of need to get away.

My cousin's gone missing. She's probably dead, but my mad aunt who isn't really my aunt says she's not because spirits told her so. Also, my other cousin just had a baby and she's moving in with a bloke who isn't the babydaddy. It's a lot right now.

Wow. Are you OK?

This is standard. People disappear a lot here, in case you were thinking of it as a holiday option.

So you're not OK?

I'm fine. Just need to do family shit. I'll message you.

I'm coming. Get ready.

There are threads of cloud up the river, lying in the last of the sun. Khadi stands by the bedroom window, wondering why, when Farah finally decides to run, she wants to run to Saltash. Her parents seem nice. Normal. If she needs to cry on someone, why not her mother?

Down below in the garden, Carol is smoking over the wall. Her third of the day, assuming she wasn't lying earlier. The low sun throws a long afternoon shadow from the house, over the wall and beyond her into the shadow of the road bridge. Khadi looks out at the overlapping squares of darkness and wonders about the place Farah could have gone back to. What is the precise shape of the skeleton of steel and concrete she came from? Where do people fall there?

Chapter 29

The busker hands Alice off to a woman called Amanda who shows her an empty landing and points out which takeaways will let her use their toilets without asking for anything.

'They'll be cooking up downstairs. Just stay put till they all nod off.'

'That bloke said he was taking me someplace with no druggies.'

'Don't worry, people here are cool.'

'Yeah, that's what he said.'

Amanda says she's from Essex. Says her parents threw her out when they retired to Southwold.

'They're religious but it doesn't exactly make them charitable.'

'You don't sound like you're from Essex.' She sounds posh.

The ketamine heads are on the ground floor and a bunch of women have the first landing, sharing a bag of fruit. The second and third floor landings are full of stuff but no people. Alice steps carefully over all of it, climbing behind Amanda.

'What do you do for clean pants?'

'Sometimes you don't, lovely. You can find some water and wash them out, but where will you dry them? No one ever gives pants to the shelter. Change your trousers instead.'

'Great. OK.'

'My parents didn't like the people I hung around with.'

Amanda is about five minutes from thinking they're best friends.

'No offence, but I don't care. 'Night.'

She isn't the type to kick off; doesn't care enough about herself. Alice can tell. She looks hurt, but not offended, drops her head and walks away down the stairs.

Alice sits down on the all-weather carpet and pulls the dark up to her chin, pushes everything visible into the square of street light across from her. There is a bubbling of voices from below, made up of singing and slurring and earnest assurances. If she is very still, she can make the whole car park forget her until the sun comes up.

She read in a book once that junkies never get bored or agitated. Everything is smooth for them, apparently, time just flattens out. The meds are a bit like that. Alice thought drowning would be an even better version. Wrong again.

She has been out in the wide world for a week when the whole thing turns over. Her skin and her clothes are beginning to wear thin and the fire in her hair has burned away. It's gone dry and full of breaks, brown like she's anyone. Everyone. You'd only know her by her veins. Those are even bluer now, closer to the surface.

She is alone on the car park landing, doing her best to experience junkie time. Things become very loud very suddenly and then her body refuses to hold together. When she tries to use her arms to lift herself off the carpet they convulse.

That sky is only there because the roof came off the room. The roof came off the moon.

I wanted to cut her.

Do you want to cut it, Dad? A laugh and a woman's soft sobbing.

Space opens up between Alice's bones. Water rushes over the landing. She pushes one foot against the floor until the force raises her up above the surface.

I can't forget, Craig Kennedy says. *I can't sleep. I can't see.*

His voice inside all the voices like a cold current brushing past. Then gone again.

This isn't light. This is the blankets. You're tangled in the blankets.

Come back, Alice. Don't tear your skin, don't fall apart now. Come breathe in the water and go to sleep.

'This isn't water! It's air.'

Mud, Craig says.

Mud is the terrible truth Alice has been holding since she was nine years old. It has grown inside her like a tumour, sometimes speaking, always silting up in her organs, her veins. She has tried to bleed it out like people used to do with fevers, tried to bury it in the smell of Charlie, tried to drown it now.

Mud in Craig Kennedy's nostrils, filling one of his ears. Cold water lapping at the crown of his head.

Alice, Craig says.

Then a baby cries and a whole gaggle of them are talking at once.

It's cold up there. You'll hurt someone; you know you will. Your bones won't work. Someone will steal your eyes. You'll hurt someone.

You never existed; this is someone else's delusion. You're lying with a needle in a bedsit. You're in hospital with your head split.

Now someone is puking. There is so much blood, and something creamy all over Alice's skin.

Hello.

It's Jo.

Hello, little Ruby Mae.

Chapter 30

Khadija stands in the little shelter on the train platform, breathing the smell of piss until she hears the London train squealing on the bridge. It slows to a stop and Farah climbs from the first carriage, all the way down the end under the viaduct. She looks half like the person she was in the first year, in skinny jeans and Chuck Taylors, but then she has a new mac and a rolling suitcase that matches it exactly.

The moment she sees Khadi, Farah stops beside the rotting boat full of flowers and waits with her arms out. Khadija walks past them and takes hold of the suitcase.

'Jesus!' Farah looks at the crumbling station house surrounded by barbed wire, then over at the bridges. 'Don't you find it soul-destroying?'

'Yes.'

'Just before the bridge the train went through some freakish wasteland of terraces and tower blocks that looked like it's where they filmed *The Firm*.

'That'd be Devonport.'

'And you think *London* eats people? What the hell?'

'Well, this is my home.'

'OK, sorry. But seriously, Khadi, I'm worried about you.'

'Why? People live here. You used to live someplace like this, remember? Most of the country is like this.'

'Wait, we're arguing already? I didn't mean it, Khadi. I was trying to be caring.'

'On your best day, you got nowhere near enough sympathy for this, babe. You came down on the London train; wanna know what the train that doesn't go all the way to London is like?

'All right, I get it.'

'There's shit smeared in the toilets and weird mysterious stickiness all over the lino floors and half the seats are covered in hazard tape because they're broken. There's no free wi-fi and no food and drink. Sometimes you get stuck for an hour between stations because kids have stripped the copper wire out of the points. Because they need the fucking money, because *your* neighbours sold their jobs to their mates overseas and took all the money out of the counties so they could build a shitting garden bridge over the Thames.'

'Khadi! Please can we start over?'

'OK, give me a minute. You kind of sprung yourself on me and then started judging.'

'I need you, Khadi. Can't do this one on my own, OK?'

'How about sorry?'

'Yes, I actually am. And you're right. I came from someplace pretty much like this. That's why it freaked me.'

'The actual word sorry wasn't in there. You get that, right?'

'Sorry. Sorry. Sorry.'

'Let's go. My mum's over the moon you're here. She's making homemade pasties. It's creepy.'

'Your mum's a sweetheart. Give her a break.'

'You give her a break. Make her feel useful. You owe me already.'

'OK, done. Also, I want to see the bits you love. I get that we all crawled out of different hellholes, but this is your hellhole. Show me.'

'Let's go inside. It isn't far.' Khadija waves a hand across the tracks. 'I only live just there, under the bridge of destroyed souls.'

Later, after pasties and being nice and showers and an awkward telly session, Khadija climbs onto her bed and leans against the wall. She'd pulled the curtain back, then half closed it again because seeing Farah in front of the bridges was too unsettling.

'Wow!' Farah says. 'People would pay big for a view like that in London.'

If it were London, Khadija would use Farah to lean on so she could tilt her head and line up the bridge with the windowsill. But if it were London the bridge wouldn't be there. Or the sky.

'It is beautiful in an odd way,' Farah says now.

'Sublime, in't it?'

'I wouldn't go that far.'

'I mean sublime like in English class. It's a bit too big to get your head round. If you picture yourself out there you lose your breath a little. It makes you feel time and death and the shape of the whole earth.'

'Huh. I'm glad you're still you, Khadi. I was worried you might be different here.'

'I never changed. I came away so I could stay who I was.' Which is what she wishes were true, not what is.

'Right, let's talk about you,' Farah says. 'Tell me what's been happening. Your cousin's gone missing. Tell me.'

'They all think it's my fault, but no one's saying that.'

'How? You haven't even lived here for the past six years. She must have been nine years old when you left.'

'I'm kind of like a curse around here. But also everybody expects me to save them. It's messed up. It's why I went to London in the first place.'

'Don't take this the wrong way, but you *are* one of those saviour people. You're always taking in strays. Including me.'

'Yeah but I don't want to, Farah. They grew me like that, this lot. They're all bloody lost-its and people are always dying everywhere, suffocating and falling into the river and mysteriously fucking disappearing. Every time it happens, somebody calls me.'

'Uh, stop answering?'

'Wow, thanks. I never thought of that. It isn't that simple. I love them.'

Khadija leans just a little to the left, close enough to feel the buzzing between them, to see the bridge at ten degrees from the windowsill, then she throws herself across Farah's legs to reach under the bed.

'There was this guy,' she says. 'He got a little obsessed with me, then he joined the army. He came home safe but then he died anyway.'

She pulls the Cadbury's tin up onto the bed and takes off the top. There is a picture of everyone in swimsuits on Town Quay. Jo is small and Khadija and Beth Kennedy are standing against the railing with their wet hair hanging in strings.

'Holy crap, that's you!'

'Yep.'

'And that's the guy? The one with the shorts? Were you in love with him?'

'No, Farah, I wasn't. But he dumped it all on me anyway. Like I was some sort of Virgin in a church, some kind of cross between Morena Baccarin and his mother. It was creepy and I didn't like it.'

'You say that every time someone fancies you.'

'Because it is. People are always looking to quarry each other, trying to open each other up and lift out the precious shit.'

'That is the most glass-half-empty bollocks I have ever heard.'

'Tell me to my face it isn't true. Even I do it. If I ever ran away from anything, it was myself doing that.'

There is a long minute then, and maybe some pieces come together. Maybe they don't come together and carefully not moving them into place is how the two of them have learned to care.

'Listen, there might be something you could help me with,' Khadi says.

'Wait, hold up. I think I just felt hell freeze over.'

'Ha ha. It's about a company hiding money. Washing it, maybe.'

'Laundering, Khadija. You launder money. And how would I know about that? I project risk; I'm not an accountant. Also, I'm quitting.'

'Wow. Congratulations.'

'Don't take the piss. I'm going through shit.'

'No, I mean it. I'm happy for you. It's a good move.'

'Let's get back to you.'

'OK, I'm sorry, but this is really important. See this letter? It's from a company called Rame Holdings.'

'This is about your serial killer map, isn't it? Is this one of the companies you had written up on your wall in London?'

'No actually, it wasn't. That's the thing. This is new. They sent Craig a cease and desist, not long before he died.'

'That sounds like your territory.'

'No, look. Why was he bothering them, though? He must have known something, or thought something anyway.'

'About asbestos, right? This is the asbestos crusade.'

'Sort of. Could you just check if Rame Holdings has anything do with a limited company called Slate Group?'

'Financial filings are at Companies House, Khadi.'

'Those don't show anything worth looking for. Isn't it your job to make sure of that?'

'It's to do with the bloke, innit? Jesus, Khadi. Why didn't you tell me this five years ago? We were supposed to be best friends.'

'You were kind of busy refusing to live your own life.'

'Your polite-request game needs a bit of work, lovely.'

'OK, OK. Sorry.'

'How about actually talking to me?'

'You know what. I do feel guilty. Don't laugh but I didn't even realise it till I came back here.'

'Guilty why?'

'The night Craig died, I was pissed.'

'So he died because you did some shots? That's a stretch, Khadi. Even for you.'

'No, but— He was in love with me and I was leaving. I didn't want to deal with saying goodbye to his puppy eyes. He came round and I brushed him off. I went and got pissed with a bunch of people instead. One of them was his sister.'

'So you have to take down six or seven major corporations before you feel OK about acting like a normal teenager? The bloke was creeping on you, Khadi. Not your fault.'

'I get that. In my head I get that. There's more but it's hard to explain. So anyway, all you get at Companies House are board members and dates. There are some financial filings, but not always and they don't have enough detail.'

'OK, and?'

'Holding companies are about risk, right? Distributing risk.'

'In theory, yeah. But that isn't complicated. You don't need an actuary for that. The idea is that a company that holds parts of several other companies distributes shareholder risk. On the surface, that's it.'

'And underneath?'

'You can use them to hold assets. Stuff you don't want to disclose to directors and shareholders of the other companies. Patents, that kind of thing.'

'So, you could move your assets in to protect them from liability?'

'If you were avoiding something specific like that you'd have to be really crafty about it. Anyway, they'd just offshore. And you'll never see that. Whatever they did will be technically legal.'

'Actually, there's a limited called Resolve Logistics, as well. They could be connected.'

'What's the gain for you here, Khadi? What good is this information gonna do?'

'I need to know, Farah. I need to know exactly how it works. How it happened. I just do.'

Khadi puts the letter back and hands over the little nest. She doesn't explain, but when Farah holds it, she has the right gentleness. She really looks, turning it over and moving it under the lamp. Running the tip of a finger over the white fluff at the edges. This, the way Farah pays attention, is the healing thing.

Go figure.

'You sure you didn't love this guy?'

'No, Farah. Never been like that, sorry to disappoint. I liked Craig, though.' Khadija puts the lid back on the tin and stands to put it on top of the chest of drawers. 'He was another messed up sweetheart. We grow a lot of those round here.'

They no longer sleep like twins in the womb. It might be the time passed or it might be Saltash. It might be just the electric heating. At 2.30 in the morning Khadija wakes up to turn it off and Farah is standing at the window, looking out at the bridge. She stares up the river like there is something important hiding there, turns her ear to the glass so the bridge lights gild a line around the edge of her face while her hair spiderwebs against the glass. Like a net for catching ghosts.

'Go back to sleep, Farah.' Khadija rolls over and pulls the duvet up. 'It isn't real.'

Farah is at the window again when Khadi wakes up. Or maybe she's been there all night, standing in her sheep pyjamas with the curtain pushed back over one shoulder.

'This place is kind of ... I don't know, dramatic.'

'Yep.'

'It is literally like the sky fell down,' Farah says. 'Look.'

There is a blanket of cloud sleeping on the cold river while the rest of the world warms up with sunlight, pylons on the road bridge rising up out of an opaque mist. The ground could be any distance away, like they live on the surface of a gas giant.

'Oh, yeah. I like when that happens. Put a coat on, we'll go outside.'

'I can't go out like this. I need to shower and stuff.'

'This is Saltash, Farah. Put a coat on over your pyjamas. We're only going down the green.'

Carol is up and out already. She's left scones on the side and put out instant cappuccino sachets. Khadija loves her all the way for one sharp second, then pushes everything aside and makes tea.

Farah comes down in skinny jeans and her pyjama top.

'Bring this with you.' She hands Farah a Cornwall Air Ambulance mug.

Down at sea level, it is still a soft morning. Drops form on their clothes and they can't see the sun. Farah turns around every couple

203

of metres or so, trying to figure out when exactly they've moved from one kind day to the other. The harbourmaster blokes are drinking tea outside their pre-fab, beside a pile of kayaks. Khadija leads Farah to a bench facing north, up the invisible river toward Cargreen.

She wipes the drops off the bench with her sleeve. 'So, you gonna tell me what you're doing here?'

'What if I wanted to see you.'

'OK, but why now all of a sudden?'

'You've been here less than ten days, Khadi.'

A red shadow leaks into the mist up the river, too faint at first for Khadija to know whether it's real. She watches while it hardens into the shape of a sail, then two. A little wooden boat, junk-rigged, slides down from Parson's Quay. It could be from any time in the past three hundred years.

'My annoying mad cousin ran away and my fun cousin just had a baby. That feels like enough right now. Sorry if I was rude about you coming. I'm happy to see you. I am.'

'So talk to me. You ever think maybe that's why I'm here?'

'I came back home and literally nothing is different. Not even me.'

'You are, Khadi. You're different than the person I met. She was a teenager, for starters. You're a woman. Also, you're a solicitor.'

'Almost a solicitor. Final exams in six weeks. Mostly I'm bad luck. Ask anybody in Saltash.'

'I need to leave Will. It's been fairly dramatic.'

'Well … duh.'

'Fuck off. It's fine, actually. I just need to leave. I was waiting for my promotion so I could go straight into a new flat.'

'You did the financial math on your relationship status? OK.'

'All right. Don't come on with that you're-such-a-soulless-London-sell-out high and mighty thing. We had a marble floor in the foyer and a bunch of Le Creuset crap Will's mother kept sending over. I'd come home at night and order shit online and then never even open the boxes.'

'Oh my God, that sounds awful. My next-door neighbour suffocated to death because poison particles clogged up his lungs and he couldn't cough them out. My cousin probably threw herself in the river because the waiting list for counselling was eight months long. People around here pretend they can talk to the dead, because otherwise the size of their loss will shrivel them up and their souls will just blow away while they're still alive. They've been jumping to their deaths past my bedroom window my whole life.'

'None of that is my fault.'

'No, but you're choosing to live inside the M25 where you don't have to see it or think about it. You're choosing that on purpose.'

'So, you left London because of your steadfast principles? I was there, Khadija. I am the one person who knows that's not true.'

'I couldn't watch what was happening to you. I couldn't help. Helping is who I am and I couldn't.'

'Well, I'm done with it and I nearly killed myself getting out of it.'

The boat with the red sails burns a trail into the mist, leaving an open path of clarity behind it. Khadija expands her lungs to breathe in the second-hand light and the brackish air, the smell of cut grass and metal. *Home is where the hurt is.* She looks at Farah and smiles.

'I'm sorry I couldn't be your manic pixie dream girl,' Farah says.

'No worries, bird. You turned out to be well boring anyway.'

'Thanks.'

'I don't have to hold you up. You are one thing I do not have to hold up.'

'I'll just check in here and point out that I never asked you to. Love you though, mate.'

Farah catches the up train in the afternoon. She'll glide up through Devonport with the setting sun at her back and free wi-fi, put on her mac and wheel her matching suitcase through the ocean of sound at Paddington, catch the Hammersmith line west and wait for her bank account to free her.

Khadi waves her up and hands in the little suitcase. The gap is extra wide because the trains don't fit properly into Saltash station. Farah looks past her at the derelict station house, the buddleia and the razor wire.

'I actually like it here,' she says. 'I get it.'

'Fuck off back to St Margaret's, you.'

'Love you.'

'Love you too, actually.'

The train sits waiting for the bridge signal in the sharp sun. Khadi turns her eyes away from Farah stowing her suitcase and finding her seat. And there is Mr Osborne, climbing the mews through to Forder, heading to his mother's house. What do they tell each other every Sunday? How much do they say?

Khadija turns back at the sound of the whistle. The guard flips her paddle and the train begins to edge forward. She looks up but all the train window shows her is a curved version of the A38 bridge against the blue sky.

Khadi's phone vibrates in her pocket. It'll only be Farah, taking the piss and texting from her seat.

Then there is a hand among the reflected suspension wires, moving slowly back and forth. She stretches her own hand up toward it and some part of whatever weight has been settled inside her escapes out the ends of her fingers. Particles of soot and sadness evaporate from her blood into the mirrored sky. Farah's face appears against the window and Khadi smiles at her.

You are not my fault and I am not yours.

Chapter 31

Alice has been in Poole two weeks when someone fills the bottom of the stairwell with blood.

You *can* wash your pants out, for twenty pence in the public toilet. Amanda just doesn't. Alice got an extra pair at Primark and now she hangs the spare out the window of the landing, raining or not. If it's raining you don't need the twenty pence. She drinks a lot of coffee because there is always coffee. Her skin is going yellow, but there are no mirrors anyway. Her face doesn't mean anything anymore, but the rest of the world gets very close in the absence of mirrors.

Now there is Ruby Mae, and one of the voices is Charlie. Charlie calling her through an open vein. The thing she didn't bargain for. Boy like the antidote to his own father, like the opposite of poison and the answer to the question she didn't ask.

It is a rainy Monday when she writes the date on the landing wall, using a pen she took from the reception desk at St John's. Next to her initials and the date she writes, 'I can breathe without existing. I can be invisible. I can walk through walls.'

The guitar-and-dog man is on the floor below her. They are almost friends but he still won't tell her his name. She did hear someone say it, but then forgot it again. One day when Alice was out with the guitar man and his dog, not busking, the women from the first floor left. It is harder to hide with them gone. People wander up into the quiet the way they wouldn't if there was noise. While the women were there, the druggies stayed downstairs. Nobody argued, or spoke at all. On the streets everyone makes boundaries out of nothing for all kinds of reasons and without any words. You learn where they are because you have to.

Today, the falling rain takes all the sound out of the air, safer in so many ways than the sun. Everyone comes out in the sun, everyone sees, everyone wants to clean the place up. It must be horrible in sunny countries. Where does everyone hide? The wet, closed sky puts Alice to sleep in the afternoon.

Her head has been quiet all day because there's so much else to think about. Where to eat? Will anyone hassle her tonight? Could she stash her stuff in those trees for a bit while she goes to the library computers? There is no room in her thoughts for anything else. Right up until everyone starts shouting at once, inside her and out.

At first, it's the noise from below that wakes her up. The sky is dark.

'I didn't even give it ya!'

That is a woman called Sheila who talks Croydon and has a tattoo of holly around the base of her neck. The thorns look like they're pricking into her skin. People like to get tattoos that fool your eye into thinking their skin is broken, pierced. They like to pretend there are painful extra holes in themselves.

'You fuckin' did give it me. And you took it out with you again and all.' The voice of a bloke Alice doesn't recognise.

'OK, chill. Let's calm it down. Everybody take a breath and wait two minutes.' One of the ketamine heads from the ground floor.

A minute or two of silence then, but Alice can feel them all breathing. There are four people in the stairwell below her. She counts the separate sounds of their lungs before they are drowned out by the shouting in her head.

Get out, Alice.

This is where your bones come apart.

Breath in, maid. Deep breath. Nice and calm.

Don't. Someone will steal your eyes. Get out.

She listens and the deep breaths come anyway, because your body does those things if you can manage to leave it alone. Blood pumps around and your lungs fill up and empty out and sometimes nothing piles up inside you.

'Shit!' That's guitar man. 'All right, come on now. No need for that.'

'You did and you fuckin' know it.' The first bloke, shouting.

Now Sheila says it, 'Shit,' and then 'come on now.' And then nothing.

'Shit. Shit. Shit. Time to go everybody!' Guitar man shouts it up the stairs and down into the back.

Alice opens the window to get her pants and the rain falls onto her paper skin, onto her veins holding everything in. She breathes again and packs the breath down as if she's about to dive off Town Quay, then runs down the stairs, stuffing her spare wet pants into her back pocket.

Shit shit shit shit shit. They're all saying it now, inside her and out. There is blood sprayed up the wall and over the ceiling two landings below hers, interrupted by the ceiling light and then dripping down the opposite wall. It looks like enough for three people, and it makes a lot of noise. So many people are talking inside her it almost freezes her legs. She almost sinks into the floor. Her mouth fills up with harbour water and the clouds above the car park turn orange. She knows without looking that the sky is on fire.

'It's Robert.'

Alice pulls her head out from between her knees because whoever said that is outside her head, looking down. She is sitting at the edge of a pavement with no idea how she got there. It's the guitar man speaking.

'Sorry?'

'My name is Robert. Have you got a fag at all?' He looks away down the road.

'What? No, I don't have a fag. You know that.'

Shit shit shit shit shit, they're all singing in her head like a cathedral choir.

The soup people are in two cars, pulled over by the edge of Alexandra Park with the boots open. Alice goes to the back of the queue and someone brings her a coffee while she waits. More coffee. There is already something chalky and corrosive running up and down her spine, like the stuff they threw over bodies in the plague pits, lime like they burned in the kilns up the river from home. Coffee is the last thing she needs, but she drinks it for the burn in her throat.

Once she has some soup and an apple, Alice sits back down at the edge of the road. There are five or six people from the car park but they're all pretending not to know each other. Robert stands by a car boot looking through a pile of books. He has left his guitar behind.

But he's only pretending. He waves her over and then says under his breath, 'She wasn't dead and I knew that, so don't take me for a complete cunt. I called 999. You need to leave Poole now. Go somewhere else, right?'

'Alice. I'm Alice.'

'Walk away now, Alice. Go home and get yourself back on your meds. Let your parents look after you.'

It takes Alice all the next day to get the coach fare. There is a rain so warm it's like blood running down her arms. Sometimes it is blood, just for a second, blink and you miss it. It comes down like a curtain over the doorway of the empty shop where she spends most of the morning. Everyone from the car park is gone, as if some kids' book magic spirited all the homeless away overnight to an arctic farm where they separate them from their souls and use the energy to drive their non-specific evil machines. Or just transformed them into golden retriever-walking Waitrose shoppers, maybe. There are still plenty of those. And cops.

'Hello, love.' It doesn't sound friendly. 'Got a name?'

'I only just got off the coach. I'm meeting my cousin here.' She widens her eyes and turns her toes in toward each other, but she doesn't even find it convincing herself.

'So, this afternoon I won't see you anywhere around here? Is that right?'

'Yep, 'cause I'll either have gone to Axminster for my holiday or

210

disowned my cousin.' She laughs absently, distracted by the blood raining down over the cop.

By lunchtime, Alice has coach fare. She is still good with people. People who don't know her, anyway. She saves out two pounds for a library computer and can only get a ticket as far as Exeter. The coach station is full of foreign language students speaking Italian and French. They've come to look at the fossils and have cream teas in cottage gardens, dipping into Englishness like it's a paddling pool. No idea what's at the deep end.

Another hour and forty minutes until the Exeter coach, so she goes into the library, where it's almost as damp as outside. There's a lady taking a bloke through a job skills tutorial online, and another behind the desk trying to talk to someone about a library card. Behind the crime section there's a computer on its own, where no one will be able to see what she's doing.

She types the message before adding the number of the sender.

There is so much blood inside us.

No. Not that.

I can't figure out how to drown.

No.

Tell them I'm OK. I don't know how to be sorry.

Alice only knows one number off by heart, and it isn't her mother's or Charlie's.

Make something up and tell it to them, Khadi. Don't hate me.

Chapter 32

Jo is waiting on the bridge walkway, bent over the baby's pram with her hood up.

'This is weird, Khadi.'

'I had to talk to you. I couldn't do it in anybody's house.'

Khadija leans over to look at Ruby Mae, lying with one fist smashed against her face and a bubble of snot moving in and out with her sleeping breath. Something inside her inconstant body expands, some liquid rushes somewhere and leaves her off balance.

'Is it OK for her to be outside? She's only a week old.'

'Now you're asking? It's fine.' Jo turns her face and presses her cheek against the walkway cage. 'She's all wrapped up and the air is good for her. In Iceland they leave their babies out in the cold for hours, to make them healthy.'

'Please tell me you're not reading parenting books. Will you look at those nutters?' Khadi points down to Brunel's pylons.

'Tombstoning already?' Jo lifts her face to look, little square depressions on her skin turning pink as the blood rushes back. Boys are jumping off the dock that sticks out from Town Quay under Brunel's bridge. 'It's March for fuck's sake. That water must be absolutely freezing.'

'It makes me feel so at home, though. Mad boys with their wet suits half hanging off, hurling themselves off things. Pretty much the meaning of Saltash, in't it?'

Every once in a while, somebody climbs the side of a pylon and throws themselves off. Ben used to do that, and Jo's eyes would shine with satisfaction. Soulmates. One way or another Ruby Mae is the result of that shit.

'So,' Jo leans her head toward Khadija, 'is there some sort of code word before I get to hear what's up? You gonna hand over a secret package, or something?'

'I got a message.'

'OK. Wait, you... what?'

'Yes, Jo. I got a message from Alice. I don't know what to do.'

'You fucking tell someone, Khadi! What do you think? Let's go.'

'No, wait. She said not to. She said if she came back someone was gonna hurt her.'

'It's Alice, you dozy cow. She'll say literally anything to make people do what she wants. You bloody know that.'

'Why would she message me and then not want me to tell anyone?'

'Because she doesn't want to come home and deal with what she did to her parents. I thought she left her phone in her room. She email you or what?'

'It came by text but the return number's unknown. She must have done it through a website.'

Shouts rise up from the water. There's a boy clinging like a monkey onto the pylon. The sun sinking over Trematon throws the shadow of the bridge and its bump of a boy out over the river.

'I'm angry at her too, but think about it for a minute. She must be in hell.'

'She's put everyone else through hell, Khadi. She does that when she's here and all, mind. You fucked off and I been dealing with it.'

'Neither of us should have to deal with it, Jo. She's not our kid.'

'Well, you got the message so it's on you, bird. Do the right thing, not the thing Alice wants you to.'

'She thinks I'm in London.'

'Crap, 'course she does.'

'Why the hell me, Jo? Why did she message me? Everyone already thinks I'm some kind of Jonah on a boat. Now I'm gonna rock up at Debbie and Pete's house like, *Nah she's fine. She text me?*'

'Well, you've told me now, so you're going to have to. Unless you're planning to push me off the bridge right now.'

'What am I gonna say when they ask why she messaged me instead of them?'

When the sun drops behind Rame they're still arguing. Ruby Mae wakes up and the halogen lamps settle into her eyes. She opens her toothless mouth and gives them back their light, shining like two stars.

On Fore Street the chippy glares out into the bus shelter and the cider heads are settling on the cement block across from the Co-op. Comfortable people are buying upmarket ready meals and bottles of rosé to take back to Landrake. Twice a minute Jo leans over to adjust something in the pram that doesn't need adjusting. She just wants her hands on her baby.

'By the time they track down the message,' Khadi says, 'she'll be gone from wherever she sent it from. They won't find her till she wants them to.'

'Yeah, Khadi, but you can pass it on. You don't have to hold onto it. It in't yours; you just said so.'

When they cross the road by Victoria Gardens, the dark relief from the High Street makes their voices sound clearer and their steps ring out into the shadows. There are dozens of begonias in perfect rows, looking small and exposed in a patch of dry earth. Jo leans over to pull the blanket up to Ruby's chin, even though it's already there.

'I don't know how you do it.'

'Do what?'

'Need people. I tried it one time. Done.'

Later, when Khadija goes over every second of their walk, she is almost sure it happened in this moment.

Something moves under there in the dark and draws her eyes. She looks over behind the club house in Victoria Gardens, to the place where the shrubs are overgrown and the ground is covered in damp mulch.

Then the sirens. It isn't even clear where the sound comes from,

214

right then. It could be from the A38, or from North Yard. It's the kind of night when the air is full of enough moisture to carry the sound anywhere.

It's not coming from either of those places, though. The sound of sirens is coming from Torpoint, twisting around up the river from the ferry landing.

Chapter 33

They're all pissed, but it's only seven o'clock. Ben is happy because Jo had a baby that in't his. Well, it is, though. But technically it isn't. Biologically.

Jo didn't come out with them because of Ruby Mae, but they're getting a flat and Ruby will call him Daddy. So he's celebrating his girlfriend shagging someone else and having a baby, but it's Saltash so everybody gets it. You take care of the people you love. Ego bullshit don't come into it.

It's windy on the top deck, and the taxis waiting on the road at the Torpoint slipway have their windows up. The air feels good under the sky because everything is put back right again. While Jo was gone the whole world felt like he was indoors and couldn't get out, even when he climbed the bridge or stood on the top of the ferry.

Sometimes, last year, he went over Plymouth and got pissed, got off with a few birds, but it didn't help.

He saw somebody get glassed down Union Street one night. He was in a doorway with some girl he didn't even know her name. They were getting off with each other until Ben got sick. There was shouting all around but he didn't pay attention. There was always shouting. When he started to be sick she laughed. He was looking at her thighs, puking on the step next to her, when a splatter of blood came past him and hit the door. Not a spray, mind, a splatter. Big gobs of it the size of fifty pences. Chappie must've lost half his face.

People have so much more blood in them than you think.

The thing is, it wasn't funny and he didn't want to sit around telling stories about it later. He didn't fancy the girl with the thighs and he's never been raged enough to want to glass somebody. He could be, mind. He just in't. He stood in that doorway off Union

Street thinking he wanted to go tombstoning from the pylons even though it was January. He was sick of the smell of amaretto and perfume, sick of being on the ground.

He only wanted to be over the river, maybe in Victoria Gardens with Jo, hiding behind the house with some fags and a bottle of cider, listening to her talk about being a filmmaker or a chat show hostess. Whatever she was gonna be that week. He wanted to smell the burned ends of her hair and her mum's washing powder that always made him feel a bit sick, too. Which is maybe what reminded him, that night in the doorway off Union Street.

He wanted to go to work with his dad and bring home a pay packet so he could take her to Exeter or Truro and buy her something. He wanted to stand on the bridge walkway with her and look down at the R.A.B.I. until they felt dizzy.

Now she was back and Ruby Mae was born, he was so happy he wanted to wait between trains and walk out the railway line with Connor until the hill fell away under them and they were up over the water in a trough made of steel. Maybe five centimetres of metal between them and the drop. That is the only feeling that will match his happiness.

Everyone shouts when Ben climbs the railing on the top deck of the ferry, pulling himself up by the radio mast. All laughing and cheering over the sound of the chain clunking through the motor. It leaves a foamy wave where it drops through the surface and back to the bottom of the river.

'I had a baby!' He throws one arm out and leans over the water.

'You didn't though mate, did ya?' Everyone laughs. Connor don't mean nothing.

Ben takes a second to balance, feeling how the weight falls on the soles of his feet, how gravity works around the top bar of the railing.

'Guard's coming!'

That girl's thighs were red from the cold and covered in bumps, but she still wasn't wearing a coat. Ben was thinking how the bloke's blood would be frozen onto the door by morning. Somebody would come to work and have to prise off little frozen fifty-pence pieces of it before they could open for custom. The gobs would skitter out onto the pavement all full of some bloke's iron and alcohol and DNA. Wonder what his face looks like now? Don't matter, he probably deserved it. They're all cunts over the river.

On the top deck of the ferry, up on the railing, comes the moment when everything balances. The world weighs itself into two perfect halves with his body in the middle, his feet on the dividing line. He can let go now. This is the feeling, when Ben knows the earth is a planet in space, the sky is a void full of invisible force. Fuck surfing in the sea, you can ride pure gravity like a wave on anything high enough. Ben's been doing it since he was little. He can ride the sky.

'Get down, *bhey*. Seriously. Guard's coming.'

'I did, though. I had a fuckin' baby with Jo Sleep. I'm gonna look after her and make her happy and that means they're mine.' He waves an arm.

The sky tilts, and the engine houses on the slipway turn away from the surface of the river. Then the river is a wall. The moon pulls him up by the feet, and his body is two seconds behind. By the time he pulls back the muscles in his legs, they are moving in the wrong direction. He's going to get soaked. Jo'll be fuming, and the ferry guard will probably call the police. They're nearly across now, good thing the tide's in. He won't hit the mud and break a collar bone.

He'd forgot about the chain.

The ferry chain relieves Ben of his happiness the way the river puts other people out of their misery. Between 7:01pm and 7:02pm, Ben Jinks is replaced by a blank space the size of the sky, and all of the gravity inside it.

By 7:23pm the sirens moan down the slipways on both sides of the river, but Ben is long gone down the channel. The river lies smooth and open to the halogen light, asking for more.

2010

Chapter 34

The first time he snuck up on her, Khadija was still seventeen. She'd gone out onto the dock, just to be away from her mother and sit in the dark for a bit. Down there, she could hide inside the shadow of the bridges and the anonymous noise from the pub. The tide was all the way in, lapping at the dock a few inches from her legs, and the air was clear all the way over to Barne Barton, sparkling on the hill.

'Khadija.'

She whipped her head around, but there was nobody there.

Khadija knew more about disembodied voices than most people. Since she was five, she'd been sitting on Aunt Tammy's kitchen stool while women gasped and wept. Sometimes she'd make the tea, other times just sit and listen, pretending to read while they talked about their odd little fears and their enormous sorrows. Tammy would cock her head and go still, then the messages would come out of her mouth.

'It's all a show,' her mother would tell her after. 'There's nothing to be afraid of. There's nothing there, maid.'

She'd grown up believing them both.

So when that voice called her out of the distorted darkness it flipped the world around and made her mother a liar. Everything was instantly different, but also it had been there all along.

'Sorry.' Craig Kennedy stepped out of the shadows at the side of the Union Pub.

'Shit! I thought you was a ghost.' *Were* a ghost.

'Been in the army but I didn't die.' That was meant for a joke.

'Why ya acting like a ghost then?' Khadija said.

He wasn't someone you'd notice. No one paid much attention to Craig when he was living. He was just there, the sad boy with the dad who was taking ten years to die. He was out of uniform that

221

night, discharged two months before, back in his trainers and a jacket with a sheepskin collar. The army had laid him back down on the Hamoaze like a stripped screw they couldn't use anymore.

'I was just getting a breather. I didn't mean to startle ya.'

'If you don't want to startle people, maybe leave off the spooky whisper, mate. Call me out loud next time.'

He didn't laugh, or even smile. Maybe sneaking up softly was a habit with him, since he'd spent his childhood twitching with his dad.

'Mind if I sit here, too?'

Khadija waved a hand and shrugged. He'd come back with just the whisper of a limp, walking not quite straight but you had to squint to notice it. Or you'd think it was just him leaning into the side of the hill how he always was, bent a little sideways from growing up in Saltash.

He sat down two yards from her as though she might startle if he came any closer. For a while it was fine saying nothing. The air was clear, the river was full, and they both belonged. They went on for half an hour like that.

'You come out for a breather, too?' Still speaking soft. Low. Birdwatching speech. Maybe he ran those things together in his mind. Birds and birds. Thought you should go about them the same way.

'I was trying to revise, but my mum's a nightmare.'

'Hassling you?'

'Trying to "help". Cleaning all round me and trying to make me take weird capsules from Barrett's she says make you clever.'

'Have you tried 'em?'

'Fuck, no. I'm really sorry about your dad. I like him.'

'Blokes don't last long on the Hamoaze, in't it?'

'Some do.'

'Not ours.'

'Anyway, he's not some bloke. He's your dad. It doesn't matter what happens to other people. Not right now.'

'It does, apparently. There's union solicitors and all sorts, saying they knew this would happen.'

'How's Beth?'

'You know my sister. She's pretending nothing's wrong, then randomly shouting at everybody all the time. I feel bad for my mum. She don't need that right now.'

Something unsettled the surface of the river and broke up the light.

'I remember how Tammy was, with Micky.'

'You must have been small.'

'I'm gonna be one.'

'Sorry?'

'Solicitor. I'm gonna be a solicitor.'

A second ripple in the water, with a sound like a hiss. Maybe stars were falling from somewhere behind the filthy haze in the sky. Or maybe someone was dropping fag-ends from the bridge.

You couldn't have called it a mundane conversation. It was about families and pain and horrible death. Still, none of it matched the way he was looking at her. Like he could lift her up with just his eyes. Like he had some power that could reshape the water around them and carry her away on a wave of his own making.

Chapter 35

Jo had been thinking.

'I'm not gonna be like All Saints,' she told Khadija. 'I'm gonna be like Dido.'

Because looking at Khadi always made Jo think about being famous. It was like looking at an arrow pulled back in the bow, a star falling up instead of down. You knew she was on her way up and out, shooting for somewhere else.

They were in the Tregidgas' kitchen. The mums were all out together and Alice was playing up in her room. They were putting pizza and chips in the oven for tea while sheets of falling rain washed over the concrete patio outside in the security light. *Top of the Pops 2* was on, but they weren't really watching it.

'Dido's a bit posh and whingy, don't you think? I feel like you're tougher than her.'

'She don't sound posh.'

'That's an act. The music business is like that.'

'I'm gonna be an act.'

'You are an act, you nutter. Get some plates.'

Dido had nice hair, though, so blonde and straight. If Jo had Dido's voice she'd feel smaller, prettier.

'What about Duffy?' Khadija said. 'At least she actually sings instead of whinging.'

These were the best nights, when everyone went out and they could pretend to be anything. It was good when Khadija babysat. She was half like a mum; Jo did what she said half the time.

'You just think Duffy's pretty, in't it?'

'Maybe. Maybe I also have musical taste.'

Then they heard the thumping, something banging against the wall over their heads. Jo wouldn't have noticed the sound, if it weren't for the look on Khadija's face.

'Alice? You OK?' Khadija ran for the stairs.

Jo pulled out her new phone and followed.

Alice's room was still on the first floor then; Aunt Debbie and Uncle Pete hadn't done the loft yet. Jo stretched up to look over Khadija's shoulder into the bedroom. The overhead light was on, and for some reason Alice had the window open. Rain was pouring in onto the duvet, and there were drops of blood dripping down the wall. She sat on the bed, up against the pillows with the rain soaking into her socks, staring at the chest of drawers with wide, watery eyes.

I'll use the flash, Jo thought. Spookier.

'She bit me.' Alice said.

'Who bit you?' Khadija went calm like a mum does when you're bleeding really bad. 'What was that noise?'

Jo framed the bloody wall through her phone. The phone was good, because if you got too close to Alice with nothing in between you, the world stopped making sense. She touched the screen and lit up the room with blue flash.

'Jesus, Jo! Stop it. Alice, let me see your hand.'

'Look, though!' Jo turned the phone around so Khadija could see the streaks of gore, lit up and contrasty.

'Who lets a thirteen-year-old have a smartphone? Bloody hell.'

Alice's index finger was bleeding and the blood had soaked into her lap.

'What happened, maid?' Khadija's comforting voice. 'Come on, let's get that washed out.'

Jo would never sound like that. Didn't want to.

It took a few tugs for Khadija to shift her, but then Alice followed to the bathroom like a sleeping child on automatic.

'Jo, shut the window.'

'Crap, that's a lot of blood.'

'Jo!'

Everything was wet. Jo used a pillowcase to wipe away the blood on the wall, then realised she'd ruined the pillowcase.

'What happened, lovely?' Khadija said in the bathroom.

Jo leaned in to ask what to do with the pillowcase and saw Alice staring at herself in the mirror, hatred in her eyes. Her mouth looked wired shut, and she glared at her own reflection like she could strangle it. Khadija put TCP and a plaster around two puncture wounds on the pad of Alice's finger. So much blood for just those two little holes.

Back in the bedroom Jo could see two wells in the carpet where the legs of the chest were supposed to be. It was shoved away from the wall on one side. When she went to put it back she saw Sally, Alice's new hamster. Jo chucked her phone onto the wet bed and crouched down.

'Khadi?'

'Just a minute, babe.'

Sally was crumpled into the space between the leg of the chest and the skirting board, still with frozen violence. Jo could only count three little sets of claws. The fourth foot was twisted underneath her, or maybe ground into the carpet. There were little beads of blood in her nostrils, but the rest of her was intact, her pristine belly and her sandy head uncrushed.

'Khadija! Shit.'

'What? And will you please stop swearing.'

'She's dead,' Alice said from the bedroom doorway. 'I killed her.'

The banging they'd heard was Alice, slamming the chest into the wall over and over again because Sally was crouching behind it.

'She bit me,' Alice said.

Jo went still, waiting for Khadija to make the world stop moving around her. She didn't though; she just turned her back on both of them and started stripping the bed. Jo felt like she was standing on the bridge walkway, yellow warning for wind and the roadway shut.

'Why was the window open, sweetie? It's rainin'.'

'I wanted to go out.'

'You're on the first floor, Alice,' Jo said.

'Never mind,' Khadija said. 'You sit here. I'll get you some dry things. Jo, go down and get the pizza.'

'Hang on.' She picked up her phone.

'Stop it!' Khadi slapped Jo's arm and then said sorry.

She was acting like Alice had just wet the bed or had a nosebleed or some other kind of everyday thing. She was acting like Aunt Debbie.

'Come on, Khadija. No one's gonna believe this without pictures.'

'No one's gonna believe this anyway, because you're not telling them. Get the flippin' pizza.'

Jo came back up with the pizza, remembering the plates and ready to go back for the chips. She found Khadi in the airing cupboard. Aunt Debbie's house had everything it was supposed to; she was the mum who had things like spare duvets and TCP. On the other hand, she had Alice.

Jo put the pizza on the chest, which was back in its exact place with its legs in the carpet holes.

'Alice, look at me.' Khadija pulled the dry duvet over her and held her shoulders. 'Come on.'

'I'm not sorry.'

'It's OK, bird. You got hurt and you panicked. It's OK.'

'Why in't I sorry, though, Khadi?'

'You look sorry.'

'I'm not! I hate Sally. She bit me.'

'OK, let's don't think about it for a bit. Can we all eat pizza in your bed?'

By the time Jo and Khadi went back downstairs it was Yorkshire on the telly. A girl was crumpled into the boot of a car with rope burns on her wrists and purple stains on her throat. A recently bereaved man with stubble and a flight jacket was about to spend an hour finding out why. There would be flashbacks. The girl would run frightened through some trees, lose a shoe, gasp rhythmically and finally whimper and beg.

'Don't look at that, Jo.'

Khadija switched it off and then there was nothing to look at but rain and privacy fencing. She made strong tea and got Jo to rehearse the story.

'That doesn't make sense, Khadija. If the hamster was dying, why would it bite Alice?'

'It was trapped. It got scared. When Alice tried to help, it bit her.'

'Alice won't say that. You know what she's like, Khadi. She'll go around telling everyone she's a murderer for the next six months.'

'She's nine years old, Jo. No one will really listen. They'll just think she feels bad.'

'She doesn't though, does she? Pretend what you like; me and you are always gonna know she did that on purpose.'

'Stop for one second and think what it feels like to be her right now, Jo. We need to look after her. You have to help, OK, maid?'

Jo saw right through that *be a big girl and help me* swiz. Her mum did it lots after Dylan arrived, puking and yelling all the time. 'Look at this, Khadi.'

'I don't want to see the picture! It's in my brain already, thanks. Delete that.'

'There's kids like Alice on the internet. They like this stuff. I could get loads of likes.'

'You're serious, in't ya? You're all as twisted as each other. I can't wait to get out of this place.'

See? Khadija was born on her way up. Sometimes you could almost see her wings.

She didn't make Jo dry the dishes. She only stared at the wall behind the kitchen sink, washing them by hand with her back turned to the room. Jo posted the picture of Alice's bed and then made a video of the rain on the patio.

'Take me with you, Khadi.'

'What?'

'Let's move to London. I'll never get famous here.'

'I'll be going to uni, bird. You can't come with.'

'What like, you're gonna live there?'

''Course. Can't ride up and down every day, maid. It takes hours and costs seventy quid a go.'

The mums came in pissed. Khadija's carefully made-up story went straight past them. They didn't even ask to hear it again the next day. Debbie never bought a new hamster.

The next day, Jo got in-school detention for her uniform and the deputy head grilled her about being late three times a week. Which was because of Dylan.

Saturday, her mother told her to visit Khadija and Aunt Carol while she got some sleep with the baby. *Fuck the lot of 'em*, Jo thought, and followed everyone who hung out up behind the school, messing about. There was a ship in the Lynher the exact same colour as the sky. It was a cold day, but the air was so heavy you sweated under your jacket. Everyone leaned around on the goalposts, smoking rollies and looking at nothing.

She was thirteen and Khadija was going away. Everybody would expect Jo to look after Alice and Dylan, to stay home while the parents went out to work or to drink. What was *she* gonna do, next time Alice killed something or tried to climb out the window? Jo had already looked inside herself and knew she didn't have that thing Khadija had, that stream of calm mother shit Khadi turned on like a tap.

Colin Williams was there behind the school with John Killian, who was older and had hardly any teeth left. John Killian was the sort of lost-it who hung around teenagers well into his twenties. They had some cider and John always had gear.

'Who's the little one?' He looked at Jo through his one clear eye like she was lowering the tone.

'John, meet Jo Sleep. Ben Jinks says she's his *soulmate*.'

'Soulmate?' John laughed.

'I in't, by the way,' Jo said. 'I'm my own destiny. Gonna leave you lot in the dust.'

'OK, me lover. Sure.'

Beth Kennedy came and stood at the edge of the group then, wearing a studded belt and a Ramones T-shirt. Her hair was mousy and she still had her baby fat, so all of that emo shit just made her pink cheeks look betrayed. Alice would be pulling the whole thing off much better real soon. With actual animal torture and scarring.

Jo took a photo, put her phone in her back pocket and looked away at the ship in the Lynher, because just looking at Beth made her rage. Which she shouldn't, because everyone said Beth's dad would be dead any minute. Jo's mum said that would be a mercy, the sooner the better. Jo should feel sorry for Beth, but she was fed up with high drama.

'Ya'right?' John Killian said to Beth.

'Hiya.' She twisted one foot against the pavement and looked him in the eye.

'You want a cider?

Don't, Jo thought. *Don't take it.*

'Cheers, lover.' Beth took a can and shook it, then turned round to hold it away from her while she popped it. It sprayed out over the grass and she sucked the foam off the top.

Jo's life was full of emo birds and their attention-seeking bullshit. Talking to Beth was like babysitting Alice. She might start crying and scratch some girl's eyes any minute, or have a mini breakdown behind the school so everyone had to stop drinking and deal with her. Guys loved it as well, always tried it on with mad girls. It was like tombstoning, they could hit bottom if they didn't judge the tide just right. If they did though, they could jump into Beth and right back out again. The noise in her head would be so loud she'd barely notice.

'You gonna sit down?' John did that smile men do that's an invitation and a threat.

'Nah. I'm OK.'

'Those new jeans or something?'

'I don't want to sit next to you is all. Don't have to, do I?'

'You took my cider; don't be a bitch.'

Beth smiled. She was going to get a fight. 'I've got no interest in being close enough to smell your breath.'

People started to shift back on their arses and feel in their pockets for fags.

'You.' John Killian pushed Jo's arm. 'Hold her still.'

'What?'

'Hold this bitch still so I can give her a good slap.'

Beth was looking back and forth between them like she'd spun the roulette and was waiting to see where it would land. She was excited. Mad cow.

So, Jo held her. Pinned Beth's arms against the studded belt and tilted her chin away from Beth's shoulder so she wouldn't have to smell the washing powder on her T-shirt, the perfume from the sale basket at Accessorize, the No 7 liquid foundation or the cider that had sprayed the sleeve of her jacket. The oxygen smell of her dad's breathing machine.

John Killian slapped Beth one time, hard enough to leave finger marks. Jo let go. Beth smiled at him again and walked away with the bruises she'd won. He laughed and shouted, 'You're welcome for the cider.'

He thought he'd frightened her.

If only Jo had taken another photo. She could have had Beth's face before and after. Blank and then with the imprint of John Killian's fingers. She went home and posted the first one on Deviant Art, titled it 'Before the Bruise'.

Years later, if you slapped Beth Kennedy you'd hurt yourself on her bones. The heroin would make sense if you'd seen the way Beth threw herself at things back then, even before Craig died. Whatever was inside her, blankness must be so much better.

And, years later, if you asked Jo to hold some bird down while you hit her, Jo would slap you instead. But there was nothing going to erase it, that moment when someone asked Jo to help, and she did.

Chapter 36

After Khadija started working weekends at the R.A.B.I., Craig came every Saturday and Sunday. He didn't always speak or seem to notice her; just all the time tried to make himself part of the furniture of her life. Hoping she'd come closer if he stayed still long enough.

He'd been and gone already, the Sunday Mr Osborne came in for a roast on his own. She said hello and Mr Osborne told her Charlie was doing a woodcraft weekend with the school and his mum had gone with him to Plymbridge.

'Fending for myself today.' His smile almost seemed pitiful, a little bit crumpled up and out of focus.

The gig rowers were out on the river and a bunch of people were watching from the tables out by the slipway, even though it was freezing. April freezing, with the sun out but a cold wind underneath it taking your breath away.

Mr Osborne watched from the window. When she brought him his beef and swede and a yorkie with a second half of bitter, she stopped a minute because he seemed lonely. She felt bad for him.

'You're at Devonport High now, eh, Khadija?'

'Yeah, just finishing my A2 year.'

'And what are you studying? English? Drama?'

'History, Sociology and Psychology. I did an AS in English but I'm not carrying it on.'

He looked taken aback, but even that didn't stop her being sorry for him. That kind of thing was normal as the cold wind from Plymouth Sound. She barely noticed.

'Will you go off to university, then?'

'I got accepted at City. It's a bit daunting to be honest. I don't do so well in strange places.'

'You could go to Plymouth. Then your mother wouldn't miss you so much.'

Odd thing for him to say. Nobody spoke about Khadija's mum that way, as if she had feelings. His voice went too soft and too close, like someone running their hand up your back in a crowded room. A little creepy, but maybe you'd imagined it.

She went outside to collect glasses and let the wind into her sleeves and around her ankles. The gig rowers were heading up into Kingsmill Lake in a long streak of sunlight.

The dishwasher was down the hallway past the loos. On the way back she found herself in the passageway with Mr Osborne.

It wasn't that he touched her. And you couldn't say he threatened her either, not to someone who wasn't there. If you'd told it after, it would have seemed like nothing. At least that's what Khadija thought at the time. She only told it once, and that turned into a different kind of nothing altogether.

'You have wonderful hair,' he said, because everyone always said that.

'Thanks.' She stopped there in the passage because there wasn't enough room to go past without touching him. She was afraid if she asked him to move he wouldn't, and then neither of them would be able to deny what was happening. You couldn't say he was blocking her way, though.

'Your mother is very good looking, but you are something else.'

She couldn't help laughing then, out of embarrassment mostly. 'Too right. I'm something else, I am.'

She actually felt bad for being sarcastic, like she'd been rude and he was obviously just lonely.

He was still speaking.

'Sorry?'

'I said, you can always ask for help if you need it. I have friends at the council and the LEA. If you have any trouble with grants and whatnot, I'll see what I can do to help.'

'Thanks. That's really sweet, Mr Osborne.' Because that was what you said to men like Mr Osborne when you wanted to say, *back the fuck up out my personal space and mind your own business, you patronising twat.*

'I think you can call me Anthony, Khadija. You're pretty much a woman now. We're both adults and I've known you all your life.'

Jerry the landlord came around the corner then, and Mr Osborne stiffened up and took half a step back, said 'excuse me' and moved past without even stopping for breath. That was what made her sick to her stomach. If it hadn't been for that, she would have told herself she'd imagined the whole thing. That he wasn't creepy, just being kind and a bit clueless.

Later when the pub slowed down, she asked to leave early so she could walk across the bridge before it was all the way dark. There was a feeling in her veins like after you touch nettles, like when you run your biro down the fence on the bridge walkway and the vibrations ring all the way up into your head.

She walked on the outer edge of the bridge walkway, laying the edge of her right trainer along the painted line with every step. She pretended everything could fall away but that line, that it was a tightrope. That she could move through the sky without falling.

At home, she went in the front door and headed straight up the stairs, ignoring the sound of her mother's voice talking to someone on the landline and the smell of her fish pie in the oven.

She let the hot shower run while she got undressed. Mist rose up and sat in the bathroom just like it did on the river when the temperature changed. She could feel it opening up her pores and lifting out the dirt. Fog clung to the walls and covered the window, covered the mirror until Khadija looked like a ghost, trapped on the other side. In the shower, it ran off her and down the drain into the river looking deceptively clear.

Tammy used to tell her the old people thought a witch couldn't cross running water. She said they had that backwards. That cats were fascinated by it for a reason, sitting on your worktop dipping their paws in and out the running water like it was a candle flame.

234

It was the water that had the magic, not the women they called witches, Tammy said.

The whole of Saltash poured itself away into the Tamar, all the blood and cheap wine and snot, the car exhaust that clung to you after you'd walked on Fore Street, the cement dust and the dregs from the wine glasses and the undigested excess of every drug that came out in people's piss. The lager, lager, lager and the fag ash. Gravity took it all through the pipes and down the hill while Khadija wrapped a clean white towel around herself. Her towel, the one she kept in her room so her mother couldn't use it. She folded another one up onto her head and opened the curtains.

She lay down and rested on the special extra pillow that lifted her head just enough to line up the world. Then there was nothing to tip or spill, nothing to stop the bridge from holding up the sky.

Craig would be back at the R.A.B.I. next weekend, sitting in the corner and looking at her like he was in church. What about Mr Osborne? There was a trick her mother did, where she could balance two men against each other, then lift herself right out of the space between and take off. It looked easy from a distance.

Craig's father finally went just before exams. Khadija had sat her GCSEs and done most of her A-levels in between Micky Williams dying and Craig's father dying. Everyone went to the funeral, even old Mrs Osborne. And Tammy, who sat next to Ben looking like she wasn't sure which funeral she was at.

The photo by the casket was Mr Kennedy out twitching with Craig. The hymns were the same as always, the same as Micky. When Khadi was little, she used to look out her window at night, listening for the sound of Micky's wheezing next door, his strangled little cough. In her sleep she'd imagine her own organs hardening up. Bodies all around her were killing themselves trying to put walls around a threat that was already inside them. Nature backfiring all over the place.

How was she supposed to say no when Craig asked her to walk

over to the R.A.B.I. with him? He'd just put his father in the ground. His mother was home staring at the refrigerator and his sister had run off to Plymouth somewhere. Guys always liked Craig, but he never seemed to have actual friends.

He didn't come looking for her, just waited at the side of the Union until she got out of her black skirt and wandered down to Town Quay. He had on a Rame Festival T-shirt and jeans. He hadn't shaved; you'd never see the army on him if you didn't know. How long had he been waiting there?

'Don't flatter yourself,' he said, like he'd been inside her head, listening. 'I only come out for a smoke.'

The wake was carrying on inside, a load of friends from the dockyard.

'Since when do you smoke?'

'Since you have no idea how boring war is.'

'Don't look boring on the adverts. What will you do now?' The worst possible, most clichéd question but it came out before Khadi could stop it.

'I don't know. I still have some disability, but it in't permanent.'

'Don't you think it would've been better to join the Navy?'

'The Navy killed my dad, Khadi.'

'The army kills lots of people's dads.'

'You wouldn't understand. You got brains. You passed the eleven plus. What am I supposed to do, spend thirty years breathing in poison till I die like him?'

That was more words than she'd ever heard Craig say before. More anger, for sure.

'Are those the only two choices?'

'Pretty much, yeah.'

They went around the bridge office and over to the top of Normandy Hill, then turned until the wind was behind them. Tears dried on their faces while they looked across at Lowhill and the railway viaduct.

'Tell me a better story.'

'Sorry?'

'Tell me something, Khadi.'

'A lady came to see Tammy yesterday. She had a dog she thought was her dead granddad.'

'Fuck off.'

'No word of a lie. She brought it with her, said it had the granddad's expression on its face and kept trying to drag her to his old allotment.'

'Tammy Williams encourages people to be mad. You get that, right?'

'See, I think she helps them. They're already mad, clearly, but it in't permanent. She helps them sort through it, like.'

'I need a drink. Come on.' Something about the funeral had made them easier with each other, for a little while.

The hill down to Saltash Passage was so steep every step was like falling and then catching themselves with their feet. Halfway down, Craig stretched a hand out in front of Khadija and then pulled it back again.

Why her? Of all the people they knew in Saltash, why did he want to spend those three hours with her? It felt like a deliberate mistake, like he'd driven the wrong way down a one-way or tacked a sail face to the wind on purpose. He watched her tipping and swerving sideways down the hill and smiled.

Jerry didn't say anything when Craig ordered her a shandy, though it was another three weeks till her birthday.

'What was it like?'

'He went quiet, at the very end. People'll call it peaceful, but he was struggling. It was just on the inside because he couldn't move at all.'

'I'm so sorry, Craig.'

'Everyone is. No offence, but so what?'

'Well, it's all we got. I meant the army, though. What was it like?'

'What? Afghanistan? Dusty, I guess. Bombed out. I didn't see much of it, to be honest.' He wouldn't stop staring at her. She had

237

to look out the window to keep him from barging into her eyes. 'The hospital was grim.'

'Would you do it again?'

'Nah. Let's talk about something else, yeah? Tell me about uni. You're gonna be a barrister?'

'Solicitor.'

He was still staring. She wanted to shout at him, *Fucking hell, Craig! We just put your dad in the ground. Your mother's at home speechless and your little sister's getting legless in Plymouth with God knows who.* (Whom!) *Why are you choosing this moment to try to crawl under my skin?*

'Are your mum and Beth okay?' she said.

'I guess. How would I even know? Mum spends all her time talking to solicitors. We're part of the class action now, but they say it can take years. That'll be you soon, I guess.' He made it sound like it was something she was doing to hurt him personally.

They peeled off their coats and played pitch penny. The windows steamed over and the pub smelled like cabbage and parsnips, but neither of them was hungry. It got blue outside and then black, and the purple lights on the Ferry Inn shone down onto the road. The river slipped back from the mud and all the boats in Saltash Passage tipped over sideways.

'I need to go home and revise, Craig.'

'Yeah, you do. Let's go.'

He took her hand and pulled her back up the hill. She laughed and stumbled like girls do, then she realised what she was doing and stopped.

'You are not a barmaid, Khadi Sleep.'

You're not your mum, is what he meant.

'Being a barmaid's not a condition you're born with, Craig. It's not a state of being. It's a bit of cash for uni, that's all.'

He was still looking, just kept on until she hunched her shoulders up and turned her face away. *Please don't be your mum,* he meant. *Turn yourself into what I need instead.*

Craig went up Normandy Hill and back over the bridge on his own two feet that night, the limping one and the working one. That night he was his own self, a little soft but basically good. Apart from the limp and the hole his father had left in him, he was still functioning, a young machine in perfect order, in nearly perfect health. Food for the river, almost ripe.

They stopped on the bridge walkway to put their fingers through the cage and look out at Wilcove. Out over Trematon the sky was the colour of empty flesh. The wind kept pushing them sideways. It tasted like metal being forced down their throats.

'I took the offer at City University.' The words had been jammed in her windpipe like broken glass all night. She spat them at the river like a cat spitting up bones.

'What offer?'

'The Law course. I'm going to City. It's in Islington. I'm gonna live in halls and all that.'

'Well,' he said. 'You were always brainy. You can come back and open your own chambers.'

'It won't be a chambers. I'll be a solicitor. Just a plain office, and it won't be here, mate.' Some people you knock down just because it's easy. So easy it makes you furious.

He just stood there like the whole of him was one held breath, until she felt she'd suffocate if she didn't give him something.

'I can't live in the house with my mother forever, can I? I'll end up murdering her.' She laughed, but it got lost in the sound of the up train, crossing the bridge in front of them.

Give him credit, he kept the melodrama under control. You could see him trying not to make her feel bad about the fact that she was destroying him. Whatever else Craig was, he wouldn't stand in a dark hallway between her and the exit. He wouldn't offer to buy her.

She leaned forward into the cage and spoke to the boats down below.

'It's like I can't turn around here without someone trying to suck the life out of me.' She meant Craig and all, and he probably knew it.

'Maybe people just care about ya, Khadi. It's not that odd.'

'You don't get it. Why would you? Mr Osborne from over the road was creeping on me only yesterday. He's at least forty and he's married with a kid.'

'He what? What are you saying?'

'It wasn't anything, really. It isn't like he touched me or threatened me. It was all in between his words so you'd only get it if you were standing there. That's how they do, the old married ones. When they put their hands on you, maybe they're just being nice and you're the one with the dirty mind.'

Silence. She strained her ears to try to catch the sound of his breath.

'I would have thought I imagined it, but he jumped when Jerry came round the corner. It was like he'd been caught at something. He offered to help me pay for uni.'

Craig breathed out, loud and all at once, then turned away toward St Budeaux.

'He used to come round randomly, making shit up about parking and the post. I thought he was creeping on my mum.'

'He probably was and all. There's no bar low enough for the Osbornes.' The words were flip but there was a drag underneath them like the tide in the channel pulling out.

She should stop and she knew it.

'I just feel like I could stay in the shower for days and I'd never be clean.'

She should have minded where those words were landing, but they were pushing up out of her like bile and river water, like whatever you cough up instead of drowning.

He came close again, stood just behind her and to the side. She could feel the dark electricity ringing between them like the air between two struck bells.

Then Craig said, 'Saved you something.' He held out a tiny nest made of lichen and fine twigs and white feathers.

'You brought me a bird's nest?'

'Goldcrest.'

The nest wasn't what drew her in, not exactly. It was beautiful, but so was the air around it, the space around him. She'd forgotten how it crackled. How it sparked. Up above Forder there was an electrified fence. When they were little, Craig's sister Beth showed Khadija how you could feel it buzz up your arm if you lay a blade of grass against the wire. When Khadi showed Alice, Alice waited till no one was looking then lay her arm there instead of the grass. It burnt a long rusty line onto her skin. A year later Alice still had the scar.

'How big are the eggs?' You couldn't lay fifty pence flat inside that little bowl of grass and fluff.

'Bigger than you'd think.'

Khadi turned the nest over and wondered how it felt when birds landed on that fence. Could they feel the electricity even though they weren't grounded?

'Bigger than mini eggs?'

'Yes.'

Craig laughed and Khadija leaned into the buzzing.

Chapter 37

Jo finally agreed to be Ben's girlfriend in May. He was doing his GCSEs, and he spent lots of time pretending he didn't care about them, powering down green-lanes with some blokes from Tideford. He got six Bs, but he didn't tell nobody but her. That was later. First, they got some guy off the street to buy them cider in the Co-op and Ben kept smelling her hair, said he liked the smell of burning from the straighteners. One stifling night in early September, he came round to help her look after Dylan.

Jo put the kettle on because she didn't know what else to do. She was only fourteen. There was something coming off him that made her feel important, but she didn't know what it was exactly. OK, she knew, but only from what people said. She'd never felt it before.

Ben said, 'Let's go in the sitting room, yeah?' and they did. You'd have thought he had a plan, that he'd slide closer on the sofa every time she wasn't looking and throw his arm over behind her like something from an 80s film. Instead, he kept fidgeting like he couldn't sit still in there either. He rubbed his hands on his jeans and asked if Dylan would wake up.

'Are you kidding? I could light his bed on fire. My mum hoovers with the telly on at one in the morning. Me and Ben could sleep through anything. He gets up and walks around, though.'

'In his sleep?'

'Yep.'

'Let's go up the hill.'

'What, now?'

'Yeah, we'll stay where we can see the house.'

That was when he leaned over into her neck. 'You smell amazing,' he said, and pulled her up by her hands before she had time to figure out what was happening in her body.

242

'Lock the door. We won't stay long.'

But she wasn't even worried. She was thinking between her legs already. It was getting cold at night, but she didn't feel it. They climbed up till they could see the Lynher, but Ben turned around to make sure they could see down into Wearde too.

She thought how he was like a bird trapped in a boy's body, or maybe born with a mismatched soul, too big for him. He always knew where the highest point was, the very top of anything. Ben liked to have air underneath him, then he liked to let go. Next to him, Jo felt like there was wind rushing past her, even when they were indoors.

There at the top of Lowhill, he put his arms around her from behind and it was like an 80s film after all. Her hair went into his mouth and he just talked through it instead of pulling it out.

'When I finish my exams I'm going away up North. Wanna come?'

He didn't mean it. He knew she couldn't and anyway he wouldn't have anywhere to put her at his cousin's house.

'What's it like up there?'

'Like here except everyone talks like they're on *Corrie*.'

'Bloody everywhere's the same, you ever think that? Except London.'

'Nah. It's us that's the same. We only go certain places.'

'I'm not, Ben. I'm going somewhere different. Don't want to spend my life here.'

'Yes, you do. I'm here.'

'Cocky little shit, in't ya? Let's go over there.' She pointed at the Osbornes' house.

'What for?'

'So we can see the old lady when she don't think we're watching.'

'Right. Creepy. Why?'

'It's not creepy,' she said. 'People are interesting. Everyone's going around their lives and no one really gets it all down, you know?'

'Nope.'

'I mean, we're all pretty much invisible. Real life is exactly like telly, it's just no one notices. No one bothers to stop and record it.'

'No one ever notices this either. Look.' He pointed out over Torpoint and then across the river. There was a thin moon, so bright it blurred over North Yard. That was before the waste incinerator, just black clouds piled up in the sky over the crematorium. He took her head in his hands and tilted it back until she couldn't see the ground. 'Imagine there was no ground. Imagine we just lived in the sky.'

She leaned back onto him and counted to ten, waiting. Nothing happened, nothing changed.

'Come on,' she said, and then realised the thing she'd been waiting for had already happened. She'd broke it before she understood.

The bridges were busy and the tide was all the way out. Jo could just make out Beggar's Island, uncovered now. She took Ben around the outside of Mrs Osborne's house.

She had the curtains drawn in the sitting room; she always did. You had to go round to the kitchen and lay behind some old paving stones piled up in the garden. Jo had started watching after old Mr Osborne died. The old lady got left alone and Jo worried about her. Not because she was a sweet old lady; she was a bitch. Mrs Osborne didn't care at all whether people liked her, that was what was so good about her. If it was warm at night, she left her kitchen door open and the patio light off while she sat there, drinking her Horlicks before bed. You could be two metres from her and she'd never know.

That night, the son was there, Charlie's dad. He was with Mrs Osborne at the kitchen table and he was fuming, sort of shouting at her. Jo lay down behind the paving stones and took out her phone. Ben put his hands on her back. After a while he slid them around to the sides of her and she felt contained, so sort of looked after she almost couldn't pay attention to the camera.

'My father's dead and they still won't give up,' Mr Osborne was saying.

'Why should they give up?'

Jo checked the screen to be sure they were both in the shot. Mrs Osborne was staring at a tea towel, kind of blank-eyed. Jo turned the flash off and held the phone in place on top of the paving stones, took a picture of them in the yellow light, framed by a world of nothing around the doorway.

'What the fuck?' Ben whispered into her ear. 'We're gonna get arrested. For *this*?'

'What more do they want?' the son said. 'They got their handout. We don't owe them anything.'

'I expect they want someone to admit that we knew. That your father knew, anyway. Those families get compensation cheques if they're lucky; we got all this, and the right not to die horribly.'

'You sound like a bloody Labour councillor.'

'I sound like a human being. You should try it.'

Ben slid his hand up Jo's back and leaned his head against her, needy but graceful. Nothing between them was awkward; from the very first time he touched her it made sense. He whispered, 'Come on, you weird bird. Let's go back to yours before your brother wakes up.'

She held up a hand for him to wait.

'Why did you hate him so much?' Mr Osborne was saying. He meant the dead father. 'He gave you a house and put food on your table for years. He paid off your father's debts for God's sake.'

'And a son. Don't forget he gave me a son.'

'We all know how you feel about that.'

'In fact, you have no idea how I feel about that. It's well beyond your grasp.'

'That Kennedy kid needs to let it go. He needs to get on with his life and stop trying to bleed us.'

'Is he asking for anything?'

'A public apology, last time I checked.'

'That's hardly bleeding us, is it? Words are free.'

'You see? Speaking of beyond your grasp, this is the sort of thing you never bother to understand. If I put an apology on record, it goes to liability. You judge us for things you don't even comprehend.'

'Have you thought about letting it go yourself?'

'Letting what go? I haven't done anything.'

'You have "materially benefitted" is, I believe, what the paperwork calls it, but that isn't what I mean. I mean the boy is grieving, and he's wounded. Let him shout about it, let him be angry. He has a right to be.'

'Hello? I'm the person he's attacking. Me. Your son.'

'Surely that makes me more responsible, not less.'

'You act like Dad and I are the immoral ones. What about you? No feeling for your own family; none at all.'

Mr Osborne was proper shouting by then, but he put his cup down very gently on the table before he stormed out of the room. His mother didn't follow; she just leaned back against the worktop and carried on staring at the tea towel. Jo zoomed in on her even breathing and took one last picture of the glitter in the old lady's eyes before she closed the phone.

Ben kept his hands on her sides while she rolled over and stood up.

'You're fucking odd,' he whispered. 'You know that?'

'You like it. Let's go.'

They half slid down through the pine trees into her back garden.

'You get that's illegal, right?'

'Only if someone catches me.'

'Nah, bird. It's illegal even if they don't catch you. What you gonna do with the photos anyway?'

'You know what I mean.' She didn't answer the question and he didn't ask again.

Dylan was sleeping on the floor when they got back. He'd got out of bed in his sleep and wound up across the room. They made tea and watched *Big Brother's Little Brother* and then they could have been any two kids in Britain.

Later, when she was alone, she scrolled through her phone. Looking at the photos, she could hear the anger buzzing through

246

their tightened lips. The sound was just colour on the surface. It didn't matter.

If you took away people's words and focused on the anger, the laughter, the drunken singing, the druggie haze, the whooping through the air just before the splash, that was when you could really see what was happening. That all the stories were the same.

Chapter 38

What if you were, then? High up and god-like on the bridge tower? What if it were that night? Late September, clear and warm.

From up there, you would take in the whole sweep of the river with one breath. The yellow-lighted balconies stacked up on Barne Barton. The green hills of Rame under uncountable colours of sky. The quiet hulk of the ships in North Yard, trying to impose themselves on all that. The immense steel arms of the bridges, succeeding.

And what if every person crawling up, down and across all that mattered, specifically and in detail. What would you see?

There is Craig Kennedy, walking mostly upright, heading for the bridge. Just that barely perceptible half circle every time his left foot swings forward, the shape of the river in his step. Craig passing through a passage between two fences and into a cul-de-sac. He doesn't notice, but of course you do, that he passes under the first-floor window where Alice Tregidga has gone to sleep. That Alice wakes then, because of the shouting that Craig can't hear.

He hears only traffic and blackbirds.

In late September, the water is at its warmest. At first, no one but you sees the fog that rolls off the sound when dark comes and the air loses its heat. You see it spill up to fill the channel between the banks, make lavender pearls out of the light from the Ferry Inn, lie like a blanket covering the river. Hushing.

Craig passes Jo Sleep and Ben Jinks, thinking maybe Jo shouldn't be out this late. Ben is with her, anyhow. No real harm.

And that is the truth. No harm for Jo here. This is her safest place and she has only just found it.

The two of them laugh as they pass, one voice under the other like two currents in the river. They've got a bottle of cider and a blanket crocheted by Jo's mum. At the back of the playing field in South Pill they spread the blanket, sit and light fags. Jo can't seem to stop talking, to stop laughing, can't keep from stretching out her arms and explaining her future. And then her other future. And the one after that. Ben can't stop watching her do it.

Until they both feel suddenly tired. Until he kisses her and they lie down to touch each other. And then somehow they are asleep in the shadows between security lights. They don't see the rising fog.

You can see Khadija Sleep on her doorstep wearing something that sparkles, an unlit fag in her hand. Waiting for a taxi full of other girls, all newly released and about to fly off. See her turn her head to watch Craig by the turnstile, hoping he won't stop and speak. See him stop, of course.

Can you hear them? What does she say?

Because Craig goes over the bridge, but he never goes inside the R.A.B.I. You see him stand outside, watching the smokers, looking fed up. Looking angry, in truth. See him pull at his collar like he's suffocating. There he goes under the bridge towers, invisible for a minute or more. Then out he comes into the security light, grabs a gate with one hand and swings himself round the fence out onto the tugboat dock.

How many lives between Craig and Tina Osborne back over the river, waking up past midnight? Tina under her brand-new roof. No one sees her but you, because she wakes up alone.

She looks at the time, half asleep but already sitting up. The curtain is open and her hair is still wrapped up after washing. Odd, she never falls asleep like that. Never has got rid of her mother's voice telling her she'll catch her death.

The air behind the viaduct is a colour Tina has never seen. Clouded like the sky is full of milk, but with something rusty spilt in it. She goes to the window, thinking there must be a fire somewhere.

What was it made her startle, made her sit up with her heart pounding? She stares out the window until Anthony comes in the front door. He's late but walking steady. Not pissed, though he's been over at the pub at least four hours by the clock.

Tina calls Anthony's name from the bedroom and he jumps. She can hear the hall table knock into the wall. She steps out onto the landing as he comes up.

Charlie breathes wetly behind his bedroom door.

She leans to kiss Anthony so she can smell him. His breath is clean, and there is a tremor going through him like the bridge extension under a heavy truck. She puts a hand on his arm and thinks for a moment that it might break into pieces. His skin is cold. Hard. And he's sober as a judge.

Even *you* feel the urge to turn away. Tina does turn.

There out the front window is Khadija Sleep stumbling through the turnstile onto Lower Fore Street, leaning on Beth Kennedy's arm. They are laughing hoarsely, having sung their way across the bridge. *Ah, Freshers' week tomorrow*, Tina thinks. *Everyone starting new lives. Good luck to her, Carol's maid.*

Even you have never seen what Khadija looks like when she isn't holding onto herself, when her shoulders let go. This is how she moves when she is full of cheap vodka, too numb and tingling to feel the air pressing in. Looking the world right in its shining eyes.

'Bloody hell,' she says, waving an arm. 'All of this will be gone tomorrow.'

'It won't, bird,' says Beth. 'You just won't be looking at it. Lucky cow.'

Tamara Williams sleeps under the roof below them. Was it you, who gave her this night? Your vision passes over her face softly, like the memory of her mother's hand. For once in her life, Tammy sleeps like an island in the river, still while the hours wash in and cover her, breathing slowly while they slip away again.

It isn't that the air is silent. They are all there tonight, shouting and laughing, whinging, crying, talking all at once. But tonight, it isn't Tammy who has to listen.

You've seen Alice when the first whispers woke her.

Now Alice looks around in the shadows for the person they belong to. She's never heard them before, how could she know? Her bedroom window is open. Why hasn't her mother shut it?

The night is cold with lots of stars. Half a moon.

Please help, I'm burning, someone says.

You're gorgeous, someone else.

He's slipping. He'll slip.

'Mum?' No sound comes out though, because of the fear squeezing the air out of Alice's throat.

It's your fault.

I'll give thruppence for the basket, shilling if it has a head inside.

He fell.

Not yet.

He'll fall.

That's what they call the autumn in America. Fall.

Six point five seconds. Five, four, three.

Your lungs are like bunches of grapes, see?

I'll give you three rivers if you take the fingers off.

Here it means the men, not the leaves.

I feel sick.

They built the bridge for them.

Slick. Sicker.

You're gorgeous. Can I touch you? Just here?

Before the bridge, it was the hoists at Keyham Steam Yard. Where they fell.

The sparks fly off and burn you.

They got pissed and chucked themselves out first-floor windows.

Three seconds is such a long time, Alice. You have no idea.

When they say her name she calls out for her mother again. No one stirs in the house below her. They are sleeping like the dead.

Sometimes they rise up again. Twisted, not near killed enough.

The dead are not. Sleeping.

The pieces are too small to see, but sharp edges. Jagged.

Nothing round here was tall enough for all that sadness.

251

Sick. It was his ticker.
Folks pull it out of the earth in Africa.
Less than two of those seconds to fall.
I can't cough it out. Alice, I can't.
And then, more than voices.
The rest of the time is for slipping under, Alice.
She sees.
Three seconds to disappear.
Alice sees everything, all at once.
Maybe she is you, for this one night? You, in a body far too small.

Chapter 39

Khadija stepped down from the train into a chamber of booming echoes, clacking and roaring. The milky light of Paddington Station all around. She turned to look back into the train and there was her mother, with her hair done and her bitten nails. Carol handed down the big suitcase and then they stood together on the platform, wondering where to go while commuters huffed at them and walked round.

That first day, Khadija had no idea what London was shaped like or where to get the 205 bus. They walked through the lines of smokers at the station entrance. Carol was so embarrassing; Khadija wished she would turn around and get back on the train right then. Also, that she would never leave.

'Mind your pockets, maid,' her mother said.

The bus sat on City Road for ten minutes and then dumped them on a corner full of posh journalists and scruffy lost-its. The halls were down a side street above the canal.

'You don't have to come up, Mum.'

'I am, though. You'll just have to live through it.'

'Look. That lot are waiting outside.'

'I need to be able to picture it later. I need to see where you'll be when you're talking to me.'

Khadija hauled her suitcase up onto the bed while her mother unloaded her cleaning potions into the en suite. She had a bag full of bedding that smelled like lemon balm, too.

It would fade. Khadi stretched her arms from wall to wall and breathed in. 'Check out the view.'

The side of a building rose up less than two metres from Khadija's new window, blinds drawn in the windows opposite and stains from the guttering running down the side. You had to stand up against Khadi's window to catch a glimpse of the canal through a crack between buildings.

'Well, that's a downgrade, in't it?'

'I like it.'

''Course you do.'

They went back out to City Road to have lunch and let go of each other, wound up in some kind of hippie café above a vinyl shop. Khadija took in a big breath above her sweet potato and ginger soup. It was time to say it.

'Mum, you stole half my life.'

'No, I *gave* you half of *my* life, didn't I?'

In half an hour Khadija would be miles away from the look on her mother's face.

'Aunt Tammy says he loved you.'

'What?'

'He loved you. Me.'

'He would have stopped, Khadi. He had lovely parents and a big job back in Morocco. The government had paid for him to come and he was supposed to go back. He would have ended up hating us.'

'Hating you, you mean. He could have left you without leaving me, if you gave him a chance.'

'How, Khadi? How would that have worked? Think about it?'

'You reckon I haven't thought about it? You stole me!'

Now it was her mother's turn to be embarrassed. She looked around at the dreadlocks on the posh people and then back at her plate.

'Well, now you're stealing yourself back. Well done. I thought I was doing the kindest thing. I honestly did. Of course, I screwed it up. That's what I do, in't it?'

'Nah, Mum. I'm not buying that 'feel-sorry-for-me-because-I'm-such-a-fuck-up' bollocks. You can sell that junkie bullshit somewhere else, thanks.'

'Please stop swearing at me, Khadi. You're the one that's gonna have to live here.'

254

'Here?' Khadi looked around at the artfully scruffy white people and the mural of Bob Marley on the wall. 'I won't be back in here. Don't worry.'

'I loved him.'

There was more feeling in that than Khadija wanted to take in. Her mother was brittle on the surface, but once you opened a hole in her, whole rivers would come out. Ghosts and cleaning mixtures, weird remedies and melodramatic distress. Saltash, basically.

'Tell *him* that. I don't want to hear it.'

'It hurt.'

They said goodbye in the street, hugging hard and silently. Khadija watched Carol diminish into the paved distance under clouds of pigeons. There were running squirrels and people on stairways covered in layers and layers of tatty clothing. Everything was like television, but then it wasn't at all, too. The air was thick with something invisible. London.

It took weeks for Khadi and her mother to peel themselves apart, to stop calling every night. That might have been because of what happened next, or it might have been like that anyway.

The first thing Khadi saw was an Instagram post. Flowers in front of the R.A.B.I. and a quote from a war poet you would have known didn't fit if you'd paid attention in GCSE English. It didn't occur to Khadija at first that the coughing boy buried far away was Craig, because he didn't cough and he wasn't far away. Or buried.

Half an hour later her phone started ringing. Her mother six times, and then Beth Kennedy. Beth never rang Khadija. Did she think they were friends now, because they went out and got pissed one time? When Tammy rang, she answered.

'Sit down, maid.'

'I'm sitting.' She wasn't.

She was standing with her shoulders wedged into a corner of the wall, trying to disappear and thanking whatever was supposed to be God that there was nothing out her window but bricks. No bridge, no river, no thirty metres of air, no thirty-two feet per second per second.

'It's Craig, lovely.'

'I know. I saw online. Tell me, Tammy!' Khadija was shouting. She was gasping and dry-eyed and thought maybe she was watching herself on a film.

Tammy told her straight, no fuss. Her mother wouldn't have, which was why she'd picked up for Tammy.

They'd found him on the mud by Saltash Passage when the tide went out. It would have been seven or seven-thirty in the morning. Khadi and Carol would have passed over him at ten to six, bitching over her suitcase or pissing in the train toilet or spilling tea. She can't even remember what they were doing when the train crossed onto Normandy Hill. She will never remember it. Whatever it was, they could have been looking down instead. They could have seen him, wet in the morning cold, without his jacket because he'd made Khadi take it with her to uni. Craig lying with his stomach down and his face wrenched to the side, lying with his lungs full of mud and heavy metals, and the cocaine that flushed from the boat toilets out into the Tamar.

Khadija could see all of it piling up right there, in her room in halls. She stretched up onto her toes, but it still pulled her under. She craned her neck and saw the canal, the kind they drag bodies out of on the news. Wherever Khadija went, there was a ribbon of deadly water lying alongside her.

Her phone went dark and the time appeared. 9:30pm. She'd been in London eleven hours before Saltash washed up and dragged her back under.

There were eight other people in the flat. The kitchen had two refrigerators and two cookers. Someone said Ewan McGregor lived just across the canal. Khadija spent Freshers' Week under her duvet, in the fading smell of lemon and vinegar. People being sick on the other side of every wall.

Her first lecture was at eleven on a Tuesday. At 10:15 she was dressed and standing in the kitchen with her tea in a plain white mug from Wilko's. The kitchen already smelled like stale alcopops and takeaways. She leaned over the worktop to open the window and then had to go back to her room and change her top.

When she came back for her tea there was another girl there.

'Hey. Lecture?'

Khadija would have backed out of the kitchen if she could have done it without being obvious. The girl had on bank teller trousers and a manga T-shirt.

'Hi. Yes. Introduction to Legal Precedent.'

'Is that your lecture or what you want me to call you? I'm Farah. It's nice to meet you, Introduction to Legal Precedent.'

In the first term, everyone picks a role. Farah had picked 'the Funny One,' which she didn't have to because she was well pretty. Much later she said, 'when I saw you, I knew "the Pretty One" was taken, so.'

'My name's Khadija. Sorry, I'm distracted. Things are a bit much, to be honest.'

Farah didn't ask why, but she sat down and put on a listening look. Khadija said she'd have to go soon, to get to the lecture on time. Then they told each other about their courses and bitched about how filthy people were. Said thank God they didn't have to share bathrooms with these pigs. It went quiet while Khadija ate some of her mother's muesli.

'So what's your story?' Farah asked.

'No story.' Not one small enough to tell a stranger over breakfast, anyway.

'Where are the parents from?'

'I'm Cornish.'

'Cornish is not a thing. Where are they *from*?'

'My dad's from Morocco, but I never met him. And it is a thing. I am that thing. My second name is Sleep. Trust me, that's as Cornish as it gets.'

'You're in London now, and your *first* name is Khadija. You don't get to be Cornish.'

Farah lived two doors down. She had a collection of boring cardigans and twenty pairs of very odd and not at all girly shoes. And a midlands accent. She had actual vinyl and a turntable.

When Khadi got back from the lecture ready to do the reading, Farah was waiting.

'Nope,' she said.

'Nope, what?'

'We're going out. Do the reading later.'

'I can't get behind in week one.'

'This year doesn't count, Khadija Sleep. Haven't they explained that?'

They went for coffee at Angel. Farah wore her cardi buttoned up. They sat outside so she could smoke. She took quick neurotic drags and said 'fuck, fuck, fucking, fuck' in the middle of every sentence, looking like a nun on holiday and talking like someone in a Guy Ritchie film. But from Birmingham.

It was 2010, literally everyone had hair straighteners and no personality. Farah was the first available thing for Khadi to hang in her empty sky.

'So. What's Actuarial Science?'

'I'm shit-hot at math. Ask me anything.'

'Why do you have so many shoes?'

'I worked at House of Fraser. They have this scam where they give you a store card and discounts. You're fifteen and before you know it you end up owing them more than your salary.'

People stood waiting to cross the road under the dead clouds. Behind the panes of plate glass everything inside the café sparkled and steamed.

'Why didn't you return the shoes?'

'Your turn. Why is your closet full of boy's clothes?'

'You—?'

258

'I looked when you were in the bathroom putting your slap on. You don't need it by the way.'

'I do need it. It's only a jacket and one shirt. They aren't mine. They're Craig's. It's— I do need it.'

Two people were shouting by the entrance to the tube station. One of them had backed down into the road, using his knees in that way smackheads do, like shock absorbers.

'Oh, boring. I thought you were gonna be a cross-dresser. I meant you don't need the foundation. It'll give you spots and then you'll put more on to cover up the spots and it'll be some kind of vicious cycle that lasts until you have so many wrinkles it's pointless. Then right after that you die. Think of how much you will have spent by then. Who's Craig?'

'Where are *your* parents from?'

'Egypt. They came for uni after they got married, now they work in a hospital. Nothing posh or glamorous; shit jobs in Radiology. Boring. Who's Craig?'

Khadija could have said everything then. Would it have mattered? Would it have stitched them together? Or ended everything right there? Too much drama for the funny girl, and Khadija's heart saved for later. They didn't have anywhere to be, why not? Give it all to the stranger, let go and see what happens.

'Our families were friends. Kind of. He died.' Not, *it's my fault because he was obsessed with me and I wasn't bothered.* Not, *I think I might have pushed him over the edge.*

Farah put both elbows on the table and stared for a good long minute.

'It's like there's a big hole inside you,' she said. 'Interesting.'

'Last week. He died last week.' Even Farah didn't know what to say to that.

She took Khadija's half of the money and paid, so she could keep the receipt. She brought it back to her room and stuffed it in a boot box with a pile of other receipts.

'So, an actuary is like an accountant?'

'Not really. I'll figure shit out for insurance companies. So they don't have to pay suckers whose houses fall down, basically.'

'But I mean, you have to be organised, right?' Khadi leaned over Farah's shoulder to look at the box full of crumpled up paper.

'This is different.'

'Okay...'

Farah's room had a proper view of the canal. Lights rippled onto the water from all the impossible back gardens across the way.

'One day, years from now, I'll be able to dump this out and reconstruct everything I did today. I rode the tube and bought some conditioner; we had a coffee; maybe tonight we'll have a drink. I'll know all of it happened, and exactly what time.'

'You remind me of my cousin Jo.'

'Right, where are we going tonight and what do I wear?' Farah pulled off the cardigan and the top underneath and started to climb out of her skinny jeans.

Khadija turned from the box of receipts and found herself inside the invisible circle of Farah's space. She had a birthmark on one thigh bigger than a ten pence. There were three red strings and an old festival bracelet on her bare wrist. For the first time in her life Khadija didn't back up, or want to. London fell open, like the city was so full it couldn't hold itself in.

Anything could happen.

2016

Chapter 40

Alice climbs over a garden wall and sits behind it, hiding from the road. The pubs in Saltash Passage are full and people have spilled out onto the tables in front, blowing fag smoke into the purple light. The sound of sirens rolls up the river, coming from both banks. Something big has happened, down at Torpoint or Pottery Quay.

Waiting there in the shadows, Alice forgets the rain turning red on a policewoman's shoulder, sheds the sight of blood in a car park stairwell and the choir swearing in her head. For now.

There is a reason for being here and it sharpens her. Alice needs to go home. She has something to tell, which is what Tammy Williams has been saying all along.

The designated drivers leave the pubs first, with their cars full of pissed people laughing. Little knots of walkers pass by on the other side of the wall, singing badly; Alice then stands up in the dark of the empty road. The moon has moved toward Lowhill, picking out the petals on the clematis blooming beside her and the ripples around the bridge towers. She swings her legs over the wall, takes a last breath of Devon and heads for the mud.

There she unties a rowboat, pushes it out of the shallows and climbs in. It rocks with the weight of her. One thin girl. Woman. One changing female and the size of the invisible things she carries tipping the fiberglass side to side against the black water. The boat has no oar. She wades back for one, steadies it in the mud and rolls back on board. She paddles carefully, slicing into the water without a sound and then turning wide.

Below the middle of the railroad bridge, the returning tide catches the prow and points her north. Time to swim. She doesn't dive, doesn't take a deep breath or shiver, simply rolls down the oar and into the channel without seeming to displace any river at all.

Nothing on her skin rises up against the water. Her lungs close up quietly and then wait to be released.

The Tamar rolls Alice once and then again. The first rush of memory, eddying up out of the stones and the mud below, almost makes her gasp. She holds herself steady just under the surface. The muscles and bones of the river move in the quiet below, back and forth around spikes of rusted metal left from forgotten quays. The river remembers every atom of falling iron and every morning full of exhaled petroleum mist. Every hollow it has opened for a jumper, just before they hit. The way the water laughed itself up around each one.

The river remembers Alice, too.

You, with the rusty hair, with your little head full, your wishing to be dead pull. You got stuck. We coughed you up.

She isn't stuck now. She swims like an eel, baring her teeth, sparks along her spine. She turns over below the surface just to feel the water between her shirt and her skin, tucks her hair back and opens her ears.

Your veins were the colour of the ships and the stones in your pockets weren't real. You didn't want to feel, but we fooled you.

You didn't carry stones at all. You carried people in your pockets.

You tried to weigh yourself down with ghosts.

Silly bird.

The water is neither cold nor warm; it is the temperature of Alice. She can't feel her own surface, where she ends and the currents begin. The difference is, it doesn't frighten her now. Alice is carrying something, something for everyone. The truth.

We took the other one. They'll be needing you.

Her fingers brush the mud; the surface of the river takes her hair and spreads it out under the sky.

Are you ready to remember now?

'Yes,' Alice says, and rises up on the rocks by Town Quay.

River water bubbles from her mouth. The wind blowing up from Looking Glass jetty dries the silt on her skin into scales. In the yellow street light the wet ropes of her hair are no colour at all. She shakes drops of water like sparks onto the wood, turns her back on the bridges and takes the road toward Wearde.

Alice crosses the mud under the viaduct while the up train swings round from Anthony Passage above her. She spits river water at it and climbs the far side. In the line of trees above the estate, a pair of crows startles up. They should be sleeping. She turns away from the moon and laughs then, but the river throws the sound back from its surface, keeping its quiet for the sleepers underneath.

Alice laughs again because she knows where she is going. It's quiet there, too. Tammy always said so.

'What have you come here for?' Charlie's grandmother stands in the crack of her front door, looking annoyed but not at all surprised.

Alice pushes the bell again so she can hear the tune. 'I like that.'

'I don't. It's absurd. Also, it's the middle of the night. What are you doing here?'

'Sorry, I guess it is. I've been away.' She smiles like a person possessed of joy instead of like a person possessed.

'Ah,' Nora Osborne says. 'You've changed.'

'Please can I come in, Mrs Osborne? I'm cold.'

'Your people will want to know where you are, changeling.'

'Could we not tell them yet? I did let them know I'm safe. I just want a little time, Mrs Osborne. I need to sit up here and look down, just for a bit.'

'You're not lying. That's new. And they don't know you're safe. They know you're alive. That is quite the opposite of safe.'

'I am, though. Lying. I'm always lying a bit, or I wouldn't be able to be around people at all.'

'Come in, then. And I'll ask again, what have you come here for?'

'Tammy said it was quiet. She was right. You can't hear them in here.'

'You can't hear them anywhere, Alice.'

'You know that's not true. Is Charlie OK?'

265

'Charles is fine, thank you. In spite of whatever you've done to him.'

'I really didn't mean to, Mrs Osborne.'

'You'd better call me Nora. What is that you're soaked in? It hasn't rained all day.'

'It's the river.'

'Good Lord. Why have you brought half the river into my house? That water is full of things that kill people. Believe me.'

'I'm sorry, Nora. Everyone says it's bad luck, but the river is good to me.'

'Rivers are neither good nor bad. Really, it's as if the Age of Reason never happened around here.'

Nora brings her a man's dressing gown and tells her to put her clothes in the tub down the hall. Then she opens the curtains and pours them each a cognac.

'Let's hope that'll kill some of whatever is in the water. You'll be sick for days.'

'I won't. The river won't hurt me.'

'You sound like a madwoman.'

'I am a little, but it's OK. It'll be OK now.'

They sit together looking over at Barne Barton and across to the darkness around Antony House. Cloud is piling up to the south, the moon behind it now, covered but lighting the edges.

'Gibbous,' Nora says.

'Sorry?'

'That's a gibbous moon behind there, in between half and full. You can tell it's waning because the dark is on the right-hand side. My father taught me that when I was very small. No one learns it now.'

'I'll have to go home in a day or two. They'll probably put me in hospital.'

'Well, you'll need a world of antibiotics at the very least.'

'No, I mean for the stuff going on in my head.'

'Tamara says there's new medication for you. She has worried the whole time you've been gone, you horrid girl. She's been talking to doctors and all manner of interfering types.'

'I am sorry, Mrs Osborne.'

'Nora. I believe you actually are.'

'Nora. I'll take medication and do whatever. All this was easier for Tammy.'

'Perhaps we could not use those American nicknames. What do you say, piskie?'

'Sorry, *Tamara*. It was easier for Tamara. The voices are nice to her.'

'There are no voices. They cannot be nice.'

'There are.' *Ask your grandson.*

Alice doesn't say it out loud, but Charlie's image falls between them anyway. And then Mr Osborne's. Anthony's. Nora stands up and takes Alice's glass away, even though it isn't empty.

Mrs Osborne knows; she remembers. She's scared, but she's happy about it too. Thrilled even, looking at Alice and the truth inside her the way you look at Adrenalin Quarry right before they release the zip wire. She closes the curtains on Barne Barton, on the steep drop and the welcoming surface of the river.

'Tamara won't be here tomorrow,' Mrs Osborne says. 'You can have two days.'

'Thank you, Mrs Osborne. I'm different. You'll see.'

'Well, it isn't up to me, is it? Charles thinks you're some kind of muse. I'd just as soon try to hold back water.'

'You're gonna like me in the end. You'll see. I'm good with people.'

'I thought I'd be alone,' Nora says.

'You won't, though. There's me and Charlie and Tammy. *Tamara*.' Alice's laugh falls incongruous onto the closed curtains and the furniture.

'You'll be here after I'm gone, I suppose.'

'Well, I hope that's a long time from now.' Alice means it. She isn't charming anyone.

267

'I suppose you should know about the house,' Mrs Osborne says.

'Well, it isn't haunted. I can tell you that.'

'Of course it isn't. There are no haunted houses. Charles' mother and I have put the house in a trust. For Charles.'

'He loves you so much.'

'His father will make trouble, no doubt.'

'He'll be happy here. Because of you.'

'Lawyers and a lot of rows, I expect. You ought to stick by Charles for that, since you seem to comfort him.'

'He'll always be able to remember you, being here.'

'God knows why. You are the most unsettling person I've ever met.'

Nora opens the door of the guest room and pushes the switch by the door. The light bulb kindles the smell of dust and mushrooms, hiding under carpet cleaner.

'I thought from now until the end I'd be allowed to sit quietly alone,' she says, 'but the house just keeps filling up.'

Chapter 41

At six in the morning Khadija is awake because she hasn't been to bed yet. Well, she has but only for half an hour, and that was a lifetime ago. A lifetime.

Jan gave Jo one of Aunt Debbie's pills and pushed Khadija out their door saying, *go home to bed*. Khadija walked down Lower Fore Street while it was still dark, hearing Jo's voice blowing over from the bridge. 'I'm gonna be an act.'

These past few weeks Khadi believed her, then the sky dropped on Jo like an axe. Trusting fate is literally the same as stepping in traffic.

Years ago, Jo filmed Khadija over the river at Manadon Roundabout, where there's a dizzy walkway suspended above the A38. Khadija had to walk across while Jo lay on the ground at one end, behind her phone camera.

You step onto that walkway and startle the pigeons. They all take off and flutter up around the edges of your vision and you're in the sky, nothing but fifteen metres of air between you and the rushing cars below. The whole of Britain's travel infrastructure is built to encourage suicide.

When Khadija reaches the top of the hill, she sees Tammy below on her front step. Six weeks since the last time she walked down Lower Fore Street into Tammy's arms, ushering in a whole new world of grief. She walks with her arms at her sides until she is inside the circle of Tammy, being held and breathed on and murmured at, still frozen.

'I'm so sorry, Aunt Tammy. How is Ben's dad?'

'Pretty much as you'd think, maid. I think we all knew, in one way. He was born falling, Ben. My stomach pitched every time he climbed on something.'

Khadija puts her arms around Tammy and squeezes until she can feel her little bones. 'It must be so hard.'

'Well, grief's no stranger, eh? We'll keep going, won't we, bird?'

'No, I meant feeling like you can see things coming and then they happen anyway. It must be so awful, Aunt Tammy. I never thought.'

'I wish I could just wash my head out sometimes. People talk about their mind going blank like it's a bad thing.'

'Oh no, I'd love that too.'

They laugh one soft laugh together.

'He was such a good boy, Khadi. If anybody got hurt anywhere near him, he'd reach out a hand without even thinking.'

'I know. He was like that when we were all little, even.'

'She's here.' Tammy's voice sounds like tissue paper in the wind.

'All right, lovely. Let's get you inside and make you a cuppa.'

'Alice. She's here somewhere, but I can't see.'

A down train goes through Saltash station without stopping, the blinding lights shining inside it. Khadija looks over Tammy's shoulder to count the carriages. *Five, six, seven, eight.* She rests her chin on Tammy's head.

'One out, one in, in't it?' Tammy says.

'Let's go in, old bird.'

For some reason, Tammy lies down in the guest room. The death room. Khadija brings a cup of tea and tucks her in, lies alongside on top of the blanket and puts her arms around Tammy.

'You got smaller. You fit right under my arm.'

'No maid, you got big. People grow taller in all they other places. You must have caught it in London.'

'You're funny when you're sad.' She puts one small kiss in Tammy's parting and lets go. 'I'm going to shower and get myself together. You come round if you need us meanwhile.'

At home, the light in the kitchen is on and the back door is open.

'You all right, babe?' Her mum's been awake all night. Death does that.

'Fine, mum. It isn't me you need to worry about. Jo was like the walking dead.'

'Come in here and sit for a bit.'

'Later. It's six thirty in the morning. I haven't been to bed yet.'

'Two minutes. Come give me a hug.'

She's leaning against the worktop, smiling like it's Christmas morning.

'What's up with you? Someone's dead, Mum.'

'Hug first.'

'Bloody hell.'

'You got a letter,' Carol says into Khadija's hair. Then a little kiss just like the one she'd given Tammy.

Khadija backs up and Carol holds out a thin little envelope. The stamps have pictures of kids' paintings. They say something in Arabic at the top and *Royaume du Maroc* at the bottom.

'Shit.'

'No idea how he found us.' She can't keep the smile off her face.

'He didn't. I found him. Well, people helped.'

'Oh, maid. You should've told me. What if it went wrong?'

'Goodnight. Good morning. Whatever.'

'Aren't you going to open it?'

'Not here. It's none of your business. If you'd had your way, we'd never have spoken at all.'

'Well, I'm happy for both of you. Sue me.'

Khadija lifts a cushion off the sofa and takes it upstairs. She undresses with the curtains open, piles up the pillows and lies down so that the bridge walkway sits along the horizon.

You nearly got my friend Tom sacked. Happy? It's Farah.

Dunno. Did he deserve it? Who's Tom?

No! He's an accountant. He was feeding your OCD. Self-blame, whatever it is.

…

You were right, incidentally.

Will's a twat and you never loved him? Duh.

271

No, they hid assets. Slate Group.

Shit!

They moved all of it through like three companies and disappeared it. Before the class action was filed.

Which means they knew. Bloody hell.

No, it means there's nothing anybody can do about it.

I owe you, bird.

Bird?

...

Glad you owe me, cause I'll be skint by the time I ever need a lawyer. What else is going on with you?

Nothing. I'll tell you later.

She might, too. Khadija puts the phone on the chest of drawers without closing anything, lies back and waits for it to go dark. The letter smells like nothing but paper and glue, paper that feels too light to hold anything. She puts it unopened beneath the pillows and sleeps for ten hours without dreaming.

Three Saturdays later, Khadija walks through Forder with Jo and all of the lightness and the overly formal English of that letter inside her. They will write now. Someday, they might meet.

'I can't believe it worked,' Jo says. 'You have a dad. That's nuts.'

'I need to go to the mosque downtown and do some work. Wanna come?'

'Don't tell me you're getting religion. I can't cope.'

'Calm down, bird. It was folks at a mosque in London who helped me find him. I want to pay it forward. Do some *pro bono* work, like.'

'Am I allowed in there? Will I have to wear a dress and cover up?'

'You watch too much telly.'

'Nah, mate. I *make* telly. Anyway, this is twisted.' Jo waves the tobacco tin in her hand and leans back into a hedgerow.

'Aunt Tammy was trying to help. She knew you'd want to say goodbye.'

'Goodbye to what? Ben's left foot?'

The tin says *Anstie's Golden Flake*. Inside are some of Ben's ashes. Khadija is fairly certain Tammy stole them from her brother's sitting room when no one was looking.

'How much does it weigh? Half an ounce? Ben weighed eleven stone two. This is a little burned piece of him. It don't mean anything.'

It's been three weeks and Jo has started sleeping again, three or four hours at a time. She wakes up angry and Ruby cries all day, feeling it.

'You know that jasmine at the back of Aunt Tammy's garden?' Jo asks.

'Yeah?'

'Ben and his dad cut it back every year, as soon it gets cold. Got cold. They used to, I mean.'

'Yeah, I know. Ben was in there the day after I got back, changing Aunt Tammy's ceiling fixtures and fixing the lock on her upstairs window, bless him.'

'There used to be a trellis under the jasmine but it rotted. The vines are still all shaped in twists that used to go around it even though it's disappeared. I'm like that, Khadi.'

'Yeah, OK. I get it.'

'I'm just the space around Ben. Not like I'm not myself, but like we grew in the shape of each other. Even when I dumped him and got pregnant with Ruby, it was only part of the story of me and Ben.'

'Sucks for Max, eh?'

'Max is fine, he just in't for me. What am I supposed to do now that I'm all twisted around an empty space?'

They head down the hill into Forder, then have to move back up against the hedgerow for a Range Rover. It slides past them in the narrow road and the driver raises his hand in something that's almost a wave.

'Hey, you know that thing you always say about people and their stories?'

'I don't really care anymore, to be honest,' Jo says. 'I mean, I suppose I will, but I can't even remember what it feels like.'

'Yeah, but you will. What if you tell the one about us? I mean all of us. It's like you said, it's as big as all the famous stories, in't it?'

At the bottom of the hill by the little church the road splits. They take the left fork and then walk off onto the lane that runs along the lake.

'Sit here.' Khadija gestures to a downed beech tree.

Someone's Labrador runs out from the scrub across the lake and startles the birds picking in the mud.

'You know you asked me about that night?' Jo says, 'The night Craig died?' She puts a hand on the log and lowers herself like an old woman, looks down at the tin in her hands.

'It doesn't matter now, babe.'

'It does, though. I was with Ben. We fell asleep.'

'You and the rest of Saltash. You were only fourteen. What the hell were you doing out?'

'Thinking with my fanny, obviously. Your body just throws you at something and you don't even know what it is, in't it? I mean, I could've drawn you a diagram, but I didn't *know*. You get it though, right?'

'Not really. The first time, did you not think, *that's it? Seriously?*'

'No! What the hell did you do up there? I thought the sex was supposed to be better in London.'

'Why would it be better? The population density? The money?'

'The pills, maybe?' A soft laugh comes out of Jo like a dead moth.

'Very funny. It was OK, if you must know. I just don't get why someone would trade their life away for it.'

'Holy crap, you're serious, aren't ya?'

'I really am. Every once in a while you feel like doing it and sometimes it's nice. That's all. Also, FYI, I'd rather do it with a bird.'

'Duh. I hope you weren't looking to make a dramatic announcement, 'cause literally everyone knows that about you already.'

'Doesn't matter, does it? I'm here now.' Khadija gestures like she lives just here, in the mud at the bottom of Forder.

'So? You need to go out and get something better than nice, Khadi. Stat. You'll be old in a minute.'

'Ta. What time was it?'

'Huh?'

'When you fell asleep that night? What time was it?'

'Dunno. I got home after midnight. My mum was fuming.'

'Well, I guess, you were fourteen. You could've made up a lie, said you were staying at ours or something.'

'I didn't think. Then I tried to explain it to her and that just made her more cross, because it was odd. She thought I was making it up.'

'Not odd, just stupid.'

'No. I mean, OK, I was a bit pissed and all the other stuff with Ben, but it was like one minute I was looking at the Tavy Bridge and the next minute I was opening my eyes an hour later. It felt like when they put me under for my appendix, like a piece of time just folded up and skipped.'

'Ben could have been a bastard, you know. You were lucky he wasn't, meeting up in a field with some bloke and a bottle of cider when you were fourteen.'

'Don't be ridiculous,' Jo says. 'He was Ben.'

'Yeah, fair. He was.'

'Let's go.'

Behind the lake there is a green lane that winds up the hill to the old quarry. Ben and Connor used to speed down it in their scatty Ford with the mounted lights and the doors off. Jo runs right up like someone who never smoked a fag in her life.

'Slow down!'

'No. You keep up, city bird.'

'So, I'm thinking about publishing something in the paper. Thanks to you.'

'You what? What did I do?'

'Well, you and Ben, really. It was the name on his payslips that put me onto it. They're doing the same shit again, with the academies. Paying their friends for supplies that cost ten times what they're worth. Thing is, some of them are the same people.'

'See, you should be a private detective. Also, what are you talking about?'

'Well, anyway, law certainly won't work on these people. I'm talking about these logistics companies. Suppliers and companies on the boards of the companies. When you look up the academy trust it's the same as with the dockyard. They paid the compensation to people like Micky and then just kept on doing it.'

'Standard. That's not really news, Khadi.'

'Thing is, my friend Mo works at the *Financial Times*.'

'Which literally no one reads. You might as well put it in the *Guardian*.'

'People like Anthony Osborne read it. Whoever's making the real dosh would make him resign.'

'YouTube, mate.'

'Eh?'

'I'm saying, forget the papers. You need to put that shit on YouTube.'

The cow parsley and the campion are open all over, making the hedgerow look soft. If you weren't from the West Country, you'd never know there was a stone wall under there. In the home counties they make the hedgerows out of shrubs, branches all twisted together like Jo and Ben.

'Also, I shagged him,' Khadi says.

Jo stops on the rise and holds the tin out in front of her, little green pieces of shadow and sunlight falling over her shoulders like lace.

'Shagged who? I thought you just told me you didn't shag blokes?'

'Mo. I wanted to see what it was like.'

'That was mean.'

'Nah. It's cool. He's getting married.'

276

Khadija leans over with her hands on her knees, lungs expanding and collapsing without her permission, dragging her bones open and closed.

Jo says, 'Ready?'

'Hang on. Let me catch my breath.'

'No. This is for Ben, remember? Whatever you do, don't catch your breath.'

The air is full of pollen and moisture and all the thousand poisons rising from the landscape around them. Without asking, Khadija's body trades all that with her blood. She is home.

'Go!' Jo heads full tilt down the hill, raising the open tin above her head. They run with their heads thrown back, watching the incomplete particles of Ben puff out above them like smoke, knowing either of them might hit a rock and fall any second, twist something vital and leave more blood in the dirt. Feeling Ben's favourite feeling.

But neither of them falls until they're back down by the pond where the mud is soft. Jo trips and Tammy's tin flies out toward Beggar's Island when she puts her hands out to stop herself. She kneels there panting with her fingers sinking into the mud.

'Jesus. You OK?'

'Shit,' Jo says, and falls over onto her side.

Khadija stands above her, not knowing whether to put out a hand or say something. Jo rolls onto her back and her eyes glisten up into the trees, tearless. One side of her is clotted with mud.

Look at her. The familiar outlines of her little cousin have opened and shifted, a person has come out of her and another is buried there. Jo's eyes sparkle up the same colour as the Saltash water and the Saltash sky. *Look at her. Of course he loved her.* The thought sounds in Khadi's head like a stranger's.

Chapter 42

Alice is with them the night Tammy does a group reading at the Drake Social Club, home from residential care. They all pile over the river to help. Sitting inside the club, you wouldn't know it was over the river, or anywhere. All you can see out the window is a wall ten metres high looming over the road, asking to be smashed into, maybe waiting to fall down and flatten the world. The Drake is full of jobless men whose granddads worked at the dockyard. The only gainfully employed people in the front room are a couple of housebreakers drinking on a deal with a fence at the end of the bar, and a table full of chippies at the back. Strangers wouldn't know the difference between the working girls and the rest of the women in here. They work indoors, instead of walking around the back alleys in Millbay.

Alice has come to the reading with them, though she isn't technically old enough to be in here. They don't serve food. She looks undeniably fifteen, but also well fed and like maybe she even slept a little at the residential place. The medication always puts a little weight on her, but she needs it. Jo has come along too, slowing them all down with the weight of her over-full breasts and her limping soul. She sits inside a circle of silence by the karaoke machine, shedding whatever light falls on her off onto the dance floor. That leaves Khadija and Alice taking tickets.

They're raising money for a grieving families fund, otherwise Aunt Tammy wouldn't be here at all. She doesn't normally do group events, or even read for strangers. Most of the time she's their own private madwoman.

But it's a 'good cause' and it turns out people will pay a tenner for somebody to tell them life lasts forever and has nothing to do with blood or breathing or being able to touch things.

'Pepsi's out!' someone shouts from behind the bar.

Khadija is busy herding people toward the function room and isn't really paying attention. Anyway, if you aren't expecting to hear someone's voice you don't recognise it.

The veneer is stripped off one side of the function room door and someone has painted the chipboard underneath. In the hallway to the toilets there is an empty cigarette machine no one's allowed to use anymore.

'Kevin!' the woman behind the bar shouts. Khadija looks then. 'Pepsi!' It's Beth Kennedy, waving a nozzle at some guy in the doorway behind her.

Surely Tammy must have known. Somebody must have known. Khadija forgets about the grieving punters and the donation container in her hand, lets go of the door without looking to see if anyone is still walking through it.

Beth is kneeling down behind the bar, unscrewing the hose on the empty syrup canister.

'Hello?' Khadija whispers.

Beth has thrown her hair back across one shoulder to keep it out of the way. The word 'Craig' in blue ink twists around her bare arm and into the dark under the bar. The muscles inside Khadija contract upward and the edge of the bar cuts into her stomach. Something forces all the sticky air back down into her while she's still trying to get more words out.

'Hello, Khadija.' Beth doesn't look up. 'I thought you were too embarrassed to come say hello after you had the cheek to come down Millbay.'

'I was worried about you. Sue me.'

'Always worried about people, in't ya? Anyway, you were only trying to pump me for information.'

Khadija straightens up and looks away through the window at the dockyard wall. 'I honestly don't understand why you're angry with me.'

'Sorry?'

'When did you start working here? Are you stayin'?'

'Yeah, I'm staying. How do you think it should end? Me strangled and dumped at the tip?'

'Stop it, Beth. Jesus!'

'Maybe you thought I was only on the game so I could pay my uni fees and become a surgeon? Hooker with a heart of gold type of thing? Or maybe me dead in a bathtub with a needle in me?'

'Any of those things could have happened, Beth.'

'Your Aunt Tammy's started back there.' Beth tosses her head toward the door to the function room. 'I'm coming through in a minute.'

'Be pissed off at me if you like, bird. I'm glad you're OK.'

'Turns out I'm not your own personal tragedy, eh?'

'I never thought—'

'That was just my brother.'

There are about thirty people in the function room. It's Devonport, so twenty of them belong to one family. Twenty-nine of them are women. There is one reluctant husband, clutching onto his pint for dear life. Tammy stands in front of a stack of folding tables, looking sideways at the door to the alley like maybe she could escape if she catches the right moment.

Everyone settles in their plastic chairs, turning off their phones and whispering until Kathy the landlady shushes them.

'Thank you all for coming,' Tammy says. 'I'll do what I can to help you. None of this is predictable; you all probably know that.'

Women around the room nod and trade looks. Khadija sits at the side, hoping she can think her way through the significant case history on tort claims for loss of bodily integrity while Tammy gives the room an hour of false hope. She has LPC exams next week.

'Can I come to you?' Tammy looks down on a lady wearing a fringe jacket she obviously borrowed from 1973.

'I want to give you a doll, a little doll sitting in the window looking out. That's what they're giving me. Have you gone places? Have you been to lots of places? Yes, you're more settled now, but you'll go again. I see that little girl, they're giving me that girl in the window with the doll. And leaves, leaves falling down, someone leaves. Someone left. (Here is where the lady starts crying.) Now that I'm saying that they're giving me a street corner. Left. Right. Left. You might be at a crossroads. Not like in your life, like a real crossroads. An intersection with a traffic light. Look both ways, they're saying. Don't forget to look both ways.'

There is a rustle in the back row as Beth moves past people's knees to sit beside Alice. Alice puts a hand on Beth's arm, like there is comfort to be given and she is the one who knows how. The gesture hits Khadija like a sudden loss of gravity, harder to comprehend than the truth.

Tammy extends one hand now, to a girl with dyed tips and a jumper that says 'Nope' in sparkly silver across the front.

'Can I come to you? Yes, you do something with needles, don't you? Is it knitting? Sewing? Needles, they keep saying to me.' Tammy folds her hands like a prayer, then puts them to her lips, bows her head and closes her eyes like she's listening. People in the back are gesturing and whispering at each other. Someone's going for another round.

'Ah, it's a hospital. There are needles, big needles. They're so big it's like you could knit with them. (Quiet laughter.) He felt it at first. He was so uncomfortable. Something in his left arm, yeah?'

Some relative that could be a mother, an aunt or a grandmother puts an arm around the girl. There is no one in this room who hasn't thrown their heart off the edge of something, who doesn't spend their dreams measuring the distance from the bridge to the surface of the river. That is what they have in common, and it's why they need whatever it is Tammy is giving.

'Now, they're giving me an Angela? Angie? Maybe a little Daisy. Daisy, yeah? And red. The colour red.'

'Jesus, Tammy.' Khadija whispers it under her breath, but the lone husband hears and looks over. She scans the room for Jo and only then realises she must not have come through with them from the bar, must still be crumpled into the corner, shedding the spangles of light from the disco ball and trying to blink away the dryness in her eyes.

'Not like a traffic light,' Tammy is saying. Not like a fire engine. Red like— Oh, he coughed. There was blood. I'm so sorry.' Tammy's face crumples up and her eyes fill with water, but the girl just stares. All the tension goes out of her face, until it looks like there's no one inside her at all.

'I'm so sorry. It frightened everyone, the colour of it. It was so bright, like a fire engine. Like a traffic light. It frightened little Daisy. I'm so sorry.'

All around the room, women take tissues from handbags. Whoever it was that coughed blood into that sanitised room, he is a connecting thread here. He's one reason this family full of brittle women have come together to be soft. To believe, because they can choose to, and no one can stop them.

Tammy tells them about her counselling and how she sometimes struggles to cope. About the time she tried medication. Alice watches with settled eyes, looking neither up nor down and never taking her hand from Beth's arm. Khadija leans to the side and pushes the alley door open, hoping a breath of air will be enough.

It isn't. She stands and slips through, reaching the alley before she is all the way upright. The lights from the rugby pitch pass above her onto the roof opposite without disturbing the shadows full of empty kegs and discarded chairs. She walks out to the road and back into the bar through the front door, stepping aside for a woman with an open-front dress, leaving with a bloke who looks like he'd help you get rid of a stolen telly.

Jo isn't in the corner shedding disco light; she's at the bar talking to Kathy.

'Too much?' Khadija pushes a stool aside so she can fit in beside Jo and put her empty glass on the drinks mat.

'I can have Aunt Tammy twenty-four seven,' Jo says. 'I don't need an audience.'

'They do though, don't they? It's all part of it, everybody whimpering into their hankies together.'

'People have died, Khadi. Show some respect.'

'Sorry. I just meant, is it really helping? Even Beth is in there, sitting with Alice and Alice acting like the concerned grown-up.'

'She's all right, in't she? Alice. Who'd have thought?'

'I guess I'm being flip because the whole thing kind of freaks me out.'

'You talking about just now, or your life in general?'

'I haven't heard you be sarcastic in a while.'

'Ben'd be well pissed off if I spent more'n a month crying.'

'Devastated if you spend less than a month, though.'

And then they can both laugh. Khadija pushes her palms onto the bristles of the drinks mat and looks down. How is it that everything she touches falls? Or is it maybe just that everything around here is falling all the time anyhow? She's only put her fingers in the way of gravity and thought she was dropping things.

'Beth is not my fault.'

'What?'

'Whatever happened to Beth, it isn't my fault, Jo. She's just angry at me because I'm convenient.'

'Here's a thought. Maybe it has nothing to do with you. You ever think of that? Maybe Craig was nice to you and Beth is someone whose brother died horribly and you're not in the middle of it at all.'

'I was sort of thinking that. Wouldn't that be lovely?'

'Tammy's in there helping those people. Maybe she's mad and maybe she's special, what difference does it make if it helps? Quit acting all Home Counties about it.'

'You're right. And it's really annoying. Could you stop being right now?'

They head to the back room together, so they can pick Tammy up when she's finished. She'll be exhausted and need water. She'll need tea in bed at home after. The two of them shuffle along the wall by the door. Jo leans in and Khadija puts an arm around her, even though she's so tall now it's a stretch.

'I haven't been to you yet, have I?' Tammy says, leaning toward one end of the front row. She's swaying on her feet and her voice is small and gravelly now. The lady in front of her could be anywhere between fifty and seventy-five, depending on how little she ate as a child and how much she smokes.

'You went to Scotland in the winter, didn't you? You made snow angels, you and someone else. They're saying Jon. Jonathan? Also Iain and Gordon. Gordon. Oh, he went down in the snow. You were frightened weren't ya? But he was all right. They're telling me, *it's all right, it's all right.* They want you to know that. Here or there, body or spirit I don't know, but it's all right. They're happy.' Tammy closes her eyes and bows her head again.

'Is there anything you wanted to ask me? No. Well, I'll just say God bless. Oh wait, they're giving me wind.' *Laughter.* 'A strong wind. Snowflakes.' Tammy makes a complicated shape with her fingers. 'They're giving me those snowflakes, blowing sideways right into someone's hands. Or maybe it's crochet? You had someone who crochets? All the string,' she wiggles her intertwined fingers, 'it's like cat's cradle. You know cat's cradle, with the string? Now that I'm saying that, there is a cradle. One of they old-fashioned cradles, you could rock them with your foot while you knit or you crochet? Someone is doing that. With the needles. Needles again. Need, maybe. Needless needles. Don't let them give him the needles anymore, he says. They didn't help, he says. But he wants you to know he's happy now.'

All around the room, shoulders drop. The everyday poison of exhaled breath fills the air.

Jimmy Squires' mother sends him over the bridge with the taxi to pick them up. They all pile in, Jo and Alice either side of Tammy in the back, Khadija in the front passenger seat, taking on the small talk. Tammy leans her head on Jo's shoulder just like Jo used to do to Khadija when she was little and tired.

'You missing Ruby?' Tammy sighs.

'It's been three hours. Never left her that long yet.'

'She won't know the difference,' Alice says. 'She doesn't know about time yet.'

'Yeah well, my tits know about it. It's blimmin' agony. Sorry, Jimmy.'

'That's all right, me lover. I used to be a baby and all.'

Everyone is quiet on the way through St Budeaux. Two blokes are playing cricket on the waste ground, whiling away their shift at the all-night petrol station. At the square Jimmy slows down to let a bus out. Someone's having a domestic in front of the chicken place. Two girls are waiting in the shelter across the way for their bus back to Ernesettle, sharing their muffin tops with the world. They are maybe fourteen and probably spend their lives in bus shelters, doing things they don't even understand themselves.

'I know a lady that lives back there,' Jo says, pointing. 'I went to a knitting circle with her.'

'You what?' Khadija turns to stare into the back seat.

'She's cool. I made a video about her and she thought it was funny.'

'You're so much more odd than people realise.'

'I realised,' Alice says. 'She got like it while you were away.'

Normandy Hill is quiet. If you didn't live here you wouldn't know the size of the drop behind the houses, or the length of the distance that opens out to Wearde behind them as the car climbs higher. Imagine passing through a place at night, only once. Everything sparkling and you never come back to fill in the shadows, never have to see the light that washes up over the bodies, the polluted mud when morning comes.

'It was nice what you did tonight, Aunt Tammy.' Alice sounds so different, sort of humble and thoughtful. You could almost believe what she says. Is it the drugs, or is it her?

'Well, I only try to help,' Tammy says. 'Have you talked to your mum and dad, maid?'

'A bit. Mum thinks the medication will just make it all disappear. I tried to explain.'

'You'll come see me and tell me about it?'

''Course. If there's peanut butter cookies.'

'Hey!' Khadija says. 'Back off, you.' Everyone laughs and they are almost normal.

The driver lets Khadija and Tammy out first. Tammy's door is unlocked; it always is.

'Stop a minute, maid. Come in and take a breath.'

'You bet I'm coming in,' Khadi says. 'I want to be sure you lie down. You must be exhausted.'

'You're lovely, you. I'm fine.'

The two of them go up to stand in the front bedroom, looking down at the purple lights on the Ferry Inn, the pools of dark water around the bridge supports, the tide pulling on the weeds.

'What happened to Alice, Aunt Tammy? She seems so different.'

'She's gonna be OK. Ben died and she came through. Nothing comes for nothing round here, bird. Never has, not for centuries.'

'I wish I could join everything up the way you do. In a way, that's what I went to uni for, but it didn't work.'

'Just you wait, lovely. Alice has something she's been carrying for you and all. You'll see.'

'I'm gonna stay here in the front bedroom, otherwise I'll worry about ya.'

'What about your mum?'

'I texted her. She said give you some peppermint and thyme.'

''Course she did. You're not going to make me drink that, are you?'

'Nah, I'll make you a proper cuppa. Go get in bed.'

Once Tammy is tucked in with a hot water bottle, Khadija stands in the doorway of the spare room, looking down the river at North Yard. Maybe she can feel Micky Williams beside her, pointing out the long-gone boats. But anyone would feel that, wouldn't they? People stay half pressed on your mind like ghosts in the air.

Weston Mill Lake is empty tonight, apart from whatever timeless things are falling through the shadows from Barne Barton. Falling from the bridge, too, and the trees behind Normandy Hill, from the ferry and the dockyard wall, from the ghosts of the invisible ships.

There is a new quilted blanket on the bed, but the lamp is the same one she used to read to Micky by. The picture of Tammy's mother and father is still hung on the side wall behind the door. Behind them the railroad bridge curves up, but the rest of the sky is empty because the picture was taken before 1961. There was only one place for people to throw themselves from back then. The rest of them had to do their dying far away across the ocean, or in the steam machinery at Keyham Yard.

Khadija gets under the blanket without drawing the curtain. She answers a message from her mother and another from Mohammed Magdy. Then she nestles into the shadow of Micky Williams and sinks into sleep.

Chapter 43

'Khadi up yet?'

It's Jo, standing in front of her house. Must have been the knocking that woke Khadija, but she can't remember it. There are fewer noises here than in London, but each one is louder and sharper in the wet open air.

She rolls over and rests for a minute with her eyes open, then stands up to put her head out Tammy's front window. There is her mother in nothing but a T-shirt and pants, again. 'Hello, you weird birds,' Khadi says. 'What the hell time do you call this?'

'Wait till you have a baby,' Jo says. 'You have to sit around for three hours every morning waiting for all the other adults to wake up and talk to ya. It gets boring. What are you doing in there?'

'I stayed with Aunt Tammy. Duh.'

Carol is smiling from one to the other of them like she has a lovely secret. Like maybe it's Easter and there are nice things hidden in the back garden. It isn't and there aren't, but she doesn't care. Nothing Carol Sleep feels ever lines up with the rest of the human race, and she isn't budging.

Bless her, actually.

'What you looking so smug for, Mum?'

'I just love you lot. Both of ya. That a problem?'

'Hang on. I'm coming down.'

Tammy has gone up to Mrs Osborne's already. Her back window is open and the house is full of sad light. You can see the dust on the leaves of the angel wing begonia and the fingerprints on the glass shade in the sitting room. The signs of her grief.

Her mother's kitchen smells like something new. Something green and a little musty. Jo has brought the whole pram right in and squeezed it behind the table.

'I need a bit of help with Ruby next month. Can you, Aunt Carol?'

'Of course.' Carol is talking to Jo, but in baby talk while she leans over Ruby Mae. 'What about your mum?'

'She'll do most of it. It's just she has a catering job two of the days. Dylan's a sweetheart, but I ain't leaving him alone with Ruby Mae. He'll spill Red Bull on her while he's reaching for the game controls and not even notice.'

'Two of which days? What've you got on?'

'Filming. I won a script contest with my friend Nathan. They gave us dosh and training. I missed the training because, you know.'

'You're making a film. What the hell!' Khadija reaches past her mother and lifts Ruby Mae out onto her lap. 'You didn't even mention it.'

'I applied for it before, then when I heard we'd won I didn't want to be bothered. Nathan said Ben would want me to. 'Course he's right. Ben'd be raging if I sat around moaning about him instead of doing this.'

'Crap, you actually are gonna be famous.'

'I'm not, am I? I don't belong in front of a camera. I belong behind. It's what I've always been good at.'

'Well, you've been keeping all this close to your chest.' Carol is still looking starry-eyed at Ruby Mae. 'Got hidden talents have ya, maid?'

'You have no idea, Mum. Jo has a whole other life, involving knitting circles and weird old ladies from St Budeaux. Videos of you and me and everyone. It's well creepy.'

'Nah, it's just this life, in't it? Not so much glamour, but you can't say there's no drama.'

Carol starts moving everything off the worktop onto the top of the fridge, because there might be a molecule of dust underneath something that she hasn't yet annihilated.

'What will you do about the flat, Jo, my lovely?' she asks the front window.

'I took my name off already. I'm staying with Mum and Dylan for now.'

Carol turns to look up the hill and then stills her whole body, one arm reaching out and the light falling on her like it's travelled a long way and wants to rest there. 'I'm so sorry, Jo,' she says, just as a knock comes on the front door.

Jo lifts the baby off of Khadija's lap and lays her down like she's made of glass. Khadija goes for the door.

'Hey, Khadi.' Alice looks all fresh and filled in, standing on the doorstep in a tartan flannel shirt and a pair of Charlie Osborne's jeans.

'Why the hell is everyone up so early? You're sixteen; people are supposed to have to drag you out of bed.'

'The medication makes it hard to sleep. Aunt Jan said you lot were round here. Can I come in or what?'

Khadija stands back against the wall so Alice can pass. In the kitchen, Carol is already reaching for some jars of leaves she keeps at the top of the cabinet.

'Mum.'

'Yeah, love?'

'Put some trousers on. Seriously.'

'Calm down, Khadija. I've changed the nappies of every bird here. Except you, Ruby Mae.' She puts a finger on the baby's hand, but Ruby is fast asleep.

'You're embarrassing. Just get dressed. I'll boil the kettle for your weird shit, OK?'

'It's not weird shit,' Carol says. 'It's just kava kava. It's a kind of wild lettuce. Calms you.'

'Have a seat so mum can boil you some lettuce, Alice. Aren't you glad you came round?'

'Fine,' Carol says, 'I'm going up to get dressed. You do the tea, two teaspoons in the little brown pot for Alice.'

Alice sits in a chair by the table and never looks once at the baby in front of her. 'I'm going up to Nora's,' she says. 'Would somebody come with?'

'Who's Nora?'

'Mrs Osborne. Not Tina, the old one. Charlie's nan.'

'She don't like me,' Khadija says over her shoulder.

She never has. There are times when Khadija can almost feel Mrs Osborne above them on the hill. On winter evenings, her sitting room windows shine out over Wearde like a lighthouse beacon. Her judgment radiates out with the yellow light.

'Me neither,' Jo says. 'She don't like anybody, does she?'

'She likes Aunt Tammy. And Charlie. She hates Charlie's dad, though. You gotta respect someone for that.'

'I can't go with you, anyhow,' Jo says. 'I came round to talk to Aunt Carol.'

'Oh, nice. Thanks.'

'Pipe down. You know I don't mean it like that.' But she does, in a way. Jo and Carol are together on the other side of birth now, a place Khadija and Alice both hope they'll never be.

'Come with, Khadi.' The small happiness on Alice's face is so strange Khadija can't place it at first. 'Leave these two motherly types to their pathetic cooing.'

Alice can feel the water left in her lungs by every exhaled breath. The morning is what people call 'close'. There will always be river condensing inside Alice anyway; she is half fish, but people don't know. Maybe this is what they meant in old stories about mermaids. Women throw themselves at the water, and some of them it throws back half changed.

'We can go across under the viaduct. The tide's out.' Speaking to Khadija's back, she realises they are the same height now.

'I'll ruin these shoes,' Khadi says.

'Take them off, then, city bird.'

'You lot really need to stop calling me that. You gonna tell me why we're going up there? Aunt Tammy'll be home in an hour, anyhow.'

'She's all right. Nora, I mean. She's cool.'

'Seriously? Why are you on a first-name basis? She is one of the nastiest people I ever met. And I lived in London for six years.'

'She's not, though. You'll see.'

Khadija stands on the little quay, lifting one foot and then the other to take off her sandals. She twists her hair round over her shoulder so it doesn't get in the way of her feet.

'Khadi?'

'Hmm?'

'Jo said you came back and started asking everyone about when Craig died.' Alice looks out at the water draining out of Wearde through channels in the mud.

'You were nine years old. I don't expect you to remember anything.'

'I do though, Khadi. I remember everything. Nobody remembers but me.'

Khadija doesn't answer until they've navigated the mud under the viaduct. If you grew up here you know where the soft spots are, but you still have to pay attention.

'Maybe you're mixing up the memories?' She grabs a buddleia branch and pulls herself up the far side. 'It was a long time ago and you were little.'

'Khadija, listen to me. I was awake. I was the only one awake. I heard all of it. I heard so much I sicked up my dinner and went deaf for three days.'

'Oh, babe. I know you've had it rough, but you really seem better now. You never went deaf, though. We would have noticed.'

'OK, I don't mean deaf exactly. I mean there was so much noise in my head I might as well have been deaf. He fell, Khadi. He didn't jump.'

Khadija sits down on the edge of the pond with her hair still twisted behind her and her feet in the mud, morning light from Upper St Budeaux giving her a halo.

'I heard everything,' Alice says. 'I didn't even know what it was. It's taken me years to sort it all out, but I know exactly what happened to Craig.'

'You don't though, hon. I'm sorry, but you were little and you weren't there. You have a problem and you're getting help now. It'll be OK.'

'He didn't fall, but Mr Osborne was standing right there watching. I get that no one will believe me. That's what they invented madness for. Also, I am actually mad. That part's not easy at all, but you can take the pills and all the shit you hear doesn't bother so much anymore.'

Khadija moves through the long grass and up toward the road. She wipes her feet, then looks at them in disgust.

'I can't put these back on.' She waves her sandals. 'Listen, bird, you've only been on the medication a few weeks. It'll get better.'

'Yeah, I've gained half a stone already and they're all still talking in here. That's not the hardest part.'

'What's the hardest part?'

'For me and Aunt Tammy, half of what they say is true. Time is not the same for us as it is for you, everything sort of happens at once. You feel all the time like you know what it's going to be already. It's confusing.'

'I know, babe. I'm so sorry.'

'You're always sorry about stuff that's not your fault.'

'It's just an expression. It means I care.'

'It's not just an expression for you though, is it?'

'You're right. You and Jo have everything sussed now. It's well creepy.'

'The last thing he thought of was you.'

'Enough now.'

'I don't mean it to make you feel guilty. He was happy about everything, because he was dying with you in his eyes.'

'Fuck, Alice! Ease up.'

'That's how he put it, not me.'

'You know what? It actually sounds like him. Crap poetry and heaps of emotional blackmail. That was Craig Kennedy.' She strides away up the hill.

293

Alice watches Khadi move up the hill like she's walking down a city street, like gravity is nothing and the swampy grass is solid as pavement. The sun comes over Higher St Budeaux and blazes into the side of her, painting a gold edge onto her hair and all down her left arm. And then Craig is there, inside Alice. The sight of Khadija Sleep moving through the air above the river makes her want to fall on her knees and thank God.

Khadija can see Mrs Osborne as they come up the side lawn, framed in her front window, watching her son rake up the cut grass. Tammy must be somewhere indoors, carefully dusting around things. The sight of Anthony Osborne stops Khadi there on the walkway. She supresses the urge to smile politely and turns to Alice. But Alice is not behind her.

'Khadija,' Mr Osborne says. 'Welcome back. Didn't London agree with you?'

'I didn't agree with London, actually.'

'Well, it would be tough on a girl like —'

'You were there!'

They both turn toward the sound and see Alice's head and shoulders rising above the lawn at the bottom of the slope. Mr Osborne shakes his head, visibly tossing off the sight of Alice and whatever she is saying.

'What will you do now?' he says to Khadija, like what he means is something else entirely. 'You always were clever.'

'I'll work now. At my job. As a solicitor.'

'She's gonna catch people like you. And put them in gaol.' Alice moves up the freshly cut lawn, a new tightness in her eyes and the flushed skin rising out of her flannel shirt, her hair falling around her blue eyes like anaemic blood.

Mr Osborne looks back at Khadija. 'You'd better take her home.'

'She's fine, Mr Osborne. How are you?'

'You stood there and watched,' Alice says. She isn't shouting anymore but her voice carries right up to the house. 'You were arguing. You were yelling at each other, in between the lights on the tugboat dock. It took me ages to figure out where it was.'

'Really, Khadija. The girl is ill. Why are you people letting her wander around ranting at everyone?'

Khadija doesn't apologise. Instead, she says, 'Why do you have a guy who owns a plumbing fixtures company on the board of a comprehensive?'

'There are so many misconceptions in that question I don't know where to begin.' He isn't shaken at all. Yet. 'Let's begin with the fact that it isn't a comprehensive. It's an academy.'

'And why, Mr Osborne, does the logistics company who pays your estate staff have two directors who were also on the board of Slate Group. That's just sloppy. Or maybe shameless.'

There is movement at the side of Khadija's vision. Nora Osborne easing the casement window open.

'We were bankrupted once already by people like you,' he says. 'It isn't going to happen again. You may be a solicitor, but we have plenty of those.'

He's rattled now. If he weren't he'd never speak like that to anyone but Nora. You can see the old lady flinching at his tone.

'You were shouting and he slipped.' Alice has reached them now. She stands on the lawn breathing faster than she did coming up the hill at Wearde. 'It wasn't far; it wasn't the bridge. It's hardly ever the bridge, is it? Everyone just thinks it is because that's where the Samaritans put their signs.'

Tammy is at the window now, in the shadow behind Mrs Osborne.

'Well?' Khadija seems to be ignoring Alice too. She isn't. 'How about the part where your new head of IT Services used to work for Resolve, who you just paid ten times the going rate for that new server?'

'I see you think you're clever, Khadija. Sadly, you really don't know how these things work. We've done nothing illegal.'

'Oh, I know that.' Khadija shakes her head and reaches into her back pocket for her phone.

'There wasn't even any water,' Alice says. 'The tide was out. His head hit the dock and he landed face down on the mud. You stood there for ages, just looking at him.'

'Really…' But Mr Osborne doesn't finish his sentence. He's trembling now. Even the sneer he was born with starts to slip from his face. 'Khadija, if you don't take her away from here, I'm going to call the police. The girl is clearly a danger to herself and others. She needs help. Listen to her.'

It's a long speech and he can't get it out without fumbling some of the words.

'OK, just let me read you a little something first. "Academies Face Growing Scrutiny over Procurements," that's the headline, page three. By Mohammed Magdy, he's a mate of mine. So you see, I do know how these things work.'

'You think you'll cause me trouble posting an article on some conspiracy theory website? Sad, but ineffective.'

'This is a copy edit for tomorrow's *Financial Times*, Mr Osborne. "One secondary academy in East Cornwall, whose head teacher (earning £164,000 per annum) also sits on the board of Rame Holdings … Osborne was formerly among the directors of a limited company found liable in a class action suit for knowingly exposing workers to fatal asbestos-related illnesses."'

'And you're the source? You've just got yourself a lawsuit, young woman.'

'Now that, I do know all about. Please sue the *Financial Times*. Then we can go let a court decide whether or not it's all true. Spend some time looking at the evidence.'

'I'm fairly certain I have more friends in the legal profession than you do, Khadija Sleep.'

'At least until tomorrow you do. Let's see how fast they drop you, eh? I'm gonna go ahead and guess Simon Orcutt won't be posing for a photo op with you at this year's regatta.'

The window opens wider and Mrs Osborne says, 'Come inside, Alice. Tamara can make us all some tea.'

'He was lying there for hours,' Alice says from the doorstep. 'All night long they were shouting at me and I didn't know why. I was nine years old, you fucking bastard.'

'Mother! You can't—'

It's true, what Alice is saying. Khadija can see it on his face. She falls back against the house and puts a hand over her eyes.

'Craig knew, didn't he? How you hid the assets.'

'You cannot invite these people inside, Mother. It's my house too, you know.'

'It really isn't,' Mrs Osborne says. 'Be quiet now. Perhaps go home and ask Tina about the house. You seem to have missed a memo there.'

'Good God, we're surrounded. Hysterical woman are in the House of Commons talking about their bodily functions; teenage girls are spouting nonsense and pretending its prophecy. If I go home, my wife will try to poison me with an overdose of household cleansers.'

'You're raving, Son. I'm worried you may be a danger to yourself.'

'Me! The world has gone mad. What happened to all the men?'

'They're dead.' The words come out of Khadija's mouth like used bullets, heavy and flat.

In the front hallway, four women find each other's eyes from their places in the light and shadow, breathing the golden moisture and the smell of cut grass.

'Come on then,' Aunt Tammy says. 'Go through. I'll make the teas.'

Mrs Osborne sits in the wingback chair with her shoulders curled forward and her head down between them, weeping without sound.

'I brought you some Garibaldis,' Alice says, like Mrs Osborne is her best friend. 'They've been inside my jacket though. I think they're a bit the worse for wear.'

Mrs Osborne doesn't look up. 'I thought he'd pushed him. All this time, I thought Anthony had done it.'

'How did you know, Alice?' Khadi sits on the edge of the couch so she doesn't have to let go of her muscles. 'Tell us how you really knew, bird.'

'I spoke to the coroner,' Mrs Osborne says. 'I'd met him a few times with Jon at charity things. He said, "Don't worry, the death will be ruled accidental." Like that was what I'd be worried about.'

'He stood for a long time, just looking,' Alice says. 'Then he went away and Craig was alone and they were all shouting at me. I didn't understand. The water came up over him and lifted him away. He only—'

It might have gone past but it doesn't. Tammy stops in the doorway with the tea tray. The rest of them raise their heads and go still.

'Only what?' Khadija already knows the answer. And she knows that what Alice said about time is true for all of them. The difference between the women in Saltash isn't measured by what they hear or how they feel time pass. The difference is who admits it and who doesn't.

'He only died when the water covered him. That's why they were all shouting at me. I'm so sorry, Khadi. I didn't understand for ages. I could have helped.'

'It was because of me,' Khadija says. 'Craig was all worked up because Mr Osborne creeped on me. I shouldn't have told him. I knew that and I told him anyway.'

'He stood by,' Mrs Osborne says.

Tammy puts the tea tray down on the carpet and moves across to the sofa. She kneels down so she can look Alice in the eye. She's talking to them both, though.

'You listen to me, you two. You weren't to know. How are you supposed to understand a thing like that at nine years old, Alice?'

'I could have helped. It wasn't fair.'

'They aren't always fair, but only because they get so desperate. Khadija Sleep, it in't never wrong to tell someone you're frightened, that you were made to feel small.'

'I was relieved for a moment.' Mrs Osborne uncurls her shoulders.

She sits tall, holding up something invisible with her spine, just as her mother taught her to. 'But that's what we do, isn't it? Stand by and watch, then say we didn't do it. We didn't actually push.'

'Well,' Khadija says, 'you usually say it's our fault and we fell on purpose.'

'All right, maid.' Tammy stands up, knees clicking. 'Steady on.'

The sun burns through the mist and into the window. It falls on the tea tray, forgotten by the doorway. Khadija looks at her bare feet with the mud dried on them. She wants to apologise about the carpet but it isn't the time.

There are four women crying for four different reasons, but you'd still be able to hear a pin drop on that carpet. No one makes a sound to trouble the dead air.

They tremble in silence while the sun wheels round and burns the mist off Mill Pond. An aircraft carrier is tugged round to Weston Mill Lake and the local train screeches to a stop below them, not fitting along the platform. Alice's collar is wet. Nora Osborne reaches into her sleeve for an actual handkerchief and holds it out to her. Tammy's tears are running in the ready channels at the sides of her mouth. The water in Khadija's eyes is about to spill over. It softens the room and makes the sunlight splinter out in front of everything.

This is how they wash the dead. Their tears are brackish like the river, watered down with rain and hiding the taste of the sea.

Salt. Ash.

Acknowledgements

I lived in the Plymouth dockyards for thirteen years. Thanks to all my friends and neighbours there. Thanks especially to Maia Pollio for constant encouragement and for her clear-sighted reading of draft material. For love and support, my heartfelt thanks to Lully, Dan, Shamira and Diana. Thanks always and forever to my family. I finished this novel in Wales, where I am lucky enough to live and work now. Diolch o galon i bawb yn y cwm, am groesawu fi mor gynnes yn eich cymuned.

Thanks so much to Rebecca, Gemma, Lynzie and all the wonderful women at Honno for making this the best publishing experience I've ever had.

According to the Office of National Statistics, 327 men in the Plymouth area died of asbestos-related illness, and 629 of mesolthelioma, between 1981 and 2021. In total, there are currently over 5000 asbestos-related deaths in the UK annually. These are caused by previous asbestos exposure at work, mostly between 1950 and 1980. The first study proving that asbestos exposure caused illness and death was submitted to the UK government in 1894. Most of those who died were laggers and fitters in Britain's dockyards.

Also according to the ONS, the rate of suicide has increased markedly across the UK since 2016. If you are not coping, please ask for help. Good people like Tina are on the phone twenty-four hours a day at 116 123. Llinell Gymraeg 0808 1641023.

ABOUT HONNO

Honno Welsh Women's Press was set up in 1986 by a group of women who felt strongly that women in Wales needed wider opportunities to see their writing in print and to become involved in the publishing process. Our aim is to develop the writing talents of women in Wales, give them new and exciting opportunities to see their work published and often to give them their first 'break' as a writer.

Honno is registered as a community co-operative. Any profit that Honno makes is invested in the publishing programme. Women from Wales and around the world have expressed their support for Honno. Each supporter has a vote at the Annual General Meeting. For more information and to buy our publications, please visit our website www.honno.co.uk or email us on post@honno.co.uk.

Honno
D41, Hugh Owen Building,
Aberystwyth University,
Aberystwyth,
Ceredigion,
SY23 3DY.

We are very grateful for the support of all our Honno Friends.